HONOR

BOUND

Book I

ATHENA RYALS

First Printing, 2020

ISBN 978-1-7346805-0-8

Edited by Kylie R. Bean

Cover art by www.ebookorprint.com

Author photo by Lucy Schulz Photography

Chapters 53 & 54 of this publication appeared in a somewhat different form in *Erato: Flash Fiction (2020)*

www.athenaryals.com

Thank you to Dotty, for being this story's first cheerleader. Without your invaluable friendship and generous support, this story may never have come to be.

Thank you to Bristol, for caring about these characters so much. The fact that I have made something that touches someone else so deeply astounds me every day. I am so grateful for your friendship.

Thank you to Sable, for helping me craft this story into what it became. The chemistry we have when we're deep into our creativity helped shape the story into what it is today.

Thank you to Katie, for being willing to celebrate this story with me when it was still a secret. I am so grateful that we can share our dreams with each other.

Chapter 1

Gavin knew it was too late to make a getaway with Sam. He had to admit, he hadn't exactly expected their family to call in the cavalry. *Maybe Sam means more to them than I thought.*

He glanced at them, slumped and tied to a chair with their arms bound behind them. *No. I'm not wrong.*

Sam had been so easy to break. So easy it almost wasn't fun. The location of their home base? He knew now. The names and weaknesses of every member of the team? Carefully recorded for future use. Gavin knew how much the team knew about him. He knew what the team was going to do next. Where they were planning on sabotaging him next. Their strategy on weakening his family's operations. All of it. *Why did they keep such a liability around? I would have put a bullet in their head to prevent them from revealing all that.*

The sound of gunfire grew louder. They were getting closer.

Gavin sighed. He couldn't bring Sam with him in their state. He'd have to leave them behind.

It didn't have to be a total loss, though.

"Sam."

A groan.

Gavin approached them as they slumped unmoving in the chair. "Hey." He smacked them lightly across the face. "Sam. Rise and shine."

A whimper. "No… please…"

"Hey, hey, chill out. I'm not gonna hurt you. I'm done with all that." He gripped Sam's hair and lifted their head until he could see their eyes. "But you know who's coming for you now?"

He relished the briefest flicker of fear that flashed across Sam's face. "N-no…"

Gavin smiled crookedly, looking almost sympathetic. "It's your team! They're coming for you. They're almost here."

The look of hope that brought some life into Sam's eyes was even more delicious. Dark delight curled in Gavin's belly. "They… they're…"

"Yup." He let go of their hair and let their head drop. Sam struggled to lift their gaze to Gavin, their eyes hopeful and broken. Gavin frowned. "That's not good for you though, is it?"

Confusion. Eyebrows drawing together above wide brown eyes. "But… why?" Sam's eyes had a glassy sheen to them that made them look so vulnerable.

"Oh, honey." Gavin ran his fingers through Sam's hair. They cringed away from his hand. It was still stained with their blood. "What do you think they're gonna do to you when they find out everything you told me?"

Sam's face shattered into agony as the realization came crashing down. "No… I told… no…" A high, keening sob started in their throat. *"No…"*

"Yes." Gavin continued his gentle touch, running his fingers through their hair. His fingers caught on tangles of sweat and blood. "They're gonna be so unhappy with you. They might even do to you what I did. They might *hurt* you, Sam. And you'd deserve it, right?" He waited for an answer. There it was: a miserable nod of the head against his hand. He smiled. "There's nothing you can do to stop that from happening. Unless…"

Gavin pulled a knife from his pocket and cut the rope tying Sam's wrists. They slumped forward. He pushed them upright and drew a gun from the waistband of his pants. He pressed it into Sam's hand. "…unless you protect yourself. You can defend yourself against them. Kill them when they come for you, and you can avoid more pain. You don't want more pain, do you?"

Sam's lip quivered as their eyes turned once again to Gavin's. Delirium clouded their face. *Is it the dehydration, or the shock?* From the way they were trembling it was anyone's guess. *It might just be the pain. I may have just completely broken them.*

Gavin guided Sam's hand around the gun and moved their finger over the trigger guard. "Okay? Shoot your team when they come for you. If you don't, I wouldn't want to see what they do to you for betraying them."

Gavin backed towards the door. He took one long, lingering look at Sam as they stared at the gun in their hands. They were shaking so badly he doubted they could actually hit anyone if they tried.

It's worth a shot. Gavin turned and ran.

∴

Isaac burst through the door. His weapon swept the room as he looked for Sam. He blinked as his eyes adjusted to the dark. His heart caught in his throat as he saw Sam, teetering on the edge of a chair in the middle of the room, shaking from head to toe. They cringed at the sound of gunfire coming through the open door.

As his eyes adjusted more, he saw them more clearly. Their arms and legs were a mess of lacerations and burns. Their hair hung limp and bloodied, dripping with sweat. *Or water?* As he took a step closer, he heard Sam draw a wet, painful-sounding breath. It was all he needed to confirm his suspicions. *They were waterboarded.* His stomach burned with rage. The sound of gunshots stopped.

"Guys! I found them! I found Sam!" he called over his shoulder as he holstered his weapon. Vera and Gray stepped into the room behind him. "Hey Sam…" he murmured in a low voice. "Sam, are you…?"

That's when Isaac noticed the firearm clutched in Sam's hand. He heard Vera gasp behind him, heard her gun finding its way into its own holster. He knew Gray would watch the door.

"Sam…" He took a step closer, hands outstretched and empty.

Sam jerkily stood and lifted the gun to point it squarely at Isaac's heart.

Everyone froze.

"Hey Sam," Isaac murmured, soothing. "You're okay. It's us. You're safe. We're here to get you."

3

Sam's hand shook. "Gavin said you would come for me." Their voice was thick with tears.

"Yeah," Isaac said gently. "Yeah, we came for you." Another step closer.

"Stop." Sam's hand spasmed on the gun. Tears leaked from the corners of their eyes. "Please. Just let me go. Please don't... please..." Their face contorted as they choked down a sob.

Isaac's stomach filled with icy dread. His eyes roamed over Sam's body again, looking for whatever he was missing. Sam's hands shook. Their eyes were dull and unfocused. Their skin was too pale, much too pale, and slick with sweat. They stumbled as sobs wracked their body. *What did Gavin do to them?*

"We can't let you go, Sam. We have to take you back home and get you cleaned up. You're hurt. Let us take you back—"

"No." The word tore out of them with another sob. "You can't go back there. I told Gavin... I told him *everything*. He knows where you are now. He knows *who* you are. I'm sorry... I... I didn't want to. He... He hurt me and I... He tortured me and... and I..."

"I know what he did, Sam," Isaac whispered, swallowing a lump in his throat. "I'm so sorry I let him get to you. Please let us take you home. We'll find another safehouse. Let us help you, please."

Sam's body convulsed with sobs. "Please, no..." They took a faltering step back, the gun still pointed at Isaac. "You can't... I betrayed you all. I told him... I told him everything. Please just let me go. I'm sorry. Gavin said I had to kill you or you would hurt me... Please don't hurt me, please just let me go..."

"No, Sam." Isaac's voice was low and husky as he fought back tears. "I can't do that. I won't hurt you. I promise. It's... it's *me*." Sam swayed on their feet. "Give me the gun. I won't hurt you."

Sam took one shuddering gasp as a sob tore through them. "I can't," they moaned. They put the gun to their own head.

"NO!" Isaac bellowed. He lunged at them. Isaac's hand closed around the gun. He forced it away from Sam's head as they pulled the trigger. The bullet went wide and buried itself into the ceiling. The shot was deafening.

4

Sam collapsed against Isaac, sobbing. "No…" they moaned. "Please…"

"Come on," Isaac whispered as he gathered them into his arms. "It's okay. I got you. You're okay."

Sam weakly pushed against his chest. Isaac lifted them up and carried them out of the room, forcing his eyes away from the dark stains on the concrete floor. Vera drew her weapon again and went first. She cleared the way as they stepped into the hall, back the way they came. Gray took up the rear. Isaac kept his eyes averted from the bodies on the floor. *They should never have touched Sam.*

Isaac whispered soothingly to Sam as they went, quieting their cries from their jostled wounds. Sam took another rattling gasp and coughed on their tears and the water still in their lungs. They huddled against Isaac's body heat as his arms tightened around them. Sam's quiet sobs echoed off the walls of the hallway as he carried them out of the compound.

Chapter 2

"How're they doing?" Isaac's voice was brittle with worry as he glanced in the rear-view mirror. His hands tightened on the steering wheel.

Vera turned from her spot in the passenger seat and reached a hand back towards Sam. They lay across the back seat, their head in Gray's lap. Gray stroked their hair away from their face. Sam shuddered away from the touch, their tears soaking into Gray's pants.

"Not good," Gray said. "I don't know what's wrong..." They stripped off their jacket and laid it over Sam. Sam pulled the jacket closer and curled in on themselves.

"P... please..." they mumbled, lips trembling. "Please..."

Isaac swallowed hard. "We need to get them someplace safe. Somewhere Finn can look them over. But this deep in Stormbeck's territory, I don't..." He shook his head. "Where can we...?" His eyes lit up in realization. "There's an old safehouse I used to use. It's not far from here. I never told Sam about it, so Gavin can't know either. I haven't used it in years, but... Gray, you good with that?" Isaac found Gray's eyes in the rear view. They nodded.

Isaac thrust the radio at Vera. "Radio Finn. Tell them to meet us at 2208 Pineview Lane." Her hands shook as she held the radio to her lips and relayed the address.

Isaac's knuckles were white on the steering wheel as he accelerated. "It's only about twenty minutes away. I can't believe I didn't think of it before."

"Hey—" Gray spoke up from the back seat. Their voice shook. "I can't wake Sam up."

"What?" Isaac threw a glance over his shoulder. Sam was limp in Gray's arms. "No no no no..." He slammed the gas pedal down. He clenched his jaw against the wave of nausea that ripped through him.

"Sam," Vera breathed out in a half sob. She reached back to them, her hand trembling. Her eyes were wide and desperate.

"We can't stop," Isaac said through gritted teeth. "Every syndicate family and bounty hunter will be after us now that—" He bit his lip.

"But Finn and Ellis are at least an hour away…"

"We'll do the best we can with what we have." His eyes were fixed on the road in front of him. He tried not to let the tears in his eyes blur his vision.

∴

Isaac slammed the car into park and jumped out, ripping the key from the ignition. The safehouse looked like it hadn't been touched in years. *Thank god.* "Stay here with Sam until I clear it," he ordered.

He pulled his gun and carefully made his way into the house. He swept it room by room, finding no signs that anyone had been there since he abandoned it years ago – since he'd been on the run again, alone. Isaac sighed. He leaned out the door and signaled the others to come inside.

While they carried Sam in, Isaac went to the closet he remembered held the blankets. He pulled a few out and shook them. Some dead insects fell out, but the blankets were dry. *They'll do.*

The front door opened and Isaac rushed to the living room with the blankets. "Here, on the couch." He beckoned them over. Gray carried Sam gently, their arms and head hanging limply down. Isaac's heart constricted with worry. *I'm supposed to protect them.* They looked so small in Gray's arms. *I'm responsible for them.*

Gray laid them on the couch, trying not to jostle their wounds. Sam moaned weakly as Gray put them down.

"We have to get these wet clothes off," said Isaac. He pulled at the sleeves of Sam's shirt. As he and Gray guided the shirt over Sam's head, Isaac gasped. Bruises covered Sam's chest and abdomen. Isaac glanced up at Vera where she stood behind the couch, her hands squeezed into fists.

Sam whimpered as Isaac and Gray stripped away their clothes. "No… please…"

"It's okay, Sam. It's us. We have to get you out of these wet clothes." Isaac spread a blanket over them, and then another.

Sam's eyelids fluttered open.

"Hey," Isaac whispered soothingly, his voice weak with relief. He sank to his knees beside them and gently ran a hand through their hair. "Hey, Sam." He stroked their face with his thumb.

Sam's eyes slowly focused. "Isaac?" Their voice was ragged.

Isaac laughed, the sound twisted around the lump in his throat. "Yeah Sam, it's me. We've got you. You're gonna be okay."

Sam's eyes filled with tears. "I gave you all up," they whispered, their lips trembling. "I told Gavin everything. I didn't want to... I just wanted him to stop hurting me."

Isaac stroked their hair. "Hey. Don't worry about that now. We're all okay. We're safe and we'll find a new house. What matters is that we got you back..." The unspoken word hung in the air: *alive*.

"He wouldn't stop hurting me," Sam sobbed quietly. "I tried to hold on but he just... kept... torturing me." Tears rolled down their cheeks.

"I know." Isaac's voice broke. "I know he did. But I'm not angry with you for what happened."

Sam swallowed hard, pressing their lips together. "I'm sorry," they whispered. A choked cry tore out of their throat and they began to shake with sobs.

"Hey, hey, it's okay." Isaac pulled Sam into his embrace. They threw their arms around him and clutched at him.

"I'm sorry," they wailed. *"I'm sorry."* Their shoulders shuddered. Their body convulsed with sobs as their fingers dug into Isaac's shirt. *"I'm sorry."*

Gray crouched on the floor next to Isaac, their joints creaking a little as they did. They laid their arm across Sam and trailed their fingers gently up and down their back.

Vera leaned over the edge of the couch and stroked Sam's damp hair. She pressed her mouth against her sleeve as tears rolled down her cheeks. She squeezed her eyes shut as Sam wept into Isaac's shoulder.

"Shh, I got you." Isaac rocked Sam as they choked on their tears and coughed. "We've got you."

Chapter 3

The phone rang. Isaac jolted awake. He looked over at the others, all asleep in a pile on the couch. Sam was huddled between Gray and Vera, sound asleep. They looked peaceful.

Another ring. Isaac patted his pockets, searching for the phone. He pulled it out and stared at the number. It was unfamiliar. *It might be Finn or Ellis on a burner phone. They should be here by now.*

He hit the answer button and put it to his ear. "Hello?"

"Hello, Isaac."

His blood chilled at the voice over the phone. "Is... is this... Gavin? How did you get this number?"

"Oh, Sam gave it to me. I guess I should say, they begged *me to let them give it. I don't think they would have lasted much longer if they'd forced me to keep beating them."*

Isaac's throat constricted. "What do you want?"

"I want Sam back. You interrupted me getting to know them. Breaking them was fun. Easy, but fun. I want to see them again. You're going to give them to me."

"Like *hell* I will," Isaac hissed. He got up off the nest of blankets on the floor and stalked to the kitchen, not wanting to wake the others. "You'll never get to us. Sam didn't tell you everything. We're somewhere you will never find us."

"So, you're not at 2208 Pineview Lane?"

Isaac's body locked into an icy panic. "N... no."

"Hm. The GPS tracker I forced Sam to swallow begs to differ."

All the blood ran out of his face. He stumbled and caught himself on the counter. "...what?"

"The tracker. In Sam's system."

"I... no..."

"So, here's what you're going to do. You're going to send Sam to me. You don't have to tell them why, just... send them out to the main road. I'll be waiting there. If you don't..." Isaac held his breath as Gavin paused. *"I am ready to blow the whole house to hell, right now."*

Isaac swallowed hard. Gavin could do it. Isaac knew enough about his operations to know that. "No. You can't have them. They... they're *ours*..."

"Then you choose for everyone to die?"

Isaac took a deep breath as his free hand clenched into a fist. "Take me."

There was a pause over the line. *"...excuse me?"*

"You heard me." Isaac's voice was urgent. "Leave Sam alone and take me. You want someone to, to *play* with..." He swallowed his disgust. "I'm fresh. I can take more. Sam's broken, they won't..." He shivered as he said the words. "They won't be any fun."

A delighted laugh came over the line. *"Take... you? Wow. I've heard so much about you. Your bravery... Sam had wonderful things to say. I guess they must be true. I accept."*

"How do I know you'll leave Sam alone if you take me?"

"You don't. But the tracker will work its way out of their system in the next few hours. As long as the others leave after it happens, that's it for me. I won't be able to find them after that."

I have to take that chance. I can't let him have Sam. "Okay. I'll meet you at the road."

"Can't wait." With a click, the line went dead.

Isaac felt his stomach drop to his shoes. *I can't let him have Sam. I can't. It was my mistake that let them fall into Gavin's hands. It should have been me the first time. It should have been* me. He pressed his face into his hands, feeling the burn of tears behind his eyes. *I have to go. It should have been me.* He turned away from the kitchen towards the door—

And nearly collided with Sam.

Sam swallowed a sob. "You... you can't..." they whispered.

Isaac's hands fell to his sides. "I don't have a choice, Sam. I have to go. I *have* to. I can't..." His breath caught in his chest. "*Can't* let him have you."

Tears streamed down Sam's face. "Isaac, please... please don't. Just let me go. He can have me, he can... I already told him everything. It wouldn't put anyone at risk..."

Isaac stepped forward and gripped Sam's shoulders. Sam winced, but they didn't pull away. "*No.* Absolutely not. You've been through enough, Sam. Stay here. Tell the others what happened once I leave. Did you hear the part about—"

"— the tracker, yes. I heard. I..." Sam sobbed quietly. "I led him straight to you... I'm sorry, I didn't know. He... he *forced* me to... He told me it was poison, I thought— He put the pill in my... mouth, and... wouldn't let me... *breathe* until I... I'm so *sorry*..." They crumpled in on themselves.

"*No, Sam,*" Isaac whispered fiercely. "None of this is your fault. But I..." He took a step towards the door. "I have to go."

Sam moved in front of him. "No. I won't let you. Please..." Their hands tangled in his shirt. "Please don't do this..."

Isaac wrapped his hands gently around Sam's wrists and guided their hands off his shirt. "Let me go, Sam."

They took a shuddering gasp. "I'll wake the others. We'll all stop you. You can't leave. Please Isaac, don't..."

Isaac felt like a stone had settled in his stomach. "Don't make me hurt you, Sam." His throat ached with the strain of keeping his voice even. Tears pricked at his eyes. "You need to let me go."

Sam opened their mouth to shout.

Isaac lunged forward and clapped his hand over their mouth. Their eyes went wide. They weakly pulled at his arms as he moved behind them. He grabbed both of their wrists in one hand and pinned them down. Sam struggled and screamed under him. *They're still so weak.* Isaac hated himself as he felt their struggles become lethargic and slow. *I have to do this.* Tears burned on his face and fell into Sam's hair.

Sam slowly grew still. *That's it, tire yourself out.* Isaac pulled his hand away from their face and their head drooped back on his shoulder. He placed them on the ground in the nest of blankets he'd made on the floor and covered them with one. They were already starting to stir again. *I have to go. Now.* He dashed to the door, grabbing the car keys on the way out.

Chapter 4

Isaac swallowed a sob as he pulled away from the house. *I hurt Sam. I hurt them. I'm no better than Gavin.* He wiped his face with his hand. *I had to keep them safe. This is my job. I make the hard calls. I have to keep them all safe.* He bumped along the dirt path winding through the trees leading out to the main road. It was just a few miles. It wouldn't take long.

He felt a rising wave of nausea in the pit of his stomach. *What is he going to do to me? He beat Sam, and cut them, and burned them...* He shook his head. *If I think about it too much, I'm going to turn back.* He knew he wouldn't. Not really. It just hurt to think about.

His hands tightened on the wheel as he thought about leaving the others without a vehicle until Finn and Ellis got there. *Maybe they'll find it at the road. Maybe one car is enough. They'll be taken care of.* His throat constricted. *I'm not going to be there to protect them. But... this is how I keep them safe. Keep Gavin so distracted with me he won't look for them.* He pulled in a deep breath. *This is how I keep them safe.*

Soon, far too soon, he broke the line of trees and pulled onto the shoulder of the main road. He shuddered as he saw a car already there waiting for him. *Gavin said he'd be waiting for me.* He shut the car off and pressed his forehead against the steering wheel. *This is how I keep them safe.* He calmly got out of the car, leaving the keys on the driver's seat.

Three people got out of the other car. Two large men, obviously guards. *I could take them both...* The one that had to be Gavin was the last to get out. He was beaming, almost giggling with excitement. Isaac clenched his jaw and walked towards them.

"Oh my god. Oh my *god*," Gavin said, smiling. "Oh my god. I got Isaac Moore." He laughed. "This is so unexpected. I wasn't even sure if you were going to come. Thought you would maybe make some stupid attempt to save everyone. But you didn't... you're *here*..." Gavin clasped his hands together under his chin. "It is so great to meet you."

Isaac met Gavin's gaze with an even stare. His arms hung limp by his sides. "I'm here. You have me." His lips trembled. He pressed them together in a hard line. "Let's just go."

Gavin grinned at him. "Oh, sure. But how do I know you won't attack us as soon as we turn our backs? You decimated my people at the compound. You might be able to overpower us here, too."

Isaac gritted his teeth. "I won't. I told you that you could have me, and here I am. The longer we stay here, the greater chance the others show up and try to stop me. So let's… just…" For a moment, an image of his family asleep on the couch flashed through his mind. "Let's just *go*."

Gavin cocked his head. "I need some kind of insurance. I can't just have you in my car… unfettered." He waggled his eyebrows at Isaac.

For a moment Isaac stood rigid in front of Gavin, clenching and unclenching his fists. Then, with a deep breath, he held out his wrists.

"Uh-uh." Gavin shook his head. "On your knees."

Isaac's throat tightened with humiliation. He closed his eyes and again pictured his family. *This is how I keep them safe.* He lowered himself to his knees.

"And?" Gavin's eyes shone with excitement.

Isaac was resigned as he held out his wrists again.

"Perfect." Gavin stepped forward and pulled a length of rope out of his pocket. He wound it a few times around Isaac's wrists, knotted it, and pulled it tight. "Let's go." The two guards pulled Isaac to his feet and guided him into the car.

Chapter 5

One of Gavin's men drove while the other sat in the back seat with Isaac, his gun trained on Isaac's heart. He looked a little like Gavin, with the same strong jaw and full lips.

It was the second time in five hours that Isaac had had a gun pointed at him. Gavin was babbling away in the passenger seat.

"I can't believe, I seriously just *cannot* believe you came to me. Here I was, thinking I'd be dragging Sam with me back to base, but instead I have *you!* You just... you can't know how excited this makes me," Gavin gushed. He turned and grinned widely at Isaac. "I mean, I've been making a habit of hurting people for a long time. Fun as it is, it kinda loses its appeal after a while with the same weak people. But with *you*—"

"Sam's not weak." Isaac's voice cracked like a whip.

Gavin paused, a smile drifting across his face. "Oh?"

"They're *not* weak."

Gavin laughed. "I beg to differ. You've seen them at their best, maybe at their worst too. But I've seen them at their *lowest*." His voice dropped to a low murmur. "I made them *scream*. I made them *beg*. I'd challenge you to tell me you've seen them in such a vulnerable position. At the rate I was going, they would have given me your damned *life* if I asked it. You have *no idea* how weak they are. They let you come to me in their place, didn't they?"

Isaac didn't care about the gun pointed at him. He launched himself across the car, his bound hands reaching for Gavin's throat. The man with the gun slammed one arm across Isaac's chest and knocked him back against his seat. The man threw his weight on top of Isaac and pressed the gun to the side of his head. Isaac gritted his teeth, bracing for the shot.

"No no no!" Gavin screamed. "I swear to god Mark, I don't *fucking* care if you're my cousin, if you shoot him I will *fire you*."

16

After a moment, Mark grunted and pulled his gun away from Isaac's head. He settled himself back in his own seat and stared Isaac down with a glower.

"Mark, if you shoot him, I will be so..." Gavin squeezed his hands together like he was crushing an imaginary windpipe. "Did you not just hear me say I was looking forward to this one?"

"Sorry, your highness," came the unapologetic reply.

Isaac glared at Gavin, his eyes shooting daggers across the car – a safe distance for Gavin. "Sam is *not weak*. They tried to stop me. They tried to go to you. They tried not to let me take their place. So how... *dare you...*"

"I'm the daring type." Gavin grinned at Isaac. "And yet you still came. They must not have tried very hard."

Isaac swallowed his hatred and sat still, shaking. "Sam has more courage in their little finger than you do in your entire goddamned *life*."

Gavin snorted. "I adore your loyalty to your little team. It's cute, it really is. You're so... *protective*. Is that why you came in Sam's place? Wanted to protect your little family?"

Isaac swallowed hard. His voice was barely above a whisper. "It should have been me. I messed up on the raid. Left them unprotected. You should have taken me."

"And now you're punishing yourself for your mistake. Adorable. I assure you, though..." Gavin's lips pulled into a wicked smile. "By the time I'm done with you, you'll wish you had let them come to me. I only had them for, what, two days? Three? But you I'll have for a long, long time."

"You had them for sixty-three hours," Isaac said, his jaw tight. "And when will you be done with me? What exactly do you have in mind here? You just gonna..." He tried to steady the tremor in his voice. "...torture me forever?"

Gavin grinned. "Yeah, something like that."

Isaac fell back a little more into his seat. *I just have to make it... maybe... eight hours. Long enough for the tracker to leave Sam's system. Then I can think of escape.*

17

"Still think you made the right decision?" Gavin mocked.

This is how I keep them safe. "Yes."

The car had cleared the line of trees miles ago. It pulled off the highway and turned onto a county road that stretched as far into the horizon as Isaac could see. Isaac's eyes widened.

Gavin watched his reaction. "What? I couldn't very well take you back to the same place. I'm taking you back to my... headquarters, I guess you'd call it? I have more... facilities there." He giggled. "You didn't manage to find this one too, did you?" Isaac shook his head stiffly. "Thought not."

Isaac tried to look directly in front of him, nowhere else. *We only found his other compound because one of his people made a mistake. Didn't check to see if they had a tail. How are they going to find me at this place?* Then, with a chill: *Are they even going to come after me?* He swallowed hard. *Doesn't matter. This is how I keep them safe.*

He closed his eyes and let his head fall back against the headrest. He was exhausted. He wasn't too worried about Gavin killing him while he rested. Not after the tantrum he'd thrown about Mark nearly killing him.

Isaac had only gotten to sleep for about two hours after they had brought Sam back to the safehouse. *It was a long sixty-three hours.* Patrols, searches, waiting for one of Gavin's men to move and lead them to Sam. The worrying. The guilt. *It should have been me.*

His mind wandered to his family. Vera, with her nervous tics and intensity under pressure. Gray, with their nurturing and strong presence. Finn, their medic, always champing at the bit to be in the thick of things with the others. Finn's partner Ellis, sarcastic and guarded. *They're my family and I'd do anything for them.* He shuddered as he pictured the bruises across Sam's chest and back as he lifted Sam's shirt. *Anything.*

He drooped in his seat, exhaustion overtaking him. He didn't know how long he drifted.

"Wakey wakey!"

He jolted awake and threw his hands in front of his face at the sound of Gavin's voice. He remembered, in one horrifying moment, that they were bound and why.

The car was stopped. Gavin was staring at him with an irritated and expectant look on his face.

"Wha...?"

"We're here! Home sweet home."

Isaac looked out the window at an industrial building in the middle of nowhere. "This is where your operations are based?"

"Yup! My branch, at least." Gavin sounded proud. "To the outside eye it looks like a warehouse, although *why* there would be a warehouse out here is beyond me." Gavin winked at Isaac. "Kinda conceals the several underground floors for fun stuff, don't you think?"

Isaac drew in a deep breath. "Sure."

Gavin jumped out of the car and motioned to his bodyguards. "Come on, get him out."

Isaac pulled at the door handle with his bound hands, groaning as his body unfolded after being in the car so long. "I can get out myself, thanks." The two men quickly closed on him and grabbed his arms. "How long was I asleep?"

"About three hours." Gavin raised his arms theatrically. "You ready to get this show on the road? Or do you want me to go grab Sam instead? You can totally leave, if you want." He paused and glared at his men. *"You can leave if you want."* He motioned them away from him with one hand and rolled his eyes in mock annoyance as they stepped away from him. "Final offer, though. Once we pass those doors, you're mine forever and Sam's free. What do you think? Are you *absolutely sure* you want to do this?"

Isaac cast a glance behind him, at the way they had come. He couldn't see anything but the road stretching into the horizon. He turned to look at the imposing structure in front of him. He flexed his wrists, feeling the rope tight on his skin. He drew in a slow, deep breath and met Gavin's gaze.

"Let's do this."

Chapter 6

Gavin grinned. "Excellent." He motioned with his head to his guards. "Mark, Leo, let's do it." They grabbed Isaac's arms and began to march him into the building.

Isaac's heart sank as the building loomed above him. *No no no...* Isaac had been roughed up by goons before, thrown around during training with his old team— He shut the thought down. He'd even been stabbed once on one of his first raids. But he'd never been captured by the syndicates he spent his life fighting. He'd never been so helpless.

And he'd never been at the mercy of an unhinged sadist.

He shivered.

Gavin's lips quirked up into a smile. "Aw, come on. It's gonna be fun." Gavin snorted. "Well, maybe not for you. But I am gonna have the time. Of. My. Life." He jabbed his finger into Isaac's chest with each word. As he reached the door, he pulled it open for the three of them, motioning them all in with a flourish.

The inside wasn't nearly what Isaac expected. He was greeted by the brightly lit interior of a warehouse bustling with people, vehicles, and equipment. Before he could look around to take in any details, Gavin began to laugh.

"Not as scary as you thought, right?"

Isaac looked straight ahead and said nothing.

Gavin cuffed him on the shoulder. "Don't worry, the scary stuff is all a few floors down. That's where we're going." He led them down an aisle bordered on both sides by stacks of boxes. *DANGER: EXPLOSIVES* was printed in big letters on the sides. Gavin turned to relish Isaac's wary look. "Oh, relax. This stuff only goes boom out there." He gestured vaguely towards the door they had come in.

He marched them to an elevator and pressed the call button. As he waited for the elevator to arrive, Gavin turned to shoot a satisfied glance at Isaac. "Nervous yet?"

Isaac's jaw clenched. "Nervous isn't the word I'd use."

Gavin's eyes widened. "Aw, are you *scared?* Are you seriously *scared* right now?" Gavin's jaw fell open like he'd been mortally wounded.

Isaac's eyes snapped to Gavin's. "Of *course,* I'm scared. I didn't do this because I thought it would be a good time. I did it to save my *family.*"

Gavin's open-mouthed gape pulled up slowly into a smile. "I... love that, actually. You're terrified, but you're here anyway. For the good of the *team.*" He drew out the word mockingly. "Do they know you're such a softie? Do they appreciate you the way they should?"

Isaac turned back to the elevator, his face like stone. "I might have rethought this if I'd known you were going to *talk* so damned much."

"Rude." The elevator doors opened. The bodyguards pushed Isaac in and Gavin followed, pressing *B3.* He typed a six-digit code into the keypad on the wall and the elevator started to move down.

As the floors went by, Gavin whistled a few notes. It didn't sound like a song. When the doors opened again, he stepped out and Isaac was pushed out right behind him.

This was more of what Isaac was expecting. The hallway was narrow, with pipes running the length of it on the walls. The fluorescent lights flickered on the ceiling as Gavin guided them to a door a few dozen paces down the hall from the elevator. *I'll need to remember this for when I escape. Five hours and then I can try.*

Then Gavin pushed the door open and Isaac's stomach dropped.

The room was dimly lit, but Isaac could still see what was inside. Chains hung from the high ceiling on pulleys, out of reach now but ready for use at a moment's notice. The floor sloped just slightly towards a drain in the center of the room. An empty table stood against the wall to the left. There were no windows. *Of course, we're underground.* But the thing that made Isaac's stomach pitch in revulsion and terror was the table at the far side of the room. It held every imaginable torture instrument and some Isaac couldn't even guess the purpose of. Isaac swallowed the bile rising in his throat. He turned his face away from Gavin, who seemed to be drinking in Isaac's fear like cool water on a hot day.

"Much as a love a self-sacrificing idiot all tied up," Gavin mocked, his voice sickly sweet, "I need to get you into something a bit more... sturdy." He went to the table and picked up a pair of manacles. He slowly approached Isaac, closely watching his every move.

Isaac's instincts kicked in and for a moment, he forgot why he had come. He pulled against his captors with eyes fixed on the manacles. *Once he gets me in those, I'm trapped.*

Gavin held up one finger. "Ah ah ah, I thought you were going to play nice?"

Isaac froze, trembling against his captors' grasp. *This... is how... I keep them... safe.*

Gavin smiled. "Much better. Hold out your hands."

He held them out. They were trembling.

Gavin snorted and locked the manacles around Isaac's wrists. He held out a hand to Leo. "Knife." Leo pulled one out of his pocket and handed it over. Gavin cut through the rope on Isaac's wrists and slipped the knife into his own pocket. He stepped back, admiring the look of Isaac in chains. "You just look so much... *better* than Sam did. A broken little thing all tied up is just... pathetic. But you..." Gavin took a step closer, his eyes dancing over Isaac. "My guys tell me you killed some of my people when you came in for Sam. You, personally. Killed my guys." He patted Isaac roughly on the cheek. "And now you're here, in my basement, chained up and ready to take torture for your family. It's just... so... good!"

Gavin turned away and moved to a corner of the room where a chain hung from the ceiling. He guided it up through the pulley system, lowering the other end of the chain almost directly over Isaac's head. It had a hook on the end of it. Isaac could guess what was coming next.

The guards pulled his arms up over his head and hooked the manacles to the chain hanging from the ceiling. Gavin pulled down on his end of the chain, lifting Isaac's hands higher above his head. Isaac was seized with panic for a moment. *I can't let him do this. I could run, I could fight this.*

The look on Sam's face when they realized they were rescued flashed across his mind and burned into the backs of his eyes like he had been staring into the sun. He let his body go slack. He felt the manacles pull tight against his wrists. *Even if I tried, I couldn't get away now. Sam is safe. Sam is safe from me and my weakness.* Gavin's men let go of his arms and stepped away.

"Thanks guys. That'll be it for now." Gavin looked practically giddy. Isaac heard the men leave the room and pull the door shut behind them. It closed with a forbidding *thud.*

Gavin slowly sauntered up to Isaac, relishing every moment of his fear. Gavin's gaze danced over him as Isaac's eyes went wider than before, his breaths coming a little faster. Isaac tightened his fists in dread and anticipation. Gavin's lips pulled into a grin. "Wanna know what I'm gonna start you off with?"

Isaac glared at him, his jaw tightening. "Just because I came willingly doesn't mean I have to play your games. We both know what you're going to do. So just... do it."

Gavin rolled his eyes. "Okay fine, no guessing game." He walked slowly around Isaac. As he moved into Isaac's periphery, Isaac turned his head to follow him. Gavin's hand shot out and grabbed him by the hair, turning his head away from him. Isaac jumped as he heard the knife open again. He felt the cold on his neck as Gavin cut away his T-shirt. He shivered as the blade moved from the neck of his shirt down his back until it stopped almost at the hem. Gavin tore the last few inches of fabric himself. He cut down the back of each shoulder. The shirt slid off him and made a small heap of fabric at his feet. Isaac trembled at being so exposed.

Gavin stalked to the table, his hand moving across his instruments. He stopped on a long, heavy-looking length of leather. His fingers curved almost lovingly around the handle and he wound it a few times around his hand as he approached Isaac again. "We can start with the next thing I was going to do to poor Sam before you interrupted me."

23

Isaac's blood ran cold. "You were going to whip them? *Seriously?* What's *wrong* with you?" He swallowed hard. "How far would you have gone with them if we hadn't come? Would you have... would you have killed them in the end?"

Gavin's hand fisted in Isaac's hair as he dragged him forward. Isaac could see now that he had two inches on Gavin, easily.

"Honestly..." Isaac shuddered as he felt Gavin's breath on his face. "I'm kinda surprised *you* didn't kill them after everything they told me." Gavin tossed Isaac's head back and moved behind him again.

"Gavin, *please*," Isaac whispered. He heard Gavin stop behind him. "*Please* don't do this."

"Are you fucking *kidding* me?!" Gavin again appeared in front of Isaac and slapped him across the face. Isaac rocked back, gasping. "Are you *kidding* me right now? You're *begging*? Already?" He grabbed Isaac's face and pulled him close. "If I wanted some pathetic whining and begging, I would have stuck with Sam! I wanted *you*—" His hand tightened on Isaac's jaw. "— because I wanted something *different*. I thought you would be *different*, Isaac. Sam told me all about how brave you are, that you wouldn't break if it was you I was torturing, that you'd come for them. That you'd *save* them."

Tears pricked at Isaac's eyes.

Gavin smiled. "Oh, you didn't know about that? They didn't tell you how they screamed for you, begged me to stop and begged for you to save them, how they sang your praises after I cut them over and over again?" A feverish light danced in Gavin's eyes. "They *idolize* you, Isaac. You're their *hero*. How would they feel if they saw you now, begging like they did?" He pulled Isaac so close their noses were almost touching. "I will hear you beg, but after I've *earned* it. Do you understand?"

Isaac nodded slowly.

"I haven't even *touched* you yet. I can go get Sam instead if you can't take this for them."

The tears threatened to spill over. Gavin released Isaac's jaw with a shove and moved behind him again.

"Now." Isaac heard the length of the whip smack against the ground as Gavin released it. "You ever been whipped before?" Gavin's manic tone was back. Isaac shook his head, afraid that if he spoke his voice would shake.

"Ooh, excellent. You have no idea what to expect. Perfect. Well, I haven't tried it myself but if my prior experience with *other* people means anything to you, apparently it's… excruciating."

Nothing could have prepared Isaac for the first blow. The impact stunned him first, made his breath freeze in his chest before he even felt the pain. It came a moment after that. A line of fire arced across his back and he gasped.

Before the sting of the first blow had a chance to fade, Gavin whipped the leather across his back again. Isaac cried out as the whip drew another line of fire across his back, diagonal to the first. *If I'm weak, he'll go after Sam.* He bit down on his lips and tried to hold back the scream that tore from his throat on the third swing. On the fourth, Isaac's broken sob echoed off the walls.

Gavin laughed. "Much better. Come on, Isaac, be strong for me. Be strong like Sam thinks you are."

Crack.

Isaac tried to force down his anguished cry.

Crack.

He couldn't draw breath. His chest was frozen in agony.

Crack.

He saw a blinding flash of light as the pain crashed through him.

Crack.

He didn't try to hold back his scream. He couldn't.

Crack.

He squeezed his eyes shut against the pain. *No no no no I can't be weak, can't let him go after Sam—*

Crack.

He sagged against the manacles around his wrists. He pressed his mouth against his arm and sobbed. Each time he breathed his chest was wracked with pain. He felt the warm trickle of blood down his back over the searing agony of each lash.

It took him a moment to notice the lashes had stopped. His eyes fluttered open and he gasped to see Gavin's face only inches from his own. He pressed his face against his arm, trying to hide the tears burning his cheeks. *I can't be weak; I can't let him get Sam...*

"Oh no no no no, don't hide from me." That hand was in his hair again. "That was just getting really good."

Isaac frantically shook his head. "No, I can do this, I can..."

"I know. You're doing great."

Isaac dragged in a shuddering breath. "You... you were going to do this to Sam..."

Gavin grinned. "Yup. Can't you just imagine how they would have screamed?"

"No..." Isaac shook his head. He *could* imagine it. He couldn't bear to think about it.

"That was ten."

"...what?"

"That was ten. Lashes. Think you could take another ten without breaking?"

Isaac couldn't catch the sob on its way out. He didn't think he could take another *one* without breaking, let alone *ten*.

"Oh come oooon, Isaac," Gavin whined. "Come on. Please? Pretty please?" He pouted his lips.

This is how I keep them safe. Isaac tried his best to stop his lips from trembling. Then, slowly, he nodded.

"Excellent."

Isaac squeezed his eyes shut and felt the air move as Gavin disappeared behind him again.

"Brace yourself, hero."

Isaac gritted his teeth as the lash came down.

Chapter 7

Crack.

"Twenty-five." Isaac had long since abandoned his attempts to hold in his screams. They seemed to shake apart the room.

Crack.

"Twenty-six. Holy shit, Isaac, are you seriously going to make it to thirty?"

Crack.

"Twenty-seven."

Crack.

Isaac broke. *"PLEASE!"*

The whip fell to Gavin's side as he lowered his arm. "Aw. Twenty-eight. So close."

"Please," sobbed Isaac. "Please, I can't…"

"You want me to stop?" Gavin's voice tightened.

"Y-yes, please, please stop, please…"

"We're so close to thirty. Two more."

"NO!"

Crack.

"PLEASE!"

Crack.

"No no no god no, please..." Isaac trailed off into whimpers. He hung limp from the manacles, his legs shaking too badly to hold him up. The steel dug into his wrists until he thought they would bleed.

"Hey, chill out. You're done." Gavin placed his hands on Isaac's face and pulled it up. Isaac shuddered as Gavin's eyes moved over him. Isaac's face was haggard with agony, his cheeks wet with tears. His skin shimmered with sweat and blood. His eyes were glassy and unfocused.

Isaac choked out a desperate sob. "I... I'm done...?"

"Yeah." Gavin grabbed Isaac's face in one hand. "That... was... *awesome.*" Confusion moved over Isaac's pain-drawn features. "Don't get me wrong, you had me going for a minute there. I was really worried you'd break too fast, beg, but... wow. You lasted *twenty-eight lashes.* You know the next-highest number anyone's ever gotten through with me was seventeen?" Isaac's eyes rolled back. "*Seventeen.* You did that plus eleven more." Gavin shoved his face towards Isaac's. "I really am so, so impressed."

Isaac groaned. "I... had to keep them... safe..."

Gavin patted his face. "Look at you. You did great."

Isaac looked at him, trying to focus his eyes. He realized the right side of Gavin's face, chest, and arm were spattered with his blood.

Isaac licked his lips. "How long has it been?"

"Since... what? Since we got here?"

"Since you started... torturing me?"

Gavin's mouth slid into a wicked grin. "Now... why would you want to know that?"

"I... just..."

"Because you want to know how much longer you have to hold on before there's no risk of me going back for Sam?"

"No..."

Gavin stepped behind Isaac again. Isaac pulled at the manacles, cringing in on himself. Gavin pressed the flat of his palm against Isaac's back. Isaac cried out, pulling away from Gavin and stumbling. His weight fell hard on his wrists again.

"Don't tell me you're powering through this because you think you only have to last for a few hours." Gavin pulled his hand away from Isaac's back and smacked him over the bleeding welts. Isaac *screamed*. "Because that would be so, *so* disappointing."

"No no no no…"

Another slap. Another tortured scream. "Good. Because I want to remind you that I only had Sam for sixty or so hours, however many you said. And look how *broken* I made them. I broke them so hard, they truly believed you were coming to kill them."

Isaac whimpered.

"I didn't know if they'd even be capable of killing you in the state I left them in. I figured it was worth a shot, at least." Gavin snorted. "So to speak. So I want you to forget anything about holding out until they're safe. Fact is, if I *want* to find them, I *will*. I'll only leave them alone if *you* prove to be more interesting than they were. And I want to make something very clear." Gavin walked around to stand in front of Isaac. His hand gripped Isaac's hair and pulled his head back. "If I could convince Sam, sweet, innocent, loyal Sam that their friend was coming to punish them, to *kill* them for breaking under torture after just a few days, what do you think I'll be able to do to you after, say… a week? A month?" He scoffed. "A year, if you live that long? I intend to keep you alive as long as humanly possible and I happen to have a kickass medical dude on my staff who can help me with that." He grabbed Isaac's face in a vise-like grip. "What I'm trying to say is, don't worry how long it's been. That's not your concern. Your concern is this: remaining worth my while."

Tears ran silently down Isaac's face.

"Did you really think you were going to escape this after a few hours? You figured you'd just hold out for a few hours of torture and then fight your way out?" Gavin laughed. "No no no no. You are gonna be my plaything, my stress relief, my entertainment, for as long as you stay interesting. As soon as that stops being true…" His mouth slid into a wider grin. "…I'm going to kill you, the way you should have killed Sam for betraying you, and hunt them down so I can take them back."

"No."

The power in Isaac's voice surprised him. Gavin stared at him. *"No?"*

Isaac set his jaw and met Gavin's eyes. "You're never going to look for them. You're going to keep me. I can give you what they couldn't." He trembled and the power in his voice faltered. "Please. Keep me."

For a moment, Gavin was enraptured. "Oh. Do that again."

"Do… what?"

Gavin's smile turned dark and terrifying. "Beg me to torture you. Beg me to torture you in every way you dread."

Isaac's voice shook. "Please… I want you to…" His throat worked around a soft sob as it made its way out of his chest. "Please hurt me like you hurt Sam. Tie me down. Beat me. Please. Whip me, chain me up, waterboard me…"

Gavin nodded quickly. "Don't stop, keep going. If you run out of ideas, just say the same ones again."

Isaac blinked tears out of his eyes. "Gavin, please… hurt me. Make my life a misery, make me wish for death, beg for it, torture me, torture me, Gavin, please…" He had to stop to take a gasping breath. "Just torture me, leave them alone. Don't hurt them. Hurt me, please. I'm the one you want. Don't look for them. Please." His voice broke. "Please," he whispered.

Gavin looked beyond pleased. He looked ecstatic. "Okay." He walked to the wall and jerked down on the chain attached to Isaac's manacles, releasing it from its catch. Isaac crumpled to the floor. He grunted as the impact sent pain lancing through his wounds.

Gavin kicked him hard in the back. Isaac cried out, dragging himself away from Gavin, gasping against the pain. Gavin watched him for a moment as he tried to crawl away with his hands still chained together. Gavin aimed another kick at his shoulder and pitched him onto his side. Isaac began to sob.

Gavin bent over and patted Isaac's face, streaked with blood and sweat. "You have a deal. You're too much fun." He stood to leave, stepping over Isaac's body. Isaac laid on the ground and cried.

Chapter 8

Sam groaned and rolled onto their side. Their mind spun. *What was I...? What just...?* They heard the car start and it all came back in a rush.

They stumbled to their feet and threw themselves at the front door. *"Gray!"* they screamed, their voice cracking. *"Vera!"* The two others on the couch jumped at Sam's shout and staggered towards them.

"What?" Gray's voice was thick with sleep. "What is it?"

Sam didn't stop. They hurled themselves out the door, stumbling as they tried to run. *"Isaac!"* they screamed, tears pouring down their face. "Isaac, *no!*" They chased after the car as it pulled onto the trail and out into the woods. *"Isaac!"* The car turned a corner and disappeared into the trees.

Sam tripped and splayed out into the mud. It was cold and gritty on their hands. Their eyes were fixed on the spot where Isaac had disappeared. They began to sob, their body rocking forward with each painful breath. They felt Vera skid to a halt beside them. Her hands were urgent on their shoulder.

"Sam!" she panted. "What happened?!" She pulled them up roughly by their shirt.

They collapsed again, their knees hitting the cold ground hard. "No... no..." They clutched at Vera's hands.

"What happened?" Gray was right behind her, breathing hard. "Sam, what is it?"

Vera's voice was strained. "Why did Isaac leave with the car?"

Sam tried to calm their breathing. "He..." They gulped and heaved another sob. "He went..." A wail cut off their words.

"It's okay, Sam." Gray's voice was low, right in their ear. "Just breathe, take your time. Tell us what happened."

Sam pressed their hands to their face. "G-G-Gavin called him, told him to send me back to him and Isaac..." They curled in on themselves, trembling violently. "Isaac... went in my place... He wouldn't let me stop him... I tried to... I tried..." Their throat felt like it would tear open.

"What?" Vera's eyes followed Sam's gaze into the woods. "No, why would he...?"

"Gavin found us," they moaned. "He made me swallow a GPS tracker. I'm so sorry, he said it was poison and he'd only give me the antidote if I... told him more about you..." Vera and Gray looked at each other. Their faces bore twin expressions of horror.

Sam ducked their head. "He tracked us here and... I don't know what he was going to do, I don't know, but Isaac said he would take my place because I'm too... *broken*..." Their sob drew out into a scream.

"Oh my god," Gray breathed. "No..." They turned their gaze to Sam and helped them up out of the mud. "Let's get you cleaned up, and we'll make our plan from there."

Sam was inconsolable. "If I had just... no... If I had stopped him, if I had gone... If I had... *died*... under his torture... Isaac wouldn't be..." Their legs wouldn't hold them up. "Isaac... *no*..."

Gray gathered Sam up in their arms and carried them to the house. Sam didn't seem to notice. They continued to sob into Gray's shoulder.

"I'll get Finn and Ellis on the radio," Vera said, voice pitched high with strain. "They should have been here by now." She jogged back to the house.

"Gray..." Sam sobbed. "I'm sorry, I'm so sorry..."

"Shh..." Gray whispered. "It's okay. It's not your fault, Sam. It's not your fault. We'll get Isaac back."

"We'll never get him back," Sam wailed. "How will be get him back with just us?"

"We'll figure something out." Gray pressed their lips into Sam's hair. "We'll get him back. He's strong. He'll survive until we get there."

34

"You don't know that…" Sam whimpered. "You don't know what Gavin does, what he…" They swallowed a sob. "He got inside my head. And he hurt me… It didn't stop, he just kept hurting me… I thought he was going to kill me but it just didn't… *end*…"

"Shh," Gray murmured. "Shh. We're going to find him." They climbed up the steps and ducked under the doorway with Sam still tight in their arms.

Vera spoke quickly into the radio. "That's what I *said*, Finn. Gavin has him. We need you to get here as soon as you can so we can start strategizing his rescue."

"We're getting there as fast as we can. Can you tell us anything else?"

"Not over the radio. We don't know what's compromised and what isn't." She threw a glance at Sam and Gray as they came through the door. Gray set Sam gently on the floor. They swayed, but stayed on their feet. "Just… get here, okay?"

"Okay. See you soon."

Vera blew out a slow breath. "They're about half an hour out, still. They nearly ran into one of Gavin's patrols and had to take another route." She pulled her hair over her shoulder with a trembling hand.

"They're probably…" Sam's voice shook. "Probably protecting Gavin. He met I-Isaac out by the main road. I wonder… if they…"

"…if they're protecting him as he falls back," Gray finished. "Maybe. We'll have to ask Finn and Ellis which route they were taking. Might give us a good starting point for at least the direction they took him." They pinched the bridge of their nose between their thumb and forefinger. "Our raids must have been sending a message if a damned syndicate *son* feels like he needs that much protection this deep in his own territory."

"Should we…" Sam stared at the floor. "Should we move once they get here? Since G-Gavin knows where we are?"

Vera shook her head. "No. If he's got a tracker in you, might as well stay here. He had the option to come here and kill all of us, and he didn't. Once you… uh… pass it, then we can move." Her eyes moved between Gray and Sam.

"Either of you two have any secret safehouses you haven't thought to mention?"

Gray shook their head.

"If I did, they wouldn't be safe anymore," Sam said, their voice weak.

"Don't do that." Vera's voice was harsher than it ever was when she talked to Sam. Sam flinched. Vera looked cowed. "I'm sorry, just… Don't you *dare* hate yourself for this. Gavin captured you and tortured you. You did…" Her eyes were far away and brimming with tears. She blinked them from her eyes and focused again. "You did so well, Sam. We're proud of you. But we need you at your best right now. Isaac…" She swallowed hard, tears shining in her eyes again. "Isaac needs you. Okay? I know you want to help him. And the best way you can is to… I need you to keep being strong for him, okay?"

Sam nodded miserably.

Gray knelt beside them and ran their long fingers through Sam's curls. "I know you just want to break right now. We're going to help you as much as we can. I wish we could just… care for you and take care of you the way you deserve. But we need to focus on the next step, okay? And the next."

Sam struggled not to let the tears in their eyes roll down their cheeks.

"Hey." Gray wiped Sam's tears away with gentle hands. "We are going to be here for you. We are. You are not forgotten."

Sam shook their head. "I'm not worried about me. I'm f-fine. I just want to get Isaac back. You don't know what it's like, what Gavin will do to him…"

"Stop." Gray took Sam by the shoulders and shook them once, gently. "If you need to talk about what you went through, we are happy to help you and hear it. But don't get lost thinking about what Isaac is going through. We need to think about his rescue. Okay?"

Sam wiped their nose against their muddy shirt. "Okay."

Gray wrapped their arms around Sam. "We're gonna get him back, okay?" Sam felt tears drop onto their shoulder. "We have to get him back."

Chapter 9

Isaac groaned at the sound of the door opening again. "No…"

"Oh, come on," Gavin huffed, walking into the room with Leo close behind. "I gave you twenty minutes to recover. And didn't you *just beg me* to torture you? Come on, Isaac, mixed messages here." He grinned and turned to Leo. "Get him up."

Leo yanked him up to sitting. Isaac cried out weakly as the welts on his back stretched and bled a little more with the movement. Leo pulled a key out of his pocket and unlocked one of the manacles. Confused, Isaac raised his eyes to Gavin. He paled when he saw that Gavin was carrying a bucket of water.

"What… No…" The tears started again as Leo wrenched Isaac's arms behind his back and shackled his hands behind him. "Wait…"

Gavin set the bucket on the floor and pinched the bridge of his nose between his fingers and thumb. "I swear to god, if I have to remind you about Sam every damned time I start into you, I'm gonna get *real* tired of that *real* fast."

Isaac's eyes were wide and fixed on the bucket. "I… I can be scared and still know why I'm here…"

Gavin rolled his eyes up to the ceiling. "And why are you here? I'm sure we could all use a reminder."

Isaac swallowed hard and closed his eyes. "Sam. I'm here for Sam."

"Good. Come here."

Trembling, Isaac drew himself to his feet. He stopped in front of Gavin, staring at the water.

"Get on your knees."

Isaac fought back a sob. Of all things, of *all things* Gavin could have done, he decided to do *this*...

"Get on your knees. I'm not going to ask again." Gavin's voice had a hard edge to it that made Isaac's chest tighten.

This is... This is how... Isaac couldn't think straight. He couldn't think of his family. He couldn't picture their faces. The only thing that occupied his mind was the bucket of water in front of him and what he knew was about to happen.

Isaac went down as Leo kicked him in the back of the leg. Leo forced him to his knees and yanked his head back with a hand in his hair. He could barely draw breath past the sobs. "No no no no no no..."

"Isaac."

"No no no no please no..."

Gavin slapped him across the face. *"Isaac."*

That brought him back, a little. "What..."

"You're the one psyching yourself out right now. Have I done anything to you? Seriously."

"No... No, I..."

"Then chill out. I'm just talking to you right now."

Isaac nodded, shaking from head to toe.

Gavin laughed. "Well, if I doubted you were scared of drowning before, I wouldn't doubt it now. Christ."

Isaac did his best to draw in deep inhales and blow out slow exhales.

Gavin waited a few breaths. "Isaac."

Isaac tremulously met his gaze. "What?"

"Do you know why I decided to do this next?"

Panic clutched at Isaac's stomach again. "No..."

Gavin's slap knocked his head to the side, despite the hold Leo had on his hair. He cried out. Gavin's hand shot out to close around Isaac's neck as he trembled in Leo's grasp. "I swear to god, Isaac, get your shit together *right now* or I kill you right here and go after Sam."

Not Sam.

Isaac blinked the tears out of his eyes and dragged in another breath. "No."

"Okay then. Can I continue? Please?"

Isaac nodded and pressed his lips together.

"Thanks so much." Gavin rolled his eyes and sat cross-legged on the ground in front of him, the bucket between them. "Let's talk."

Isaac watched him warily, his head still pulled back by Leo's hand in his hair.

"Do you know how I knew bringing this in here would freak you out?" Gavin nudged the bucket with his foot. Isaac flinched away as the bucket moved and stiffened as Leo tightened his grip on his hair.

"No," he whispered.

"Oh, come on. Not even a guess?" Gavin grinned up at him.

Isaac felt a chill creep into his stomach. He kept his eyes fixed on the wall behind Gavin and pressed his lips together.

Gavin glanced up at Leo and nodded. Without hesitation, Leo forced him forward and plunged his head into the bucket.

Panic gripped him immediately. The cold on his face made him gasp and he drew water into his throat. He bucked hard against the hands on his shoulder and hair, but Leo's grip was like iron as he held Isaac's head under the water. He screamed as his pulse raged in his ears. His lungs spasmed as he choked, dragging more water in.

His head was pulled from the water. He dragged in a ragged gasp and coughed until his ribs ached. Water poured from his nose and mouth. Tears mixed with the water on his face.

Gavin reached out and grabbed Isaac's chin. "That is gonna happen every time to refuse to answer me."

Isaac's chest heaved with each breath as he began to sob. "You'll... never... get anything out of me."

Gavin tilted his head. "Aw. There's that courage Sam kept going on about. But I don't want information from you. Even if you do know things Sam doesn't, I don't really feel the need. I'm content I have enough if I ever need to hunt them all down."

"No..."

Gavin held up a finger. "I'm not here for information. Like I said, I just want to talk." Water dripped off Isaac's face, onto his bare chest and onto the floor. "So. Do you know why I knew to do this?"

A whimper made its way out of Isaac's throat. "Sam told you."

"Bingo!" Gavin laughed.

Isaac shook his head. "I don't blame them for that." His knees were already beginning to ache.

Gavin grinned wickedly. "Oh? Would you blame them if I told you they *volunteered* that information?"

Isaac swallowed hard. "There's... no way."

He laughed again. "Think again! I *told* you they broke, and they broke fast. This was, like, day one." He gestured to the bucket. "All I told them was to tell me something interesting about you. They volunteered your greatest fear all on their own."

Isaac clenched his jaw. "They're young. And inexperienced. It's not their fault."

"Oh, please. How old are they? I know every single thing they're afraid or ashamed of and yet... their age just never made it into the conversation."

Isaac hesitated before speaking. "They're nineteen."

Gavin snorted. "Okay, yeah, that is pretty young. Five years younger than me. But still, aren't you even… the *slightest bit* mad at them?"

Isaac shook his head. "You tortured them. It's not their fault."

Gavin's eyes narrowed. "What are they to you? You're so god damned protective of them, to the point of idiocy. There was absolutely no need for you to take their place. If anything, you've left your family vulnerable without you. So why?"

"They…" He swallowed. "They're *Sam*. They're just… good. They didn't deserve this."

"People don't go to their deaths for people who are just *good*."

Isaac's voice shook. "I didn't know you were going to kill me."

"Would that have changed anything?"

"…no."

"You know what I think?" Gavin scooted himself closer until his shins were pressed against the bucket. "I think you would have done this for Ellis, or Gray, or anyone else on your team." He grinned as Isaac's eyes grew wide. "Yes, of course I know all their names. And do you know why?" Isaac glared at him. "This team is all you have. And I don't mean just, 'they're family' or anything like that. No. You came because… What else do you have to offer them, besides your life?"

Isaac swallowed.

"Really, I mean it. If Gray's in charge, Finn's medical, Vera is… operations, I guess? And Ellis sounds like they've got a sense of humor, so they've definitely got you beat there." Isaac's eyes grew wider. "Oh, come on. I had almost *three days* with Sam. You think I didn't get to know your little family *intimately* well?" He cocked his head at Isaac. "But what do you bring to the table?"

Isaac's throat bobbed. "I…"

Isaac's head plunged into the bucket again. He did his best not to breathe the water in, but his body betrayed him. He yanked hard against the hand in his hair. It was unrelenting. When the hand let him up again his lungs were burning for air. He choked on the water in his throat.

"What do you bring to the table, Isaac?"

He couldn't answer. His throat was too constricted from coughing.

Gavin sighed. "I'll wait."

When Isaac could finally catch his breath he gasped out, "I protect them!"

Gavin rolled his eyes. "That doesn't count, because you obviously suck at it." Isaac bit his lip. "So, what do you actually *do* for the team that no one else does? More importantly…" He adjusted his seat. "What it is about your life that makes you so keen to give it for another?"

Tears burned in Isaac's eyes. "I… don't…"

"Let me tell you what I think." Gavin's voice was intense. "I think you know you're not the hero Sam thinks you are. You aren't even a particularly *good* guard dog. After all…" Gavin clicked his tongue. "I took Sam because of a mistake *you* made. I think you came to me because you know that's all you're good for: dying so someone else doesn't have to."

The tears spilled over.

"Aw, someone's sensitive. I'm right, though, aren't I?"

"You don't know what you're talking about…"

"Oh, yes I do." Gavin got up on his knees, at Isaac's eye level. "I think you know, deep down, that you're not the person Sam thinks you are. You came here because you wanted to *earn* that place in their eyes. With Sam, with everyone. Deep down, you know you're as weak as they are."

"Sam's *not* weak!"

"You keep saying that with all evidence to the contrary. But I'm not talking about them. I'm talking about *you*." He tapped Isaac on the nose. "See, by coming here you guarantee the last thing your family remembers about you is this incredibly brave and selfless thing you did for your sweet and innocent Sam. Everyone will love you for it. Sam will hold you in their mind as their

42

hero forever. And your family doesn't ever have to see you when you're at your weakest." He grinned. "They don't have to see how you begged before the whip even touched you. Or how you begged just because you saw a bucket of water. They don't have to see how terrified you are…" He made a beckoning motion to Leo. Leo slowly forced Isaac's head down to the water.

"NO! No no no, please, *please*, don't…" Leo stopped with Isaac's face an inch from the water. Isaac sobbed and writhed against his grasp. *"Please…"*

Gavin chuckled. "See? My point is made." He placed his hand on the back of Isaac's head and dunked his face into the bucket. Gavin allowed him right back out of the water and Leo drew Isaac back upright.

Isaac coughed and spluttered. Gavin's eyes moved over Isaac's face. "And I think you refuse to believe that Sam is weak because you want to believe you sacrificed yourself for someone good. Because if your sacrifice means nothing, and you are nothing without your sacrifice—"

"You're wrong. Sam *is* good. And brave. And kind."

"…that's all you're gonna correct me on? Does that mean everything else is true?"

"You're a coward," Isaac spat through his teeth.

Gavin's face slid slowly into a smile. "Wow. You're really taking this personally. Methinks I hit a nerve." Isaac clenched his jaw shut. "You didn't correct me, though. Which means you know. Deep down, maybe, but you know that you're weak, you're nothing, and this was the only thing you could think to do to convince your family that you're worthy of the trust and love they give you. Or maybe you needed to convince yourself."

Isaac held his gaze with a glare.

Gavin smiled. "Tell me who you really are, Isaac."

Tears dripped off Isaac's face onto the floor.

"Isaac, you have a choice here. You can either…" Gavin put his hand on Isaac's head and forced his face down toward the water. Isaac cried out. "…drown again, or tell me the truth about who you are." They stood still for a moment,

Isaac whimpering as he stared down into the water. "Wow. You would rather face your worst fear than tell me the truth about yourself?"

It's not the truth. Isaac tried to steel himself for the water, tried to push down his panic. But he broke. "Okay," he gasped. "Okay." Gavin released his head.

"Yes?"

Isaac swallowed hard. "I don't know what you want me to say."

"Dunk him," came the order. Leo shoved Isaac forward and forced his head into the water. He tried to hold his breath. A hand pressed against the welts on his back to keep him there. For one beat, two, three...

He was pulled up again. He gasped and coughed. When he opened his eyes, Gavin was leaning towards him.

"This isn't complicated. I want you to tell me why you're really here."

"Is this what you did to Sam?" Isaac panted. "Tried to get inside their head?"

Gavin smiled. It didn't reach his eyes. "Oh, I didn't just try. I convinced them you were there to torture and kill them, remember?"

Isaac pulled against the man restraining him. "What did you do to them?" he growled.

Gavin laughed. "It didn't take much. I just helped them realize they were weak and a liability to their team."

"Fuck you," Isaac spat bitterly.

"Should you be so lucky," Gavin murmured, leaning closer. After a moment, he sat back. "But I digress."

Isaac struggled against Leo's hands. "What's the point of this? You want me to say I believe my life is worthless? That I came here to try to make it up to Sam for failing them? Fine. If you want to put words in my mouth on pain of torture, fine. There you go. I said the words."

That terrifying smile again. "I never actually said *those* things. You came up with them on your own." Gavin signaled to Leo again.

"No!" Isaac screamed. Before Leo could get his head under the water, Isaac threw himself to the side and slammed his leg against the bucket. It tipped over and splashed everyone with water. Gavin shouted and fell backwards away from the spray. As Isaac fell to the floor Leo's weight crashed on top of him, pinning him to the ground. He cried out as Leo dug his knee into Isaac's lower back. Leo's hands pinned Isaac's head to the floor and his hands against his back.

Gavin laughed, looking down at his wet clothes. "Fair enough."

Isaac's face was pressed against the wet concrete floor as the water rushed to the drain. He groaned at the weight on his back. Gavin got on his hands and knees beside him and smiled, bringing his face so close to Isaac that he could feel his breath. "Alright. No more drowning for now. I'll have to move on to something else." He got to his feet. "I'm going to go change. Leo, tie him down. I don't want metal on him for the next part."

Chapter 10

As the door closed, the pressure on Isaac's back let up. He groaned in relief. Leo jerked his arms back and dragged him to his feet.

"No no no…"

"Shut up."

"No…"

A punch smashed into his stomach. Isaac doubled over, eyes streaming with tears. He dragged in a choked gasp. He hung limp from Leo's grip. Leo wrestled him to one side of the room. As Isaac tried to pull away, Leo picked him up and slammed him back onto the empty table against the wall. The impact drove what little breath Isaac had out of his lungs. He could feel the table was made of wood, not metal. His chest heaved and he dragged in a ragged breath.

He felt one manacle coming away from his wrist and his hands being yanked up over his head. The other manacle dropped away. His chest ached with the effort of pulling in each breath past his spasming throat. He felt the bite of rope around his wrists and the tension as they were tied down to the top of the table. Then Leo was at his feet, binding his ankles together and securing them to the bottom of the table. Isaac pulled uselessly at the ropes. Tears of rage burned hot on his cheeks.

"So this is what you do?" Isaac spat. "Do whatever he tells you to do? Hurt people? Kill people?"

"Uh huh." There was no emotion in Leo's voice as he stepped away from the table and leaned against the wall.

"And that makes you happy, huh? You content to torture people for him?"

That made Leo turn and look at Isaac. The cold look in his eyes pinned Isaac to the table as much as the ropes. "Yes."

Isaac gulped and turned his gaze to the ceiling, the metal beams and cement that held up the floor above. He wondered how many beams there were from one side of the room to the other. *I'm guessing I'll be intimately familiar with every aspect of this room by the time he's done with me.* He shuddered. *He'll be done with me when I'm dead.*

Isaac's mind wandered. He didn't mean to think about them. He didn't want to let them in, not now. But the faces of his family invaded his mind. Vera. Gray. Finn. Ellis.

Sam.

Sam, who didn't deserve this. Sam, who survived three days of this. *I wonder if I broke faster than they did.* His stomach welled with shame. *I'm supposed to be the strong one. I was supposed to protect them.* Another tear rolled down the side of his face and into his wet hair.

The door opened. "Knock, knock!"

Isaac swallowed the whimper that rose in his throat.

"Oh, nice. Thank you, Leo. Perfect." Isaac heard Gavin walk closer until he was at his side. Gavin bent to place something he was carrying on the floor. He straightened and put a hand on Isaac's shoulder. "How you holding up?"

Isaac refused to look at him, staring at the ceiling.

"Oh, so now you're deciding to go all stoic?" Gavin snickered. "Okay. Suit yourself. I'll have you screaming in a minute anyway."

Isaac closed his eyes. More tears ran down into his hair.

"So." Gavin reached for whatever he'd dropped at his feet. He picked up a towel and quickly dried Isaac off. Isaac shivered at the touch. "This is why I didn't want manacles on you. This little box…" He bent over to pick something else up and set it on the table beside Isaac's head. "…is what I like to call the 'shocky box'. It's kind of like a taser, but more painful. It delivers a shock to your body that is excruciating, but completely harmless. Well, unless one of the spasms breaks a bone, of course. By harmless, I mean it won't stop your heart or cause any brain damage or anything. Something about direct voltage and alternating charge and… something…" He threw up his hands. "I don't really know how it works. All I know is, it won't kill you."

It was so hard to hold the sobs down. Isaac shuddered, his eyes still tightly closed. He gasped as he felt two clips bite into his skin, one on his shoulder, and one on his waist.

"Hey. Open up."

Isaac slowly opened his eyes, blinking the tears away. Gavin held a rolled kerchief in front of Isaac's face. He realized Gavin meant for him to open his *mouth*. He shook his head.

"Believe me, you want this." Gavin smiled. "The last thing you want is to break a molar or bite your tongue. This baby's got kick." He patted the box almost affectionately.

Isaac rolled his eyes up to the ceiling, resigned. He opened his mouth. Gavin stuffed the cloth between his teeth. He lifted his head and let Gavin tie the gag behind his head. He let his head drop back to the table. *At least I can't beg like this.*

Gavin looked down at Isaac almost gleefully. "Oooh… I love this thing. You ready?"

Gavin pressed a button. Isaac's world shattered into pain.

Every muscle in his body spasmed as the electricity gripped him. He heard an agonized scream tearing through the room. He couldn't tell where it was coming from. It couldn't be *him*. The muscles of his chest were frozen, locked in place as the current coursed through him.

Then, it was over. His body fell limp against the table. He sobbed weakly, the gag muffling the sound as tears poured down his face. He couldn't move. He couldn't do anything but focus on the air moving in and out of his lungs and weep.

Gavin was laughing. "Really kicks your ass, huh? That wasn't even the highest setting. That was about middle of the road. Wanna feel it higher?"

Isaac weakly shook his head, his breath hitching in his chest. A moment later the pain shattered him again.

48

His muscles strained against the ropes. His entire body was wracked with agony. Every nerve was on fire. He tried to draw breath, tried to move, tried to scream. He was locked in his body, in a prison of pain.

Then it ended. He pulled in a shuddering sob. His skin was slick with sweat. He tried to move his wrists against the rope. The skin had torn, he'd been pulling against the rope so hard. He moaned helplessly.

"You done?" Gavin's face loomed over him. "You had enough?"

Isaac sobbed through the gag. *I can't take it.*

Gavin toweled Isaac off again and patted his face. Isaac weakly turned away from his hand. "Isaac, do you want me to stop?"

Isaac nodded. He trembled.

"I'll tell you what. I'll stop when you tell me to stop." Gavin reached for the button.

Isaac roared, pled, tried to beg, tried so desperately, *no, please, I can't take it, stop, I can't take it, it's too much.* The gag muffled his words until he trailed off into broken whimpers.

The pain tore through him again. He screamed, the sound forced out of his spasming chest. *It hurts, it hurts, it hurts, it hurts.* It was beyond pain, beyond agony.

Stillness again. He felt scraped hollow. He couldn't hear anything but the roaring in his ears and the sobs that forced their way out of his throat.

Again. The world was on fire. It was crawling into his veins and setting him ablaze, too. It was hell. It was...

Relief. His hair was soaked with sweat now. It dripped down his face, his chest, soaking the pants he'd been captured in, making him shiver.

Pain. He was torn apart. There was nothing left of him. He was pain; he was *nothing*; there was nothing but this...

Relief. He tried to beg. *Please. I can't take it. I can't take this. Please. Kill me, let me die, just stop this pain.* He could get nothing past the gag.

His skin tingled as he felt the towel move over him again. "This is as high as it goes."

Every fiber of his being cried out. His body spasmed and yanked against the ropes tying him to the table. A scream tore out of his throat as the electricity crushed his chest. He tried to draw breath, to refill his lungs, but his chest was trapped in a vice. It was *agony*. It was *torture*. It was *death*. His lungs screamed for air. He panicked, trying to move or breathe or *think,* but he was trapped in the prison of his own body, trapped without air. A buzzing began in his head. He felt dizzy. The world started to spin. *I'm going to die it hurts it hurts I'm going to die.*

Then it was over. His mouth gaped open uselessly, his chest heaving. His eyes rolled back in his head. He couldn't get air. Couldn't get air.

"Isaac..."

He pulled uselessly at the ropes. *Can't breathe.*

"Isaac, breathe."

He fell back against the table, gasping.

"Isaac, I am *not* doing mouth to mouth on you. Breathe, or you're going to die here on this table."

His chest, gasp by gasp, began to release. He could draw small breaths. Then bigger ones. It wasn't enough, wasn't enough, but he could breathe. He trembled against the ropes holding him to the table. He was drenched with sweat. Tears rolled down his face.

"Isaac..."

He moaned.

A finger tapped his face. "Iiiiiiisaac..."

He willed his spasmed chest to expand, then fall. Air moved around the gag. He kept his eyes closed. Helpless.

Gavin pulled the gag from his mouth. He giggled. "I don't know if *you* had a good time with that, but that... was... *awesome.*"

50

"P… please…"

"Yeah, you're done for a bit. I can't do that one for very long. Something about electrolyte imbalances and heart de-rhythms and stuff… I think. You should really meet my medical dude. He's great."

"No…"

Gavin laughed. "Oh, you'll meet him at some point. Believe me, you will. I don't play nice and you will absolutely need him soon. Be grateful. I could just… leave you to suffer without medical care…"

Tears rolled down Isaac's face from his closed eyes. "Please… please kill me… I can't…"

"Oh, sure you can. I won't make it that bad again for a while. I just wanted to give you a taste of what real pain is. Maybe you won't complain so much next time I whip you, or when I waterboard you, or beat you, or… What else did you ask me to do?" Gavin shrugged. "We'll get to it all eventually. For now…" Isaac felt the ropes snap under Gavin's knife. "I'll leave you with food and water. Make sure you eat and drink. I don't need you passing out on me." He laughed, patting Isaac's face. Isaac heard him walk to the door, conversing quietly with Leo. Then the door closed and he was alone. He sobbed.

Chapter 11

The front door slammed against the wall as Finn kicked it open. Vera jumped, swiping her hand at the tears on her cheeks. She crossed the room in three strides and threw her arms around them. "Finn. Thank god." Ellis was right behind them. She turned to them and pulled them a little more hesitantly into her arms. "How you two holding up? You okay?"

"Yeah." Finn's usually cheerful voice was low and frightened. "Yeah, we're fine. Glad you're okay."

Gray poked their head in from the other room at the sound of voices. They heaved a sigh of relief and crossed to them. "Oh, thank god." They put a hand on each of Finn's and Ellis's shoulders, their gaze flicking between them. "We were worried we lost you, too."

They all flinched.

"So... how's Sam? They okay?" Ellis shuffled anxiously, their hands in their pockets.

"Yeah," said Finn, twisting their hands together. "I need to go check them out. They doing okay?" No one would meet their gaze. They pressed their lips into a line. "...as expected?"

Gray nodded. "They're in the bedroom. Asleep, finally. After what they've been through..."

A grave silence fell on them. Finn ran a hand over their face. Stress etched lines around their eyes. It made them look so much older than their twenty-seven years. "Okay. I'll let them sleep for a bit. I want to take a look at them as soon as they wake up. I want a good idea of what I'm dealing with, what... Gavin... did to them."

Ellis ground their teeth, hate burning in their eyes. "I can't believe he took Isaac. I cannot... *fucking* believe he took Isaac." They leaned their elbows on the counter and pulled their hands through their short black hair. They looked to Vera and Gray, desperate. "How did this happen?"

Gray barely kept their voice steady. "While Gavin was… When he had Sam, he forced them to swallow a tracker. He told them it was poison. Sounds like some mind game, because he told them he'd give them the antidote if they gave up more information about us."

Finn paled.

"We'd only been here for a few hours when Gavin called Isaac and demanded he give Sam back. Sounds like he…" Gray's face was twisted with disgust. "…he wanted Sam back because they were… fun."

"Son of a bitch," Ellis whispered.

Gray leaned against the counter. "Isaac said he would go in their place. He sacrificed himself. I don't know what Gavin threatened. It must have been something terrible for Isaac to have gone to him."

"Isaac's never been one to avoid pain for our sake," interjected Vera. She rubbed the back of her neck. "It doesn't matter what Gavin threatened. There's no way Isaac would let him take Sam back, no matter what."

Gray pushed out a slow breath. "You're right."

Finn looked around at everyone. They all wore the same horrified expression.

Gray continued. "Isaac took the car and went up to the main road to meet Gavin."

"We saw it as we came in." Finn had their arms hugged tight to their chest.

"After that, we figured Gavin headed east if you almost ran into his people coming from where you were. It gives us a good starting point to start going after Isaac," Gray said.

"Is that the plan now?" Ellis looked from Gray to Vera and back. "Going after Isaac?"

Vera spoke up. "The tracker Gavin placed is still in Sam. We don't go anywhere until it's out of their system."

"And then after that, yes, the plan is to go after Isaac," Gray finished.

Finn nodded. "Well, you know I'm in. But we have nothing to go on. Where do we even start?"

Gray was staring at the floor. "We start with 'east.' It's the only thing we have for now." They raised their eyes to the group.

"What about Sam?" Finn's voice was low. "Can they travel? How badly hurt are they? Can they walk? What do they remember about being with Gavin?"

"I remember everything."

They all jumped at Sam's voice and turned to see them leaning against the wall, pale and trembling.

Finn rushed to their side. Their hands were on Sam in an instant, feeling for injuries. "Hey, Sam. Hey buddy. You doing okay? You need to sit down?"

"No, no, I..." They swayed on their feet. "I'm okay..."

"No, you're not." Finn's voice became gentle and steady. "Let's get you to the couch."

"I'm... fine..." A thin sheen of sweat appeared on Sam's face from their effort to stay standing.

"No, you're not. Couch. Now." Finn grasped Sam under one arm and guided them to the couch. Sam sank into it. Finn knelt in front of them and brushed sweaty hair away from their forehead. "You've got a little bit of a temperature."

Sam shook their head, whimpering. "No... No, I'm okay... I have to be okay... We have to get Isaac..." They bit down hard on their lip. Gray and Vera appeared over the back of the couch, and Ellis took a seat beside Sam. "We have to focus on Isaac."

"We don't have to focus on anything but you right now," Finn insisted gently. "Until that tracker's out of you, we can't do anything for him. Right now I need to make sure you're going to be okay."

Tears ran down Sam's face. "I'm sorry. I'm so sorry. I tried to make him stay…" They turned and looked back at Gray and Vera. "I tried to wake you…" They sobbed miserably.

Ellis jerked their hands towards Sam and then pulled back, uncertain. Always uncertain with everyone but Finn.

"We know you did, honey." Vera's voice cracked. "We know. But don't focus on that right now, okay? Focus on getting better. Focus on the next steps." She squeezed Sam's shoulders over the back of the couch.

Sam took a shaky breath and coughed wetly. They gasped as their chest heaved with each spasm.

Finn glanced at Gray. "Waterboarding," Gray murmured. Finn looked back to Sam, eyes wide with concern.

"Sam." Finn rubbed Sam's back in soothing circles as Sam took deep, shuddering breaths. "Can you tell me what Gavin did to you? Or do you want to go back to bed?"

"I can tell you," Sam said miserably, folding in on themselves. "I'll tell you everything."

Chapter 12

Isaac quivered on the table, exhausted, skin prickling still from the electricity. The rope fell away from his wrists and ankles as he moved. His fingers shook as he fumbled for the wires attached to him and hissed as the clamps came free from his skin. He rolled to one side, muscles twitching. The welts on his back left streaks of blood on the table. *He said he'd leave me water.*

His eyes were blurry with tears as he looked towards the door. Gavin had been true to his word, at least. There was a bottle of water and a sandwich on the floor. Isaac groaned as he grasped at the edge of the table. He tried to swing his legs over the side. The rest of his body followed and he collapsed in a heap. His legs felt like they were made of putty. He sobbed weakly and dragged himself across the floor.

His mind was blank as he made his way to the door. The only thing he could feel was the uncomprehending, tremulous shock of what Gavin had done. *I can do this. I can take it.* His hand closed around the bottle. He pulled himself up until he was sitting and cracked the seal. He downed the bottle in seconds. He turned to the sandwich, gritty from being on the floor. He didn't even dust it off. He ate the whole thing in five bites.

Breathe in, breathe out. He felt a little stronger. *I can do this.* Vaguely, he wondered if the others were safe yet. *Is the tracker still in Sam? Have they started running?* He felt tears in his eyes as he pictured their faces. Now it was safe. Now, while he was alone, he could be with them.

He wrapped his arms around himself and tried to quiet his sobs. *They're my family. They're the only family I have. And I'll never see them again.* He briefly wondered how long he would survive. He supposed it didn't matter now. *I just hope they're smart enough to get as far away from Gavin as they can.*

A terrible thought crept into his mind. *I want them to come back for me.* He pressed his face against his hands and curled in on himself, shaking. *I can't want that. I want them to be safe.* As much as he hated himself for it, though, he wanted them to come for him. *I don't want to hurt anymore. It hasn't even been a day and I just want it to stop.* A sob made its way out of his throat. *I just want to be with them again.*

He crawled to the other side of the room, as far as he could get from the door, and slumped in the corner. Tears poured down his face even as he tried to stop himself from crying. *Maybe it's okay if I'm weak when I'm all by myself. If I don't let Gavin see, maybe I'm not betraying them.* He bit down hard on his hand. The sobs kept wrenching themselves from his chest. *Maybe it's okay.*

He pressed his face into his arm. It didn't feel like he had a choice to be strong anymore. His stomach dropped through the floor as he pictured his team, his *family*, separately, together, laughing, sleeping in a pile, packed into their car and running for their lives, building fires in the woods when they couldn't find somewhere safe to stay for the night, doing odd jobs together just so they could eat, sabotaging the syndicates, protecting each other, fighting with each other. Loving each other. His heart ached to be with them again. He wrapped his arms around himself and wept, and wept, and wept.

Chapter 13

The sound of Sam's labored breathing woke Finn up. They turned on the lamp beside the bed and rolled over, feeling blearily for Sam. When Finn touched Sam, Finn flinched away. Sam's skin was *burning*.

"Oh no, no no no, no, Sam…" They sat up and rolled Sam over onto their back. Sam's skin was slick with sweat, hair plastered to their forehead, clothes soaked beneath the blankets. Their eyes were glazed over and unfocused. In the light of the lamp Finn could see their pulse jumping in their neck. Too fast. They felt Sam's wrist. *Way* too fast. "Shit, shit, *shit.*"

They pulled the blankets off Sam, exposing them to the chilly air in the safehouse. Sam shivered and blindly reached for the covers, eyes lazing over the ceiling, unseeing. Finn dashed to the living room where Ellis and Vera were slumped on the couch asleep and Gray was stretched out on the floor. They all had decided to give Finn and Sam the bed so Sam could be comfortable, and Finn could monitor them during the night. *I was supposed to watch out for them, and I failed. Shit!*

"Ellis," they hissed. Ellis stirred on the couch, slowly lifting their head and looking around. "Ellis," they whispered louder. "Get up, I need you." Finn didn't look back as they rushed out the door to the car, grabbed their med kit, and dashed back inside.

Ellis was still sitting on the couch, groggy and confused.

"Come on." Finn grabbed their arm, pulling them up off the couch and into the bedroom, Ellis weakly complaining the whole way. As soon as Ellis saw Sam they fell silent. Frozen.

They were shaken out of their reverie by Finn tossing the blood pressure cuff and stethoscope at them. "Get me a blood pressure," Finn said without looking up from the bag. Ellis shook themselves and jumped onto the bed beside Sam. They pulled Sam's arm out of their sleeve.

Finn pulled out an IV kit and tied the tourniquet around Sam's arm. Sam stirred, mewling weakly at the touch and the cold. While the veins filled, Finn passed a thermometer over Sam's forehead. Then again, disbelieving. They shook their head and mopped Sam's forehead dry with the comforter. Measured again. *"103.2. Shit."*

Finn assembled the IV set-up and sanitized the inside of Sam's elbow. Too quickly for Sam to even flinch, Finn had the needle in, withdrawn, and connected to the extension set. They taped the IV down and turned to Ellis.

"What have you got?"

Ellis shook their head, taking the stethoscope out of their ears. "Um… 84/48?"

"Take it again."

Hands shaking, Ellis pumped up the cuff and tried again. Finn's heartbeat deafened them as they watched Ellis, holding their breath.

"88/50."

"Shit." Finn felt for a pulse. "124 on the pulse. No no no…" Their hand went to Sam's forehead and swept the hair back from their face. They held out their hand for the stethoscope and listened to Sam's lungs. The lower right side rumbled with infection.

"What are we gonna do?" whispered Ellis.

"They're septic," moaned Finn. "They need antibiotics. And a lot of other things but… antibiotics mostly. And I don't have any…" Their face fell into their hands. "None of the last four groups we ran into were selling, either. But I…" They looked helplessly at Sam. "If they don't get them, they'll die. Maybe tomorrow. Maybe sooner."

Ellis reached for Finn's hand. "Let me go find some."

"No." Finn's voice was hard. "It's too dangerous. Gavin's people are probably out there looking for us right now. No way."

Ellis squeezed their hand. "Either I risk that, or Sam dies. Right? There's no way they could survive without antibiotics?"

Finn shook their head. "Well... probably not, but... we could find... we could do something..." They grabbed Ellis's hand with both of theirs and stared at them desperately. "You're my *partner*."

Ellis smiled crookedly. "Don't I know it. I can't get rid of you." They got off the bed. "But I'm going. I love Sam, too, just as much as you do." Their eyes swept Sam's body, hot and flushed and trembling on the bed.

Finn opened their mouth to protest. They let it close with a sigh. "You're right. Let me follow you out so I can grab my stuff. Take a radio with you. Don't go far. If you're gone for longer than a day, it won't matter." Their breath caught in their throat, shame chilling their insides. "I mean..."

"I get it." Ellis took Finn's chin and made them look at them. "I know you have to be that way with patients. Right now, Sam's your patient." They turned to leave the bedroom. Finn followed right behind.

Finn was proud of their cache of equipment. It had taken them a long time to collect and had cost more than all the family's other needs combined, but it was worth it in times like this. They grabbed their sack of saline bags and the cardiac monitor they had had to trade a car for. Ellis grabbed the oxygen concentrator – Finn's prized possession – and the extra batteries for it.

As they carried the equipment inside, Gray stirred. "What's goin' on?" they mumbled. Finn walked right past them into the bedroom.

Ellis dropped to one knee and whispered so as not to wake Vera. "Sam got worse. Finn is gonna do what they can here, and I'm gonna go get antibiotics."

"I'll go with you." Gray clumsily got to their feet, joints protesting.

"No." Finn poked their head into the hall. "Too dangerous. I hate risking Ellis. I can't risk you for this, too."

"I'm of more use helping Ellis than I am here," Gray whispered back.

"No." Finn's voice had a deep, steady pitch that they only got when they were with a patient.

Gray's voice was low and even. "It's not your decision to make, Finn."

Finn hesitated in the doorway for a moment. They sighed. "Take the radio, for if you have questions. Don't be gone longer than twenty-four hours or it won't matter anymore." They disappeared back into the room.

Ellis and Gray left silently, trying to let Vera sleep. It had been days since any of them had gotten proper rest. No use in waking her up if it wasn't necessary.

Finn looked down at Sam and watched their eyes move slowly under the lids. They swallowed hard and got to work.

Finn covered Sam back up with only the thinnest blanket on the bed. Sam was already starting to shiver, but it was better to let them cool off a bit than to let them sweat under the covers. Finn spiked a bag of saline and hung it from a nail in the wall. They assumed the nail once held a picture, but whatever was there before was gone. They attached the saline to Sam's IV and let it run wide open.

Finn dug a portable pulse oximeter out of their bag, a small box with a screen on the side that opened like a clamp for Sam's finger. Finn waited for the little machine to beep, normalize, get a reading... *89%.*

They cursed silently and reached back into their bag for a nasal cannula. They put it on Sam's face and plugged it into the oxygen concentrator. They turned it on and within minutes the number on the pulse ox was rising. *91%... 94%... 96%...* Finn got out some Tylenol, checked the dose, and ran it into the IV.

None of the others had ever been this sick before. Finn had treated scrapes and cuts, broken bones, even sutured a graze from a bullet that nearly killed Ellis when they first met, but they'd never done anything like this.

Finn wasn't deluded. They knew their family trusted them too much to take care of them as they all threw themselves into danger fighting the syndicates. Finn knew if someone took a bullet to the gut, or got a concussion bad enough, or got an illness that couldn't be treated with Tylenol, fluids, and very little else, they would die without a hospital. And hospitals were run, almost without exception, by the syndicates. The only safe hospitals, the hospitals for civilians and refugees, were inordinately expensive. Finn shook their head wearily. *I'm a stopgap. A glorified band-aid distributor. The pharmacy aisle at a convenience store could help more than I can.*

Most of the medicine they knew was what they had picked up along the way. The only difference between them and anyone else in the group was three weeks of training they'd had ten years ago – and that had been stopped short. *A monkey could do what I can do and be almost as successful.* A tear ran down their cheek.

Snap out of it, idiot. Sam was dying. Finn couldn't do much without antibiotics, but they might be able do enough to keep Sam alive until they arrived.

Finn turned to their bag to do a quick inventory. Aside from their regular med kit, they had twelve bags of saline left, four lithium ion batteries for the oxygen concentrator, and one extra battery for the heart monitor. They did some quick math in their head. *If Sam is sixty kilos, give or take, they'll need 1800 mL fluids in the first three hours, or is it 1200 mL, shit, why can't I remember this right now…? This is when I need to know this stuff…* They glanced at the liter of fluid hanging from the wall. Half of it was already gone. *Screw it. I'll get their blood pressure up. If they need the same amount of fluids after that then I'll have a little less than twenty-four hours before I run out.* They closed their eyes. *I guess it won't matter after that. I told Ellis they have twenty-four hours.* Finn's hands reached vaguely towards the lithium batteries as they stared at the wall, thinking. *Each battery lasts for four-ish hours, give or take, so including the one already running we'll have… twenty hours of O2, max.* They ran a tense hand through their hair. *That's more than cutting it damned close.*

They pumped up the blood pressure cuff and took another pressure. *90/54.* They could pretend it was an improvement.

I can't think of another damned thing I can do for them. Most of their equipment was for trauma, anyway. They wracked their brain again before they slumped, giving in to their worry.

They crawled into bed next to Sam and lay down next to them, flinching at the heat coming off Sam's skin. They laid their head next to Sam's and draped one arm across their waist. Finn reached across them and held their hand.

"You know," Finn whispered against Sam's ear, "we're gonna get through this. You're gonna get better, we're gonna get Isaac back, and we're all gonna run away together somewhere safe. Somewhere Gavin can't find us. Someday this is all gonna be some terrible memory. Maybe there's somewhere else in the world where the syndicates can't reach us. Maybe there are places out there just like the way Gray says there used to be. Maybe you can go to college, would you like that? I could *actually* become a medic. Or maybe even do doctor school. Who knows? Vera could get that dog she wants, and we could all go over to mine and Ellis's house on the weekends to have cookouts and go swimming in our pool and watch movies. Ellis could be safe, they could go to therapy, they could... I don't know, maybe write a book?" Finn laughed gently. "Isaac can finally relax and figure out what he wants to do. You know, I've never once heard him talk about what he would do if we were safe? Anyway, we'd be far away from the death and the running, we'd be safe, maybe we could have a garden, a cat... What would you go to school for? I don't think I remember. I know we've talked about it. You'll have to tell me when you get better." They pressed a kiss against Sam's temple.

Finn's eyes closed. "You know I hate it when they leave me behind? Drives me insane. I just want to help, I just want to *contribute* like they do, and they say it's because I'm an asset, but anyone could do what I do. Honestly, not complicated. Maybe if I had some actual medicines to work with but with what I have to work with...?" They sighed. "I just want to be in it with you. I want to feel how it feels to raid a compound, pull the trigger and watch some piece-of-shit murderer go down. I want to feel the way you all do when you work together and pull off a plan." They pressed their lips together and tried to ignore the tears running down their face and into the pillow.

"I'm so sorry we let this happen to you." Finn's voice shook. "I know Isaac blames himself, but it's all of our faults. We all left you unprotected. We should never have expected you to..." They shook their head. "Once we get you better, I swear to you, we will keep you safe, we'll never put you in danger again. Just... hold on for us, Sam. Hold on for me. You just have to hold on until they get back with the antibiotics... Just for a few hours, I promise." They soothed Sam's sweat-soaked curls away from their face. "Please, Sam. Please just fight this. Please stay alive."

As they put their hand back in Sam's, Finn felt them squeeze weakly. They smiled through their tears and squeezed back.

Chapter 14

Years ago

"Hey, Dunham!"

Finn's head snapped up from where it had been drooping on their hand. "Huh? Yes. Sir. Hello."

The instructor's mouth turned down a little at the corners. The tension in his lips betrayed his amusement. Finn smiled.

"Dunham, were you sleeping in my class again?" A shadow of a smile flashed over Instructor Grant's face.

Finn grinned. *Channel your dumbass energy. Channel it. He thinks it's funny.* "Um. No, sir. I was practicing a comatose state." They tapped their finger against the open book in front of them. *Traumatic brain injuries.* "Research, sir. Helps me better understand what I'm treating."

Instructor Grant took another step towards Finn, his boots making a dull tapping sound on the linoleum floor. The other students were watching him intently. Their eyes flicked between him and Finn. Finn had to suppress a smile. *Maybe they think I'll get kicked out today. Maybe they think this is it, I'm done.* There was a brief flutter in their chest as they considered it. *Probably how I end up leaving Junior Defense Corps, if we're honest.*

"How old are you, Cadet Dunham?"

Finn swallowed. "Seventeen, sir."

"And how is it, Dunham, that in seventeen years you learned how to be such an absolute, monumental pain in my ass?"

"Um..." They swallowed. *Here's the gamble.* "Practice? Sir?"

Instructor Grant cleared his throat. "You're dismissed from medical training today." Finn's stomach dropped. "I think the quad needs to be swept."

"The... quad... sir? The dirt quad?"

"Yes, Cadet Dunham. The dirt quad. Get a broom and start sweeping. I need it spotless by the time this class segment is over at 1600."

Finn swallowed hard. They searched Instructor Grant's eyes for a hint of good humor. A hint of a joke. *I was a smartass in front of the class. I guess I would understand if he was kinda pissed.* But there it was. A glimmer in his eyes, a twitch of his lips. Finn's heart stuttered and slowed.

"Yes, sir. Understood. Would you like me to wear my pack the whole time?" Finn carefully put their textbooks into their bag.

"You read my mind, Dunham. Wear your pack. And when you're finished, I'd like you to explain to me in detail the pathophys behind a diffuse axonal injury and how you would treat one in the field. Put your research to use." Instructor Grant walked back to the front of the room and turned around. "You're dismissed, Cadet."

"Yes, sir." Finn jumped to their feet and saluted smartly, clicking their heels together with just the slightest hint of overdoing it. *Yeah, I'm getting kicked out.*

Finn flung their pack over their shoulder and walked from the room. They headed for the utilities closet near the door leading outside and selected a broom. They chose one with a wide brush at the bottom. *Perfect. Perfect for sweeping the dirt fucking quad.* They wandered outside and looked around.

The quad had to be a half acre, at least. It was huge. Other cadets jogged by them wearing their own heavy packs. Sweating like pigs. *I could be there. Fuck, I'm glad I got accepted for the medical program.* They sighed and got to work.

At least he's not having me mop up the rain.

It was mindless. Push the dirt this way, push the dirt that way. Make a pattern. Right angles, swirls. Kick up the dust for fun. *My boots are gonna take forever to polish tonight. Dammit.*

Back and forth across the quad. Finn figured if they started at a corner and spread out that wouldn't exactly be very orderly. *And if he wants the quad to be swept spotless, dammit, I'll do it in rows like a goddamned professional.*

Back and forth. Back and forth. They paused and wiped their brow. Their wrist came away a little muddy. *Delightful.* They looked at the sun, past the noon point. *Only three or four more hours, probably.* Back to sweeping. *Diffuse axonal injuries. Fuck. Um. That's like... worse than a normal concussion. And it... hurts the axons? That's gotta be it, they wouldn't put axons in the fucking name if it wasn't about axons. Christ, I wish I'd been paying attention.*

They bit their lip. *I'm here so I can get into Defense Corps. I'm here to fight the syndicates. I should be paying more attention. I'm lucky to have been put in medical.*

Sweeping this quad is still dumb as shit, though.

They heard a faint popping sound in the distance, across the base. *Must be shooting practice. I wonder when I'll get to do that.* They shrugged and kept sweeping.

The popping sound got closer. Finn raised their head in the direction of the sound. The hair on the back of their neck stood up. *Hm. I wonder if it's a moving drill?* They hesitated for a moment and went back to sweeping.

Boom.

That was not a shooting drill.

Finn's head snapped up. They were instantly alert. *Something's wrong.* They turned in the direction of the classroom.

The popping sound was so close now Finn could feel the concussive force in their ears. They didn't know guns super well yet; they were pretty much only familiar with their own M16 replica at this point. Which was back at the armory right now, because rifles weren't brought to class. Behind a lock they didn't have the key to. And didn't shoot real bullets anyway. And whatever was being fired right now was *heavy* fucking artillery.

Fuck this.

They dropped the broom where they stood and dashed towards the armory. They skidded to a halt. If there was no one at the armory right now, it wouldn't matter.

If they were under attack, whoever it was would go straight for that building.

And they were under attack.

They spun and ran back towards the classroom. *I can at least warn Instructor Grant and the rest. He'll know what to do.* They were halfway across the quad now. Their heart was pounding.

The doors of the classroom banged open. Finn's classmates ran out, followed by Instructor Grant. Behind them was an army of people armed to the teeth, wearing bulletproof vests and helmets and masks that hid their faces.

Instructor Grant cleared the door. He turned and fired at the men – mercenaries, had to be – with his sidearm. Finn stood frozen. One mercenary went down. Then another. The next shot went wide. And the next. A bullet tore through Instructor Grant's leg and he collapsed into the dirt.

Another student – Kasey – screamed and grabbed at Instructor Grant's arm. "NO!" he bellowed as he shoved her away. He thrust his sidearm into her hands. "Go! Fucking go!" She wept as another student tore her away from him.

Finn cried out weakly as the mercenaries descended on Instructor Grant. They screamed at him, *"Hands up! Do it now! Fucking do it!"* One of them slammed the barrel of his rifle into Instructor Grant's gut. He doubled over onto his hands and knees. Finn took a step towards him on legs made of jello.

One of the mercenaries stepped over Instructor Grant. He leveled his weapon at Instructor Grant's head.

Finn took another step forward. *No. Fuck no. No no no this is not happening.* Instructor Grant's eyes snapped to theirs and held their gaze for a moment. Finn could have been imagining it. They *swore* they imagined it. But they thought they saw Instructor Grant move his head to the left, then the right. *No.* Finn froze.

Run, Instructor Grant mouthed.

The mercenary pulled the trigger.

Instructor Grant crumpled to the ground. Finn let out a ragged scream. One of the mercenaries spun around and saw them. They raised their gun to fire at Finn.

The spell was broken. Finn turned and ran. They heard the shots, *felt* the bullets as they whizzed by. Their legs burned. They realized they were still carrying their heavy pack with books in it and tore it from their shoulders. They looked to their right and saw Kasey running too, Instructor Grant's pistol held tight in her fist. Tears were streaming down her face. To their left, a building caught fire. The mess hall. They looked straight ahead and ran faster.

They were approaching the fence the separated the school from the rest of the world. Finn used to think it was a pretty pathetic fence, for protecting the future defenders of the country. *We're just fucking cadets. We aren't even real soldiers yet.*

We're officially in peacetime.

It was chain-link, ten feet tall, with a line of barbed wire at the top. Finn grit their teeth and threw themselves at the fence. Their fingers clawed at it as they climbed. They reached the barbed wire and hesitated for a moment.

Thirty feet to their left, another cadet was climbing the fence. They were bleeding from a wound on their arm. They didn't even seem to notice. They threw themselves on top of the wire as they scrambled up and over.

There was a spray of blood. The cadet flinched and slumped against the wire. Finn blinked and it took them a moment to realize what they were seeing. Blood poured from a gaping hole in the cadet's chest. *Oh, god.*

They whipped their head around and saw another mercenary running towards the fence. Leveling their weapon at Finn.

Finn clawed their way over the wire. Their uniform caught and ripped on the barbs. They could barely feel the pain that lanced through their hands as they climbed over. A barb caught their thigh and cut deep. In their panic, one thought pushed out all the others for a moment: *DID I GET MY TETANUS SHOT? FUCK FUCK FUCK I CAN'T REMEMBER.* They dangled over the other side of the fence and *dropped.*

They didn't take a moment to catch their breath. They staggered to their feet and took off running again. Tears poured down their face. Their lungs were on fire.

Chapter 15

Isaac was woken from a deep sleep by a rough hand in his hair. He was dragged away from where he was slumped against the wall and thrown across the floor. He cried out and threw his hands over his head.

"Wakey wakey!" Gavin's voice was cheery. Aggressively so.

Isaac scurried away from him towards the door. He collided with a pair of legs and Leo's hands closed around his shoulders. Leo dragged him back to the table and slammed Isaac onto his back. It knocked the breath out of him. He gasped, stunned. Leo locked his hands around Isaac's wrists and wrenched them up over his head.

"No no no…" Isaac whimpered. He tried to yank his hands out of Leo's grasp. He kicked at him frantically, his foot catching Leo square in the chest. Leo let out a grunt. Isaac struggled with renewed force, straining against Leo's grasp.

Isaac felt a hand in his hair and the cold, sharp edge of a blade under his chin. He instantly went still.

"As much as I love watching Leo throw you around," came Gavin's cool voice in his ear, "let me make a small suggestion: don't move, let him tie you down, or I cut right *here*—" He pressed the tip of the blade against Isaac's throat, right over the pulse. "— and watch you bleed out on this table."

Leo guided Isaac's wrists up and Isaac pulled against him. The hand in his hair tightened and the knife pressed harder against his skin. "You think I'm kidding? Try that again and this story ends right here." Gavin jerked Isaac's head up and thumped it back against the table for emphasis.

"What does it matter?" Isaac spat through his teeth. "You're just gonna kill me anyway. Why not let it be now?"

Gavin smiled. "Okay, I'll call that bluff. Go ahead. Try it."

For a moment Isaac lay frozen, still straining against Leo's grip. Then, with a whimper, he surrendered. He let his hands be pulled above his head. He shut his eyes against the tears threatening to spill. Gavin stepped back.

Leo quickly bound his wrists together and tied them to the table. "Feet, too?"

"Naw." Gavin looked down at Isaac with amusement. "He's gonna hold still, right?" He winked at Isaac.

Isaac stared straight at the ceiling, burning with shame.

"I take your silence as an emphatic yes." Gavin twirled the knife in his hand. "Can you guess what we're going to do today?" Isaac remained motionless, lips pressed together. Gavin stepped closer and stabbed the knife into the table, inches from Isaac's head. He grinned at the little jump it caused. "I said," he murmured, leaning close, "what do you think we're going to do today?"

Isaac said nothing.

Gavin chuckled. "You're confusing my admiration of your strength for a desire for you to be silent. I want you to scream, yes, but I also want to have a *conversation* with you, Isaac. Where's the fun if you just lay there and don't talk to me? What?" He pouted. "Am I boring you already?" He watched a moment for a reaction. "What is this, like... a pride thing? You upset that I broke you and now you're trying to make up for it? Do you honestly think it matters to your family how you take this? They have no idea what I'm doing to you. You could be dead, as far as they're concerned. What's the harm in just... *talking* to me?" He sighed and tapped the side of the knife against Isaac's cheek. Isaac flinched. He forced down a whimper.

Gavin rolled his eyes. "Fine. I can work with this. I'll make you a deal. I'm gonna cut you with this knife. Obviously. If you move, try to kick me, do anything like that, I cut your throat and you bleed out." He waited for a reaction. "Anything? No? Yikes, you're already boring me. Anyway, other option is you take the pain and I stop when you beg me to. Sound good?" He waved a hand in front of Isaac's face. "You home?" Isaac's jaw tightened. "Jeez, are you seriously just gonna lay there and take it just because of your *pride*? Whatever." He set the tip of the knife against Isaac's skin, just below the left collarbone. "I can take this as a personal challenge."

Gavin drew the tip of the knife down Isaac's chest, down his abdomen to his waistband with a feather-light touch. He looked up at Isaac with a playful grin. "Don't wanna beg yet? No? Yeah, I'd be disappointed if you did." He returned the knife to the same spot and drew the knife along the same path, the tip leaving a white scratch as it went. "No? Sweet."

He placed the knife in the same spot and began to scrape it down Isaac's chest. This time it left a raised red line. Isaac's quick intake of breath was the only reaction he gave.

"Here's a fun fact for you," said Gavin. "Most of the nerve endings in your skin lie pretty close to the surface. Once you get deep enough into the body, there are hardly any nerve endings at all. So, if done right, a shallow cut can hurt more than a stab wound. Or at least that's what I've been told. Every person I ever stabbed complained quite a bit, so I'm thinking that little fact isn't entirely true." He returned the knife to the spot below Isaac's collarbone and followed the line he was making. The knife parted the first few layers of skin, leaving a line of blood welling up in the cut. Isaac gasped and squeezed his eyes shut.

"Open your eyes." Isaac kept them shut. Gavin pressed the knife against Isaac's throat again. "Open your eyes or die."

Isaac blinked his eyes open, revulsion curdling in his stomach.

"That's better. I want you to see what I'm doing, and I want to watch you hurt." Isaac fixed his eyes on the ceiling again and Gavin went back to work.

The next line began a centimeter from the first. Gavin pressed the knife down, cutting him on the first path. Isaac grunted at the pain, straining not to make a sound.

Gavin smiled. "Okay, I'm actually really enjoying this. It's adorable to see you try to keep quiet. Like it's going to matter. You are absolutely going to scream from this, no matter how hard you try. But I appreciate the effort." The knife moved down Isaac's chest again. His breath froze in his chest with the effort to be quiet. Again, the knife moved in a long line. Isaac could feel a hot trail of blood roll down his chest and dribble off his side onto the table. Gavin blew gently on the cuts and Isaac shivered.

"You doing okay still?" No answer. "Okay." Another cut. Deeper.

Isaac groaned, unable to stop himself.

"Ooh," Gavin cooed. "That one might need stitches. Maybe not, though."

He moved the knife to the other side of Isaac's chest, below the collarbone. "I'm a sucker for symmetry." Isaac bit his lip as the knife cut him down to his waistband.

Gavin smiled and the knife drew another line of blood.

Isaac felt his body break into a sweat. The salt stung the lines Gavin had made.

As Gavin drew the third line down the right side of Isaac's chest, he whimpered. Gavin grinned. "Now that's a good sound. Do you understand now why this is so much fun for me?" Another cut. The pain burning across Isaac's chest was rising, tearing through his mind, breaking through his silence. Tears began to roll down his cheeks. He sobbed quietly.

As Gavin made another cut, Isaac pulled at the ropes on his wrists. His muscles strained as he trembled under the knife, sobbing. Gavin leaned back to admire his work. "That's better, now it's even." He rested the tip of the knife in the hollow of Isaac's throat where his collarbones came together. He dragged it down Isaac's sternum.

Isaac screamed.

"There we go!" Gavin grinned. "Had enough? Want me to stop?" Isaac whimpered high in his throat. Gavin laughed and shook his head. "This really makes no sense to me. You could stop me from hurting you *right now*. Just beg me to stop."

Isaac kept his eyes fixed on the ceiling.

"Why? Why won't you just beg me, and spare yourself the pain? Your holding out like this is meaningless. Why keep hurting like this when it won't make your family safer? When it won't make Sam feel better when they wake up screaming from nightmares of what I did to them?"

Isaac's eyes snapped to Gavin's. His blood boiled with fury.

"Ha, thought that would get your attention. You're just an interesting person, Isaac. I don't get it."

Gavin turned the knife on him again. Isaac cried out as Gavin raked the blade along his ribs, blood beading immediately. Before he could catch his breath, Gavin started another cut. Isaac's chest heaved.

"Careful. Keep breathing that hard and I might cut you deeper than I mean to." Another cut. Isaac screamed so hard his throat felt raw.

Over and over again, Gavin cut him. His chest looked like he had been flayed. Blood pooled on the table and dripped onto the floor.

"It's really not as bad as it looks," Gavin said gleefully. "There are just a lot of cuts, and the skin is so thin where I'm cutting you. Bleeds easily." He cut him again. And again.

Gavin prepared to take the knife to Isaac again. Isaac couldn't count how many cuts Gavin had made already. Gavin pressed the knife in enough that it parted Isaac's skin before he started to draw the line.

Isaac screamed. *"Please!"*

Gavin pulled his hand back, the knife hovering an inch above his skin. "Please what?"

Isaac sobbed. "P-please stop, *please*, I can't do it."

Gavin grinned. "So, I was right?" Isaac licked his lips and swallowed hard. Gavin grabbed him by the hair and wrenched his head to the side, forcing Isaac to look at him. "Say it."

Tears poured down Isaac's face. "You were right."

"Right about what?"

Isaac's cheeks burned with shame. "I broke. I can't take it."

Gavin released his hair. "Yup. You broke. Again. I'm, what, four for four with you now, right?"

Rage flashed in Isaac's eyes. "How about you trade places with me, and we'll see how well you do?"

74

Gavin laughed. "There's that snark. No thanks, though, I'll pass. I'm better at this and, let's be honest, you look so much better like this than you would doing what I'm doing." He held his hand out behind him and Leo stepped forward. Isaac had forgotten he was even there. "One more thing."

Leo handed Gavin a spray bottle and stepped back again. Gavin grinned at Isaac. "Gotta keep those cuts clean." He sprayed Isaac's chest once.

"N—"

He smelled the rubbing alcohol before disintegrating into agony. Every cut was suddenly shot through with bright, hot pain that obliterated every other thought in his head. He screamed. His back arched up off the table. Over the sound of his own screams, he could hear Gavin laughing.

Chapter 16

Finn jumped at the sound of a car approaching the safehouse, gun in hand. They peered out the window. *If Gavin's come back for Sam, they'll die before he gets them back to his compound.* They let out a shaky breath when Gray jumped out of the car. Ellis got out the other side with a package in hand.

"Is that them?" Vera looked in from the kitchen. She'd been able to sleep for another few hours after Gray and Ellis left, and then Finn had explained everything. At the time, she'd been calm. Accepting. She had only become more tense as the hours ticked by. She was busy inventorying the safehouse, figuring out what they had and what they could take with them. It wasn't much.

Gray burst through the door. Ellis was close on their heels. They pushed the package into Finn's hands.

"What did you get?" Finn worked to tear open the bag.

"A... zithro...?" Ellis stumbled over the word.

"Azithromycin?" Finn was incredulous. "It's perfect. How did you find it?" They tore the package all the way off and dumped the bottle into their hand. They read the label, searching for the dosage. *Qty: 10. 250mg.*

"Is it enough?" Ellis searched Finn's face with desperate eyes.

"It's... it's perfect. I can't believe you found it." Finn rushed to the bedroom where Sam lay still in the bed. Everyone followed them in.

Sam was a little better than when they had left. Empty saline bags lay on the floor with another one running into the IV in Sam's arm.

"How're they doing?" came Gray's tentative voice.

Finn shook their head. "They're going through saline like nobody's business. I've been able to keep their blood pressure up and their fever down a little bit with the Tylenol, but... this is what's going to help." They knelt on the bed and put a hand on Sam's forehead, brushing the hair away from their face. "Help me get them sitting up."

They all jumped to help. Finn sat themselves on the bed against the headboard as Gray and Vera pulled Sam's arms up, trying to cradle their lolling head. Sam's skin was hot, not quite as hot as before, and soaked with sweat. Gray and Vera leaned them against Finn.

"Ellis, will you get me a glass of water?" Finn was busy opening the bottle of medication. Ellis was gone and back in seconds. They handed the glass to Finn.

"Hey, Sam," Finn murmured against their ear. "I've got some medicine for you. You're gonna be okay. Can you wake up and take some medicine?" Sam moaned weakly, eyes moving slowly under the lids. "Hey." Finn pinched Sam's shoulder, deep in the muscle. Sam moaned and opened their eyes. Their hand pushed weakly at Finn's. "There you go. Let's take some medicine, huh?" Sam looked around the room, dazed and delirious. "You think you could take a few pills?"

Sam nodded weakly. Their eyes closed and their head fell back against the headboard. Finn poured two pills onto the sheets and picked them up with the water in their other hand. "Hey, Sam." They pinched Sam's shoulder again. "Let's do this. You'll feel a lot better, okay?" Sam let their mouth fall open and Finn dropped the pills in. They brought the glass to their lips and let Sam take a sip. Then another. Sam swallowed the pills painfully down.

"Do you want any more water?" Finn couldn't tell if Sam shook their head. Their head drooped to the side, eyes closing again.

"Were we too late?" Ellis sounded close to tears.

Finn pulled Sam against their chest and let their head drop to their shoulder. "I don't know." Their voice was weary. "They're really sick. But... they have what they need. All there's left to do is wait. I'll keep their blood pressure up, keep their fever down. The rest is up to them." They smoothed a hand through Sam's damp hair and cradled them in their arms. "We should know in the next twenty-four hours whether it's working."

Vera sank to the bed, squeezing Sam's foot over the blanket. "Stay with us, honey," she whispered. "We love you."

Gray sat on the other side of the bed beside Finn and rubbed on Finn's back. "You've done so well," they murmured. "Sam's in good hands. They'll be alright."

Finn pressed their hands against Sam to hide how badly they were shaking.

Chapter 17

Gavin's medic had come and gone hours ago. In the end Isaac had only needed five stitches. Otherwise the lines had been clean and relatively shallow. Isaac shuddered to imagine how many people had suffered under Gavin's knife as he honed his skill.

He'd been left on the table, hands still tied and pulled up above his head. He felt so exposed. He'd remained that way while Gavin's medic – *"well, he's not technically a doctor, not anymore"* – had cleaned his wounds, stitched him up, and placed bandages over his chest. Given him water. *"I'd rather not have you free to attack my medical dude. Especially not when he's here to fix you up."* He'd lain on the table, still except for when he flinched from the antiseptic, tears of shame running down his face. *I gave up. I stopped fighting.* Isaac swallowed the lump in his throat. *He told me he'd kill me when I stopped being fun. Is this what he wants from me? Am I keeping myself alive like this?*

The door opened again.

Isaac tried to stifle a sob at the sound of footsteps entering the room. He lifted his head from the table for a moment to see who Gavin had brought. *Leo again.* He wondered if Gavin really *had* fired Mark for nearly shooting him in the car.

"Tie his ankles." Gavin had a sickening smile on his face.

Isaac gasped and sobbed in terror and despair. He couldn't hold still while Leo tied him down again. He couldn't. When he was tied down, he was hurt. He was helpless. He flinched away from Leo's iron grip on his ankle, cringing in on himself. "No no no… please…" He threw his dignity aside. He didn't care if Gavin killed him now. If the past two days were any indication of what the rest of his life would be, he didn't want to live it. Better to die now and save himself the pain.

But Sam…

He gasped as Sam's face flashed, unbidden, through his mind. *No… I don't want to think of you now, I just want to stop hurting…* But the damage was done. He surrendered to Leo's grasp and felt the rope tighten around his ankles. Leo secured the rope to the table again and stepped back into the shadows. Isaac whimpered in resignation.

Gavin approached him on the table, grinning from ear to ear. He was holding his hands behind his back like he was hiding something. Isaac rolled his head from side to side, a weak attempt at shaking his head. "No…"

Gavin tilted his head. "No what?"

Isaac closed his eyes, sending more tears streaming down his face. He said nothing.

Gavin shrugged. He leaned over Isaac, staring at the gauze on his chest. "How you holding up there, champ?"

Isaac's lips quivered. "You don't give a shit about how I'm holding up."

Gavin looked offended. "Yeah, I do! I give many shits! I want to know how close you are to your breaking point, how much more you can take. I wanna know how much longer you're going to be interesting."

Isaac opened his eyes in surprise. "What do you mean, my 'breaking point'? You… already…" *Maybe this isn't the best time to bring up the fact that he already broke me?*

Gavin laughed and stood at the head of the table over Isaac. "No no no. Yeah, I've broken you, but you're not, like, *broken* broken. Not like Sam was. You remember how Sam was, don't you? Ready to kill you just to spare themselves more pain? Because they thought you were there to torture them? Remember that?"

"*Yes*, I remember." Isaac seethed with hatred.

"Right. Like I said, not *broken*. You're not ready to give up your friends just for a break from what I'm doing to you, right?"

Isaac set his jaw. "Never."

"Aw. That's cute." Gavin brought one hand from behind his back and patted Isaac on the head like he was a child. "I'm bored with this game, though. Bored with *you*. So I'm here to break you, then go back to Sam. This was fun while it lasted, really, it was. But I'll be honest... I'm done with you." He pulled his other hand from behind his back and produced a blindfold. Before Isaac could pull away, Gavin had the cloth over his eyes and tied behind his head.

"What..." Isaac's voice shook so badly he could barely get the words out. "What do you mean you...? No... please..." Tears began to wet the blindfold.

"Exactly what I said. I'm done with you. You're just not as fun as I thought you would be. I was lying before, though. I do need some more information about your family before I go hunt Sam down like an animal and drag them back here, kicking and screaming. Might even show them your body before I start into them. That would really set the tone, huh?"

"You... you're *sick*..."

"I am *not!* I'm just bored. And creative."

"I won't give you a damn *thing*. I won't give you anything. You might as well just kill me now."

"Not just yet."

Isaac felt cold steel press against his head. *A gun.*

"No..." he whimpered. "Please don't do this... I can, I can be better, just tell me what you want, I'll do whatever you want, *be* whatever you want..."

"You don't get it," came Gavin's voice from above him. "I don't want you to *be* anything. I just wanted you to be yourself. And yourself isn't... *interesting*. Sam was."

"Please... please no..."

A sigh. "Are you begging for Sam's life? Or yours?"

"Sam's. And mine. Both. Please, please Gavin..."

A hand wrapped around his chin and pulled his head up hard against the barrel of the gun. "Decision's been made. Sorry honey, not everyone can make varsity. Gotta make some cuts." Gavin giggled. "I do have some questions about your family, though."

Isaac shook his head against Gavin's grasp. "Never. Never."

"Yeah, I can understand why this wouldn't be a proper motivator. I mean, why tell me what I want to know when I'm just going to kill you at the end?" Gavin's hands left Isaac's head. Isaac heard Gavin move to his side. "You don't need your kneecaps if you're dead, right?"

Not more pain. "No! Please!" He couldn't take it. Not now. And he absolutely knew Gavin would do it. "Please..." He dissolved into sobs. "Please... I'll tell you whatever you want to know, anything, just not about my family. I'll tell you anything else. Please. Please just... leave them alone." A pause. He held his breath, waiting for the burst of agony. It never came. Gavin moved up behind his head again.

"Hm." Gavin's hand pulled Isaac's head back by his hair and the gun pressed to him again. "Anything?"

"Yes." Isaac nodded frantically against Gavin's grasp. "Anything. I swear."

He heard a gentle laugh. "Okay, I'll bite. Tell me about you."

"...what?"

"You refused to tell me about yourself while I was drowning you. So... tell me about yourself, Isaac. If you don't, I will start at your kneecaps and work my way up."

"What do you want to know? I'll tell you anything. Please." He sobbed with terror.

"Tell me why you made the decision to come to me. Do you really love your family *that much?* Hey, that's a fair question, it doesn't betray them or help me find them, right?"

Isaac swallowed hard. "They... they're all I've got..."

"What, you seriously have *no other family?*"

Isaac sniffed. "Not anymore."

"…okay, what does that mean?"

"…why do you want to know this?"

"Okay, kneecaps it is."

"*No no no no!* I'm sorry, I'm sorry, I'll tell you. I… I don't have any other family, no. I don't have any siblings. My… d-dad was killed in a car crash." Isaac hadn't talked about this in years. It felt so strange to be telling Gavin, of all people, and at gunpoint no less.

"How long ago?"

"Fifteen years."

"How old were you?"

"I was… twelve."

"Hm. Kay. You're only three years older than I am. Continue."

"And my mom, she… she started… drinking, couldn't handle his death, and she… she'd ask me to go get more booze for her when she was too drunk to walk, told me where to go to get it. Things were just starting to get bad so it was easy to get if you know where to look."

"'Getting bad'… as in…?"

"The syndicates were taking over already at that point."

"Ah, yes. My people. 'Syndicates.' Is that really what you call us?" Gavin snorted.

"Yeah… What do you call yourselves?"

"Uh… Same thing everyone calls themselves I guess… Keep talking."

"Okay, okay. She would, um. She wouldn't hit me, but she'd tell me all these terrible things… like she never wanted me, and she should have…" His lower lip quivered. He pressed his lips together to try and stop it.

"She should have what?"

"Should have left me on the street for the criminals to find because... because it was all my fault..."

"*Was* your dad's death your fault?"

Isaac couldn't help the sob that tore out of him. "...no..."

"...that sounded fake."

Isaac tried to swallow the whine coming from his throat. "No... he... he died while he was out grocery shopping for us. He had to get milk because I finished it that morning and didn't tell them we were almost out..."

"That doesn't sound like your fault, then."

Isaac whimpered. "I know it wasn't, I *know* it, but... I still blame myself..."

"Oh, come on, don't be an idiot. I'd say that pretty definitively wasn't your fault. I would tell you if it was, believe me. You need to learn the difference, Isaac. For example: your father's death and your mother's subsequent alcoholism? Not your fault. Me capturing Sam and destroying them forever? *Definitely* your fault."

Isaac sobbed. "Sam's not destroyed."

Gavin chuckled. "Oh, I beg to differ."

"You didn't destroy them. They're strong. And... the others will take care of them."

"The fiery defensiveness is really, truly touching. Seriously, what are they to you? You having misplaced older brother vibes? You..." Isaac felt breath on his face. "You *into* them or something?"

"No." Isaac shook his head. "It's not like that. They're like... my little sibling. I'd do anything for them. I just..."

"You just what?"

"I told you before. They're good. And sweet, and honest, and brave. I love them."

A snort. "You *love* them?"

Isaac couldn't bite back his retort. "Just because you wouldn't know a fucking thing about that—" He gasped in a breath and braced himself for the pain – or the shot.

Gavin paused. "That was rude." He adjusted his grip on Isaac's hair. "So that's it? You *love* them, and you go to your death for them? That sounds… stupid. And I don't think it's just the way I'm saying it."

"I can't explain it beyond that. I just love them. I love them all."

"Would you have done this for any of them?"

"Yes." There was no hesitation.

"Huh." Gavin tapped the gun against Isaac's head. Isaac flinched. "Do you think they'd all do the same for you?"

Isaac couldn't answer as quickly. "…I wouldn't let them."

"So that's a no."

"…no…"

Gavin sighed. "It's a no. I can hear it in your voice." Tears rolled down Isaac's face behind the blindfold. "Aw. Poor Isaac. That's sad." Gavin blew his breath out from between his lips. "So, your mom. Alcoholic. Abusive. Go on."

Isaac swallowed hard. "I left when I was fourteen. I didn't want to buy her alcohol anymore. Someone tried to snatch me off the street, and I think they were planning on selling me, but… someone saved me. Rosa. Grabbed me right out of the man's hands. She took me back to her hideout with her resistance cell. Back when there were still resistance movements. They taught me how to fight, shoot, forage for what I needed… They gave me a family."

"You said you have no other family."

"I know. I left them when I was about twenty-one."

"Why?"

Isaac's stomach spasmed with shame. "They... were..."

Gavin sighed. "What?"

Isaac shook his head. "They were tired of laying low. They were going to go fight. And I didn't..."

"You were scared."

A whimper. "Yes."

"Did they all die or something?"

Isaac licked his lips. "No. Most of them came back."

"So..."

He could barely say the words. "They told me... there was no place for me if I couldn't... do what was necessary. They told me to choose. Fight or leave."

"And you left."

"Yes."

Another sigh. "And yet... you gunned down my people not three days ago."

Isaac swallowed hard. "I learned to be okay with it. Things got harder when I was on my own. I had to be okay with killing people to survive." His jaw clenched. "I wouldn't have *touched* your people if you had left us alone. If you hadn't taken Sam."

"Hey, *you* were raiding *me!*"

Isaac didn't have a response to that.

"How many people have you killed?"

Isaac whimpered. Gavin yanked his head back and pressed the gun harder to his head. "How. Many."

"Including the four of yours?" Isaac thrust his chin at Gavin.

"Yeah, including those."

"Nine."

"Seriously? You almost doubled your number with me?"

Isaac's voice was cold and hard. "I told you, you should have left Sam alone."

"Hm." Gavin shifted his weight. "Fair enough." He leaned farther over Isaac. "Well, my interest has run out. I don't want to hear another thing out of your mouth that isn't exactly how to find your family."

Isaac shuddered, nearly crying out in fear. He pressed his lips together. *Then you'll get nothing.* Gavin yanked Isaac's hair so hard his neck twisted. He groaned.

"Nothing? Not even any last words?"

Tears ran freely down his face. The blindfold was soaked through.

"Okay. Goodbye, Isaac. Five, four..."

"No..." he whimpered.

"Three, two..."

He squeezed his eyes shut behind the blindfold. *I love you all.*

"One."

Bang.

Chapter 18

Isaac jumped so hard the rope cut into his wrists again. The shot echoed around the room, vibrating the walls, the impact percussing Isaac's chest.

A blank.

He took a breath.

He collapsed into sobs. Gavin pulled the knot on the blindfold and slid the cloth off his face. He threw his gaze around the room, uncomprehending, not able to believe he was alive. Gavin leaned over him and patted his face.

"Are you kidding?" Gavin laughed, tucking the gun into the waistband of his pants. "Isaac, you are so much damned fun. How could I lose interest in you when you give me shit like *that* to work with? That was just… so fucking fun. Seriously, I've got *so much* I want to do with you. You are… the best I've had, Isaac. Wouldn't you like a t-shirt with *that* on the fucking front? How could I want to give up on you when you hold out under *that*?" He turned away, beckoning to Leo. "Cut him loose. He's earned a break, I think." He walked out of the room, laughing.

Isaac lay motionless as Leo cut the ropes tying him to the table. His sobs tore out of his throat from deep in his chest. When his hands were free, he covered his face and curled into himself. Leo walked out the door behind Gavin. Isaac wasn't sure if he was relieved to be alive or not.

∴

Isaac didn't know how long he lay trembling on the table. His wrists stung from the burn of the ropes. His ankles were raw. He pressed his face into his hands and sobbed. *How can I know what's real? How can I know what he wants, or when he's actually going to kill me?*

He tried to force the old memories from his mind. *I never wanted to think about my mother again. Or Michael, or William, or Jordan, or Lexi, or Rosa… Any of them.* He wondered if they were still alive. He wondered if they had been successful in the war they had decided to fight after seven years of laying low. *If I had gone with them, would my life have been different?*

He rolled and swung his legs off the table. Gavin's "medical dude," Ex-Dr. Bodhi, had done his best to clean and sanitize the table after Gavin had bled him all over it. There were still some streaks of dried blood in the grain of the wood. He shuddered and suddenly wanted off.

He collapsed in a heap next to the table and leaned against one of the legs, trembling. He barely had the strength to sit up. His muscles ached. His chest burned like he was lying on an open flame. The welts on his back had cooled to deep bruises marking his skin, at least where the skin wasn't broken. A few still bled. His throat was sore from screaming.

Gavin was right. He had claimed every bit of Isaac: his body, his voice, his dignity... his past. Isaac thought he had put it behind him. Forgotten. Focusing on his new team, his new family. It did him no good to dwell on the past, he knew. But his heart still ached for the homes he'd had before. With his parents. Then just with his mother. Then with the band of rebels who had taken him in. Then... *Sam. Gray. Finn. Ellis. Vera.* He'd left them. He'd left them without protection, to go suffer in Sam's place. Now he was locked away in a basement somewhere, a plaything for a monster. *I'm going to die in this room and then he'll go after Sam.* He hated the tempting pull towards death that offered him peace. *As long as I'm alive, I'll suffer.* He hung his head. *But as long as I'm alive, Sam and the rest are safe. I keep them safe by staying alive.*

He crawled to the corner of the room farthest away from the door and slumped to the floor. His body ached with every movement. He curled in on himself, trying to push the sobs down. He'd never felt so alone in his life. He shivered against the cold cement floor.

Mercifully, unbelievably, he fell asleep. He drifted. Sometimes he dreamed, sometimes he just disappeared into his own mind. Pain moved underneath the blackness like magma under the earth. He whimpered in his sleep.

Far too soon, the door swung open again. Isaac woke in an instant. He shot upright and moaned as pain lanced through all his wounds. He threw his hands in front of him.

Gavin smiled. "Aw, you're awake already! Have a good nap?" Isaac glared at him. "Enjoying the memories I dug up?" Gavin snorted. "I, for one, would think you'd appreciate the time alone with your thoughts. At least I'm not torturing you then, right?"

The thoughts you pulled out of my mind are *torture.* Gavin wiggled his eyebrows as if he could read Isaac's mind.

Leo didn't approach but stood behind Gavin with his hands behind his back. Isaac watched Gavin for a moment, measuring his intent, waiting for him to move in and hurt him.

Gavin stared straight at Isaac and said, smoothly, "Get on your knees and face the wall."

Isaac paled. "Why?"

Gavin threw his hands in the hair, shaking his head. "Does it matter? I feel like blowing off some steam, and you are here in my dungeon available for just that. I'm going to hurt you, dumbass. Does that answer your question?"

Isaac bit his lip, trembling. *This is what I'm here for. This is what I'm here to do.* He pushed himself up to his knees and turned around.

"Over here." He turned to look at where Gavin was pointing, across the room.

Slowly, he got to his feet. He wobbled as he stood fully upright and leaned against the wall.

"Doing okay?" Gavin's voice was too gleeful.

Isaac wrapped his arms around his middle, careful not to press against the cuts. He staggered across the room and fell to his knees. He looked down and noticed an anchor loop on the floor in front of him. He whimpered.

Leo moved at last, stepping out from behind Gavin and pulling a pair of handcuffs from his pocket. He snapped one cuff around Isaac's wrist. He passed the other through the anchor loop on the floor before snapping it onto Isaac's other wrist. Isaac whimpered and pulled weakly against the cuffs.

Gavin crossed the room to the table with all of his tools. He didn't browse. He went right to the whip. He ran his fingers over the handle before picking it up and weighing it in his hands. Isaac took a shuddering gasp and closed his eyes, turning away.

"I'm really a simple creature, at the end of the day," Gavin said casually. "Yeah, I've got a lot of things over here to choose from, but honestly it's more for intimidation than anything else. I like what I like. And one of the things I happen to like…" He cracked the whip. Isaac flinched away like it had hit him. "Is a good old-fashioned whipping. Let's see how long you can take this one."

Isaac could barely get words out through his sobs. "P-please, Gavin… Not again, I… I c-can't…"

"I want you to count this time. Last time I did all the work. You made it to… um… twenty-eight last time? Is that right?" He waited for Isaac's response. He got none. "I think it was twenty-eight. But you were fresh then, right? I bet you're tired. I bet you're hurting. So, we'll say… I'll go to twenty-five. Twenty-five lashes. You count."

Gavin approached Isaac from the side. Isaac could see him, and the whip. He pulled away. The cuffs tightened around his wrists and he whined softly. Gavin put the handle of the whip under Isaac's chin and tilted his head up. Isaac met his gaze with eyes wide with terror and pain. "Keep counting… or I start over." He released Isaac's chin and walked behind him.

The first lash came without warning. Isaac cried out as the pain crossed the marks already on his back. He gasped, pulling at the handcuffs, waiting for the pain to subside. It didn't. "Come on, hero," Gavin mocked. "Count it, or we start from one again."

"One!" Isaac gasped out.

Another. Isaac screamed. It hurt so much worse than the first time, the whip cutting into the bruises already crossing his skin. He felt blood begin to ooze down his back. *"Two!"*

Crack.

Isaac shook his head frantically. *I can't take it. I can't do this.* He swallowed hard. *But I can't start over. "Three!"*

Crack.

He screamed the word. *"Four!"*

Crack.

His chest heaved with sobs. He couldn't form the word. His lips were numb, his back was fire. "Ah…"

Gavin's voice was low and dangerous. "Count, or we start over."

"F-five!"

"Good."

Crack.

Isaac pressed his forehead against the wall, shaking violently. *"Six!"*

"See, Isaac? This is fun. At least, it's more fun for me this way." He laughed.

Crack.

The whip curled around Isaac to snap against this shoulder. He jumped away, his wrists jerking against the handcuffs. He looked at the mark where the whip had touched him. *It's not bleeding. "Seven!"*

Crack.

Isaac gasped desperately. He couldn't breathe and if he couldn't breathe, he couldn't count. His head spun sickeningly as the pain flooded his mind. He tried to push it away, tried to push away everything but the next number. *"Eight!"* He screamed with air he didn't know he had.

Crack.

He rocked forward with the blow. He choked on the word. *"N—"* He wailed wordlessly, tears pouring down his face.

"Please tell me you can count higher than eight, Isaac."

"Nine, it's nine, please…"

Crack.

He cried out, throat straining. *"Ten."*

"There we go. Getting into a rhythm here."

Crack.

A scream. *"Eleven!"*

Crack.

"No! Twelve!"

Crack.

Isaac gasped. "Please…" he begged. "Please no…"

"Count it, Isaac!" Gavin shouted. "Or we start over from one!"

Helplessly, Isaac sobbed. *"Thirteen!"*

Crack.

His mind was blank, flooded with nothing but pain. *What number comes next, what number…?*

"Come on, Isaac, I feel like I'm coaching you or something. Count. Now."

No no no no… Please, what number…?

"Say it or I start over in three… two…"

"Fourteen! It's fourteen, please don't…"

Crack.

Isaac sobbed breathlessly. "No…"

"Come on Isaac, you're more than halfway through. It would be a shame to start over now."

"Fif-fifteen…"

Crack.

The sound that tore out of Isaac was almost inhuman. His head spun. *"Sixteen!"*

"Not even ten more. This isn't that bad, right?"

Crack.

Isaac's breath froze in his chest and for a moment he didn't make a sound.

"Don't mess up this streak, Isaac."

"Seventeen!"

"Good."

Crack.

Isaac thought he might pass out. The room was spinning. The pain was rising in his back and he thought he might be sick. It was inescapable, unending.

What number comes next?

Isaac's mouth gaped open in panic. *No no no... I can't, I can't start over...* He cast about in his mind for the number, the damned *number*, but there was no room in his brain for anything, anything but the pain. His stomach dropped at the thought of another twenty-five lashes. *I'll die.*

"Guess we start over."

Isaac lurched forward. *"Eighteen!"*

Gavin paused. Isaac's heart pounded in his chest. He could hear every heartbeat like they were shaking apart the room.

"Okay, I'll give that to you."

Isaac sobbed with relief.

Crack.

Isaac screamed, long and broken. His throat was raw. *"Nine..."* He swallowed. *"Nineteen..."*

Gavin laughed. "Thought you were going back to nine there for a minute. We can, if you want..."

"No!" Isaac panted. "No, please..."

Crack.

He sagged against the wall. "Ah… *twenty…*"

"Last five! Let's make 'em count."

Crack.

The whip cut into him and a fresh stream of blood ran down Isaac's back. He leaned against the wall, uncomprehending. He didn't know how it was possible to be in more pain. His mouth hung open in agony.

"Are you seriously gonna make me start over *now?* I'll be honest, Isaac, I'm getting a little tired. This takes effort on my part, too. Have some fucking respect."

"*Twe*— I'm… *trying… twenty-one…*"

"Good job."

Crack.

The whip cut him again, across the back of his neck. He moaned. *I have to finish this before I pass out. "Twenty-two."*

"Three more. I'm loving this."

Crack.

The scream ripped out of his chest. His very bones were on fire. *"Twenty-three!"*

Crack.

Sweat poured down Isaac's back. It ran into his eyes and burned him there, too. It mixed with the tears on his face as he sobbed. *"Twenty-four."*

"Last one! This one's gonna hurt."

Crack.

The whip wrapped around him and struck him across the chest. Isaac's breath rushed out of him in a guttural scream. *"Twenty… five!"*

He slumped to the ground, the handcuffs pulling his arms out to the side, too exhausted to sob. Tears leaked out of his eyes and dripped onto the concrete. He was a mess of pain and terror.

He felt a hand on his head and flinched. "No no no…" he whimpered.

Gavin pulled his hand through Isaac's hair. "Have I mentioned yet today that I love hurting you?" he said fondly. Isaac lay on the floor, shuddering under the touch.

"But…" All the warmth slithered out of Gavin's voice. He yanked Isaac's head up so Isaac could see his face. Isaac's eyes were bright and unfocused. "I'm not quite done yet. Hasn't really… hit the spot. I could go for a bit more." He dropped Isaac's head to the floor.

Isaac's mouth fell open in despair. He couldn't move, couldn't get up, couldn't press himself against the wall. He moaned low in his throat.

Gavin let the end of the whip smack against the ground. "Don't try to hold back for me this time, Isaac. You can scream all you want. I just want to hear you."

The lash split Isaac's mind with brilliant agony. He felt his throat go tight and raw again, but he couldn't hear his screams over the anguish in his mind.

Chapter 19

Finn blinked their eyes open. Their gaze moved around the room, never really focusing. Landing on things and moving on. The window. The shelves on the wall. The lamp. The door. They groaned, rolling their neck. It ached from having slept in the chair all night. Finn's eyes finally focused on Sam.

Sam was awake.

They were touching the IV in their arm with one finger, following the line with their eyes up to the bag of saline hanging from the wall. Sam squinted in confusion.

"Sam." Finn lunged out of the chair. Their hand went to Sam's face, pushing back their damp hair. "Oh my god, Sam. Your fever's down." They reached with a shaking hand for the thermometer on the nightstand and swiped it across Sam's forehead. Finn mopped Sam's forehead dry and swiped the thermometer again. "Oh my god." They turned the thermometer around to show Sam. "100.2."

Sam put a hand to their head. "Ugh. What… What happened?"

Finn's eyebrows pulled together as guilt washed through them. "You got worse. A lot worse. We found some antibiotics for you. How do you feel?"

Sam squeezed their eyes shut for a moment. "Um… like I really have to pee."

Finn laughed. They felt weak with relief. "Okay. I'll help you to the bathroom." Finn gingerly pulled the blanket off Sam. Sam sat up and swung their legs over the side of the bed. They wobbled for a moment.

Finn placed a hand on their shoulder. "Whoa. You okay?"

Sam nodded. "Yeah. Just a little dizzy."

Finn disconnected the line from the IV and hung it up from the nail on the wall. Sam slowly placed their feet on the floor and stood up. Finn tucked a hand under their arm. Sam staggered, caught themselves, and took a step towards the bathroom.

Finn's eyes raked over Sam as they took another step. "How you doing?"

"I feel okay." Sam's forehead furrowed with concentration. "Just a little out of it."

Finn guided Sam to the door and held back, their hand still on Sam's arm. "You gonna be okay by yourself?"

Sam blushed. "Yeah. I'll be fine. And, um…"

"Yeah?"

"I'm kinda… hungry. Is there… soup? Maybe?"

Finn smiled gently. "Hungry's a good sign. Yeah, I can heat up some soup for you. Holler if you need anything and I'll hear you."

"Okay." Sam closed the door.

Finn walked to the kitchen. They reached for a bowl in the cupboard. The house was quiet with only them and Sam in it.

Distractedly, they reached for a can on the shelf. They didn't read the label before they peeled off the aluminum lid and dumped it into the bowl. They vaguely noticed the smell of chicken noodle. *At least I picked a good flavor.* They added water and put the bowl in the microwave.

They looked around the empty safehouse. The blankets were piled in a tangle on the couch. The others had taken all their other belongings when they had—

They shivered. They didn't want to think about it. Not until it was absolutely necessary.

The beep of the microwave saved them from their thoughts. They pulled the bowl out and stirred it. Their eyes were unfocused, distracted, as the steam rose. Their mouth watered. It had been some time since they'd eaten, too. Some time since they'd slept well. Maybe they could sleep after…

No.

They shook themselves out of their reverie and carried the bowl to the bedroom. Sam sat on the bed, wrapped in the light blanket. They perked up at the sight of the soup. "Chicken noodle. My favorite. Thanks, Finn." They reached their hands out to take it.

"Would you like to eat in bed, or at the table?"

Sam paused for a moment. "I can… I can eat at the table…" They pushed themselves up off the bed onto their feet again. They swayed for a moment.

Finn hurriedly put the bowl of soup on the nightstand and put a hand on Sam's shoulder. "Nope. Bed it is." They guided Sam back until they were sitting upright against the headboard. They handed Sam the soup and sat on the bed next to them.

Sam devoured the soup, first scooping the chicken, noodles, and vegetables out of the broth and then drinking the broth straight from the bowl. They licked their lips and wiped their mouth with their shirt, wincing a little when they realized how damp it was. They handed the bowl back to Finn.

"Thank you." They had some color back in their cheeks.

Finn reached out a hand and stroked Sam's hair. "No problem. How you feeling?"

"Better. Um." Sam's face turned a brilliant red. "I… uh…" Finn waited. "The tracker, um…"

"The tracker's gone?"

Sam nodded. "Yup."

A smile broke across Finn's face. "Excellent. That's a huge weight off our shoulders, huh?"

Sam nodded again. Took a breath. "Where's everyone else?"

Finn looked away. "They're… um…"

Sam's eyebrows rose. "What? Are they okay? Are they in trouble?"

Finn waved a hand. "Oh, no. No. They're fine. They... um..." They looked at their hands, lacing and unlacing their fingers together. "Ellis... made a plan to get Isaac back."

Sam brightened. "Great! Are we going to rescue him? How can I help? Can I—" They pushed out of bed.

Finn's hands pushed Sam's shoulders down. "No. You are going to focus on getting better."

"No, I want to... Let me talk to them, maybe I can help them..."

Finn's hands wrapped gently around Sam's wrists. "No. You're staying put. Don't make me tie you down." Their lips quirked up into a smile.

Sam stiffened. *Fuck.* Finn pulled their hands back. "I'm sorry, I didn't... I didn't mean that..."

Sam's eyes filled with tears. "I know... I know you didn't. You were joking. I know." Their lips quivered. They sagged slightly, some of the pain returning to their face. "I'm sorry... This is my fault..."

Finn reached for Sam's hand and clasped it between their own. "Nobody blames you, Sam. I should have..." They bit their lip. "We should have protected you. And... I should have... kept better watch over you. I should have made sure you were okay. You got so sick, so fast, I couldn't..."

Sam laid their other hand on top of Finn's. "No..." They fixed Finn with their wide brown eyes. "Please don't blame yourself."

Finn took a breath and blew it out between their lips. "Ellis and the others... They'll be here soon to pick us up. They'll take us to the next place for a while."

"'Next place'? Why are they gone? What are they doing? Finn..." Sam licked their cracked lips. "What's going on? How are we going to get Isaac back?"

Finn stared at the bedspread as they spoke. Their voice was low, robotic. "We know of one of Gavin's men who lives nearby. The others left to... take him... and..." They shook their head. "They're going to take him to an abandoned power plant near here. He's going to stay with Vera and Ellis while Gray comes to pick us up in the car." Since the others had left, Finn had rehearsed the plan in their head, over and over. "Gray will take us to them and we're all going to… ask him where Isaac is."

"…*ask* him?" Finn slowly raised their eyes to Sam. They looked horrified.

Finn swallowed. "Um. Yeah. We're going to ask him where we can find Isaac and Gavin. And then we're going to… call Gavin. His number is on the phone Isaac left… and we're going to… trade his man… for Isaac."

Sam took in a sharp inhale. "You're going to ransom him?"

"Trade him." Finn's voice slipped lower. "We're going to trade him. For Isaac. Get Isaac back."

"And… what if he doesn't… *want* to tell you where Isaac is?"

Finn's lips pressed into a hard line. "We're going to interrogate him."

Sam swallowed hard. "You're going to torture him."

Finn jerked their head in a nod. "Yes."

Sam pulled their hands out of Finn's grasp. Finn wouldn't meet their eyes. Sam's voice trembled. "And… this was Ellis's idea?"

Finn raised their gaze to Sam. Tears poured down their cheeks as they looked at Finn, disbelieving.

Finn nodded slowly. "Isaac is… is *family*," they said miserably.

"Isaac is family to me, too," Sam whispered. Finn looked away. "But you would do to someone… what Gavin did to me?"

Finn's mouth spasmed. They swallowed hot tears. "What else can we do, Sam?" Their face was warm with desperation. "Tell me what else we can do. Tell me you have a better plan. We're fighting people who have no qualms. Gavin will never give Isaac back. He will torture him to death if we don't save him. And… I'd be willing to bet he'd come for you before Isaac's body was cold."

Sam cringed against the bed. Finn reached for their hand. "Gavin is insane. We can't reason with him. We just have to hope…" Finn swallowed hard. "We just have to hope this guy means more to him than Isaac does."

Sam watched Finn's face in horror. "I…"

Finn grabbed Sam's wrist. Their voice was strained with tears. "What would you do, Sam? What would you do to get Isaac back?"

Sam opened their mouth, shaking their head. "I don't…"

Finn was crying now, too. "This family is all I have. All any of us have. Isaac… will… d—" Finn's throat spasmed and they choked. "Isaac will die if we don't get him back. I can't…" They shook their head violently. "We can't let him kill Isaac." Their voice dropped to a whisper. "I can't let him kill Isaac." They grabbed Sam's hands, pleading.

Sam shuddered. Finn pulled their hands back and covered their face, their body heaving with sobs. Finn's voice rose in desperate anguish as they shook in their chair. Sam's throat closed with sobs. They reached out to touch Finn's shoulder.

Chapter 20

Isaac drifted in and out of awareness. He could feel the cold cement below him. He could feel that his wrists were not in the handcuffs anymore. He wasn't restrained at all; it was an almost unfamiliar sensation now. He was splayed on his back in the middle of the floor, blood pooling slowly beneath him. It was warm, and wet, and the smell made him dizzy.

Over it all, pushing out every other sensation, was the pain. He trembled as he counted his heartbeats, waiting for the pain to ease. He remained trapped in it, unable to escape to a corner of his mind. Unable to imagine a time, a world, when he had not been in agony.

His eyes were half closed and unfocused. His breaths came ragged and harsh. Every moment hurt. Breathing was *torture*. Every movement of his lungs pierced him with pain again. Again, and again, with every breath, until he thought he would lose his mind.

Gavin had whipped him eighteen more times before he decided he was finished. Eighteen more times the whip had cut into his back, raising welts that opened up and bled. Eventually he'd stopped begging, stopped pleading for Gavin to stop. He'd stopped pleading for Gavin to kill him. Eventually he just screamed. Then Leo had unlocked the handcuffs from around his wrists and dragged him to the middle of the room. He'd thrown Isaac onto his back, wrenching another scream from him. Then Leo had stepped back into the shadows again, silent. Gavin sat cross-legged on the floor and watched Isaac suffer.

Isaac could feel Gavin's eyes on him, but he didn't care. There was no room in his mind for it. It was simply another sensation: cold cement, free wrists, warm blood, the eyes of his torturer. Pain. Always pain draped over that.

Gavin watched Isaac's chest heave with sobs. He watched as Isaac trembled in every limb, sweat beading on his forehead even though the beating had stopped a while ago. He watched his mouth open in desperate gasps, needing the air and then being torn apart by pain for taking it. He watched the blood oozing onto the floor.

Then, Gavin got bored.

He cleared his throat. "Leo, get him water. And food, please. And electrolytes."
Leo nodded and stalked out the door without a word.

"Wh—" Isaac's voice broke. He licked his lips. "Why... are you..."

"Why am I giving you water? Feeding you?"

"Please... just... let me..."

"Yes?"

Isaac trembled with the effort to speak. "Please just... let me die. I can't. If you
do that again... I can't."

"No can do, honey." Gavin *tsk*ed. "I want you strong and... you know...
alive... so I kinda have to feed you. Don't complain."

Isaac fell silent, lost in his pain. When Leo came back with water, an electrolyte
drink, and a small sandwich, Isaac didn't stir.

Leo knelt beside Isaac and placed the tray on the ground next to him. Gavin
scooted himself over to Isaac and pulled on one arm. "Sit up," he ordered. Isaac
lay still. "Seriously, sit up. Leo, help me..."

Leo came behind Isaac and pulled him up to sitting by his shoulders. Isaac cried
out as Leo placed his hands on the lash marks on his back. Leo knelt behind
Isaac and braced him against his knee. Isaac whimpered. Gavin held out a bottle
of water, holding Isaac steady with one hand. Isaac reached for it and stiffened
as his wounds protested. His face shone with tears and sweat. His hand
extended, shaking. He bit his lip. He shuddered, dropping his hand and
slumping forward.

"Whoa, whoa." Gavin straightened him upright, his hands on Isaac's shoulders.
Isaac sobbed weakly, wordlessly. Gavin pursed his lips. "Get your shit together,
Isaac. I'm trying to help you." Isaac's eyes rolled back as the pain overtook him
for a moment. "Fine."

He picked up the bottle of water and opened it. He cradled Isaac's chin in his
palm and held the bottle to his lips. Isaac took one sip, then another. It hurt to
swallow. The cool water tasted so good on his tongue. He parted his lips for

more and took in gulps of water. Gavin spilled some in his lap as he took in a gasping breath, then drank more. The bottle emptied quickly.

Gavin cracked open the electrolyte drink and held it to Isaac's lips. Isaac drank deeply, savoring the sweetness on his tongue. He hadn't realized how thirsty he was. Or hungry. He pulled away from the bottle to take a breath, and his eyes darted to the sandwich.

Gavin followed his gaze. "Hungry too, huh?" Isaac nodded slowly, too weak to lie. "See if you can hold it." He held out the sandwich and Isaac strained to take it. His hand dipped as his strength failed. "Jesus. What a big baby."

Gavin shook his head and held the sandwich out to Isaac's mouth. He took the biggest bite he could. Slowly, Gavin fed him the rest of the sandwich, and helped him drink the last of the electrolyte drink. He watched Isaac's face as he slumped back against Leo.

Gavin looked up at Leo. "You can lay him down now. Thanks."

Leo stood up abruptly. Isaac toppled backwards. He grunted as his back hit the floor and his mind was shot through with white-hot pain. He let his eyes close.

"Isaac."

He moaned. "No. I can't. Please."

"Relax, I just wanna talk."

Isaac shuddered. There was a rustling of clothing as Gavin moved. Isaac's eyes went wide with horror as Gavin stepped over him and straddled him, his hips against Isaac's stomach. He whined at the pressure against the cuts on his abdomen and the fresh wounds on his back. His hands went up to push against Gavin's chest. He trembled with the effort and his arms fell back uselessly to the floor. Gavin chuckled.

"Please..." Isaac whispered. "Please, no..."

"Oh, relax. I'm not gonna do anything to you. You don't believe me?"

Isaac weakly shook his head. "No..."

Gavin snorted. "That's fair. I've been fucking with you this whole time. I understand. This time, though…" He leaned over Isaac and drew an X across his chest, just over his heart. "I promise. No torture. Just chatting."

Isaac closed his eyes and pressed his lips together. Surrendering.

"I've really been enjoying learning about you. I wanna explore this relationship with Sam more, though. Tell me about it. When did you meet them?"

Isaac sighed. It was useless to argue. *This is better than him hurting me. I won't give him anything he can use to find them.* "About a year ago."

Gavin paused. "…'kay… Care to elaborate?"

Isaac shook his head helplessly. "They were laying low, trying to stay out of the way of the syndi— of your people. They were doing well. Staying with safe people, traveling in large groups, staying out of contentious cities… But… they…" He blinked tears out of his eyes as he thought of Sam when they first met: barely eighteen, terrified, and alone in the world. His heart wrenched. "They were caught in the crossfire of two warring syndicates. Each one thought Sam was working for the other. So… they ran. We found them a few days later. They'd been on the run and were out of supplies and they were huddled in a safehouse begging for food from whoever passed through…" He cleared his throat. "We took them in. Kept them safe. Taught them how to protect themselves."

"You clearly didn't do a good job."

Isaac grimaced, turning his face away from Gavin. "I know," he whispered.

"I'm confused, though. Why did you have to teach them how to survive? Weren't they already surviving on their own?"

"Surviving and being on the run from warring syndicates are two very different things."

Gavin nodded. "Ah. Fair."

Isaac's eyebrows pulled together. "You didn't ask them all this while you had them?"

"Honestly? Not really." Gavin shrugged. "I was more interested in the others at that point than in Sam's tragic backstory. And they broke so fast... I honestly didn't get everything out of them that I needed. I was lucky to get what I did."

Isaac squeezed his eyes shut, trembling. "Damn you."

Gavin leaned over Isaac. He twisted a hand in Isaac's hair, pulling his head back and baring his throat. Gavin's smile was venomous. "Why do you love them so much?"

Isaac shook his head and strained away from Gavin's gaze. Gavin wrapped his hand around his throat and forced Isaac to look at him.

"Please..." Isaac grabbed at Gavin's wrists, but he couldn't budge his grasp. He shuddered with exhaustion.

"Answer the question, Isaac. Why do you love them so much?"

Isaac began to cry in earnest, tears rolling down the sides of his face and into his hair. Gavin tightened his grasp on Isaac's hair and throat. "Because..."

Gavin wrenched his head back harder. "Because?"

Isaac whimpered. "Because they... are the only person... who loves me... thinks I'm good... believes in me, no matter what..." He swallowed hard. "...I never had to prove it to them. I never... had to provide, had to earn it, they just... love me... for *no reason*..." He gasped and dissolved into sobs.

"Your family doesn't love you?" Gavin inspected Isaac's face closely.

"No, they... they do..." He sniffed. "They love me. I know they do. But... I have to... I have to prove it to them... every day that I... that I *deserve* it, that I deserve their trust..." He whimpered. "I know if I failed them, if I messed up... they would... they'd stop trusting me... stop loving me..." He couldn't catch his breath. "They'd reject me..." He gasped. He couldn't breathe.

Gavin watched in fascination as Isaac spiraled into panic. Gavin turned Isaac's head back and forth, squeezing his throat, watching the reaction. He watched Isaac gasp for air, squirming under him, trying to throw him off, to get free. Gavin smiled and loosened his grip, only slightly. Isaac felt scraped hollow. He lay under Gavin's weight, helpless, thrashing weakly. He clawed uselessly at Gavin's wrists as he pinned Isaac down by the throat.

Gavin laughed softly. "*That's* why you made this sacrifice. When I broke Sam, I made them believe you had failed them. *Betrayed* them. I made them believe you were going to hurt them. And that… fucking… *destroyed you.*" He brought his face closer to Isaac until Isaac could feel his breath. "I took the one person in the world who trusts you completely and I *ruined them.*"

Isaac took a shuddering gasp and sobbed. His eyes were desperate, his mouth pulled open into a silent scream.

Gavin spoke quietly, just loud enough to cut through Isaac's anguish. "And you couldn't let that happen again, could you? You got them back. I bet as soon as they started to perk up again, they threw themselves on you, felt your protection, realized you were there to help…" He chuckled. "I bet they forgave you, took you back in an instant. I bet they blame *themselves.* Don't they?" Isaac struggled, breathless. Gavin jerked Isaac's hair. "Don't they?"

"Yes," he gasped.

"Hm." Gavin smiled. "And you couldn't stand to see it happen again. You couldn't stand to hand them over to me, knowing I'd just break them again, and harder. You couldn't stand knowing I could take them away from you again. You'd rather die. Wouldn't you?" His hand tightened around Isaac's hair in a vicious jerk. "Is that true?"

Isaac tried to nod against the grip Gavin had on his hair.

"Say it."

Isaac clenched his jaw. "I'd rather die."

"Say the whole thing."

Isaac sobbed. "I'd rather die than lose Sam's trust in me again."

Gavin laughed. "There it is. *That's* why you're here." His hand softened in Isaac's hair, but his other hand remained locked around his throat. "Did you at least leave on good terms? Did you share a tearful goodbye?"

Isaac squeezed his eyes shut and pressed his lips together. Gavin's hand tightened cruelly in his hair again. He cried out.

"Isaac, answer the question."

He whimpered. "We... we didn't."

Gavin grinned. "Oh? Tell me about it."

Isaac stared at the ceiling above Gavin's head, sobbing helplessly. "They..." He pulled once again at Gavin's wrists, trying in vain to escape.

Gavin pulled his hand away from Isaac's grasp and slapped him across the face, hard. Isaac cried out. He shuddered and fell still. Gavin's hand returned to his throat. "Continue."

"They..." He swallowed hard. "They *tried* to go to you. Everyone else was asleep. I told them to let me go but they... they got in my way. Threatened to wake the others, make me stay. So, I... I grabbed them..." His sob drew out into a whine. "I grabbed them... I hurt them; I know I did... I kept them from screaming... and they were still so weak so I... just waited for them to pass out... left them there, took the keys..." His mouth pulled open into a choked scream as he remembered it. Shame burned in his chest.

Gavin was smiling wide. "Wow. So, the last time you saw them, when you left them forever, you *hurt them.*"

Isaac nodded, sobbing.

"That's the last thing they'll remember of you." Isaac felt like he was being torn apart from the inside. "The very last time they ever saw you, you were hurting them. Holding them down." Gavin's grin pulled bigger, showing his teeth. "Just like I did."

Isaac whined as he squeezed his eyes shut.

"I wonder what they think of you now."

"No... no..."

"No, I'm serious. I wonder what they think of you. Their best friend. Their hero. You hurt them, then you abandoned them."

"No..."

Gavin chuckled. "How do you think they feel about you, now that you've betrayed them like that?"

Isaac's eyes opened to stare at the ceiling as he wept bitterly. "They hate me. I know they do."

Gavin smiled and nodded at the admission. "Oh, I don't know if it's that bad. You really think they hate you?"

"I... I know they d-do. I can't believe I... after everything you did to them, and I..."

"Not only did you sacrifice your life for them, you sacrificed their trust in you, too. I wonder who they can trust now? I wonder who will keep them safe?"

Isaac thrashed on the floor. "Please..."

"I don't know what you're begging *me* for. It's Sam you should be begging. For forgiveness. I doubt they would, though. You hurt them and they'll never forget it. Do you understand me?" He pulled Isaac's face close to his. "Even after you're long dead, if they live that long, if they can somehow escape me..." His lips slid into a wicked grin. "They will never forget how you hurt them. *Never.*"

Isaac twisted against Gavin's grip on his hair. His chest heaved with sobs, long and tortured.

"You should be grateful. They'll never see you again. I'm doing you a *favor*. Can you even imagine what they would say to you if they got the chance to see you again? Would they even want you?"

Isaac's misery was beyond words. Grief tore at his chest, made it hard to breathe.

Gavin leaned back and released his hold on Isaac's hair and throat. He shook his head. "You're a fucking mess, Isaac." Isaac pulled his arms into himself, shielding his head from blows that weren't coming. He turned away from Gavin as far as he could with Gavin's weight still pressing down on him.

Gavin grabbed Isaac's hair and yanked his face towards him again. "Honestly, I feel really bad for you. You gave up your life for someone who hates you. How does that even feel?"

Isaac whimpered. "Don't... care..."

Gavin blinked. "Say what?"

Isaac weakly shook his head. "Don't care. Doesn't matter. They're safe… They can hate me if they want… but they're safe…" A whine pulled painfully at his throat.

Gavin smiled, hostility coiling in his eyes like a snake. "Keep telling yourself that, hun. Whatever you need to believe." He stood up and dusted himself off. "Anyway, I have shit to do. Thanks for the talk. It's been fun." He stalked out of the room with Leo in tow, carrying the tray and empty bottles.

Chapter 21

The man didn't look scared. His face was pulled into a mask of seething smugness as Ellis paced back and forth in front of him. When Gray walked in carrying Sam, Ellis sighed with relief. They went to hug Finn as Finn walked in behind Gray. "Thank god. We were worried…" Vera crossed the room to Sam and Gray as Gray set Sam gently on their feet. Vera folded into Gray's arms for a moment before bending down and wrapping Sam into a hug.

Finn cast their eyes down and avoided looking at the man tied to a chair. "We're fine. Just… took a little bit to convince Sam to come with us."

Ellis looked to Sam as Vera helped Gray sit them down against the wall. Sam was pale, but they looked so much better than when the others had left.

Sam's gaze was fixed on the man in the chair. Their eyes were wide with horror and fear. Vera squeezed Sam's hand and walked past Ellis to stand behind their captive.

Ellis looked back to Finn, caressing their cheek with one hand. "You saved them, Finn. It'll be okay. This is just the next step. This is how we save Isaac."

Finn didn't want to see the coldness that had settled in Ellis's eyes. They looked down as Ellis pulled their face up. "Hey." They slowly raised their eyes to Ellis. "I can handle this if you need to go."

"No," Finn whispered. "I… need to be here. I need to make sure we get Isaac back."

"Glad the family reunion's going so well," the captive said sharply.

Ellis stiffened and slowly turned to look at the captive. "For those of us who just showed up… this is Mark." Their lip curled with contempt. "Gavin's cousin."

Finn forced down a gasp. They hadn't known the man was a *relative*. That made this worse. *No. It's better. Gavin will want his cousin back. This helps guarantee Isaac's return.*

Mark looked back and forth between each of them, eyes burning with hatred. Ellis pressed their lips together and crossed their arms over their chest.

"Let me very clear." A chill raced through Finn. They had never heard Ellis's voice so full of hate. "This can be a simple process if you let it. It's entirely up to you. How familiar are you with Gavin's movements, whereabouts, plans...?"

Mark snorted. "If this is about Gavin, you're all fucked. He's going to find you and I'm not going to tell you a damned thing before then."

Ellis lunged forward and punched the captive squarely in the jaw. He cried out and slumped to the side. Ellis shook out their hand. Vera pulled Mark upright again without a word. "Apparently I wasn't clear enough." Ellis towered over Mark as he moved his jaw from side to side. "I'm trying to make this simple for you, but I can make it *very* complicated if you don't cooperate. Gavin has one of our people. We want him back. Tell us where to find him, and we'll make a trade. No one else has to get hurt."

Mark's shoulders shook with silent laughter. "Oh, you truly *are* that stupid. You think you can torture me and hand me over to Gavin and he'll just... what... let you *live?*"

Ellis seized a handful of Mark's hair and yanked his head back. "I have not *begun* to torture you," they hissed. "Right now, we're having a conversation. Believe me, you will *know* if I decide I need to torture you."

Sam whimpered from across the room. Gray stepped in and put a hand on Ellis's shoulder. "Ellis." Gray's voice was even. "Take a breath."

Ellis pulled away from Gray's touch and fixed them with a glare. "Take a step back, Gray. I'm good."

Gray held Ellis's gaze for a moment longer, then stepped back. Gray crossed their arms over their chest. Vera watched Ellis carefully.

Mark's eyes were fixed on Sam. "Guess not everyone's on board with this plan, huh? You don't look too good, buddy. This making you nauseous?" He leaned forward in the chair, arms straining against the ropes tying his wrists to the back of the chair. He grinned at Sam.

Ellis stepped in front of Mark. "They are irrelevant. Try to stay on topic." They swallowed hard. "Tell me where Gavin is keeping Isaac, and this all ends."

Recognition dawned in Mark's face and his lips pulled back over his teeth in a wicked grin. "*Isaac*. Where have I heard that name before? Isaac…" He cocked his head. "Oh, right. Isaac *Moore*, right? I helped transport him a few days ago. He's the idiot who traded himself for one of Gavin's playthings. I'm guessing…" He leaned around Ellis and pinned Sam down with his gaze. "…that plaything was *you*."

Sam cringed back against the wall, crawling backwards on their hands to get away from Mark's stare. Gray knelt down in front of them and cradled Sam's face in their hands. "If you need to go, we go," they whispered.

"No," Sam whispered back, trembling. Their breaths came in gasps. "Have to get Isaac back. Wanna stay here."

Mark laughed. "Had some time with Gavin, huh? Yeah, he will fuck you up for sure. Did you get in his way? Or was it just for fun?"

"Shut up." Ellis's voice was brittle.

"You know what he's doing to Isaac right now, right? Well…" He threw a glance at Sam. "*You* do. But have you told *them*?" He looked at each of them in turn. "Have you told *them* what Gavin's doing to Isaac?" Sam stared at Mark. "I know what he's doing. Hell, I've helped him do it a few times."

"Stop." Vera spoke for the first time. Her hands were squeezed into fists.

Mark turned to look back at her, amused. "Or what?"

She stared him down, a flush rising in her face. Her lips trembled and she looked like she was on the brink of furious tears. "Isaac means a lot to us. I'll let you decide whether it's a good idea to continue down this road."

Mark smirked. He turned his gaze back to Sam. Gray knelt in front of them, pulling them into their arms. Sam shook like a leaf. "I wonder if Gavin's killed him yet. Sometimes he'll get bored. Sometimes someone won't break the way he wants. I'm guessing he enjoyed you. He usually kills his playthings within a few days if he doesn't enjoy them. There are only so many things you can do to a person before they just—"

Ellis slapped their hand over Mark's mouth. Their other hand yanked his head back as they leaned into him. Finn saw tears glinting in their eyes.

"Shut up," Ellis growled. For the first time, Mark's eyes betrayed a hint of fear. "Shut the *fuck up*. Tell us how to get to Isaac *right now* or we walk out and leave you here forever. You'll live for three, maybe four days? Maybe all of Gavin's people are as careless as you, you *asshole*. We'll take another one to make the trade. I don't care. I don't care how many of you I have to go through. I'm getting Isaac back. You have three seconds to decide whether you stay alive for that process."

Ellis's tears fell on their hand as they pulled it away from Mark's mouth. Something deep inside Finn twisted at the look of satisfaction on Ellis's face as fear tensed Mark's features.

"Okay." Mark cleared his throat, forcing a smile across his face again. "I'll tell you. I'll make the trade."

Chapter 22

Gavin threw the door open so hard it banged off the wall, swinging back and nearly hitting him as he stormed in. Isaac was huddled in the corner. His hours-old blood was congealing on the floor.

"What—"

Gavin smashed his hand across Isaac's face. Isaac flew to the side, stunned, raising his hands uselessly to defend himself. Gavin's grip tightened around Isaac's hair as Gavin wrenched him up off the ground. Isaac cried out and grabbed Gavin's wrists. His feet scrabbled against the cold cement floor as he tried to stand. Gavin slammed him hard against the wall, forcing a scream from Isaac's chest as the lash marks broke open and bled again.

"What do you know about this?!" Gavin screamed.

"I don't know what—"

Gavin threw a vicious backhand across Isaac's face. *"Shut up!* My cousin is missing. His post was just a few hours from the safehouse where your *family—*" His lip curled around the word. "—was hiding out. And I know, I *know—*" He slammed Isaac's head back against the wall. "—that your people had something to do with it. So, what did you do, huh?" One hand wrapped around Isaac's throat, choking him. Tears began to stream down Isaac's face. "Did you plan this with them? You figured you'd take Sam's place, wait a few days, and then snatch my fucking *cousin* to make a trade? Huh?"

Isaac's eyes rolled back as he tried to drag in a breath, weakly shaking his head. His mouth gaped open.

Gavin released his throat. As Isaac coughed and gasped for breath, Gavin drilled a punch into his abdomen. Isaac grunted against the pain and doubled over. *Can't breathe can't breathe.* Gavin threw him to the ground. Isaac lay on his back, gasping. *Can't breathe.*

Gavin knelt beside him and jerked Isaac's head up. His eyes blazed with rage. "You better fucking *pray* that they want to make a trade and they didn't just kill him. Because I swear to *god,* if he's dead, I will tear you apart, do you *fucking* hear me?"

Isaac sobbed, choking on the air as he dragged it into his chest. "I didn't... I swear, I didn't plan this... Please..."

Gavin jerked Isaac's head back against the floor and stood up. He threw a kick at Isaac's back. Isaac screamed and curled in on himself.

"I'll be back as soon as I know for sure it was your *family* who did this," Gavin spat over his shoulder. "You better fucking *hope* he doesn't die. You will die screaming if he does." He slammed the door behind him. Isaac sobbed.

Chapter 23

Isaac lay beaten on the ground, wrists bound behind him. He listened distantly to the blood dripping off his back and onto the floor. The seconds ticked by, seconds becoming minutes, minutes becoming hours, hours becoming days. Have I been here for days? I think so. *His eyes swam with tears. Had he ever been anywhere else but here?*

He heard the door swing slowly open behind him. He whimpered, curling in on himself. I can't take any more.

"Isaac?"

His heart stopped. Sam. *He tried to sit up, tried to raise his head to see, but he couldn't. His limbs felt leaden. Steps approached him slowly. Many pairs of feet, not just one.* They're all here?

He felt a hand on his back and cringed away, crying out softly. The hand moved to his hair and stroked gently through. He melted into the touch. He turned his head towards the person kneeling over him.

"Sam," he breathed.

They nodded. "And Vera, and Gray, and Finn and Ellis. We're all here."

They all knelt around Isaac and gently placed their hands on him. Gray massaged the back of his neck, avoiding the lash mark there. Finn squeezed his calf. Vera grasped his hand, still bound behind him. Ellis stroked their fingertips along his arm.

"I missed you all," he whispered, weeping.

"We missed you too, Isaac." Sam ran their fingers through his filthy hair. They looked whole, healthy. "Thank you. Thank you for doing this in my place."

Isaac gazed up at Sam, tears pouring down his face. "Of course. Anything for you." He looked around to the others. "For any of you." His head dropped to the floor. He pulled weakly at the rope binding his wrists. "I'm so tired." He whimpered. "It hurts and I... I'm so tired..."

"We know you are, Isaac." Ellis smiled down at him. "You've been so brave."

He leaned into their touch. "Are you here for me? Did you come to get me out?"

Sam's eyes were sad. "No, Isaac." Their hand continued to card through his hair.

He shivered. "What..." He gazed at Sam, imploring. "Please. Please. It hurts, Sam. Please help me..."

Sam shook their head gently. "Isaac, we can't save you." They scanned his body. "Look at you. You're too badly damaged. Gavin destroyed you."

"No... please..." His lips trembled. "Please... Don't leave me here, I don't think I'll survive."

"You won't, Isaac." Gray's voice was gentle. Their fingers worked into the tired muscles of his neck. "That's why we're here."

"We don't want you to suffer anymore." Vera squeezed his bound hand and smiled at him.

"Then please," he begged, "please, please don't leave me, please take me with you..." He pulled against the rope. "Please untie me and I... I'll walk out, you don't have to carry me if you don't want to..."

"This is the kindest thing we can do for you now." Finn's voice was soothing. Their fingers tightened on his calf.

Sam pulled a knife from their belt.

"No... no..." Isaac sobbed, trembling.

Sam bent over and pressed their lips against his hair. "You're dying, Isaac," they whispered. "Gavin will make it hurt. He'll make you suffer. I want to do it this way. It'll be a mercy." Sam's face betrayed their pain. "Believe me. I know."

"Please…" Isaac sobbed. One by one, they kissed him. On his cheek, his shoulder, his forehead. Gray ran their fingers down the back of his neck. He shivered. "Please don't do this…"

Sam eased his head into their lap and pressed their lips again to his forehead. "I love you, Isaac."

"Please no…" He closed his eyes as Sam held the knife to his throat. He gasped as he felt the blade cut into his neck, tried to twist away but the knife cut deeper. He choked as blood poured into Sam's lap. It stained their pants and spilled across the floor. Tears wet his cheeks as he pulled weakly against the rope around his wrists. He shuddered and bled.

Chapter 24

Isaac woke with a scream. His hand flew to his throat. He winced as his back and chest flared with pain. He erupted into sobs. *They weren't here.* He pressed his face into his hands to muffle the sound. *They weren't here. They wouldn't kill me.* He trembled. *They wouldn't kill me.* His mind swam with pain. *I don't think they would kill me.*

He pushed himself up to sitting and froze as he heard raised voices coming from beyond the door. He pressed himself into the corner, as far away from the door as he could get. The door flew open. Gavin stepped through, his eyes fixing immediately on Isaac. Leo followed quickly behind. Gavin threw his bag to the ground and crossed the room in three strides. His hand closed around Isaac's hair. Gavin heaved him out of the corner into the middle of the room.

"No—"

Gavin's hand whipped across his face. Isaac was stunned for a moment as Gavin pushed him on his back and straddled his chest, pinning his arms under Gavin's legs. Both hands went around Isaac's neck.

"I was right," Gavin growled. Isaac whined and tried to twist out of his grasp. "Your people just called me, demanded a trade. Said I'd never see Mark again if I didn't agree." He sneered. "Who'd have known they'd be so damned resourceful? Although, you *did* track me back to my compound when I had Sam." He leaned over Isaac, his voice mocking. "They're still at least five hours away, though. I figure, why not light a fire under their asses? I've got nothing better to do until they get here."

Isaac's eyes were wide as he frantically shook his head. "No no no… please…"

Gavin's hands tightened around his throat. "Shut up." With one hand still around his neck, Gavin pulled his phone out of his back pocket. "Just before I got down here, I sent a link to the phone they called me from. The link connects them to a live feed that I am turning on…" He pressed a button on the screen. "Now." He held the phone up in front of his face. "Hey team, Gavin here." He grinned. "Just spending some quality time here with Isaac. I wouldn't want you to get bored on that long car ride over here, so I figured I'd provide some entertainment for the drive." He shoved the phone into Isaac's face, the camera staring straight at him. "Say hi, Isaac." Isaac closed his eyes and tried to turn away. "Aw, he's being shy. Leo…" Gavin passed the phone to Leo. Leo took it and kept it centered on Isaac.

Gavin released Isaac's throat and stood up. Desperate, Isaac turned his face towards the camera. "No," he begged. "Don't come, please, he'll hurt you, he won't let you—" Gavin kicked him in the ribs. He screamed and pressed his face into the ground. Gavin yanked him up by his hair. "I'm okay," he moaned. "It's okay, please don't—"

Gavin threw Isaac to the ground again. "Does he look okay to you?" Gavin mocked, addressing the camera. He dragged Isaac forward on his hands and knees, exposing his back. "We've had a lot of good times already. I've whipped him a few times, beat him… oh!" He wrapped a hand around Isaac's neck. "Check this out!" He tore the gauze away from Isaac's chest, revealing the mess of cuts underneath. Isaac choked back a sob. "Let's see, what else have we done…?" He loosened his grip on Isaac's throat. Isaac slumped to the ground. "Oh! I drowned him… Thanks, Sam, for spilling the beans on his fear of drowning…" Gavin winked. "I electrocuted him…" He grinned. "Oh, right, I made him think I was going to kill him for not giving me more info on all of you! He didn't break, though. Take a page out of his book, Sam." He chuckled. "He's been telling me all about how he doesn't think you guys care enough about him. It's been really heart-wrenching stuff. Seriously, you should appreciate him more." He grabbed Isaac's face and lifted it from the floor, pointing him at the camera. "He's a really great guy. Loves you all to death. Especially you, Sam. Oh man, the torture he has taken without complaint for *you*…" He shrugged. "Anyway, I'm not used to having an audience. So, I'm gonna just… do my thing. I know you can't send your own reactions through, since this link is one-way and I have no service for phone calls down here, but I can just… picture it."

He turned away from the camera towards the table, running his hands back and forth in front of his tools. "What do I want…?" He turned to look over his shoulder. "Hey, Isaac. I can't decide. Should I whip you again, or—"

"No!"

122

Gavin smiled. "…or waterboard you?"

Isaac whimpered. "Please…"

"Make up your mind, Isaac, or I'll do both."

"Please… Don't come for me…"

Gavin balked. He turned away from the table and approached Isaac. Isaac tried to crawl away from him on his hands and knees. Gavin held out a hand to Leo. "Leo, do you still have your handcuffs? I'm not fond of the idea of him roaming about."

"Sure thing." Leo pulled the cuffs out of his pocket and dropped them into Gavin's hand, keeping the camera trained on Isaac.

"Thanks." Gavin bent over and pulled at Isaac's arms. He snapped the cuffs onto his wrists. Gavin went to the wall and lowered a chain over him until it was almost touching the ground. Isaac could hardly move from the pain wracking his body.

Gavin clipped the handcuffs into the hook dangling from the end of the chain and pulled, lifting Isaac from the floor by his wrists. Isaac groaned as it stretched his arms up over his head and pulled him up onto his knees. Gavin secured the chain to the wall. He left Isaac kneeling. Isaac shuddered from the effort of trying to stand, trying to take the weight off his wrists. He could barely raise his head.

"Choose one, Isaac." Gavin sounded almost bored. "Choose or I do both. Whipping or waterboarding. What will it be?"

"Please," Isaac begged to the camera. "Please stay away, please… don't come for me… please. He'll kill you…"

Gavin shrugged. "Waterboarding first, then." He pawed through the bag and pulled out some water bottles and a washcloth. He poured water over the cloth, soaking it through.

Isaac's pleas rose in pitch as he struggled against the cuffs. *"Please,"* he sobbed. "Please don't come, I'm not…" He pressed his lips together.

Gavin paused, momentarily seeming to forget the cloth in his hand. "You're not what, Isaac?"

Isaac shook his head. Gavin grabbed his hair and yanked his head back. "You're not *what?*" His smile was too wide. "Suit yourself." He slapped the soaked washcloth over Isaac's nose and mouth.

Isaac thrashed against the hand in his hair. "Something really interesting," Gavin taunted over his desperate gasps, "is that I don't even have to pour water over this for you to feel the effects." He let Isaac try to drag in one more tortured breath before he let him up. Isaac coughed and gasped, eyes wide with panic. "Now, you were saying something. You're not *what?*"

Isaac sobbed and gasped out, *"worth it."*

Gavin's mouth fell open as he threw his head back in a peal of laughter. "Oh, that was good. Say it again, say it again. I want to make sure nobody missed that."

Isaac squeezed his eyes shut and hung his head. Gavin grabbed his hair and yanked his face up with a ferocious jerk. *"Say it again."*

His chest heaved with sobs. "I'm not, I'm not worth it. Please just leave me here. Don't come for me."

Gavin laughed. "God, this is so much fun. I should have thought of the link sooner." He waved. "Hey there, cuz. Hope they're treating you well. For their sake." He turned back to Isaac. "Let's continue, shall we?"

Gavin put the cloth over Isaac's face and pulled his head back again. With his other hand, he slowly poured the water over his face.

Isaac stiffened and spasmed as he pulled against Gavin's gasp. His scream was choked off. He strained against the handcuffs, trying to stand, trying to give himself leverage against Gavin. He tried to duck his head but Gavin kept it back and held it against his chest to keep him still.

Gavin let go. Isaac pitched forward with a shudder. He coughed up water and dragged in a desperate gasp.

Gavin's hand was in his hair again, stroking it almost gently. "What do you think?" He smiled. "Worse than drowning? Better? I've heard it feels pretty similar."

Isaac sobbed, sagging against the handcuffs. His cheeks were wet with tears and water.

Gavin pulled his shirt away from his chest and laughed. "You got me all wet, Isaac. Still, I prefer this to drowning you. It's more… I don't know, intimate? I can see your eyes as you fight. It's good stuff. Again?"

Isaac desperately shook his head. Gavin pulled his head back with the cloth and began to pour the water over his face again. Isaac's body shook with panic and strain. When Gavin let him up again his chest heaved with each breath, each breath coming too fast.

Again. Isaac screamed as the cloth covered his mouth until the sound was drowned by the water. His eyes rolled back as he convulsed mindlessly, fighting the torture and trapped in it.

Gavin released him. He couldn't slow his panicked breaths down enough to get a proper breath in. He was dizzy. His head lolled as he sobbed.

Gavin walked in front of him and pulled his head up. Isaac's eyes were wide and unfocused. Gavin *tsk*ed disapprovingly. "You having another panic attack?" Isaac desperately drew in a breath and nodded weakly. Gavin sighed. "Okay. We'll take a pause on that. If you pass out it's no fun."

Isaac sagged with relief as Gavin threw the washcloth into the corner with a wet *smack*. He willed himself to slow down his breaths. His throat kept spasming from the water he'd inhaled. He gagged and shuddered. Slowly, slowly, he was able to take a breath that properly filled his lungs. He opened his eyes to see the camera in his face. He hung his head.

"No," he moaned. "Don't do this. Stay away from here, don't do this…"

He shuddered as he heard the now-familiar slap of the whip against the floor. He cringed into himself, a sob tearing out of his throat.

"Beg them to come for you, Isaac."

He shook his head, gasping and coughing between his sobs. "No, no no no…"

"Beg them to come for you, and this ends."

He wailed helplessly. "I can't, I can't, please…"

The first lash tore him open from right shoulder to left hip. He screamed against his arm, dizzy with agony.

"Oops. That was a little deeper than I meant it to be. Sorry."

Crack.

His throat went raw with his next scream.

Crack.

"Do it, Isaac. Beg them to come for you."

"No no no, please…"

Crack.

Another scream. He looked at the camera with streaming eyes. "Don't do it, *please* don't do it…"

Crack.

His head spun uselessly as he bit his tongue, trying to bite back the scream. A strangled cry tore from his throat.

Crack.

His scream was long and tortured.

"I can do this all day, Isaac."

Crack.

He gasped desperately. "Stop! Stop, please, I can't…"

Crack.

"*No!* God, please, no…"

"It's not me you should be begging, Isaac. It's them."

Crack.

"Please!"

"Please what?"

Crack.

"No no no no no no—"

Crack.

"Scream for *them*, Isaac."

He sobbed wordlessly.

Crack.

"Please… Please don't…"

Crack.

Isaac whited out for a moment. His eyes rolled in his head.

Crack.

"This is pretty easy, Isaac. Beg for them to come for you and I stop this."

Crack.

"No… Ah…"

Crack.

I can't.

"Please!" he screamed, looking at the camera. Gavin paused for a moment. He walked around in front of him and pulled his head up. His face was wet with tears and sweat.

"What was that?" Gavin was grinning.

Isaac sobbed. "Please…"

"Please what?"

"Please… just… Just kill me, please, I can't…"

Gavin's face fell. "You weren't begging them? That's goddamn disappointing."

Isaac weakly shook his head. "I can't let them die. I can't let you have them but… please… I can't do this… Please just kill me, I just want…"

Gavin released Isaac's head. It slumped to his chest. His mouth hung open as he sobbed. Gavin sat back on his heels and looked at Isaac, a smile plastered to his face. "I'm wondering," Gavin said, his voice low, "if this little display would dissuade them at all." He turned over his shoulder to address the camera. "Would it? I mean, you've gotten this far, you have my *cousin*…" His lip curled. He turned back to Isaac. "Have you considered, Isaac, that you actually *do* mean a lot to them?"

Isaac sagged against the handcuffs, barely able to breathe through the agony.

Gavin smiled at him. "Do you think you've earned their love *now?* I mean, look at you…" He motioned up and down Isaac's body with his hand. "Look at what you've taken for them. What you've taken for *Sam*." He grinned, looking at the camera. "Hey Sam, do you forgive him? Do you forgive him for hurting you and abandoning you?" He laughed. "Do all of you forgive him for abandoning you? Leaving you vulnerable?" He shook his head and playfully slapped Isaac across the face. Isaac didn't respond. "Has he suffered enough for you to love him now? Or are you mad at him for making this stupid decision?" He leered at the camera. "If he'd just let me have Sam, this whole thing would have been so much easier." He shrugged. "Oh, well. This did turn out to be a lot of fun."

He stood up, wiping his hands on his pants. "Well, I'm gonna get back to it. If I only have a few more hours with Isaac, I'm gonna make them count." He guided Isaac's face up. "What do you think? You ready to keep going?" Isaac moaned, his face contorting with agony. Gavin smiled. "Sweet." He let Isaac's head fall.

Chapter 25

"So you'll do the trade?" Ellis's voice was hard. Their fingers tightened on the phone.

A low laugh. *"Yeah, I'll do the trade. Let me hear from him. I need to know he's still alive."*

Ellis tore the tape from Mark's mouth and held the phone close to his face. "Say something."

Mark sneered. "I'm here, Gavin."

Ellis slapped the tape back over his mouth and stepped away from where he still sat in the chair, hands bound, but no longer tied to the chair. "There. He's alive."

A sigh. *"When should I expect you?"*

Ellis's jaw flexed. "A little more than five hours. Be ready with Isaac or you'll never see your cousin again."

"Can't wait." Gavin hung up.

Ellis squeezed their eyes shut and tapped the phone against their forehead. They drew in a deep breath. Let it out. They turned to see the others all watching them intently. "It's happening. Let's go."

Everyone seemed to let out a breath.

"He really agreed?" Sam's voice shook.

Ellis blew out a steady breath. "Yeah. He agreed. Let's get moving. I don't want to leave Isaac with him any longer than we absolutely have to." They turned to Mark and reached out, grabbing him by the shirt. "Get your ass up. Try anything and I swear to god…" Mark laughed past the tape and shook his head. He stood and started to move. Vera fell in beside him and Finn walked behind. Gray held a hand out to Sam, still slumped on the wall.

"I'm okay," Sam whispered, and pushed themselves painfully to their feet. "The antibiotics are working. I'm feeling better."

Gray wrapped their arm around their shoulders. "Okay. Just let me know if you feel like you can't make it, and I'll carry you. No problem." They both followed the others out of the room, down the hall, and out of the building.

They blinked at the sun in their eyes. As they approached the car, Mark snorted. *"Shotgun,"* he mumbled through the tape.

Ellis glared at him as they opened the trunk of the car. Mark's face fell a little as he climbed in. As Ellis slammed the lid down the phone in their pocket buzzed. They pulled it out and opened the notification.

Vera looked up. "What is it?"

A chill ran down Ellis's spine. "I don't know. I got it from Gavin's number."

Gray leaned into Ellis, trying to look over their shoulder. "But what *is* it?"

"It's... it's a link." Ellis's hand shook as they tapped it. It opened to a blank screen with a small circle spinning slowly above the words *please wait*.

Finn swallowed hard. "That's from Gavin?"

Ellis nodded slowly.

"What does it mean?" Sam's voice was strained with dread.

"I... don't..."

The link loaded, and Gavin's face filled up the screen.

Sam gasped and jumped away like Ellis was holding a snake. Their eyes were fixed on the phone as they dragged in panicked gasps. Gray pulled them into their arms as Gavin began to speak.

"Hey team, Gavin here. Just spending some quality time here with Isaac. I wouldn't want you to get bored on that long car ride over here, so I figured I'd provide some entertainment for the drive."

The screen went black for a moment and Isaac's face appeared. Vera let out a scream as her hands flew to her mouth. Gray cringed back, holding Sam tighter in their arms as Sam began to sob.

"Say hi, Isaac."

"No," Finn breathed as Isaac turned away from the screen. Gavin's hand was wrapped tight around his throat. His face was ragged and drawn with pain. His lips were cracked, his eyes raw from crying. Red marked his cheek in the shape of a handprint.

"Aw, he's being shy. Leo…"

The camera jostled as Gavin handed it off to Leo, whoever that was. The image zoomed out until Isaac's whole body was in the frame.

Gavin was straddling Isaac, his legs pinning Isaac's chest and arms to the floor. They all watched in horror as Gavin stood and revealed a mess of gauze and tape on his chest and abdomen. Isaac rolled to the side, his eyes fixed on the camera in hollow desperation.

"No. Don't come, please, he'll hurt you, he won't let you—"

Gavin kicked him viciously in the ribs and he cringed onto his side, pressing his face into the floor as he screamed. The air rushed out of Sam's chest like they'd been kicked, too. They watched as Gavin dragged Isaac up by his hair, showing his bandages more clearly.

"I'm okay. It's okay, please don't—"

Finn hung on Ellis's arm as Gavin threw Isaac to the ground.

"Does he look okay to you?"

Gavin dragged Isaac forward onto his hands and knees, and they all gasped. Angry purple bruises and bleeding welts crisscrossed his back.

131

"We've had a lot of good times already. I've whipped him a few times, beat him... oh!"

A cry rose from Sam's throat as Gavin wrapped a hand around Isaac's neck, wrenching him up. He tore the gauze and tape away from Isaac's chest.

"Check this out!"

Sam gaped as Gavin revealed the mess of cuts across Isaac's chest and abdomen.

"Let's see, what else have we done...?"

Isaac slumped to the ground as Gavin released his throat. Vera was weeping softly.

"Oh! I drowned him... Thanks, Sam, for spilling the beans on his fear of drowning..."

Sam slipped out of Gray's arms and fell to their knees with a scream, nearly drowning out what Gavin was saying. *"No..."* they wailed. Gray tried to pull them back up into their arms, but Sam was inconsolable, hands pressed against their mouth, unable to look away from the screen Ellis clutched in their shaking hands. "I... I *told* him about that, that's my fault... *no...*"

Ellis's hand shot out and grabbed Sam's shoulder. Ellis's eyes were still fixed on the phone.

"...I made him think I was going to kill him for not giving me more info on all of you! He didn't break, though. Take a page out of his book, Sam. He's been telling me all about how he doesn't think you guys care enough about him. It's been really heart-wrenching stuff. Seriously, you should appreciate him more."

Sam cowered on their knees, incoherent wails pouring from between their hands. Finn's mouth was open in a silent scream of despair. Vera wobbled once and stumbled against Gray. They held each other as their faces burned with tears.

Gavin pulled Isaac's face up and pointed it at the camera. Isaac seemed lost in his agony.

"He's a really great guy. Loves you all to death. Especially you, Sam. Oh man, the torture he has taken without complaint for you... Anyway, I'm not used to having an audience. So, I'm gonna just... do my thing. I know you can't send your own reactions through, since this link is one-way and I have no service for phone calls down here, but I can just... picture it."

He turned away, moving towards a table they couldn't see clearly in the dim light. It broke the spell for a moment.

Ellis pulled their fingers away from the phone. Their hand spasmed from how tightly they'd been gripping it. Their voice was icy. "We have to go. We have to go *right now*. We can't let him do this." They lurched towards the car and thrust the phone into Finn's fumbling hands.

Everyone stood frozen for a moment.

"Hey, Isaac. I can't decide. Should I whip you again, or—"

"No!" Isaac screamed, his voice ragged.

"...or waterboard you?"

"Please..."

"Make up your mind, Isaac, or I'll do both."

"Please... don't come for me..."

Ellis's shook as they looked at the others, still frozen. "Come on!" they shouted. "We're going!"

Finn tripped forward to the passenger seat. Vera walked to the back on shaking legs. She looked like she was going to be sick. Gray lifted Sam from the dusty concrete of the parking lot. They were limp in Gray's arms, weeping bitterly. Gray eased them into the middle back seat and climbed in after them. The door wasn't even fully closed before Ellis turned on the car and slammed the accelerator.

Finn held the phone in numb hands so everyone in the back seat could see. Ellis kept their eyes firmly on the road as tears poured down their face. They scrubbed their nose with their sleeve.

Gavin had handcuffed Isaac and was pulling him to his knees with a chain clipped to the cuffs. Vera bit her lip as Isaac's injuries were displayed for them, rivulets of blood running from some of the cuts and lashes. Gray's arms were wrapped tightly around Sam, like Sam would fly apart if they didn't have something to hold on to. Gray watched as Isaac gasped in agony and tried to lift his head.

"Choose one, Isaac. Choose or I do both. Whipping or waterboarding. What will it be?"

"Please."

His eyes bored into the camera, bright with pain.

"Please stay away, please... don't come for me... please. He'll kill you..."

"Waterboarding first, then."

"No!" Sam lurched forward, hands outstretched like Gavin could see them plead. "No no no..."

"Please. Please don't come, I'm not..."

"You're not what, Isaac?"

Ellis's eyes flicked between the phone and the road as Gavin jerked Isaac's head back by his hair.

"You're not what?*"* A pause. *"Suit yourself."*

The sound of Isaac's choked scream cut through them all like a knife. Ellis's hands jerked on the steering wheel. The sound filled the car as Isaac gasped wetly through the soaked washcloth. Sam sobbed desperately.

"Something really interesting is that I don't even have to pour water over this for you to feel the effects."

Gavin finally let Isaac up. Gray and Vera took in a breath as Isaac gasped for air.

"Now, you were saying something. You're not what?*"*

"Worth it," Isaac sobbed.

"No," keened Sam. "I can't, I can't I can't I can't." They pressed their hands against their face and sobbed against Gray's shirt.

"We can't stop watching, Sam." Vera's voice was hollow and haunted.

Sam turned their eyes to her, desperation making them wild. "Why?"

She pressed her lips together as she slowly turned to look at them. "We need to know if Gavin kills him."

Chapter 26

Isaac could barely keep upright. Gavin had him gagged, with his hands tied behind him. The elevator walls swam around him. His head spun. He fell to his knees, bracing his head against the wall of the elevator. *They'll be here soon. They're going to try and trade...* Leo bent down to pull him back to his feet. Gavin stopped him.

"I like him like that." Isaac looked up at Gavin. Gavin had a sick smile on his face.

Every fiber of his being was agony. After Gavin had gotten bored with the whip, he had let Isaac down and taken the knife to him again. This time, Gavin had heated the flat of the blade up over a lighter and pressed it to Isaac's flesh again and again, one burn right next to the other, down the length of his arms. Gavin had held him to the floor, pouring water slowly over his face, not quite enough to drown him but enough to make him frenzied with panic. During it all, Gavin had whispered in his ear that his family was coming to get him. Rescue him. *"If you just scream to them, beg them to help you, I'll stop this. Why won't you beg, Isaac? Are you ashamed to ask for help? Or are you afraid they still won't come if you do? Come on, Isaac, stop screaming and* beg.*"*

He trembled as tears ran down his face into the gag. *They're coming for me and Gavin's going to kill them. They're going to die and it'll be my fault.*

He had begged in the end. Gavin had shoved him to the floor and leaned against Isaac's back, marking his hand with Isaac's blood in intersecting stripes. He'd pinned Isaac to the floor as he dripped rubbing alcohol over his wounds. Isaac had screamed, whiting out from the pain, before he'd wailed *please, please come, please make him stop this...*" Gavin had straightened up and wiped his hand on his pants, grinning from ear to ear. Isaac's wounds burned still. Blood soaked through the shirt Gavin had given him.

As the elevator reached the ground floor, Leo's hand closed over Isaac's hair and he dragged Isaac to his feet. Leo prodded Isaac down the hall and he stumbled ahead of his captors. They forced him to walk down a long hallway and stopped him in front of a door at the end of the hall.

Isaac nearly fell again and Leo jerked Isaac upright. He opened the door and shoved Isaac inside. The room was empty, just white walls and a linoleum floor. So different from the dark basement Isaac had been kept in for... Days? Four days? Five?

Isaac fell to his knees in the center of the room. This time, Gavin let him stay. Gavin walked to his side and dragged him around by his hair to face the doorway.

Isaac swayed and fell against Gavin's legs. Gavin nudged him upright. "Whoa. Personal bubble." He grinned down at Isaac. Isaac's eyes were half closed as he sobbed weakly through the gag. Gavin checked his watch. "Tristan said five minutes. It's been six. What the fuck—" He stopped short as the door opened.

Isaac dragged his head up as his family appeared one by one through the door. His eyes fell on Ellis as they pushed another man into the room, his hands tied behind his back. Isaac remembered him from the drive days ago. *Mark.*

Ellis's gaze found Isaac immediately and their eyes went cold with fury. Finn was right behind them. They froze for a moment, their gaze sweeping Isaac's injuries. He recognized the controlled look they got in their eyes when they were treating someone. *They think they're going to save me. They think I'm going to be their patient.* Vera's hand flew to her mouth and she gasped. Her eyes filled with tears as she reached her hand back for Gray. Gray was last through the door, Sam tucked firmly under their arm and supported by their grip.

"Isaac!" Sam cried out and rushed towards him.

"No!" Finn reached out and clamped their hand down on Sam's arm. Sam sobbed as Finn pulled them back into their embrace. Finn held them as they trembled. "Not yet. Not until we have him back." They ran a hand through Sam's hair and cradled their face.

Isaac's eyes were fixed on Sam as he shook his head and sobbed. *No. Please. He'll kill you.* He tried to plead with them to turn around, go, leave him there, but the gag muffled his words. Gavin laughed.

"Oh, that was as dramatic as I hoped." Sam stiffened at Gavin's voice and their eyes snapped to him. They shuddered. Finn moved in front of them.

"Leo, get the door, will you?"

Leo moved from Gavin's side and stalked around the little group to close the door and stand in front of it. They all warily moved further into the room along the wall, keeping Leo in their field of vision.

Gavin smiled at Mark. "How you doin', cuz?"

Mark smirked. "Fine. They're harmless, really. It would be cute if this whole thing hadn't been so fucking inconvenient."

Gavin sighed. "Sorry about that. I've been having the time of my life. Sorry it went all sideways for you." He looked at the others. "Let's do this." He held out his hand. "Give me back my cousin."

Ellis's hand tightened on the collar of Mark's shirt. Their eyes narrowed. "Not a fucking chance. Give us Isaac. Then you get your cousin back."

Gavin laughed. "Okay. Isaac, stand up and walk over to them. We're making a trade and you're kinda holding us up."

Isaac moaned in despair. He got to one knee, shivering in agony. Sweat beaded on his skin as he tried to stand. Tears of frustration burned in his eyes.

"Come on, Isaac." Gavin made a *let's-speed-this-up* motion with his hand. "Waiting on you. Go join your team over there."

"Let us help him." Vera's voice was thick with tears. She pressed her hands together as she watched him struggle.

Gavin grinned as he eyed them. "You really want him back?" His hand made a fist in Isaac's hair and he yanked Isaac's head back, staring down at his eyes as he smiled. "I mean, look at him. What use do you have for him in this state?" He released Isaac and kicked him to the floor.

Sam lunged against Finn's hold and cried out, drowning out Isaac's grunt as he fell hard on his shoulder. Gavin's hand closed around Isaac's hair and he dragged him back, away from his family. Isaac's legs kicked out uselessly as he tried to escape Gavin's grasp. Gavin threw him to the floor and kicked him in the gut. Isaac coughed and curled into himself.

Finn dragged Sam backwards as they fought, tears streaming, to get to Isaac. Their eyes were locked on him as he wheezed weakly on the floor.

Gavin turned to them, grinning wide. "Send my cousin over."

"No." Ellis jerked Mark backwards a step. "How do we know you'll let us have Isaac once we do?"

Gavin shrugged. "Suit yourself." He turned back to Isaac. "Hear that, Isaac?" Isaac moaned, sprawled on the floor. "They don't want to send my cousin over. It's almost like they don't..." He punched Isaac in the arm, directly over the burns he had made. Isaac screamed. "...*trust* me or something. Which I don't understand because..." He kicked Isaac in the ribs. Isaac jerked against the floor. "...I've been nothing but..." A kick to the back. Gavin raised his voice above Isaac's strangled cry. "...reasonable. I've only demanded you hold up your end of the deal you made, and you went back on it." He dragged Isaac upright by his hair and punched him, sending a spray of blood from his nose as he fell back to the floor.

"No!" Gray's voice was raw. Eyes streaming over his bleeding nose, Isaac fixed them with a look, silently begging them not to break rank.

Gavin turned to survey them. "What? We had an agreement, and *you*..." He kicked Isaac in the ribs and heard something snap. Isaac's eyes rolled back as he shuddered. "...tried to intervene. Isaac was happy to take Sam's place." He focused on Sam. "How are you, by the way? Doing okay? Have any nightmares recently?"

Sam went rigid. Their face was pale. Vera pulled them behind her and spread her arms in front of them, putting herself and Finn between Sam and Gavin. Gavin looked around her, trying to find Sam's eyes.

"What? I'm just curious. Sam obviously failed to kill you with the gun I gave them, and I'm curious as to how things have gone for them since then." He grinned. "Wanna trade places with Isaac again? We could make this a thing, like a back-and-forth type thing." He punched Isaac in his side. He jerked; his mouth pulled open into a silent scream around the gag. "Uh oh. Might have broken him." He looked back up at them. "You'd know all about that, wouldn't you Sam?" He kicked Isaac in the back. Isaac moaned weakly.

"Stop!" Isaac looked up to see Ellis holding a knife to Mark's throat. He saw a flicker of fear in the man's eyes as Ellis stared Gavin down. "Stop or I cut his throat, right now."

Gavin smiled. "Oh, really? I think you're bluffing. I don't think you'll do it."

Ellis's hand shook and they hesitated, just for a moment. Leo lunged at them. He twisted their arm and wrestled the knife out of their grasp.

"No!" Ellis clutched at Mark's arm.

Leo's hand closed around Mark's shirt and he hurled him forward, towards Gavin. Gavin caught him before he fell.

"NOW!" Gavin shouted. The door burst open and five more men poured into the room. The men grabbed everyone in the group and wrestled them to the floor.

"No…" Ellis gasped. Their mouth fell open with a devastated scream.

Vera yanked hard against her captor. She threw him to the side as she advanced on Gavin. He pulled his knife out and pressed it to Isaac's throat. She paused, flinched. In a split second, she was wrestled to the ground again. The guard pulled her arms behind her and locked them into handcuffs like the others.

Gavin cut the rope tying Mark's hands behind him. He nudged his cousin towards the door. Mark left with a grin.

Through a fog of pain, Isaac watched as his family was pulled up and dragged to the sides of the room. Sam sobbed as they were forced to their knees against the wall. Their eyes never left Isaac. "No…" they wailed. "Isaac, no…"

Isaac gasped around the gag as his nose poured blood onto the floor. At Gavin's command, Leo dragged Isaac out of the center of the room and dropped him in front of Sam. Shaking with each sob, Sam bent and pressed their forehead against Isaac's temple, tears falling into his hair.

"Go ahead and take that gag off." Gavin waved at Leo dismissively.

Sam flinched away as Leo roughly pulled the cloth gag away from Isaac's mouth. Isaac coughed up blood and dragged in a ragged gasp. He looked up at Sam, agony straining his face. For a moment, his pain was forgotten. He sobbed at the sight of Sam on their knees, hands cuffed behind them, trembling in terror.

"I'm sorry," Sam whispered. "I'm so sorry Isaac, we tried to get you, we... we couldn't leave you here. He was going to kill you, wasn't he?"

It took almost more effort than he had to spare, but Isaac nodded. Sam whined high in their throat and pressed their face into his hair. "No no no... Isaac..."

Ellis stared helplessly at Finn as their chest began to heave with panicked breaths. "I'm so sorry," they whispered. "Finn... I'm so sorry..." Finn's eyes were wide and unfocused, darting around the room.

Gray pressed their lips together as tears rolled down their face. "It's gonna be okay." Their eyes bounced frantically between each member of the family. "Just breathe," they said, mostly to themselves.

Vera had fallen completely silent. Her eyes were wide. Her lips moved soundlessly.

Gavin walked slowly in a circle around the room, hands clasped behind him and relaxed. "Thanks, everyone." He nodded at his entourage. "Everyone can go except Leo and Torren." The dismissed men nodded and walked out. Leo and Torren took stations at opposite corners of the room.

Gavin looked down at each of them as he walked past them. Finn's breaths came faster and they cringed as Gavin approached. Ellis glared at Gavin as he walked past. Vera trembled and closed her eyes, still mouthing silent words. Gray huddled against the wall and avoided Gavin's gaze.

Gavin smiled. "So. This has been fun. I'm more than a little bit disappointed that no one saw this coming, but... oh well. I'm sure you were distracted by the video I sent." He raised his hands and clapped softly in Isaac's direction. "Bravo, of course, to our star. Couldn't have done it without you, Isaac. Your begging for them at the end there really has been the cherry on top of this whole experience." Isaac whimpered softly.

"Now. Here's what I want to know: whose idea was this?" Gavin continued to pace slowly around the room, eyes moving from person to person. "Anyone?" He stopped. "Seriously, no one wants to take credit for this truly idiotic plan?"

"It was my idea." Ellis's voice shook. They swallowed hard. Finn's eyes suddenly focused and they fixed on Ellis, horrified.

"No," Finn whispered. "Ellis—"

Ellis set their jaw and met Gavin's eyes. "It was me. My idea." They thrust their chin at Gavin. "So how about we get on with things, and you let everyone else go. This is my fault and has nothing to do with them."

Gavin snorted. "Oh no no no, Ellis. It's Ellis, right? You're shorter than I pictured you. No, I'm not choosing who stays to be tortured. I'm only deciding who goes *first.*"

Chapter 27

Gavin turned to Torren. "This one first. Get them up, please." He pointed at the floor in the middle of the room. "Right there." He turned to Leo. "Get the bag." He rubbed his hands together as Torren grabbed Ellis's arm and dragged them to the center of the room. Ellis yanked against his grasp. Torren threw them to their knees in front of Gavin. Ellis stared Gavin down, jaw locked with hatred as they waited for the pain to come.

"No…" Finn mumbled. They quaked with terror. "Ellis… n-no… no… E-Ellis… no…"

"It's okay, Finn," Ellis whispered. "It's okay." They never broke eye contact with Gavin.

Leo appeared again and handed Gavin a duffle bag.

"Perfect, thanks." Gavin set it on the floor next to him and pushed the contents aside, looking for something.

He glanced at Ellis out the corner of his eye. He raised his eyebrows and grinned at their defiant stare. "You seem a little overconfident there, hun. What're you so smug about?"

Ellis didn't answer. They simply stared back, loathing twisting their features.

Gavin chuckled to himself. "I always find it funny when people think they can handle the pain at first. Don't get me wrong, it just makes it that much more fun when they break, but it's so… predictable." He pulled a manila envelope from the bag. "Ah, here." He plunged his hand in. "People are so blind to their own weaknesses. It's perpetually fascinating." He pulled a sheaf of photographs from the envelope. "For example." He got down on one knee and placed a photo on the floor in front of Ellis.

Ellis froze, shuddered, swallowed hard. A smiling picture of a man lay on the floor in front of them, with brown hair and warm green eyes. Ellis swallowed.

Gasped. Swallowed again. Then they raised their eyes to Gavin. Distilled hatred ran cold in their blood.

Gavin laid another picture on the floor, a young child with Ellis's blue eyes and the man's wavy brown hair. She was frozen in the picture, eyes wide and fixed on the butterfly that rested light as gossamer on her arm. Ellis stared at the photo as it blurred with their tears.

Another photo, this one of a boy with green eyes and black hair in a homemade baseball uniform. He had taken an exaggerated stance with a bat in his hands, pantomiming like he was about to hit a home run. His face was screwed up in mock concentration. A smile pulled at the corners of his mouth.

Another. The four of them together. The man's arm around Ellis's waist, the girl balanced on his hip, with the boy standing between them, hugging Ellis's arm as they reached down to hold him close.

Ellis took in a gasping sob. Tears poured down their face and splashed onto the photos. They blinked quickly, trying to clear the tears so they could see. Their eyes moved over the faces of their husband, their children. They could remember when that photo was taken. They'd been at a friend's house when their friend had said, *"let me get a picture of you and the kids, they're growing so fast and I haven't seen you in a while…"*

Another photo. Older. At a bar with bad lighting, their husband Christopher balanced precariously on Ellis's lap with their lips pressed against his blushing cheek, his eyes turned toward the camera with a twinkle in them like he knew a secret.

"S-stop…"

Gavin smiled. "It was your idea to try to take my family away from me, Ellis. You should have known better. You know exactly how it feels, don't you? To have your family ripped away from you?"

Ellis's voice broke with a sob. "I… wasn't… I wouldn't…" Their eyes were fixed on the pictures.

Gavin ducked into their view and guided their chin up with one hand. "I don't give a *fuck* if you never intended to hurt him," he whispered. Ellis's lip trembled.

He put another picture on the floor. A birthday party for their daughter Chloe, icing up to her elbows as she sat in her booster seat, delighted. A picture of their son Galen in the living room putting on a show, singing. Christopher standing with Ellis on their wedding day, sharing their first dance. Ellis holding Chloe tenderly in their arms as she reached for their face.

Ellis's body shook with sobs as each photo was placed in front of them. They wailed in agony as memories of their family flashed through their mind.

"It's funny," Gavin whispered. "They've been dead for years, and they still have the power to hurt you." He smiled. "I have to admit, when Sam told me all about what happened to them I didn't know what they were talking about. Makes sense, though. I was only seventeen when they were gunned down. It *was* my family, though. My 'syndicate', as Isaac calls it." He chuckled. "I made some calls, asked around. They remembered you, vaguely. Your husband stumbled across some of our business while he was out with your kids. That was back when we were still trying to stay… ah… *discreet*. I doubt he even knew what he was seeing. But we gunned him down, didn't we? Him and the kids." Ellis was choking, barely able to breathe past the sobs wracking their body. Gavin raised their chin until he could look them in their eyes. "Didn't we?"

Ellis's eyes were wild with rage and bitter agony. They wound back and spat in Gavin's face. Gavin jumped back and wiped his face with his shirt. Ellis thrust their chin at him, teeth gritted against the pain, as if daring him to hit them.

Gavin laughed. "So eager for punishment."

Ellis trembled. Their mouth fell open in a scream of desperation as their eyes went again to their dead family. Their voice trailed off in a wail and then a shuddering, silent sob.

Gavin's hand shot out and grabbed the collar of Ellis's shirt. He dragged them forward and held a knife under their chin.

Finn cried out from where they were slumped against the wall. They lurched forward mindlessly. They froze as Leo took a step towards them, hand itching for the firearm in his waistband. Their wide eyes turned back to Ellis and they whimpered.

"I don't *fucking care* if you kill me," Ellis sobbed. "Do it, I don't *fucking care...*" They trailed off into a whining sob and leaned into the blade. Their eyes were open, blazing, fixed on Gavin's shirt. Their lips twisted into a macabre smile.

Gavin *tsk*ed. "Aw, don't say that. You have a new family now, right? How do you think that makes Finn feel?" Gavin grabbed Ellis's chin and turned their face towards Finn. Ellis squeezed their eyes shut at the sight of Finn's terror-stricken and tear-stained face. They forced their head back to face Gavin and glared up at him. The knife bobbed against their throat as they swallowed hard.

"P-please," they breathed. "Do it."

"You'd like that, wouldn't you?" Gavin grinned. "To go back to your family. To see them again. It's just not the same with Finn, is it? It's tainted by the pain. You were happy and there's that part of you, deep inside, that would trade them to be with your family again."

Ellis trembled, sobbing and leaning harder against the blade. They prayed for it to break their skin, prayed for the feeling of hot blood running down their chest, too fast to be stopped.

Gavin pulled the knife away. "I could torture you for hours and you wouldn't care," he hissed, his voice thick with mocking. "You'd scream and cry, but you'd welcome it. No, I don't have to hurt you to torture you. I just have to hurt your family." His lips slid into a wicked grin.

Ellis's eyes widened. "No..." They shot a horrified look at Finn as Torren stepped up and gripped their arm. Ellis lunged at Gavin, ready to rip his throat out with their teeth. Leo's hand closed around their hair. He yanked Ellis back to their knees, pulling their head back and wrapping an arm around their throat. Gray convulsed in a horrified scream. Vera rocked forward, her eyes wild with fury. Before she could get to her feet, Gavin rounded on her.

"Anyone moves on me and Ellis dies," he snarled. Leo tightened his arm around Ellis's neck for emphasis. They froze, their mouth falling open as they gagged and choked against his hold. Vera sat back on her heels, shuddering with rage. Tears poured down her cheeks. Gray shook in every limb as they forced themselves to stay on their knees. Sam trembled where they were, eyes fixed on Finn, their body protectively, unconsciously leaning towards Isaac.

146

Torren threw Finn to the floor between Gavin and Ellis. Finn fell on their side and cried out as their shoulder hit the ground. They writhed and tried to roll onto their stomach. Their legs kicked against the floor in a panic. They groaned as Gavin pressed his knee against the small of their back and leaned in.

"Finn, no..." Ellis sobbed. "N-no... Finn... P-please no no... no... F-Finn no..." They shook their head frantically against Leo's hold as Finn looked up at them, abject panic plastered across their face. Finn's breaths came faster and faster as Ellis's voice rose.

"I've heard," Gavin said over the sound of Ellis's desperate begging, "That all a medic is, is a pair of hands and a brain and someone to drive the whole package around. Finn is your medic, yes?" He leered at Ellis. "Among other things." His hand closed around the back of Finn's shirt and he dragged them up to sitting. He pulled their arms out behind them and forced their hands flat to the floor.

"No no no..." Finn gasped. "No please... no *no no no...*" Tears poured down their face.

"Torren...?"

Torren stepped forward at Gavin's command. He knelt in front of Finn and took a fistful of their hair in his hand. Torren pulled his knife from his belt and held it under Finn's chin. They jerked their head up in terror, away from the blade. He dragged their head forward as they sobbed. They pulled uselessly at the cuffs behind them.

Gavin wrapped his hand around one wrist and dragged it back to the floor. He stepped on the chain linking the cuffs and pinned Finn's hands down. They wailed, their eyes fixed on Ellis. Ellis sobbed hard, looking down at them.

"I'm sorry," Ellis gasped. "I'm sorry I'm sorry I'm *so fucking sorry* I'm sorry..."

Gavin raised his foot and stomped hard on Finn's left hand. There was a *snap*.

Finn keened in anguish, straining hard against the hand in their hair.

"No!" Ellis screamed, throwing themselves forward against Leo's grip. He dragged Ellis backwards, his arm tightening around their neck. A whine escaped their throat and they coughed, eyes streaming.

Gavin laughed. "Are you a righty or a lefty, Finn?" Finn sobbed hard and fell against the knife at their throat. "Eh. I guess it doesn't matter." Gavin stomped hard on their right hand.

Finn's scream cut through the room, drowning out the others' cries of horror. Finn dragged in a shuddering gasp as Gavin stepped off the handcuffs. Their arms retracted to bring their hands softly against their back. Their left hand was already swollen and inflamed. They trembled as waves of pain broke over them.

"Now for the brain."

Ellis lurched forward. *"No,* please Gavin *no,* I'll do *anything, please…"*

Gavin chuckled. "Aw. They mean a lot to you, don't they?"

"Torture me, not them, please, hurt me, leave them alone, god, please… I… I'll die if you want, please, just… me, not them…"

Finn's lips trembled as they struggled to draw breath through the sobs.

"I don't want to completely scramble them," Gavin said conversationally. "I risk killing them, or leaving them some drooling, senseless vegetable. Today I'm just gonna give dear Finn a little concussion. Just a little one. And then another one tomorrow, and another the next day, and the next, and the next. You're going to notice them change. Slowly. They're going to become different. Their personality will shift. They'll become more aggressive. They'll start to forget things. They'll become confused. Eventually they'll stop being… Finn."

Ellis raged against Leo's hold. Gavin turned and flashed a smile at them. "You've already lived through losing your family once. Stands to reason that you can do it again. If I told Torren to cut their throat right here you'd watch them bleed out, they'd die in your arms, and you'd mourn them. You'd scream, cry, rage, and they'd be dead. You'd find a way to move on, just like you did before. Maybe find a new family." Each one of Ellis's sobs tore from them like a scream. "But I can kill Finn, kill their mind, and leave their body walking around like a damned ghost. It might take weeks, or even months. But I guarantee you if I give them a concussion every day, they'll stop being *them* after a while. Their body would still be with you. I wonder, would that be enough for you? Would you still hold them, love them, kiss them after they didn't know who you are? Even after I've reduced them to some simple, trembling mess, would you be able to resist taking them? It would never be the same. You'd have their body, not their mind. How long would it take before you went crazy from that?"

Ellis fought Leo with everything they had, throwing elbows back at him, shrieking like a demon as they thrashed against his grip. Finn sobbed, pale and trembling. They looked like they might throw up.

"Take the knife away from their throat," Gavin instructed Torren. Torren tucked the knife away. Before Finn could even flinch, Gavin pulled his arm back and crashed his fist into their temple.

They flew out of Torren's hands and slumped to the ground. They convulsed once and went still.

"No!" Ellis screamed, falling back against Leo's grasp. Finn lay stunned on the floor, eyes slightly open, lips parted. They flinched weakly as Torren dragged them back to their place along the wall and dropped them to the floor. Finn fell like a sack of flour from his grasp.

Leo let Ellis go. They rushed, half crawling on their knees, to Finn's side and erupted into sobs, leaning over them, needing in their bones to pick them up and cradle them. They pulled unthinkingly at the handcuffs. Their eyes were wide and staring at Finn as they groaned and began to stir. "Finn…" they sobbed. "No… please…"

Gavin turned to face the rest of the room, grinning. He rubbed his hands together. "Who's next?"

Chapter 28

"Really, no volunteers?" Gavin chuckled to himself. "Fine." He pointed at Vera. "It's Vera, right? You're up next."

"No…" Her body tensed as Torren approached her. His hand clamped down on her hair and he dragged her to the center of the room. Ellis glanced up from where they were kneeling over Finn, still stretched out on the floor. Tears rolled down their face as Torren forced Vera to her knees in front of Gavin. Gray paled. Vera's eyes fixed on theirs, wide and terrified.

"Vera…" Isaac mumbled, shuddering on the ground as Sam pressed against his side.

Her breaths came in short gasps. "No no no no no no," she murmured to herself. Her eyes were fixed on the floor in front of her as Gavin sauntered around her. Looking for weak spots. Chinks in the armor.

Gavin smiled as he returned to stand in front of her. Vera kept her eyes fixed firmly on the floor. He reached a hand out to guide her face up. She flinched away at his touch, trembling as he forced her to look at him. She squeezed her eyes shut. Her lips trembled in voiceless pleas.

Gavin watched her, amused, as her lips moved silently. "Vera." She trembled silently. He knelt, looking at her. "Vera…" He snapped his fingers at her ear. Nothing. "Vera?" She didn't respond.

His hand whipped across her face. Gray gasped and lurched forward. Their eyes remained fixed on her. She slumped a little to the side as her eyes flew open. Her lips kept moving.

Gavin inspected her face carefully. Her eyes were open, but glazed over. Unfocused. His forehead wrinkled as he watched her, waiting for her silent words to cease. He pulled her hair back away from her face. She flinched slightly, lips still moving.

"What're you *doing?*" He waved his hand in front of her face. Her eyes remained unfocused, staring straight ahead. He pulled her hair back farther as he tilted her head to the side. Thinking.

His eyes dropped to a scar on her throat. He bit his lip, leaning closer, pulling her head back to show more of it, to reveal a ring of very faint scars, curving along her throat, long-healed. His lips pulled back into a grin.

"Someone already broke you in," he murmured.

He stood and walked behind her. He grabbed the cuffs, pulling her arms away from her body. He yanked her long sleeves up her forearms. He smiled as he saw more scars around her wrists, just as old and just as faint. He dropped her hands and sauntered around in front of her.

He slapped her across the face again. Her mouth fell open into a gasp, but she didn't cry out. She didn't make a sound. He laughed softly to himself. "Hm." He paused a moment. "Vera... You can speak."

"Thank you, sir," she whispered.

Gavin jolted with the rush of excitement that crashed through his body.

Ellis gasped. Their eyes snapped from Finn, dazed but awake, to Vera, a look of new horror crossing their face.

"Oh..." Gavin crooned. "Oh, man. There's a whole slew of shit locked up in that brain of yours, isn't there, Vera?"

She nodded robotically. "Yes, sir."

He giggled. "Oooh shit. Oh god." He rubbed his hands together. "Yes. Oh, fuck yes." He cleared his throat, composing himself. "Vera, why didn't you talk when I asked you a question before?"

She shook her head weakly. "Didn't have permission to, sir."

Gavin tilted his head. "And what happens when you do something without permission?"

She shuddered. "I... There's punishment, sir."

He grinned. "What kind of punishment?"

A tear rolled down her cheek. "…whatever you see fit." Her voice wobbled. "Sir."

Gavin let his head fall back as he drank in her words. "Vera, who made you like this?"

A silent sob shook her shoulders. "I… I am not allowed to know his name."

"Uh huh. And what happened while you were with him?"

She swallowed hard. "He made me… g-good. Made me obey. Taught me the rules."

He nodded. "What rules are those?"

She stiffened and began to recite. "Never speak without permission. Only eat or sleep when told to. Never scream unless he lets me. Take all punishments without complaint. Never take off the c-collar."

"Wait wait wait, the *collar?*"

She nodded. "Yes. He gave me the collar to remind me who I belonged to. So he could chain me down when he…" She swallowed hard.

"Hm. Was this someone in… a syndicate?" Gavin threw a wink in Isaac's direction, though his gaze never left Vera. He was transfixed.

"Yes."

"Why did he keep you?"

"Because it made him happy." Her voice was strained.

"How long did he keep you?"

"I… I don't know."

"Days? Months? Years?"

"I… I think it was months. Maybe two."

"And he made you like this?"

Her lips trembled. "I…" She hung her head.

"How long ago was this?"

She was shaking. "Fourteen years."

"And you've carried this around in your head that whole time? And I activated it by…" He raised his hand like he was going to hit her again. She closed her eyes but didn't flinch away.

He let his hand drop, laughing. He turned to the others. "Have you ever seen her like this?"

Gray's eyes were wide as tears rolled down their cheeks. Their gaze was fixed on Vera. "No," they whispered.

Sam stared and cringed more into themselves. "No…" they whimpered. Finn couldn't seem to focus on her. Ellis shook their head slowly.

Gray heaved a broken sob. "I'm sorry, Vera." Their voice wavered. "I didn't know… I had no idea…"

Gavin turned his attention back to Vera. She trembled under his gaze. He gently lifted her face with one hand. "You belong to me now," he murmured softly. "I claim you. And we're going to have so much fun." He let her head drop and her face shattered into agony.

Gavin turned, his eyes locking on Sam and Isaac. Vera shook herself and her eyes focused again. "I can come back to her, though. For now, I have an itch." Gavin advanced on Sam.

Vera lurched to her feet and moved towards him. Torren lunged forward and grabbed her arms, pulling her back against him. Her hands were pressed between them both. She fumbled at his pocket. He threw her down against the floor. Her knees hit hard and she cried out softly.

Gavin laughed and turned back to Sam and Isaac. "Leo, help me with this."

Chapter 29

Sam bleated in terror as Gavin descended on them. Their eyes were wide with horror as Leo jerked Isaac to his knees and began to drag him to the center of the room.

Gavin shook his head. "No. I want to do this with just them." He leaned down to pull Sam from the floor. "I missed you," he rasped into their ear. They cringed away, wailing.

Leo dragged Isaac out of the room. Gavin was right behind him dragging Sam. They moved down a hallway to another room that looked just like the first. Leo threw Isaac down to the floor. He gasped weakly and rolled onto his side. Blood dripped off his face onto the linoleum. Leo pulled him up until he was kneeling and stepped back against the wall.

Gavin forced Sam to their knees in front of Isaac. Turning to Leo he ordered, "Go back to Torren. Keep them all in line." He turned his attention back to Sam and Isaac. Leo grunted and left the room.

Tears poured down Sam's face as they looked at Isaac. Isaac swayed where he was kneeling. Wave after wave of agony broke over him. Every breath hurt. His heart plummeted to the floor as he met Sam's gaze.

"Isaac," Sam sobbed. Isaac pressed his lips together and shook his head. "Isaac…" Sam's eyes stayed fixed on him. "Did he mean that? Was he telling the truth?" Isaac whined low in his throat, dizzy with pain. "Is it true you don't think you're worth saving?"

Isaac sobbed weakly, shoulders shaking with gasps. "Sam…"

"You have to know we love you, Isaac." Sam's chest heaved with each sob. "I love you, Isaac, I love you, I'm so sorry. We tried to save you. We…" They wailed weakly. "We couldn't let you die. I'm so sorry…"

Gavin cut them off with a slap. They gasped and cringed away, biting down hard on their lip to keep from sobbing.

"No," Isaac moaned. "Gavin, don't… don't hurt them. Please…"

Gavin laughed. "I'm not going to hurt them, Isaac. Don't worry. I'm not." He knelt and pulled Isaac's head up, gripping his hair. Isaac shuddered. "*You* are."

Isaac's eyes went wide. "No." He shook his head weakly. "No. I won't. I… I *can't*."

Gavin pulled his gun from his waistband and pointed it at Isaac's forehead. "Pretty sure you can."

"No." Tears ran down Isaac's cheeks, making clear lines in the blood smeared on his face.

"It's okay, Isaac." Sam's voice shook. "It's okay. You can… you can do it. I can take it."

Isaac jerked his head side to side. "I… I *won't*…" He gritted his teeth and leaned forward against the gun.

"Then you die. Pretty simple."

Isaac's jaw locked. "Then I die," he spat through his teeth.

"Isaac, *no!*" Sam wailed. "Please, Isaac, hurt me, please, Isaac *please!*"

Gavin's lips pulled up into a grin. "Hear that? Sam wants you to hurt them. Do it, Isaac. Give them what they want."

"*I won't do it!*" Isaac screamed, almost falling forward as he pressed his forehead against the barrel of the gun. "Fucking *kill* me, Gavin, I *won't do it!*"

Gavin's smile grew wider and he pulled the gun away from Isaac's head. "That wouldn't be any fun."

Isaac's chest heaved with each painful breath. Gavin stepped behind Sam. He pointed the gun at the back of Sam's head. "Hurt Sam, or I kill them."

Sam cringed away from the gun, crying out in terror. Gavin gripped their hair and pulled their head back against the barrel. Isaac's mouth fell open in despair. His gaze moved from Gavin to Sam.

"Sam…"

"It's okay, Isaac." They trembled as they wept, head pulled back, throat bared, helpless. "Please…"

Isaac yanked hard against the rope around his wrists. He winced as it pulled against the raw skin. "Sam… I can't…"

Gavin pulled their head back harder. "You really want them to die, then? You really want that to happen?"

Isaac whimpered, adjusting his wrists, tugging against the rope.

"You have five seconds to agree to do this, or you'll be cleaning Sam's brains off the floor. I have all six of you now. I won't cry over one dead Sammy." Gavin jerked Sam's head back and they cried out, squeezing their eyes shut as Gavin stared down at them.

"No…" Isaac's strength was fading as he twisted his wrist and yanked hard. He felt the skin at the base of his thumb begin to tear.

"Five…"

"No…"

"Four…"

"Please *no!*"

"Three…"

"No no no please…"

"Two…"

"Sam!"

"One…"

Sam forced their eyes open to look at Isaac. Isaac wrenched his wrist hard against the rope. He felt his thumb dislocate as the flesh of his hand tore deep. He screamed as he drew his hand through the rope binding him. Blood poured off his hand and down his back. He lunged at Gavin, forcing the gun away from

Sam's head as Gavin pulled the trigger. Isaac heard the shot, felt it, as he bowled Gavin over. Sam cried out as Isaac knocked them to the side.

Isaac roared with fury, drawing his hand back and bringing his fist down hard on Gavin's face. Gavin pushed clumsily against Isaac's chest. Isaac raised his fist and punched him again. Over and over he punched him, smashing his fist against Gavin's face until he felt bone begin to crack. Isaac watched as his blood dripped onto Gavin from his nose and his hand. Blood began to pool on the floor.

He pulled his fist back to strike again and he felt someone press against his side. He paused for a moment, raising his gaze to Sam. Their eyes were wide, terrified. His fist hung frozen above Gavin.

Slowly, Isaac lowered his fist. He dissolved into sobs and slumped off of Gavin onto the ground. Sam fell to their knees beside Isaac and pressed their face into his chest, taking deep, gasping sobs. Isaac numbly wrapped his arms around them and pressed his broken hand against their back. He stayed there for a moment with them, rocking them softly.

"I'm sorry," he whispered. "I'm so sorry."

Sam pulled away, their dark eyes wide. "No, Isaac. I…"

Isaac took a hiccoughing breath as his gaze moved to Gavin, sprawled on the floor, unmoving. He couldn't tell if the blood smeared on Gavin's ruined face was his, or Gavin's. Isaac shuddered, the adrenaline slowly easing out of his body, leaving him trembling and weak. "See if you can get the keys out of his pocket."

Sam crouched over Gavin and reached their cuffed hands into his pocket. They pulled out the keys and dropped them in front of Isaac. Isaac reached out with his left hand, handling them clumsily. He didn't know where all the blood was coming from. He quickly unlocked the cuffs from around Sam's wrists. As the cuffs came away, Sam threw their arms around him and nearly knocked him over. They buried their face into his shoulder, sobbing hard.

"I… he… Isaac… I'm so…" They could barely speak as sobs ripped through them. Isaac's tears fell against their shoulder.

"We have to go," Isaac whispered. "We have to go get the others."

157

Sam pulled away, nodding, as they wiped away their tears. Isaac picked up Gavin's gun with his uninjured hand. He whimpered softly as he tried to drag himself to his feet. Sam stumbled up under his arm and took his weight as much as they could. They staggered and wrapped their arm firmly around his waist. Isaac whined faintly as their arm pressed against his wounds. Isaac stooped and took a moment to steady himself before nodding. They began to move.

Sam paused for a moment as they felt a steady stream of hot blood run down their back. They pulled Isaac's arm away from their shoulders, turning it in their hands. Their fingers slipped on the blood that covered his arm. Isaac's head spun as Sam found the wound on Isaac's forearm. The bullet had hit him.

Boom.

An explosion rocked the building. The door blew open, sending them careening to the floor. Sam cried out as their leg buckled under them. Isaac grunted as the impact forced all the air out of his chest. The gun flew from his hand.

Sam's gaze found Isaac's, their eyes wide with pain and terror.

"What was *that*?"

Chapter 30

Another explosion rocked the building. Sam was flung to the ground again as the shocks rippled through the floor. They screamed wordlessly as they struggled to get their feet under them.

Adrenaline surged through Isaac. "Sam!" he screamed. "Sam get up, *getupgetupgetup.*" Isaac yanked at their clothes, smearing streaks of blood on their shirt. He cried out as his broken right hand buckled. "Come on. Get up." He got a grip on their shirt and shoved them forward through the destroyed door. "Come on, we can't stop."

Sam sobbed as they scrambled to their feet, clutching Isaac's arm. Their fingers were clumsy with panic.

"Please," they begged. "Isaac…" They tried to limp on their ruined leg. Terror propelled them forward as every step made bone crunch on bone.

Isaac drew an arm across his eyes, trying to clear the dust and smoke. He cast his memory back to when he'd first been brought to the complex. Door on the right, elevator to the left. Another door on the right. "I think it's this one!" He shoved his shoulder against it and dragged Sam down the long corridor that hopefully led outside.

Boom.

Another explosion rocked the corridor.

The both fell to their knees as the door behind them blasted open and shattered, shrapnel flying everywhere. A piece of the door flew forward, wrenching and crushing Isaac's left shoulder.

"No," Sam wailed. "Isaac, please, please get up. Please. We have to get out." Their nails scrabbled against his right arm. *"Pleasepleaseplease get up."*

Groaning, Isaac pushed himself to his feet. His left arm hung limply at his side. Sweat poured down his face. He tucked Sam under his right arm and staggered towards the double doors at the end of the hallway.

Sam sobbed and choked on the oppressive smoke. They stumbled and almost fell as their leg gave out from under them. *"Please,"* they sobbed, over and over. *"Please."* Isaac couldn't move his left arm to grab Sam. His injured right hand clamped down on the collar of their shirt as he dragged them towards the doors. So close. Just a few more steps.

Isaac slammed his shoulder through the doors, his right arm still dragging Sam behind him. He hurled them out the doors ahead of him into the dark. They went toppling into the dust. He took one faltering step and collapsed to the ground beside them. His breaths came in painful grunts.

"Isaac," Sam whimpered. "Isaac..." They dragged themselves to his side on their hands. In the light streaming from the building behind them, Sam could see for the first time that Isaac was far more injured than he let on. His left shoulder was swollen and displaced. His shirt was shredded where the debris had hit him. The flesh underneath was torn, oozing blood. His breaths came in painful, creaking wheezes. Sam distantly wondered if his ribs were broken.

"Isaac," they cried, their hands fluttering over him, unsure where they could touch him without hurting him worse. "Isaac... Thank you. I'm so sorry... Isaac..."

"Go," he whispered, rolling to his side. He pushed his hand against their chest. "You have to keep going."

Chapter 31

"No. No way. No way I'm leaving you. Isaac…"

Isaac left bloody handprints on Sam's shirt as he pushed harder against their chest. Tears left tracks in the soot and blood on his cheeks. "You have to go, Sam. Please. If they find you… If I… killed him…"

Sam pushed Isaac's hands away and clutched at his shirt. *"No.* I'm not leaving without you."

"I'll only slow you down. Please…" Isaac whimpered. He curled up on his side, doing his best to cradle his left arm with his destroyed right hand. His eyes fluttered shut.

Sam's hands tightened in his shirt. *"No,"* they hissed through their teeth. "If they find us then they find us. I'm not going anywhere without you. Come on, Isaac. You have to get up." They leaned back and pulled on Isaac's shirt with all their strength, their good foot scrabbling on the ground. They trembled, still weak from the fever. "Isaac *please*," they begged. *"Please."* Isaac lay still at their feet, eyes closed.

They heaved a sob and released his shirt, falling to their hands and knees beside him. "Isaac… *please*…" They crawled to his side, mewling weakly as their broken leg jostled as they moved. They curled up next to him on the ground. Their hand gently brushed against Isaac's forearm. Their fingers came away bloody. They closed their eyes.

"Sam! Isaac!"

Sam stirred, unsure if they had imagined it.

"Isaac!"

They raised their head.

"Sam!"

The voices were close.

"Isaac! Sam!"

Ellis. Sam sat up, stunned. The smoke was thick, even outside. "Here!" They did their best to get to their feet. "We're over here!"

"Sam!" The voices were closer. *Vera.*

Sam could just make out movement in the dark. They waved their arms. "Over here!"

"Sam!" Ellis materialized out of the smoke, supporting a dazed-looking Finn. Vera was right behind them, her hand clamped onto Gray's shirt. Ellis let go of Finn for a moment and rushed to Sam.

Ellis fell to their knees beside them. "Sam!" They turned to shout over their shoulder. "Found them! Gray, go get the car!" They pulled the keys out of their pocket and tossed them to Gray. Gray caught them and turned, sprinting as fast as they could in the other direction.

Ellis turned back to Sam, their hands moving over them in disbelief. "Sam. You're okay." Their eyes moved to Isaac. He lay unmoving on the ground. "Is he…?"

Tears filled Sam's eyes and streamed down their face. "He's alive, he's… he's hurt, Ellis…" Sam looked helplessly at Finn, who was standing with their hands outstretched, a tortured expression on their face. *They can't help him with their broken hands…* Vera knelt behind Sam and held them as they swayed on their knees.

"What happened to him?" Ellis's hands reached towards Isaac and stopped a few inches from his skin. "I… don't…"

"He tore his hand getting out of the ropes," Sam whimpered. Their hands wrapped around Vera's wrists as she held them. "Gavin was going to… shoot me if he didn't torture me. His thumb is…" They stared at him with wide eyes. "He hit Gavin. I think he killed him. His right hand is broken. And he… got shot…" They gasped out a sob.

Finn's eyes seemed to focus at that. "He got shot? *Where?*" They knelt beside him.

"His forearm. There's... a lot of blood..." Sam shuddered. "And in the explosion, he... he got hit. His shoulder..."

Ellis hissed through their teeth as they rolled Isaac slightly, angling him so Finn could inspect the wound. Blood leaked from the torn skin.

"Right off the bat I s-see..." Finn's words were a little slurred. "That shoulder's dislocated, the thumb, too, and... the gunshot wound doesn't look like it went through..." They wiped their eyes with their forearms. "I can't see it clearly, but I think it's just a graze..." They squeezed their eyes shut. "And that's all on top of his... other injuries..."

Sam's eyes flicked between Finn and Ellis. "How did you all get out? What happened?"

"Don't worry about that," Vera said soothingly against their hair. "I'll explain as soon as we're all safe. I promise."

They heard the car approaching. Ellis stood up as the headlights cut through the dark. Gray skidded to a stop beside them and jumped out. They left the car running.

Ellis stood and moved to Isaac's head. "Help me with this. Gray, can you get his hips? I've got his torso... Vera, his legs?" They both nodded and moved into position around him. Sam stood to the side on one foot, trembling. Finn reached for them unsteadily. Sam folded into their arms and wrapped their own arms around Finn's waist.

Isaac cried out raggedly as they lifted him.

"I'm sorry, I'm sorry," Ellis whispered. They moved in step to carry Isaac to the car. They placed him as gently as they could in the back seat. Gray fumbled to put the seatbelt on. Isaac slumped against it.

"I'll drive." Gray carried Sam to the front seat and guided them in, helping them slide in to the middle.

"It's okay." Ellis's voice was hard. "I can drive." They moved towards the driver's seat. Gray stopped them with a hand on their shoulder.

"I'm driving. I'm the only one Gavin didn't torture. I'll be able to focus on the road the best."

Ellis fixed Gray with a look for a moment, before dropping their eyes and looking away. "Fine."

"Ellis. Can you sit in the back with me? Be my hands?" Finn looked hopelessly down at their injured hands. Tears rolled down their cheeks.

Ellis folded into themselves. "Of course." They climbed in to sit next to Isaac. Finn got in behind them. Ellis helped them with their seatbelt. Vera jumped into the passenger seat and Gray hit the accelerator.

"Sam." Finn blinked slowly. "Did Isaac hit his head? Did he h-hit his head?"

"No. I mean, I…" Sam bit their lip. "I don't think so? I didn't see if he did. No?" They twisted around in their seat, their eyes fixed on Isaac.

"Ellis." Finn chewed their lip. "Pull his eyelids back. Look at his pupils. Turn on the overhead light."

Ellis did as they were told. "What am I looking for?"

"Are they the same size?"

"Yeah."

"Did they constrict when the light came on?"

"Um… Yeah."

"Cool. Feel his head. Feel for any bumps or soft patches or… um… crunching."

Ellis winced and ran their fingers hesitantly through Isaac's hair to his scalp. His hair was filthy and clotted with blood in some places, but felt firm and whole underneath. "I don't feel anything weird."

"Good. Now his neck. Feel the bones down the back. Keep going down his back to his tailbone."

Ellis did it. "I think it all feels okay."

Finn bit their lip. "You don't have to check his ribs too much. I heard the snap back there. I know they're broken. He seems to be breathing okay, right?"

Ellis watched him take a few breaths. "It seems normal, I think."

"Feel his abdomen. Feel if it's hot or like there's something in there that shouldn't be."

Ellis pressed their fingers gently against the skin there.

"No, you have to kinda… dig in."

"O-okay." They did it. They winced in sympathy as they pressed into the cuts there.

"Now push on his hips. Do they seem to be solid?"

"Um. Yeah."

"Okay. Feel down his legs for breaks."

"I don't feel anything."

"Okay. Now for the part I know is going to suck. Try to sit him up a bit more so I can see his shoulder."

Ellis rocked Isaac gently forward against the seatbelt. Finn couldn't tell if it was dislocated, or completely fractured. The torn flesh of Isaac's shoulder leaked blood onto the seat of the car. Finn huffed a breath out from between their lips. "I need to get in there and feel it."

"But… your hands…"

Finn winced. "I think only the left one is broken. Let me try."

Ellis moved out of the way as Finn reached across the car. Their fingers touched gingerly along Isaac's shoulder and felt the bones underneath. Isaac flinched and pulled away from Finn's touch. Finn pressed into the torn flesh as gently as they could, feeling for bone fragments and sharp edges. Their hand ached.

"P… please…" Isaac whimpered.

Sam's hand shot back towards Isaac.

"No… please…" Isaac whined pitifully, his eyes not fully open. "I can't…"

"Isaac, you're safe, you're with us!" Sam's dark eyes were riveted on Isaac.

"Gavin… please… stop…"

Finn jerked their hand back like they'd been burned. Vera squeezed her eyes shut and pressed her fist against her lips. Gray's hands tightened on the steering wheel.

Finn ground their teeth together. "I don't think anything's broken. Just dislocated. Ellis, hold him. I have to reduce it."

Ellis swallowed hard. "What if something *is* broken?"

Finn pressed their lips together. "Then I make it a lot worse. I can't be sure without an x-ray. But we can't go to a hospital… especially not now… now that…" They shook their head. "But I don't… I don't *think* it's broken." They pressed the back of their wrist against their forehead. "I… don't…" They squeezed their eyes shut. "I'm sorry, my head h-hurts…"

Ellis cupped their hand under Finn's chin and tilted their head up. Finn met their eyes desperately. "I know it hurts." Ellis's voice broke. "I know. But I trust you."

Tears formed in Finn's eyes. "Even like this?"

Ellis pressed a kiss to their forehead, their lips pulling into a watery smile. "Even like this. You just got your bell rung a little. You can do this."

Finn turned their eyes back to Isaac. "O-okay. Ellis, I need you to… to hold him down."

Ellis pressed their hands against Isaac's chest and his uninjured shoulder. Finn's hand closed gingerly on Isaac's wrist and they winced.

Finn shook their head. "This won't work. You need to be able to hold him down better, and I need room to get his arm against the seat." Finn bit their lip.

Ellis moved quickly. They swung around in front of Isaac and straddled his legs, wrapping their arms around him and the headrest behind him. Their body pressed against the length of his and held him firmly against the seat. "Does this work?"

Finn nodded. "Yeah, that'll be fine, I think. Okay. I don't know if he'll wake up, but this is probably gonna hurt."

"Have you ever done this before?" Sam's eyes were wide with concern.

Finn pressed their lips together. "...no. But I've practiced on normal shoulders, and I've seen it work." Their right hand wrapped around Isaac's wrist. They held it up so that Isaac's forearm was at a 90-degree angle from his upper arm, pointing straight in front of him. Isaac stirred and whimpered against Ellis's shoulder. Finn held their left forearm against Isaac's upper arm, holding it tight to his body. They nodded at Ellis. Ellis tightened their hold around Isaac and closed their eyes.

Slowly, gently, Finn began to rotate Isaac's forearm out to the side. Isaac shuddered and pulled against Finn's grasp. Ellis held him tight to the seat. He moaned and his voice rose into a scream. Sam pressed their hands against their mouth. They trembled and went pale.

Finn rotated Isaac's forearm until it was flush with the back of the seat. They watched his shoulder carefully as they gently began to ease it back. A slight *bump* reverberated down Isaac's arm. As Finn rotated his arm back, Sam saw that the lump in Isaac's shoulder was gone. Isaac slumped back against the seat.

Bracing Isaac's arm against Ellis, Finn ran their unbroken hand over his shoulder. The torn skin still oozed blood, but the bone was in place. Finn pressed their thumb hard into Isaac's nailbed. Isaac pulled away weakly. The skin blanched and color returned to it almost immediately. Finn let out a breath. "I think it worked."

Everyone in the car let out a breath of their own. Finn held Isaac's arm against his chest as Ellis crawled out from on top of him and settled back down into the seat.

"I need a sling for him."

Everyone cast their eyes around for something they could use as a sling. Sam started to pull off their shirt.

"No... I need the med kit. Is it still in the trunk?"

"Yes, but..." Gray swallowed. "I don't want to stop. We have no idea who's coming after us."

Finn cast a glance behind them through the rear window. "I don't see anyone. Gray, please... I need to stop the bleeding. I need my kit."

Gray pushed out a slow breath. "Okay." They eased the car to a stop. "Vera, can you—"

She was already out. The trunk slammed shut and she jumped back in, passing the bag back to Ellis. Gray started the car moving again.

Finn reached out for the bag as Ellis pulled it away. Finn paused, their hands out, before letting them drop.

"Okay. Right. Ellis, get a triangle bandage from the side pocket. It'll be— Yeah. That." Ellis unfolded it. "Tie a knot in this corner and put the knot against Isaac's elbow." Ellis followed their directions. "Now take the ends and pull them up around his neck and tie a knot." Ellis leaned forward to do it. Their hands pressed against Isaac's neck as they tied the sling.

Isaac's eyes flew open. His broken hand slammed against Ellis's chest and pinned them against the front seat. *"No,"* he growled.

Chapter 32

Ellis pawed at Isaac's hand, trying to dislodge it gently. "It's okay, Isaac," they soothed. "It's me. It's Ellis. You're safe. You got out."

Isaac's eyes were unfocused. His gaze slid around the car, as if struggling to grasp what he was seeing. "Not... Not a dream?"

"No," Ellis whispered. "We're safe."

Isaac whimpered. "I don't... believe..." He slumped back and his hand fell from Ellis's chest. "Please... don't... kill me... again."

Ellis pulled back in horror as Isaac's eyes rolled back and he sagged against the seatbelt.

"Did... did he say... don't kill him? Again?" Tears rolled down Sam's cheeks.

Vera nodded slowly. "I think so." She reached her hand back to touch Isaac. She hesitated and pulled back. "What did Gavin *do* to him?"

Finn turned to Gray. "Do you have somewhere in mind to go? I need to know how long we're going to be driving before I do anything else for him."

Gray bit their lip. "I have a friend who lives close by. I haven't seen her in years, but she might give us somewhere safe to stay... for a little while."

"How far away is this friend?"

Gray thought for a moment. "I think if we stay on this highway we'll get there in... three hours? More, if we take side roads?"

"How much more?"

Gray shook their head. "Honestly, I don't know. I've never gone that way. Maybe four and a half?"

Finn exhaled, their gaze moving over to Isaac. "I don't know how much longer he has. I can't tell how bad he's hurt with the equipment I have." They thought for a moment. "I only have eight bags of saline left. I need more room to work than in a speeding car packed with six people."

"If Gavin survived, if *any* of them survived, they'll have everyone looking for us." Vera's voice was hard. "Does Isaac have four and a half hours?"

Finn bit their lip. "I don't know. But if they catch us it won't matter. We'll all be dead."

Gray nodded once, tears filling their eyes. "Side roads it is." They raised their chin and sniffed. "Ellis, do you still have the phone? I'll have you dial but let me talk to her." Ellis nodded and typed the number Gray gave them. They handed the phone to Gray.

Gray turned up the volume as loud as they could without putting the phone on speaker and held it to their ear.

A woman answered. *"If you're calling this number this damned well better be an emergency."*

"Hey, Tori."

A pause. *"Gray...?"*

"Yeah, it's me. And... it's an emergency."

A sigh. *"What is it, Gray? What have you gotten into?"*

Gray gritted their teeth. "Short version?"

"Whatever you want to tell me. Just do it fast."

"Okay. Someone from the eastern syndicate took my family and tortured them. One of my people, he's hurt bad. I've got another with a busted ankle and a few more injuries between us all. We... could use someplace to sleep. Get our injuries properly taken care of. We... we're pretty ragged right now, Tori. The guy knows about all our safehouses and we have nowhere else to go. Just one night. Please." They swallowed hard and their voice dropped to a murmur. "You know I wouldn't call unless it was really bad."

"You wouldn't have anything to do with the explosion that's all over the radio traffic now, would you?"

170

Gray paled. "It's on the radios?"

"I figured that was you, if you were calling me now. An explosion at some syndicate asshole's place. Sounds like there were more than a few casualties; it wiped out vehicles and a good amount of explosives. Nobody seems to know who did it, or if they're still alive."

Vera stared at the dashboard. Gray shot a glance at her out the corner of their eye. Sam followed the look. "Yeah, that was us. We used the explosives to get out. What else have you heard about it?"

"That you didn't kill the guy who took your people."

Sam let out a small wail. "What?"

"Apparently he was airlifted to Central."

Ellis's eyes were fixed on the phone in Gray's hand.

"Oh." Gray swallowed. "That is…"

"Unfortunate?"

Their tone darkened. "Yes."

"Hm."

"Tori… Please. Everyone's hurt but me. And it's… it's our best fighter that's off the worst. He sacrificed himself. Please, Tori. He's good. He'll die if we don't get him taken care of, get him to rest." Their eyes burned with tears. "Please."

A long pause. Then a sigh. *"Fine. I have the room. You can stay, but only until everyone's good enough to travel. Then you're gone."*

Gray's words rushed out of them. "That's more than generous, Tori. Thank you. Thank you. We're still a few hours out."

"Call me on this number when you're close." She hung up.

Gray let out the breath they'd been holding. "Thank god," they murmured. They threw a look into the back seat. "How's he doing?"

171

Finn pressed their lips together. "I mean... I can stop the bleeding until we get there. But I can't do any suturing or really anything else until we stop."

"You can't do any suturing *at all*." Ellis's voice was strained.

"I can do it one-handed." Finn ducked their head. "If you help me." Ellis nodded once, painfully.

"I'm not hurt." Vera's voice was hollow.

Gray blinked, glancing at her. "What?"

She stared straight ahead. "You said everyone was hurt but you. I'm not hurt."

Sam watched as Gray surveyed her carefully, their eyes flicking between her and the road. "You want to talk about what happened in there? What he... what he triggered?"

She jerked her head once to the side. "Nope."

Gray's eyebrows pulled together. "You know we're going to have to talk about it at some point."

Her lip wobbled and her eyes filled with tears. "I don't think so." She crossed her arms and looked out the window.

"Vera?" Finn's voice was weak. After a moment she turned back to look at them. "I could use your help splinting Sam's leg."

Sam bit their lip. They tried to steady their trembling, to do their best to be brave.

Vera softened and nodded once. "Of course."

Finn pointed to what they needed and Ellis passed her a rolled up flexible splint and a wrap. "Okay. Take the splint and unroll it. Fold it in half, then make it into... sort of a stirrup. It'll go under Sam's heel and up the sides of their leg." She did it. "Okay. Now... make sure the leg is straight, that it's not twisted at all, and put the splint on their leg."

She looked at Sam. "Here. Can you put your leg in my lap?"

Sam winced as Vera gently helped them lift their leg. They gasped as they put their leg down. They pressed back against Gray. Gray's hand left the wheel momentarily to squeeze Sam's hand.

Vera carefully fitted the splint onto their leg. Sam sucked in a breath and pressed their hand against their mouth to keep from crying out. Vera fixed them with an apologetic glance as she arranged the splint around their leg.

"Now just… bandage it with the ACE wrap. Secure it really well in the splint. Not too tight, though. We want good bloodflow still."

"Okay." Vera wrapped the bandage around Sam's leg, stabilizing it in the splint. She pressed the Velcro end against the bandage. "Is that it?"

"Yeah, that'll be fine for now. How does it feel, Sam?"

Their tears spilled over. "It's… it's okay. It's better. Really." Their dark eyes were fixed on Isaac.

"Let me worry about Isaac," Finn said softly, reaching up for Sam's hair. Their broken hand froze just before they touched them. "If it starts to feel like it's not in the right place, tell me."

"Okay." Sam turned to face the front, shuddering with pain. Vera opened her arm to them and they curled against her side.

Finn looked back to Isaac, where he was still slumped in his seat. They pulled in a deep breath. "Ellis, will you help me with the rest?"

"Of course." Their hand tightened on Finn's shoulder.

Chapter 33

Sam jerked awake as the car slowed, pulling into a long gravel driveway. They yelped as they jostled their leg. "Are we here?"

Gray nodded. "Tori's place. I've never been here before, but she told me about it years ago."

Sam cast a glance toward the back seat. Finn was slumped against Ellis, Finn's head on their shoulder. Ellis's head rested on top of Finn's. One of Ellis's hands laid gently under Finn's and the other rested lightly on Isaac's knee.

Vera sat up and looked around, dazed. "We here?" she mumbled.

Gray nodded. "Yup. Go ahead and wake the others."

She reached back and shook Ellis's shoulder gently. "Ellis," she whispered.

Their head lifted and they looked around blearily. As their eyes focused, they shook Finn's shoulder. "Finn. Finn, we're here. I'm so sorry... I let you fall asleep; I shouldn't have done that..."

Finn's eyes opened slowly, and they smacked their lips. "That's a myth." Their voice was still slurred from sleep. "Going to sleep after a concussion is fine. I guess it just worried people because sometimes someone wouldn't wake up after they hit their head but that's probably because they had an intracranial hemorrhage and they woulda died anyway so—"

They cut themselves off as Ellis took their chin in one hand.

"It's good to know you didn't get rung too hard," Ellis whispered. Finn smiled weakly.

They all turned to Isaac, slumped against the window. His nose had leaked blood down the inside of the door. Ellis's hands hovered over Isaac's body for a moment, trying to find some place to touch him that wouldn't hurt more. Their hand landed gently on his cheek. "Isaac..."

He moaned, stirred.

Ellis's hands shook as they touched his undamaged right shoulder. "Isaac?"

He squeezed his eyes shut, pulling away slightly. "No… please…"

Ellis bit their lip as tears pricked their eyes. "Isaac, it's… it's Ellis. Wake up, we're almost there…"

His eyes blinked open and moved around the car slowly. They finally rested on Ellis, who leaned over him, their eyebrows pulled together. "E-Ellis?"

They smiled in relief. "Yeah. Everyone's here. We all got out, Isaac."

He sat up suddenly. "Sam…?"

"I'm here, Isaac." Sam leaned over the seat and reached back towards him. "You got me out." They pressed their lips together as tears blurred their eyes.

He stared at them, disbelieving. "He was going to—"

"But he didn't." They reached back farther until their fingertips brushed his arm. "He didn't. You stopped him."

His eyes went wide as he remembered. "Did I kill him? Is he… is he dead?"

Gray's lips pressed together. "We don't know. Apparently, he was airlifted to Central Hospital, but that's all we know."

"How do you know that?"

"My friend Tori told me. She offered us a place to stay until we can travel again. This is her house." As they pulled around a bend, the headlights fell on a stone house tucked between the trees. The house was two stories and extended back into the dark.

Isaac stiffened. "You trust her? I'm sure they… the Stormbecks…"

Gray nodded. "I trust her with my life. I have, multiple times. She was involved in the resistance movements, back when they existed. Now she just lays low. She'll help us. She's trustworthy." They shot a glance back at Isaac. "I promise. I won't let anything happen to you."

Isaac's eyes filled with tears. "That's my job," he whispered. "It's my job to... protect you." He looked around the car. "Protect you all..."

"What do you think you just did, Isaac?" Vera's voice was gentle. "You sacrificed yourself to keep Sam safe. You protected us. Please let us take care of you." Her eyes were wide and fixed on him.

"You..." He whispered. "Gavin did something to you. Are you alright? What was that?"

Her gaze hardened. "Nothing. It was nothing. Don't worry about it."

Gray shook their head weakly. They pulled up to the front of the house and turned off the car. "Stay here." They left the keys on the seat. "Let me go talk to her first." They unfolded themselves from the car and walked stiffly to the front door.

They drew in a deep breath, hand shaking, and knocked three times. The door swung open almost immediately. They swallowed. "Tori."

She looked Gray up and down, curly hair wild around her head, her eyes guarded. "Gray. What have you brought me?"

They spread their hands in supplication. "Tori, I... I'm sorry. I wouldn't have called..."

"I know." She surveyed them for a moment longer, her arms crossed in front of her. Then she softened and held her arms out to them. "It's been a long time."

They folded into her embrace. They towered a good eight inches over her, but Gray still felt enveloped in her arms. She had always been able to cut right to their heart with her kindness. They'd missed her. Tears burned their eyes and they swallowed them down. *I'm the least damaged. I can't afford to lose it right now.*

She pulled away, her hands still tight on their arms as she looked back to the car. "Tell me what you have. Do I have to worry about blood?"

Gray nodded and bit their lip. "Yeah. Isaac... he's hurt pretty badly. Our medic Finn stopped the bleeding as well as they could, but he still might be—"

"Oh, you have a medic! Great."

"Well… Gavin – that's who took us – broke their hands. Gave them a concussion."

She sucked in a breath. "He knew what he was doing. Hurt the medic, and they can't help the others."

"It was also to hurt their partner. Ellis. They aren't physically hurt, but… Gavin dug up some old wounds and I know they're not doing well."

"Okay. What else?"

"Our youngest has a broken leg. They… Gavin took them and tortured them for three days. That's why Isaac went in. He traded himself for them. They've been sick, but they've been on antibiotics for four or five days and they're getting better, they're just weak."

"Is that everyone?"

"No. Vera. She isn't too badly hurt, maybe got jostled in the explosion, but… Tori…" Gray's eyes were wide with quiet horror. "Gavin… *did something* to her. Activated something. She… I think she's been conditioned. Held in captivity. She said for two months. It's like she went right back there. I had no idea. Tori…" They closed their eyes. "I thought I knew her and I missed this… massive, glaring—"

Tori shook their shoulders. "Stop that. Don't do that. You said you're the only one this Gavin shitstain didn't torture?"

They nodded weakly. "Yes."

"Then I don't need to tell you how much they need you right now. I know you're a good leader, Gray. I'm so sorry this happened. We can take care of them together."

"Of course," they whispered.

"Okay then. Let's get them in here." She walked to the car with Gray right behind.

∴

Isaac watched carefully as the woman looked towards the car. She seemed... unfriendly. Hard. But Gray had folded into her arms and let her hold them. *Maybe she's safe.*

They all watched warily as they both approached the car. She opened both doors on the left side.

"Okay, who's who?"

Finn mumbled out their name first. "I'm F-Finn." Ellis's hand went to their shoulder and squeezed gently.

"The medic? Broken hands and concussion?"

"Yes..." Finn bit their lip.

"Okay. Next." Her eyes moved to Ellis.

"I'm Ellis. I'm not hurt." They swallowed.

"Not physically, right?"

"I..."

"Look. I need to know what I'm bringing into my house. Who needs what. Gavin screwed with your head, right?"

They cast their eyes down, away from Finn. "...yes."

"Okay." She looked to Isaac. "You? Isaac, I'm assuming?"

He nodded slowly. "I..." He swallowed hard. "I'm al—"

"If you say 'I'm alright', I'm going to lean in there and smack you."

Isaac's jaw flexed. He said nothing.

"What are your injuries?"

"Um," Finn piped up. "Dislocated shoulder, I reduced it though, I reduced his dislocated thumb, too, he's got some blast injuries to the same shoulder, a bullet wound – well, a graze – on his forearm, a deep laceration to his thumb, his right hand is broken, and he's got... a lot of injuries from the torture itself—"

Tori's eyebrows shot up. "Those injuries you just listed *aren't* from torture?"

Isaac's cheeks burned and he swallowed. "...no. I had to get out. Had to get out with S-Sam. I got h-hurt getting out."

Tori's eyes narrowed. "There's a story there. You have to tell me once we get inside. What actual torture injuries?"

Isaac glanced around the car. "Um..."

"I need to know, Isaac."

His stomach clenched with shame. "Can I... just... tell you privately?"

Tori sighed. "You'll tell me once we get to the house. In my opinion your family should know, too, but I'll leave that up to you." She looked to Vera. "You?"

"Vera." Her jaw clenched. "And I'm not hurt," she forced through her teeth.

Tori's gaze lingered on her for a moment, calculating. Isaac's heart quickened. *She sees something's wrong, too.*

Tori nodded once. "Okay." She looked at Sam. "Last one. You?"

They swallowed. "Um... I'm Sam."

"And what have you got going on?"

"Um... I broke my leg." Vera put their arm protectively around them as they shrunk under Tori's gaze.

"Why are you on antibiotics? I need to know if you're going to be bringing something into my house."

"Um, I have... pneumonia... from... um..." They swallowed again. "It's not contagious, I don't think...?" They glanced at Finn for confirmation.

They nodded. "Not contagious. They've actually only got one dose of Zithro left and then they're done with the round."

Tori nodded and let her gaze roam around the car one more time. "Okay. Come on in."

Vera got out first. She helped Sam slide over the seat and supported them as they wobbled on one leg. Finn slid past Tori. Ellis got out and they and Gray made their way to the other side of the car. Isaac moved to open the door and flinched back as the pain flared. Ellis opened the door.

"Let us help you, you idiot," Ellis mumbled as they moved under his right arm. He slid out of the car, barely holding back a scream of pain. His shirt stuck to the cuts on his chest and his shoulder jostled as he moved, the motion sending pain spiking through him until he thought he might pass out. Gray wrapped their arm around Isaac's waist, supporting him.

Isaac sagged against Ellis. "I'm sorry," he whispered.

Ellis gritted their teeth. "Don't do that."

Isaac hung his head as they all moved to the house.

It was cozy and warm inside, dark wood floors joined with dark stone walls. They moved through the front room, past a dining room, into a study at the back of the house. Gray's eyebrows went up when they saw four mattresses, all made up with sheets and blankets on the floor. "Tori?"

She looked away for a moment, her eyes cast down to the floor. She lifted her gaze to Gray. "You're not the only one who's been trying to do the right thing, you know."

They shook their head. "I don't—"

"My house is a… safehouse of sorts. I sometimes let people crash who have nowhere else to go. I help… well, I *try* to help… when people just need to be… safe. Safe from the syndicates."

Gray's mouth had fallen open. "Tori… I had no idea."

"You weren't supposed to. Secret safehouses only really work if they're a secret." Her lips quirked up.

Gray smiled. "Thank you, Tori. Truly. Thank you."

She waved her hand dismissively. "Don't mention it. Let's get your people taken care of."

Vera supported Sam and helped them down to a mattress. They winced as they rested their leg.

"I wasn't sure if four was enough. I guess I should have asked." Tori looked concerned.

"It's perfect," Gray said as they and Ellis moved to put Isaac down on the nearest mattress. "Finn can sleep with Ellis, and Sam... would you be okay to sleep with me?"

They nodded, looking up at Gray. "That sounds okay."

Tori closely inspected the brace on Sam's leg. She gently felt the bone. "How does it feel?"

Sam bit their lip. "It hurts."

Tori smiled and blew out an exhale. "Okay, but does it feel twisted? Do you feel numb anywhere? Tingly?"

"No, it just..." Sam's eyes filled with tears. "It just hurts." They pressed their lips together, doing their best to not cry out.

"Okay. That's good. That splint looks good for now. I'll leave it alone. Are you okay otherwise?"

Sam nodded emphatically as their eyes moved to Isaac.

Isaac moaned as Ellis and Gray lowered him down. He pressed his lips together against the sobs that rose in his throat. His back arched and he whimpered softly as they lowered him onto his back. He rolled to his right side, gasping. Tori knelt beside him and looked him over. "What hurts the most?"

Isaac shook his head against the tears running down his cheeks. "I don't know," he whispered. He swallowed hard. "I don't know..." His throat tightened with sobs.

Finn knelt next to Isaac, their eyes wide and helpless. "I..." Their hands drifted towards him, almost unconsciously.

"Hey." Tori stopped them with a look. "Your hands are broken, right?"

Finn nodded miserably. "I think just the left one. I can still help with my right; he needs stitches…"

"No." Tori was nearly glaring at Finn. "Don't touch him. Don't make your hands worse."

Tears shone in Finn's eyes. "But I—"

"Finn. For your own good, don't touch him. If you make your hands worse, you can't help your family. Do you understand? If you want to be at your best for your family, rest. Let your hands heal."

Finn sniffled and nodded.

"Let me see." She held her hands out to take theirs. Her fingers moved gently over the bones of their left hand. They keened softly as she felt the break. "Yeah, that one's broken. Second and third metacarpal. Not displaced, though. We'll see if I can whip up some kind of cast. Let's see the other one." Finn swallowed the whimpers down. "I agree, I don't think that one's broken. The bone is bruised, I'm guessing." She turned to Ellis. "I'll go find the NSAIDs in a second, but for now go to the kitchen and get some ice. Make yourself at home. Help them ice their hands."

Ellis nodded and went to the kitchen.

Tori turned back to Isaac. His skin was damp with sweat and his shirt stuck to his chest. Faint streaks of blood striped his shirt like paint as his chest heaved. Every breath made him wince.

"Isaac." Her gaze was soft and steady. "I need you to tell me what he did to you."

"No." Isaac's voice dropped to a whisper. "I don't want them to hear. I don't want them to know. Please," he begged.

Tori blew out a steady breath. "We can let it wait, for now." She slid her hand through the tear in Isaac's shirt and peeled away the bandages there. She hissed through her teeth. "Yup, you definitely need stitches. But I'm going to have to clean it first."

Isaac sagged and closed his eyes. He nodded weakly.

Tori's eyebrows drew together. She turned to Finn. "Do you have anything you can give him for pain?"

Finn looked down. "No. I'm sorry. I haven't come across anyone selling in a while."

Tori sighed. "Alright. I have something I can give him. I don't have a big supply, and I don't want to use it all." She smoothed her hand through Isaac's hair. "I'm sorry. It's going to hurt, but I can help a little."

Isaac nodded, surrendering.

Chapter 34

Isaac lay on his side, towels piled under him and over the hard floor. His shirt was off, the torn skin of his shoulder exposed.

"I know it's not comfortable," Tori said apologetically. "But I don't want to get the mattress wet." She pulled the bottle of sterile water closer and drew some into a syringe. "This is the part that's going to hurt the most." She looked up to Ellis and Gray. "I might need you to hold him."

Isaac's head spun uselessly from the pain pills Tori had given him. Ellis placed their hands on Isaac's legs and pushed gently down. Gray got on the floor next to him and wrapped their arms around this torso, securing his left arm against his chest. Isaac forced down a groan as Gray pressed against the lash marks. Sam stared from where they lay on their bed, their eyebrows knit together in concern.

Tori placed her hands gently on Isaac's shoulder and pulled the wound open slightly. Isaac hissed and tried to pull away. Gray's arms tightened around him.

Tori *tsk*ed. "Good call, Finn. It doesn't look like anything's broken." She pursed her lips and glanced at Isaac. "You got lucky, all things considered." Isaac's head dropped to the floor as he huffed out an exasperated sigh. "Deep breath." She brought the syringe to his shoulder.

She flushed the water into the wound as she pulled it open further. Isaac stiffened, shuddered, forced out a scream between his teeth. Pink water and clots of blood and dust ran from the wound into the towels on the floor. She moved the stream methodically through the wound, following the tears in his skin. Isaac's back arched and he quivered against the touch. His sweat ran into his eyes. He whimpered.

Gray held him tighter, whispering soothingly, "It's okay, Isaac. You're doing so well. She's almost done. Good job."

Tori put the syringe away. The tension in Isaac's body ran out of him and he slumped against the ground. "That part's done." Her hand moved through his hair. "You took that like a champ. Good job." She reached for her suture kit. "Last part for this one. I just need to stitch you back up."

Finn watched her as her fingers moved expertly along Isaac's skin, drawing the wounds closed. "Where did you learn this?"

Tori glanced at Finn with a small smile. "You pick up a few things when you run a safehouse. I must admit, I'm a little out of practice."

Finn looked down at their hands. "You're really good at it. I can't…" They looked at her with tears in their eyes. "I'm really grateful we're here. Thank you… for…" They gestured vaguely to their family.

"Oh, hush." She shook her head. "You'd be doing this for him if your hands weren't messed up."

Finn's eyes filled with tears. "I can't help them."

"Finn, stop." Finn started at her stern tone. Tori stopped her work to look up at them. "Don't do that. They don't need it, and neither do you. You were *tortured*. It wasn't an accident. Gavin knew exactly how to break you." She pulled the needle away from the wound. "But you're not broken. If you'd fallen and broken both your arms by accident, no one would be blaming you. And no one's blaming you now. Okay?" She nudged their chin up with the back of her hand, avoiding touching their face with the blood still on her fingers. She glanced around the room at their family. "Your family loves you. I can tell that just from watching you all for a few minutes."

Finn glanced at Ellis, who still had their hands on Isaac's legs. Ellis's eyes were fixed on Finn with a look of fierce devotion. Ellis nodded.

Tori turned back to Isaac's wound. "So don't blame yourself. You don't have to be useful to be worthy."

Finn's eyes filled with tears and they crumpled, pressing their face into their arms. Vera stood up shakily from her mattress. She sat down beside them and pulled them into her embrace. They threw their arms around her and sobbed. Her fingers carded through their hair as she pressed her cheek to the top of their head.

Tori clipped the ends of the last stitch. "There. Done. I'll get some antibiotic ointment on that after I finish the rest of your stitches. Then don't get it wet for a while, okay? Let's get you up."

Gray helped Isaac sit up. They winced as their hands pressed into his wounds. Ellis went to Finn's side and put their arms around Finn, pressing kisses against their shoulder.

Sam shuddered at the sight of Isaac's back. Dozens of angry lashes overlaid deep purple and black bruises. Tori's gaze moved over Isaac and he thought he saw the slightest hint of overwhelm in her expression, the corners of her mouth drawn down. Isaac felt like disappearing into the floor. The marks of Gavin's torture were written on his body for all to see. The bruises from the beatings, the cuts that littered his chest, the marks from the whip crossing his back. The burns down his arms. The dried blood that stained everything else. He'd begged everyone to stay away while Tori treated him, and they had all refused. *"You did this for me, Isaac,"* Sam had whispered. *"I'm not leaving you."*

Tori sighed. "Okay. Let's do the graze on your arm next."

"Do you have to clean it?" Isaac's head swam.

She lifted an eyebrow at him. "Do you want gangrene?"

He closed his eyes. "No."

"Then I have to clean it. Let's get that arm out of that sling."

Isaac moaned softly as Gray untied the sling and let his arm lower slowly onto his lap. She moved his arm gently, turning it so she had a better angle. She peeled the gauze away and pulled in a breath through her teeth. "Definitely sutureable. Don't know what we're going to do about these burns, though…" Her gaze moved up and down the length of Isaac's arms to the burns that covered them. "They've already started to scab up. I won't risk debriding them to get them clean. I'll just have to watch them closely, make sure they don't get infected."

"I… thought… we wouldn't be staying here that long." Isaac tried to take deep breaths. He looked away as she drew more water into the syringe.

She adjusted her grip on his arm. "I said you could stay until you're well enough to travel. And you won't be in shape to move for a long time." She gripped his arm tighter. "Don't pull back, okay?"

Isaac grunted as the water cleaned the wound. He was dizzy from pain and the medication. He was grateful for it, but he almost wished he hadn't taken it. It gave everything a sleepy, disconnected quality that reminded him of his dreams in the basement. *I don't want to wake up from this one. Even though it hurts.*

Tori finished cleaning the graze and prepared to suture it. Isaac felt like his skull was full of cotton. He swayed. "Um…" His mouth felt numb.

Tori looked up at him, holding a steadying hand against his shoulder. "Need to lie down again?"

He nodded weakly. She and Gray eased him back down to the floor onto the towels. He whimpered as the rough towels scratched against his back.

The corners of her mouth turned down. "We can't get you laying down without touching something that hurts, huh?"

Isaac swallowed hard against the tears. "Um. No."

She shook her head and went back to work. She was quiet for a few moments. "So what did you do to piss off the syndicates, anyway? I haven't seen someone this bad off in a while."

"My fault," Isaac whispered.

"It's not—" Sam protested.

"My fault." Isaac squeezed his eyes shut as Tori pulled the last stitch tight. She moved on to the tear on his hand.

"Hm. Anyone else want to weigh in?" She gently irrigated the torn skin.

Sam's voice shook as they spoke. "He sacrificed himself for me." Isaac opened his eyes to look at Sam. Tori's hands paused as she followed his gaze. Her eyes moved back to Isaac. Thinking.

"What brought that about?"

Isaac swallowed hard. "I—"

"Gavin took me," Sam spoke over Isaac. "We've been running small raids against him for a few months and I wanted to come along. I got separated from them and... Gavin took me." They swallowed hard.

Isaac squeezed his eyes shut. "It was my f-fault—"

"Shh." Isaac opened his eyes and saw Tori glaring down at him. "Let them talk."

Sam continued, "Gavin took me and... tortured me for a few days. Everybody tracked him down and... found me." They licked their lips. "Gavin made me swallow a tracking device while I was with him and he tracked us all back to our safehouse. He told Isaac to send me back to him. Isaac went in my place."

Tori watched Isaac carefully as she closed the tear. "Hm."

"We kidnapped Gavin's cousin to exchange him for Isaac. But when we showed up, Gavin took us all. He tortured Ellis, Finn, V-Vera..." Vera cast a furious glare at them. "Um... then he... um... t-took me and Isaac to another room and said he'd kill Isaac if he didn't hurt me."

Tori's eyebrows shot up. "Oh." She pulled the last stitch closed. Keeping her voice as casual as possible she asked, "Did he?"

"No! No, he wouldn't! But then Gavin said he'd kill *me* if Isaac didn't torture me. That's when he tore his hand, getting out of the ropes. He knocked Gavin out..." Tori's eyes flicked to Isaac's right hand. "I broke my leg in the explosion and that's when Isaac's shoulder got hurt."

"Right. Explosion. Anyone want to explain that one?"

Vera swallowed hard. "That was me."

A smile flashed across Tori's face, so fast Isaac thought he had imagined it. "Hm."

"When one of Gavin's men grabbed me, I got the keys out of his pocket. Once Gavin left there was only one of them in the room, so I unlocked my cuffs, s-subdued him, and got everyone else out of theirs." Sam stared at her with wide eyes. "When the other one came back, we… subdued him too. I had everybody make a run for the doors while I made a quick… um… bomb."

Tori turned around to face Vera, her eyebrows raised. "You made a *what*?" The corners of her mouth turned upward, just a little.

"I made… a bomb. Gavin had a lot of explosives lying around and the detonator wasn't that hard to jury rig. I knew we didn't have a chance of getting to Isaac and Sam without a distraction. But once the bomb went off all I could find was Gavin." Sam gasped. She threw them a regretful look. "I didn't kill him. I assumed he was dead, given how his face looked. The building was burning. I didn't stick around to check. I figured you somehow got free, so I went outside to join the others. That's when we found you."

"Where did you learn to make bombs?"

"I picked it up…"

"That seems to be a pretty specific skill. Seriously, where did you learn—"

"I *don't want to talk about me.*"

The room went silent. Vera looked down. "I'm sorry. I didn't mean…" She glanced at Finn. "Let me get you more ice." She stood and stalked out of the room. Tori watched her go, pensive.

"I'm sorry," Gray mumbled. "She's not—"

"She's fine." She looked down at Isaac. "When's the last time you had a shower?"

He shrugged weakly, wincing when it jostled his shoulder. "Um… A week or two?"

"Well, I think you'll feel a lot better once I get you cleaned up. I'll help you wash the blood off with a rag and get you some clean clothes. Sound like a plan?"

Isaac's eyes closed. "Sounds good."

A crash came from the kitchen.

∴

In the kitchen, Vera clumsily tried to get to her feet, her hand gripping the counter. Ice cubes littered the floor. Gray and Tori rushed into the kitchen, Ellis close on their heels. "I'm *fine*," Vera snapped, before anyone could touch her.

"You're clearly not." Tori's voice was clipped. "Let me help you up." Tori reached for Vera's arm.

Vera jerked her arm away from Tori's hand and she stared Tori down as she got to her feet. Vera stood three inches taller than Tori as she drew herself up to her full height, seeming to unfold like a cobra's hood. "I said I'm *fine*." Her lips pulled back over her teeth as she bared them at Tori.

Tori held Vera's gaze steadily. "Everybody else go back to the guest room. I want to talk to Vera alone."

Vera's nostrils flared as she watched the rest of them warily back out of the kitchen. Her eyes snapped back to Tori and bored into her.

Tori lowered her voice. "I know something happened to you. I know it got activated and you're coming down off it. But that doesn't mean you can push away your friends like this."

Vera seethed with rage. "You don't have *any fucking clue* what happened to me."

"I know, and neither does your family. Until today they had no idea one of their own had suffered so terribly."

That made Vera pause. Tori watched her carefully, like she was a wild animal about to bolt.

"Why are you looking at me like that?" Vera snapped.

"Because you're not the first person I've met who's been like this. You're showing a lot of symptoms of PTSD."

"So I have PTSD. So what? I can't fix it. I can't go back and undo it."

"You don't have to. But don't you think you'd recover a little easier if you could be honest with your family?"

190

Vera spat her words through her teeth. *"There. Is. No. Fucking. Recovery. From. This.* Gavin *slapped* me and I went right back. That's all it took to take me right back... to..." She felt a roil of nausea well up inside her and gripped the counter, her body coiling tightly.

All the while Tori watched patiently. "Someone kept you captive."

Vera's eyes flashed, dark and dangerous in a way that made her look... *feral.* For a brief moment, Vera was so overwhelmed with rage she nearly lunged forward to attack Tori.

A memory gripped Vera's mind. *Be good for me, Vera.*

Vera sank to the floor and hugged her knees to her chest, taking painful, gasping sobs. Tori knelt by her side and pulled her into her arms.

Vera didn't return the embrace, but she didn't pull away, either. She sobbed hard and deep, pressing her hands tightly to her mouth to stifle the sound. Tori pulled her fingers through Vera's hair and rocked her slowly.

"Hey, girl. I got you. You're okay, you're safe now."

"They wouldn't trust me if they knew."

"Hey. You're alright."

"They'd always wonder if I'd fall back in."

"Shh."

"They'd look at me different, knowing what happened, knowing what he *did...*" The last word was a scream. Vera shook apart in Tori's arms, gasping, gagging with the force of her body heaving against the pain. She clutched at Tori, nails digging into her arms, face pressed against her shirt as Tori gently rocked her, smoothing her hair back.

"You've been carrying this for a long time."

"Fourteen *fucking* years, and I can't ever get away from it, fourteen years and he's still there, in my head, everything he did, he turned me into that *thing* that follows commands and never screams until he lets me and wears that... *FUCKING...*" She clawed at her throat, at the ghostly pressure of the collar.

191

She choked helplessly, dragging in breath after breath and there still wasn't enough air in the room.

"Okay. Come back. That's enough, you felt it, let's come back out now."

Vera clutched Tori's hand as she shuddered, sobbing, trying to catch her breath again. "I... I can't..."

"Yes, you can. I don't want to lose you in that place. Come back here, now, where I am."

"N-no I—"

"*Vera.* Come back. I know you can do this. Come back to me, *right now.*"

Vera took a shuddering, desperate inhale and blew it out through pursed lips. "Okay," she panted. "I can... okay."

"That's right. Good job. Oh. Um... Are there things I shouldn't say?"

Vera shakily shook her head. "Nothing that would come up in normal conversation." Her lips twisted wryly as she forced out another breath.

"Hm. If anything comes to mind you *tell me*, okay?"

"Mm-hm."

Tori took Vera's chin in her hand and gently guided her face up until Vera looked her in the eye. "I'm serious. With the severity of Isaac's injuries, you all are going to be here awhile. Long enough that I could stumble on something. I need to know that I won't send you right back there while you're healing, okay?"

Vera nodded. "Okay. I will."

"Good." Tori gave her a quick hug. "Now. You didn't fall because you got upset, did you?" Vera grudgingly shook her head. "Okay. Why did you fall?"

"I... got dizzy."

"Hm. How close were you to the blast, exactly?"

"Um… Close enough that I got thrown. I didn't really hit anything but… it made me dizzy for a second. I assumed I was fine."

"Concussions can show up hours later. That's probably what you have going on. How do you feel right now?"

"Fine."

"Dizzy at all?"

"No."

"Okay." Tori nodded. "I hesitate to leave you alone, but if you feel alright, I'll leave you to pull yourself together. Throw some water on your face. I'll handle the ice for Finn. When you're ready, join us in the guest room. I won't tell them anything about what we talked about. That'll be on you, when you're ready. Okay?"

Vera nodded. "Thank you, Tori."

"Oh." Tori squeezed her hand and drew herself to her feet. "Don't worry about it." She turned to get a bag for the ice.

Chapter 35

Isaac woke to a knock at the door. He stirred, confused. Was Tori expecting anyone else? *He sat up painfully from his bed. His family slept peacefully around him, unbothered by the knock.* I guess I should go answer.

He made his way to the door, swaying unsteadily. As his hand closed around the doorknob he felt a chill down his spine like someone was watching him. He turned to look back into the house. The rooms were all dark. Nothing moved. He shrugged and pulled the door open.

Gavin stood in the doorway with a grin on his face. He raised a gun and fired. The bullet punched through Isaac's shoulder. The pain took his breath away as he stumbled back, his hand pressed to the wound as blood poured hot through his fingers. Gavin pushed him back into the house.

"Where are the others?"

Isaac stumbled, his mind reeling. "They're not here," he gasped.

"Oh, so you drove here on your own? Don't insult me, Isaac. Tell me where they are, and I might not shoot you right here." Gavin stalked down the hall toward the room where Isaac knew they were all sleeping.

"No." Isaac lurched after him, hand still pressed against his shoulder. The blood loss was making him dizzy. "Gavin, don't—"

Gavin walked through the doorway to the guestroom and looked around at Isaac's sleeping family. He smiled. "All accounted for. Perfect." He approached Vera, who was curled like a cat under the blankets. Gavin pointed his gun at her head and fired. Blood poured from the hole in her skull.

"NO!" Isaac screamed. No one stirred. He tried to take a step towards Gavin, but he felt his wrists pull against rope, tying them together behind him and holding him back.

Gavin moved to Finn and Ellis. Finn was snuggled in Ellis's arms. Two more bullets tore through their skulls.

"Gavin, no!" Isaac screamed. "Gavin no, please, no…" Tears burned his face as he pulled hard against the rope. It twisted his injured shoulder and he cried out.

Gavin finally moved to the mattress where Gray and Sam were sleeping peacefully. He didn't hesitate before putting a bullet in Gray's head. Isaac begged in incoherent sobs, falling to his knees as Gavin put the gun to Sam's head. He threw a venomous grin back at Isaac as he pulled the trigger.

Isaac dissolved into a whimpering howl as he pressed his forehead against the floor. It was wet with his family's blood. He heard Gavin's footsteps approaching. He lifted his head, a mumbled plea on his numb lips. Merciful for the first time since Isaac had heard his name, Gavin pressed the barrel of the gun against his head. Isaac squeezed his eyes shut so he wouldn't have to see his family's bodies as Gavin pulled the trigger.

"Isaac!"

Isaac drew in a painful, rattling gasp. He lurched forward and shuddered as his shoulder protested. He was soaked in a cold sweat and shivering as wracking sobs tore through him one right after the other.

"Isaac, shh…" He felt a finger on his lips. His eyes focused and Tori's face swam above his in the dark.

He pushed himself up off the mattress and cast his eyes around the room, which was dimly lit from the light of the hall. His gaze moved from Ellis and Finn, to Vera, to Sam and Gray. All alive. All breathing. The floor was clean of blood.

He fell back against the bed. He pressed his lips together and tried to quiet his sobs as Tori gently stroked his hair. "There you go. Shh. Everybody's still sleeping. Don't worry about them."

"Tori…"

"Yeah, it's just me. You were having a nightmare. I came in to check on you."

"You…?"

"Yeah. It's almost five. I wanted to get a few hours of sleep before morning."

"Oh. I'm sorry, you can…" He swallowed. "I don't want to keep you up."

"Well, I'm up now." She moved from where she was kneeling over him to sit down on the mattress beside him. "Let's talk about that dream."

Isaac shuddered and closed his eyes for a moment. "I don't want to talk about it."

Tori rolled her eyes. "I'm hearing that a lot from your family tonight. Come on. I want to let them sleep and I'm worried you'll fall back in and have another nightmare if I just leave. They don't have to hear about it. But you need to get it out." She raised her eyebrows at him, and he had a feeling she wasn't talking about just the nightmare.

"Um..." He swallowed hard. "I dreamed that Gavin came here and... killed them all."

She nodded slowly. "Oh."

"He made me watch. Then he killed me."

Her hand went back to smoothing his hair. "Okay."

Tears leaked out the corners of his eyes. "I went to Gavin to keep them safe and they still ended up getting hurt. Because of me. Because I couldn't..." He bit his lip.

"Because you couldn't what?"

Isaac set his jaw. "Gavin sent them a live video of him torturing me. He said he'd stop if I begged them to come for me."

Tori's voice became exceedingly gentle. "Did you beg for them?"

Shame settled in his stomach, cold and bitter. "Yes."

"...and you think that makes what happened to them your fault?"

His throat tightened around a sob. "Yes."

"Hm. Tell me, did he send this video before or after they called with the trade?"

"Um." He swallowed the lump in his throat. "After."

"So they were already planning on coming for you?"

196

"I… I guess they were."

"Isaac." Her hand moved through his hair. "Your family loves you. They'd do anything for you. Whether you begged or not, whether you broke or not, they were coming for you. What happened to them is not your fault. You need to stop carrying that around with you."

"I couldn't protect them." His throat pulled tight as he whispered. "That's my job and I couldn't… keep them safe…"

"Shh, Isaac."

"I just laid there and watched as Gavin pulled them into the middle of the room and tortured them one by one…"

"Isaac, stop."

"I listened to them scream and I didn't do a *damned thing* about it…"

"Isaac." His eyes focused on her as she stared him down. *"Stop it.* Sam would likely be dead right now if not for you. Finn told me how badly off they were. How close they were to dying. You…" Her hand found his uninjured one and squeezed gently. "You did an incredibly brave thing, Isaac. You willingly handed yourself over for torture and pain for your family, tried to give your life for them. Yes, Gavin took them when they were trying to get you back. But that isn't on *you.* That's on *him.* Do you see that? You didn't hurt them. He did. Then when he was going to *kill* Sam you found a way to stop him." She lightly jabbed against his chest over his shirt. *"You did that."* He whimpered at the pressure on the cut over his sternum. Tori pulled her finger away with an apologetic glance. He pressed his lips together and tried to force the sound down. "Oh, shit, I'm sorry. I honestly can't keep track of everywhere you're hurt." Her hand moved back to his hair. "Can you tell me about it now?"

He bit his lip and tears welled in his eyes. He closed them. Two tears ran down the sides of his face.

"Um. He s-started by whipping me. He chained me up and whipped me until I begged him not to. Then h-he…" He took a steadying breath as his lips trembled. "While Sam was with him, he made them tell him all our fears and I'm… afraid of drowning. He drowned me in a bucket. He forced my head under. But he…" He licked his lips. "He messed with my head, too. He got inside… told me he knew who I really was, why I was there…" He turned his head away.

"Okay. Why were you really there?" Tori's voice was soft, gentle.

Isaac's voice was raspy, a shameful whisper. "Because it's the only way I know to make my family love me."

Tori's hand froze and she bit the inside of her cheek. "Hm." Her hand began to move again. "What else?"

"He…" He squeezed his eyes shut. "He tied me down and attached this… he said it was like a taser, but more painful. It…" The memory of it left him breathless for a moment. The tears started pouring steadily down his face. "It was the worst pain." Tori's eyes were warm. Her eyebrows pulled together in concern. "Then h-he… tied me down again and cut me. That's what these are from." He glanced down at his chest. "He blindfolded me, told me he was going to kill me if I didn't tell him more about them. I refused so he asked me questions about me. He m-made me tell him about… everything. My past, what I'm ashamed of… It's like he knew exactly what to say to make me hurt. Then he handcuffed me to the floor and whipped me again."

Tori drew a breath in through her teeth. "I was wondering. The marks looked like they were from different beatings."

Isaac nodded, sniffling. "Then he… got right back in my head again. Asked me about Sam. Why I love them so much." He looked over at them in the dark, curled up next to Gray, a pillow under their broken leg.

Tori's eyes bored into Isaac. "I can tell you love them." She looked over at Sam, a small smile on her lips. "And I know they love you. They love you more than anything."

Isaac smiled and two more tears ran into his hair.

"Is that when your family got to you?"

He laughed once, wryly. "No. That's when he really got started. While he was sending the video, he waterboarded me and whipped me again." Tori shook her head slowly. "He burned me with his knife on my arms. He drowned me again."

"He did all of this with your family watching?"

Isaac nodded slowly, lips trembling. "I never... I never wanted them to see it..."

"Of course not. Of course." Tori smoothed Isaac's hair away from his face. "Did he torture you once they got there?"

"He bound and gagged me and beat me while they watched."

Tori closed her eyes. "Jesus."

Isaac squirmed uncomfortably. She looked away for a moment. "Thank you for telling me. I don't think I have to worry too much about any injuries that haven't already been treated." She looked around at the sleeping forms of the others. "Why don't you want them hearing about this?"

Isaac shook his head. "They don't need to. I can't stand to have them look at me and know... that I was weak."

Tori snorted. "*Weak?* Do you hear yourself? Did you hear the long list of indescribable torture you just told me Gavin put you through?"

He swallowed. "I broke. More than once. I went to Gavin because I thought I could be strong. Strong for them. I don't want them hearing what he did to me and... knowing I couldn't take it."

Tori leaned over Isaac, cupping his face gently. "Isaac. Sweetheart. Believe me when I tell you this, please. You going to Gavin, taking the torture you did, pulling Sam out of that burning building despite all the injuries you had... That was all an incredible act of love. But they loved you before you sacrificed so much for them. Do you know that? Do you know how much they've always loved you?"

Isaac's lip quivered and a sob ripped from his throat. He rolled to his side, turning his face into the mattress.

"Hey," she soothed. She leaned over him and covered him gently with her body, avoiding all his injuries as best she could, and held him. He sobbed as she cradled the back of his head. He muffled his gasps against her shoulder as waves of pain and terror moved through him and back out. "You're safe now," she whispered. He trembled weakly, too wracked by pain to pull her close.

His sobs grew quieter as his energy began to run out. She pulled a clean tissue from a pocket and offered it to him. "I have a feeling I'll be running out of these soon, with everything you all have been through." He whimpered softly as she leaned back and smoothed his hair again. "I'll tell you something I already told another one of your friends tonight," she whispered. "Recovery is a lot easier when you trust the people who would do anything to help you."

He sniffled. She looked him over for a moment and nodded once. "They love you, Isaac. They risked everything for you, just like you did for them. Personally, I hope you tell them. I think they should know. But it's up to you." She pushed herself to her feet. "If you're doing alright, I'm going to head back to bed. I'll try to be up in a few hours to help with breakfast."

Isaac looked up at her. "Thank you, Tori. I'm sorry I woke you."

She shrugged. "When Gray called, I knew you would all need a lot of help. Please don't apologize. I would have turned you away if I couldn't give it."

"Well… thank you."

She smiled. "You're welcome." She turned and left the room, turning off the hallway light on her way back to her bed.

Isaac settled back into the blankets. Across the room, Sam closed their eyes, tears moving slowly down their cheeks.

Chapter 36

Ellis blinked awake. They could smell something, something like cedar musk and shampoo and something else. They rolled to one side and reached a hand out for their husband. He smelled so *good*. Their fingers brushed warm skin, soft clothing. They smiled gently and cuddled closer to his warmth.

"Hey."

They gasped. Their eyes focused on the face lying on the pillow next to them, at the hazel eyes and dark hair, the bruise staining their left temple and cheek. *Finn*. Ellis swallowed the tears that burned their throat as their stomach clenched. They tried their best to smile as the wisps of their husband disappeared into their mind.

"Good morning." Ellis reached out and gently touched the bruise on Finn's face. "How do you feel?"

"Ugh. Groggy." Finn tried to push themselves up off the bed and collapsed in a yelp of pain.

"Hey, hey." Ellis grabbed Finn's wrists and pulled their hands off the mattress. "Careful." Finn's left hand was swollen, bruised from their wrist to their knuckles. The right wasn't so bad off: bruised, but not as swollen. Ellis helped Finn sit up as they cradled their hands in their lap.

"Look who's finally awake." Sam's face was pale and drawn with pain, but a playful smile tugged at the corner of their mouth. *It's so good to see them like that again.*

Sunlight streamed in through the window, illuminating the walls and the mattresses on the floor. Sam sat up on their bed, their busted leg on a pillow. They leaned back against their hands as they looked at Ellis. Isaac lay on his side, eyes half closed.

Ellis's eyebrows pulled together in concern as they got up from their mattress to make their way to Isaac. "Isaac? Are you...?"

"I'm okay," he gasped out. He squeezed his eyes shut. "It just… hurts. Just trying not to move."

Sam's face crumpled. "I asked Tori if he could have more pain medicine, but she said he can't have any more for another two hours."

Ellis's hand rested gently on Isaac's forehead. Isaac's face softened, and he pushed his head weakly into the touch. "I'm so sorry," Ellis whispered. Isaac shook his head.

"Where are Gray and Vera? And Tori?" Finn's words were still the slightest bit slurred. Ellis's chest tightened with worry.

Sam lifted their chin in the direction of the door. "They're in the kitchen. Making breakfast."

Ellis's stomach growled. "Oh." They licked their lips. *When's the last time we all ate a proper meal?* "What's for breakfast?"

"I'm not sure. I thought I heard something about eggs."

"Hm. I'll go check. Stay here, invalids." Ellis winced as the word left their mouth. "I'm sorry. I didn't mean…" Their cheeks flushed. They ducked their head and left the room.

The kitchen was a happy mess. Bowls of batter and ingredients littered the countertops. There was a massive frying pan on the stove cooking eight eggs, and a countertop griddle frying pancakes. Gray was flipping pancakes with a look of intense concentration. Tori poked the eggs with the spatula. Vera stood awkwardly in the corner. Her arms were crossed firmly over her chest as she watched the two with wary eyes. Her head snapped to Ellis as they walked in.

"Wow." Ellis's mouth watered at the sight of the breakfast. "Need any help?"

"I asked the same thing." Vera's voice was strained. "Apparently 'there isn't much left to do, and I can just relax.'"

Tori pursed her lips as she threw an amused glance in Vera's direction. "I was going to say exactly what she said." She turned to Ellis. "You hungry?"

Ellis nodded, licking their lips. Their eyes followed Gray's spatula as they scooped a pile of the pancakes off the griddle and onto a plate warming in the oven. There was a pile of pancakes already on the plate, ready to topple.

"Well, we're almost done. I hope you like eggs and pancakes. I wasn't sure what everyone could or couldn't eat, but I figured this would be an alright bet."

Gray smiled softly. "It's perfect. Thank you, Tori."

Vera ducked her head, her eyes still fixed on the floor.

Tori nodded once. "Then it's time for more help. Ellis, if you could ask the others what they want? I figured we could all eat in the guest room together. Vera, could you grab some plates? Second cabinet from the bottom, to the right of the stove."

Ellis turned and walked back into the room. Finn and Sam eagerly turned to face them. "Eggs and pancakes. How many of each?"

Finn's eyes widened. "Three pancakes, four eggs."

Ellis looked at Sam. They licked their lips. "Two pancakes, two eggs."

Ellis looked at Isaac. He trembled and curled in on himself. "I... I don't think I could eat anything."

The corners of Ellis's mouth turned down. They knelt in front of him. "Isaac... you have to eat something." Their fingers brushed awkwardly through his hair, still stained with blood and sweat but cleaner than yesterday.

Isaac's eyes closed. "I just..." They opened again and he bit his lip. "I'm sorry. It just hurts. I feel sick and so tired and it just... hurts..." A soft whimper rose from his throat.

Ellis pulled their fingers through his hair. "I'll bring you one pancake. You need to keep your strength up, Isaac. You won't heal if you don't eat." Ellis's stomach clenched with worry.

Isaac nodded weakly. "I'll try to eat."

Ellis lingered for a moment at Isaac's side. They sighed and stood, walking back to the kitchen.

"Well?" Tori took the plate of pancakes out of the oven and pulled the mitts off her hands.

"Three pancakes four eggs for Finn, two pancakes two eggs for Sam, one pancake for Isaac."

Tori's face darkened. "…okay." She grabbed one plate from the counter and began loading it with food. She passed it back to Ellis. "For Finn." She loaded up another plate and passed it back. "For Sam. How much do you want?"

"Um… Three eggs, two pancakes."

"Great. Get that to them. I'll bring yours." She deposited a handful of silverware on one of the plates. Ellis went back to the guest room with a plate full of food balanced on each hand.

"Here." They set the plates down in front of Sam and Finn.

Sam dug into theirs ravenously, bringing the plate close to their mouth so they could shovel in the food. Finn stared plaintively at the plate as Ellis sat down beside them.

"Don't worry," Ellis whispered, doing their best to sound playful. "I'll feed you."

Finn raised their eyes to Ellis, tears threatening to fall. "Thank you."

"No problem." They cut a generous bite of pancakes and held the fork to Finn's mouth. Finn took it gratefully, eyes closing as they chewed. It didn't seem to matter that there was no syrup.

Tori walked into the room with her plate and Ellis's. Vera carried her own. Gray carried theirs and Isaac's. Tori placed Ellis's plate in front of them. They looked up and smiled in thanks. Tori sat cross-legged on a mattress and looked around the room. Gray sat down next to Isaac, placing both plates on the floor and pressing their hand gently to one of the few unbroken patches of skin on Isaac's shoulder. Isaac opened his eyes, barely holding back a whimper.

Vera paused and her gaze moved around the room, flicking to each member of her family one by one. A strange look crossed her face before she crossed to Tori's mattress and sat. Tori's face remained carefully neutral.

The room was filled with the sound of clinking silverware. Gray carefully cut small pieces of pancake for Isaac, coaxing them into his mouth. Isaac obediently ate and shivered where he lay.

Tori jumped slightly. "Oh. Water. Is anyone thirsty?"

An emphatic chorus of yeses went up.

"Okay. Let me get some."

"I'll help." Ellis scrambled to their feet.

Tori held out a hand. "It's okay. You're helping Finn."

Vera hesitated for a moment and watched Tori leave the room before getting up and stalking out to follow her. Gray watched her go before turning back to Isaac with another bite on the fork.

"You need to eat, too," Isaac protested weakly.

"Isaac, don't worry about me. I'm fine. Just… focus on you."

"I don't want to," he whispered. "It hurts."

Gray sagged. Their hand moved to Isaac's hair and stroked softly through. Isaac sighed and tears rolled into the pillow.

"This is the only place we can touch you that doesn't hurt, huh?"

Isaac shuddered. "My legs aren't too bad."

Gray's mouth twisted bitterly. They cut a bite for themselves before offering Isaac another bite.

Vera and Tori walked into the room with a pitcher of water and seven cups between them. They poured the water and passed it around the room. The cups were empty in minutes. Tori got up to fill the pitcher again, and again it was drained. Gray helped Isaac lift his head and gently eased the cup against Isaac's chapped lips.

Sam sat back contentedly, sated. They wiped their mouth with their hand.

Tori smiled. "Done?" Sam nodded. "Anybody going to want seconds?"

Finn devoured every bite Ellis offered, barely pausing to draw breath as Ellis alternated between feeding Finn and eating their own breakfast. Their two plates were almost empty.

Gray's plate remained nearly untouched as they tried to coax Isaac to eat. He was taking his bites slower, head drooping to the mattress, curling in on himself and shuddering. Gray cast a worried glance at Tori and she put her plate down to kneel beside Isaac.

"What is it? You look like you're getting worse." Her hand rested gently on his cheek. Ellis watched as her hand lingered, like she couldn't tell if his skin felt warmer than it should.

His eyes fell closed and he whimpered. "…h-hurts, Tori, please… it hurts…"

"What hurts, honey?"

He moaned. "My… sh-shoulder and… my hand… my head hurts… please…"

"Does anything hurt more than yesterday?"

"Y-yes… no… I don't know…" He tucked his head against the pillow.

Suddenly the room was stifling and claustrophobic, filled with Isaac's pain. Ellis's stomach dropped as they realized Isaac had been hiding how badly he was hurt. They looked around and saw identical expressions of concern on everyone's face.

"Please, Tori," Isaac moaned. "Please… I need…" He whimpered. "It hurts…"

Gray leaned over Isaac. Vera knelt beside Tori on Isaac's mattress. Tori's hand went to Isaac's leg and she squeezed, moving her thumb in soothing circles.

"I can't give you any more pain medication for another hour. I don't want to make you sicker. What I'm giving you has Tylenol in it and I can't double up."

A small sob escaped Isaac's lips as tears leaked from his eyes into the pillow. "No…" He pressed his trembling lips together.

"I'm so sorry, Isaac. I'm gonna do everything I can to make it stop hurting but… it's going to hurt." Tori looked around. There were tears on everyone's cheeks. "Ellis," she said evenly, "let's get more ice. That should help with the shoulder and hand. I've got some anesthetic ointment I can put on the burns and lash marks." She turned back to Isaac. "There isn't much I can do for your ribs except bind them and hope that support helps. Can you hold on for me while we do those things? Try to get you through until your next pill?"

Isaac nodded and he started to sob weakly. Gray's hand pulled into a fist. Their other hand stroked through his hair.

Every sound of agony Isaac made was like a knife to Ellis's heart. They looked around and could see on everyone's faces that they all felt it, too.

Chapter 37

Vera only had to take one painful breath to know where she was. The collar squeezed cruelly on her throat, tighter than usual. Every movement made her muscles clench with panic that her air would be taken away. If he wants my air, he'll get it.

She was able to choke out a despairing sob as she sank to the floor. Chains clanked from the cuffs around her wrists. She pressed her forehead against the rough, cold concrete of the floor. It's been a long time. *She could already feel the weight in her limbs, the pull of submission, the burn of humiliation as she imagined what would be coming next.* It doesn't matter what comes next. He'll do it, and I'll take it.

She should have known she'd always end up right back here. Maybe I never left at all. Maybe all that time – fourteen years – was something I imagined. Something I made up to escape this place. *She closed her eyes.* There is no escape from this place. He made me remember that.

The door opened. She rolled to her knees, pushing herself up until her hands rested in her lap. He likes me like this, *she remembered.* He likes it when I'm ready for him.

She blinked in confusion as someone shorter than the man she was expecting walked through the door. Their curls were ringed with light from the hallway. Behind them, a much bigger presence, then two more, then another. Something twinged in the back of her mind. I should know who these people are. *She couldn't remember anything. Nothing but this room, and what happened to her in it. There was nothing else. There had never been anything else.*

"Vera." That voice. Soft, kind. Familiar. What could be so familiar about kindness? *In spite of herself, she shook her head.*

A soft hand touched her cheek. She stiffened, gasped, and held herself still. He doesn't like it when I pull away. He just hurts me more. *But the hand was so warm. So warm in this cold cell, where the only thing she ever felt that wasn't cold was when her own blood ran hot down her skin. She shivered.*

"Where have you been?" Another voice, closer to her. Deep and steady. I've never been gone.

"We came here for you. We came here for the Vera we knew. But… we never really knew you, did we? We didn't know you were…" She felt the ghost of a hand motioning down her body. "…this."

She shuddered. She wasn't enough. She had made a mistake. She must have screamed, or pulled away, or maybe he could read her mind now and knew that she had wished for something else. Death would have been enough.

"We can't take you with us." Another voice. "We can't risk it. If this is what you really are…" A rustle in the dark as the person shook their head.

A hand found its way under her chin and lifted her head. She could just make out the silhouette of someone she swore she knew, someone as close to her as family. Her sister? No. Her sister was dead. She remembered that, at least. She tried to make her eyes focus in the dark, focus on the owner of the hand that was cupping her face so gently.

"We're going to leave you here," the voice said. "This is where you belong. This is where you'll die."

She nodded. She understood. She knew her death was inevitable. She couldn't be released. Not when she could tell someone who her captor was. Not that it mattered. She was broken. What would be the point? She lowered her head again, waiting patiently. How were they going to do it? She braced for the shot, the cut, the blow.

It didn't come. One by one the people left the room and closed the door firmly behind them. Leaving her for dead.

Her heart leapt in her chest in sudden realization. She knew them! She remembered! Her team, her family! They came for her!

She screamed, her throat straining against the collar that usually rendered her silent with the threat it carried alone. She screamed for them to come back, to save her, to take her away from this place and the man who loved hurting her so much. She screamed until she felt like her throat would tear open. She screamed until her voice was gone.

She sat up with a gasp. Her hands went to her throat immediately, reaching for a collar that wasn't there. *It hasn't been there in fourteen years. It will never be there again.* Her lungs burned as she caught her breath. The soft clothes Tori had given her clung to her skin, damp with sweat. She rolled to her side and threw the covers off. She padded to the kitchen.

After four days of being in Tori's house, Vera knew her way around in the dark. She walked down the hall with her hands in front of her. Her bare feet were cold on the wood floor. It was nothing compared to the cold of the cell.

This nightmare had been different from the others. For the past three nights, the nightmares had been familiar, different versions of the same old dream she'd been having ever since she escaped: she was cold, alone, and back in that cell, under the man's knife and whip and fists, under everything he wanted to take to her. And she was silent. Always silent. Near the end she had hardly ever screamed at all, even when he permitted it. She was too gone to fight it. Too gone to do anything but disappear inside her own body and watch what was happening from the ceiling, if she was lucky.

Tonight was the first time it was different. Tonight was the first time she screamed. Tonight was the first time her family had come for her.

She shuddered and shoved the thought away with practiced ferocity. *I'm never going back there.* Then, the thought that always seemed to follow: *I'll die first.*

She reached the doorway to the kitchen and slid her hand along the wall, far enough away from the guest room that she felt safe turning on the light without waking anyone. It blazed on and blinded her for several moments as she squinted. She fumbled her way towards the cabinet where the cups were kept. She pulled one out and filled it in the sink. She took a sip, too distracted to taste the cool nothingness on her tongue. Her mind was still trapped in that cell.

"Couldn't sleep?"

She jumped, nearly dropping the cup. She turned to see Tori walking clumsily into the kitchen, eyes bleary with sleep.

"Um." She cleared her throat. "Yeah."

"Nightmares again?"

"Um." Vera cast her eyes to the floor, wishing it wasn't so painfully obvious. "What do you mean, *again*?"

Tori smiled gently. "My house doesn't have thin walls, but I know every sound that happens in it. You crying in your sleep is one that's… new. And distinctive."

Vera's face flushed, her skin prickling with humiliation. "I'm… not…"

Tori shook her head. "It is what it is, Vera. You can't control what happens when you're asleep. God knows you keep a tight lid on it when you're awake."

Vera flexed her jaw. Her eyes were fixed on a dark knot in the grain of the floor. "You weren't supposed to know."

Tori huffed out an amused breath. "I know. You've made that perfectly clear."

Vera's eyes snapped up to Tori's. Vera's eyebrows pulled together in guilt. A silent apology passed over her face before her eyes dropped to the floor again.

"You were scared." Tori's voice was kind.

"I was more than *scared*," Vera snapped. She shut her mouth, regretting the words as soon as they left her lips. Tori had kept her distance after that first night. Vera knew she was trying to give her space, wasn't trying to force her comfort on her, but she had to wonder if it was more than that. She had to wonder… "Are you scared of me?"

Tori's face betrayed her surprise for a moment before the compassionate distance she showed so often took over. "…scared of you?"

"Scared I'll hurt you."

"You… don't seem like the type, Vera."

"To hurt you?"

"Yes."

She pressed her lips together. "I… I'm not."

211

"I know." Vera swallowed. "Have you told the rest of your family yet? About your nightmares? And what's causing them?"

"I…"

"I'm just curious. I'm not judging. I just… *Help me* understand, Vera. I know you know they love you, would do anything for you. I've been watching you all for days and I've never seen a group of people that loves and trusts each other more. You know you can lean on them. Look at how fiercely they all protect and care for Isaac. So… why is it different with you? Why can't you let them help you?"

"I let you help me…"

Tori snorted. "That was different."

Vera looked down. It *was* different, but she didn't know why. She squeezed her eyes shut. "Because… they'll wonder if they can trust me. They'll wonder if it was real. Who I am, what I've told them."

"What *have* you told them?"

Vera opened her eyes to look down at the floor. "They know I was a cop. They know I left the force. I told them it was because it just didn't work out, because I saw too much… I didn't want them asking questions."

"So what actually happened?"

Vera took a deep breath. "I *was* a cop. Joined when I was eighteen. Back then they were so desperate for bodies they were taking people fresh out of high school. It was what I wanted to do, so I joined up. Spent three years on the streets before I got promoted to detective. It wasn't hard. Turnover was bad enough that you just had to not be a total fuckup and you'd get there eventually. And not get killed." Her mouth twisted wryly. "We didn't know how organized the syndicates were, even then. We thought it was just some sort of heightened criminal activity. I went undercover to infiltrate one of the more notorious groups in the area. I was supposed to collect evidence and build a case to take them down. I was doing alright for a few weeks. Then I got made."

"'Made'?"

"They realized I was a cop. I didn't know it and I walked right into a trap. One of the higher-level members decided he didn't want me killed. Wanted to keep me for himself. So, he had his people set up a usual meeting and... he was waiting for me when I got there. He took me back to his headquarters. Kept me in a cell he had especially for... t-torturing people. I wasn't his first and I doubt I was his last."

"How long do you think you were there?"

"I don't know. I've been trying to figure that out ever since Gavin asked me. I thought it was two months, but now I think it may have been closer to three." Her jaw flexed. "It doesn't matter. It was long enough that he broke me." Her eyes focused again to see Tori watching her. She blinked and looked down, embarrassed. "What?"

"He didn't break you."

Vera's voice cracked like a whip. "You don't fucking know that." She inhaled sharply, ducking her head. "I'm so sorry. I don't mean to keep doing that. I don't mean to—"

"I know." Vera raised her eyes to Tori, wide with gratitude and guilt. "I know you don't. You're unburying this all for the first time in over a decade. It's going to come out... rough... sometimes."

"I don't mean to hurt you," Vera whispered, pressing her hands together. "I don't mean to take it out on you."

"I know that. Hey." Tori crossed slowly to her and pressed her hands against Vera's arms. Despite having three inches on her, Vera felt so small in her hands. "I know you don't mean to hurt me. I know. I want to help you get better, okay? I want to help you recover from this. I want to help you feel safe again."

"Why?" Vera's eyes brimmed with tears. "Why do you want to help me?"

Tori leaned back, biting her lip. "I don't know. I just do. Do I need a reason? Some explanation?"

"No..."

"Do you need an explanation for why you deserve to be helped? Cared for?"

That undid Vera. She slid to her knees, pressing her hands against her face as the tears spilled over.

"Hey, I'm sorry, I didn't…" Tori's hands went to Vera's hair, carding through it, smoothing it down. Vera's arms wrapped around Tori's waist and she ducked her head against Tori's stomach, tears wetting the front of Tori's shirt. Tori's hand went under Vera's chin. Tori guided her head up until she could see Vera's face. "Let's go to the couch, okay?" Vera nodded, taking Tori's hand as she helped her up.

Chapter 38

Tori led Vera gently to the couch and sat down on the far end, giving Vera plenty of room. Vera paused and chewed the inside of her cheek before sitting next to Tori, close enough that the sides of their legs brushed together. Tori shook out the blanket and put it over Vera. Vera pulled it tightly around her and stared straight ahead.

"Can I touch you?"

Vera nodded. Tori's hand went to her back and made gentle circles over the blanket. Vera's eyes closed, and she melted a little into the touch.

"I get the feeling you're usually the one taking care of the others, instead of the other way around."

Vera nodded, pursing her lips. "I like being there for them. I like helping."

"I know." Tori's hand traced lightly across Vera's shoulders. Vera sighed, rolling her neck, letting her hair fall into her face. She trembled at the gentle touch.

"Is this okay?"

Vera nodded. Her eyes fluttered open, but she couldn't raise her gaze to Tori. "Why are you doing this for us?"

Tori took a deep breath in. "Gray and I go way back. Fifteen years, almost."

"Oh. ...how old are you?"

"Thirty-three. I met Gray when I was eighteen at a rally against the syndicates' creep into the government." Tori laughed bitterly. "Back when there was one. We worked together, organizing resistance, doing our best to stop what was happening. They were kind of a... mentor. And a good friend." She pressed her lips together and looked at the floor. "Then things got worse. So much worse. Gray wanted to join an armed resistance movement. I... I didn't."

Vera's eyebrows drew together. "Why?"

Tori's eyes closed and she forced out a slow breath. "I thought things would get better. I hoped. I didn't want a life of fighting, being constantly on the run and watching my friends die. I wanted to make a difference, but I thought... I *hoped*... that wasn't what was required of me to make that difference." She bit her lip. "I know better now. I regret not going with them. But... I can't take it back." She looked around the dark room. "But I have this now."

"What's... 'this'?"

Tori smiled in the dark. "My safehouse. My checkpoint."

"Your checkpoint?"

Tori shrugged. "Sometimes... when it's necessary... I help people on the run. Trying to get to a safer area, running from the syndicates. Sometimes I'll house people in the resistance movements. Give whatever assistance I can. I keep tabs on the syndicates' radio traffic, pass on their movements, that kind of thing. It might be too little, too late, but it's what I can do. It's what I'm *doing*."

Vera had to force her mouth closed. "You said you let people stay, but... you're helping resistance movements? I didn't even know they still existed. I... we had no idea."

Tori squeezed her shoulder gently. "I know. That's kind of the point. I don't broadcast it."

"Why are you telling me?"

Tori bit her lip. "I don't know. I just... I know I can trust you."

Vera ducked her head. "Does Gray know?"

Tori shook her head. "No. I don't know how to tell them. How do I say I'm trying now, *now*, when I should have done this years ago?"

Vera shrugged. "Maybe you say it just like that? We all do our best when we can. I don't think there's anything wrong with hoping for a better world."

Tori laughed once. "Yeah, here's to that dream." She fell silent, hand still moving across Vera's back. Vera shivered. "You okay?"

216

"Yeah. Just cold." Vera held perfectly still for a moment, not even breathing. Then, slowly, she leaned into Tori's embrace and rested her head against Tori's shoulder. Tori smiled and wrapped her arms around her. Vera trembled at the closeness. Tori's hand moved to her hair and smoothed it away from her face. It felt so... *good*. So safe.

"How did you get out?" Tori whispered against her hair.

Vera swallowed. "A resistance raid, actually. They weren't there for me. I don't think they even knew I was there until they found me. They were trying to garner attention through the media, prove that some people were fighting back. They destroyed the place, stealing hard drives where they found them, tearing down the décor, lighting fires. They made their way to the basement and found me. I tried to stop them from taking me because I was just..." She squeezed her eyes shut and tears ran down her face, into Tori's shirt. "I was just so br—" She set her jaw. "I was so *conditioned* at that point. I was terrified he was going to hurt me for leaving. They had to drag me out in cuffs. And... and a gag." She swallowed hard. "Because I bit one of them."

Tori made a sound low in her throat. Her hands became impossibly soft on Vera's skin, stroking along her arms, smoothing her hair. "Oh."

Vera ducked her head lower against Tori's shoulder. "I couldn't stand to stay with them. I was so scared... and hurt, *Jesus*, it hurt... So I ran away. I almost went back to him. Almost. But I figured the torture he'd put me through if he found me was worth the chance to be free. So, I ran again. I was able to keep to myself, stayed away from people... I don't know how else to explain it, Tori. I was broken. Finally, some people took me in. They helped me. Well... *she* did." She trembled and clutched Tori a little tighter. "Her husband..."

Tori went very still. "Did he hurt you?"

"He tried to." Tears ran steadily down Vera's face. "He tried to rape me." Tori's sharp intake of breath made Vera curl in on herself. "I'm sorry, I should... I'm sorry."

"No no no," Tori soothed, cradling her gently. "I'm sorry. I didn't mean to make you feel... the way you feel right now. What... what happened?"

"The wife was kind to me, helped me with my injuries, kept her distance. She knew something had happened, but she didn't know what. Her husband... took

217

a lot of interest in me. In the marks on my neck. He cornered me in the bathroom once and he said he… um…" Vera gulped.

"You don't have to talk about this, Vera. I want you to do whatever makes you feel safe."

"I want to get it out." Vera's cheeks were wet with tears. "I want to talk about it. I've never… I've never talked about this… not to anyone. Please. I just want to get it out. Please."

"Okay." Tori nodded against her hair. "Okay."

"He um…" Vera's breaths were heavy and painful. "He said he wanted to… um… help me get better. Give me… a better experience than I had with… with *him*. The other one. He put his hand around my neck and I just… turned off. Like I did with… him. He… pinned me against the wall… he… he said he was going to help me get better. He said…" She gasped. Shuddered. Gritted her teeth. Kept going. "I felt frozen. I couldn't fucking *move*. I couldn't push him away, I felt… I couldn't. But I… I felt so sick and I knew I'd rather die than let it happen again. I pushed him back and shattered the mirror. I didn't mean to, but as soon as it broke I decided I was going to cut my wrists with the glass. He slipped and fell against the sink and he hit his head and I… I realized I didn't want to die, I just wanted to… to be fucking *free*. I ran. I didn't stop to grab my stuff, or explain to his wife… I just ran. I didn't stop running. I couldn't stand for anyone else to know. I didn't want anyone to know I had that inside my head. I didn't want to find out it was all still *there*…" She whimpered. "I know my family would never hurt me, but I didn't want them to find out deep down that I'm… *broken*."

Vera choked out a sob. She buried her face in Tori's shoulder, shuddering as she let the memories come to the surface for the first time in so long. Her body shook as she cried, as the tears and pain and sounds she made moved through her and back out. Tori held her, not making a sound, letting Vera come apart in her arms as years of terror and shame and grief slowly made their way out.

After what felt like hours, Vera's sobs began to quiet. She sniffled and pulled her shirt up to wipe her face. Tori chuckled softly and passed her a tissue. Vera blew her nose and settled back against Tori. Tori adjusted so she could lean back against the armrest. Vera snuggled deeper into her embrace.

"Thank you for telling me all that," Tori whispered. "I know you don't know me that well. I understand the gravity of the trust you put in me to let me hear that."

Vera said nothing, just nodded against Tori's chest. She felt warm in her arms. Safe.

"Thank you for… um…"

Tori nodded. Her hand moved slowly through Vera's hair. Vera sagged into her embrace, exhaustion seeping into her bones. She felt like she'd clawed an unbearable weight out of her chest, and she quivered at how raw she felt. Her eyes closed slowly as the energy left her limbs. She was dragged into unconsciousness as Tori's hand moved gently through her hair.

Chapter 39

Gray woke slowly. They laid in bed for a moment, taking deep, calming breaths. Over the sound of their own breathing, they could hear their family's breaths, slow and deep and peaceful as they slept. When they were sleeping, Gray could pretend things were normal. When they were sleeping, Gray could pretend they were all safe.

They rolled to their side, careful not to jostle Sam. Sam lay on their back, peaceful, a pillow braced under their leg. Their mouth was open slightly and their eyes rolled under the lids. When Sam was asleep like this, it struck Gray how *young* they looked. Barely more than a child. The pain and fear of Gavin's torture weren't so evident on their face. They looked painfully innocent. Gray's stomach twisted as they thought about what Sam had endured.

Carefully, they pushed back the covers and stood, rolling their neck, stretching their arms over their head. *I'm too old for this.* They grinned ruefully. *I'm too old to be on the run, couchsurfing, avoiding the syndicates.* They could remember very clearly the way things were before they'd gotten bad.

They were the only one in the family who remembered the world as it had been. They'd been in their early twenties when the news had started picking up on the increasing crime, the disappearances, the rumors about syndicates amassing and making plans to take over. They'd laughed with their friends about it. *"Yeah, sure, just as long as when they take over, they'll criminalize changing lanes without a blinker." "Haha, yeah, or make letting your dog shit in someone's yard a capital crime."* They'd had no idea. None at all.

They yawned and drifted towards the kitchen. They stopped dead in their tracks as they rounded the corner, to the living room.

Tori was stretched out on the couch, asleep, with her arms around Vera. Vera was cuddled against her chest, eyes closed, looking more peaceful than Gray had ever seen her. A blanket was draped over both of them.

Gray smiled like an idiot as they headed for the kitchen. They got the coffee down from the shelf and scooped some into the coffee maker. As they waited for it to brew, they leaned on the counter.

Tori was their oldest friend. *Oldest surviving friend, anyway.* They'd been estranged for so long, but Gray still loved her dearly. Had never *stopped* loving her dearly. They'd known Vera for five years, fighting alongside her, caring for her the way she cared for them, and not once had they seen her look so vulnerable. So peaceful. Not once had they seen her without that weariness she carried around with her, the walls that never seemed to come down. Gray knew why they were there now, but it still hurt to see. Gray smiled, thinking of their friends on the couch, completely relaxed for what felt like the first time since Gray had known them.

They heard footsteps behind them and turned to see Tori stumbling in with messy hair and pink cheeks. Vera wandered in a few steps behind her, the blanket from the couch wrapped tight around her shoulders. She looked sheepish. Gray smiled even wider.

"I smell coffee." Tori's voice was thick with sleep.

Gray grabbed three cups from the cabinet and set them on the counter. "Freshly brewed. It'll be done in a minute."

"Great."

Gray glanced at Vera. "Sleep well?"

Vera blushed. "Um. Yeah." She stared at the floor, militantly avoiding Gray's gaze.

Gray shot a glance to Tori, who seemed unbothered. She smiled at them. "You?" she asked.

Gray sighed. "As well as could be expected, I guess. I'm so worried I'm going to jostle Sam's leg that it's hard to get comfortable."

"They could sleep with me for a few nights." Vera's eyes were still down. "I don't mind."

Gray swallowed and chose their words carefully. "If you really want to, but I thought it would be better if you had a bed to yourself." They filled the first cup and handed it to her. "Give you some space."

Vera took the cup with one hand, the other still clutched around the blanket. She raised her eyes slowly to Gray as they poured the next cup. She searched their face and they knew she was looking for condescension or pity. There was nothing there but quiet concern.

"Actually... the space is nice. Thank you, Gray."

Gray and Tori shared a look as they smiled, gratitude flooding Gray's face. Tori looked down, pleased.

They all looked up to see Finn and Ellis wandering into the room. Finn's hair stood on end. "We smelled coffee!"

Gray chuckled and pulled two more cups from the cabinet. "I just made it."

They poured the two cups and passed them both to Ellis. Ellis set them on the counter and went to the fridge, pulling out the milk and preparing the cups the way they and Finn liked them.

"We should bring Sam and Isaac some, too." Tori took the milk from Ellis and added some to her cup, too. "Do you know how they like it?"

"Sam likes theirs tasting more like a coffee milkshake than actual coffee." Gray grinned. "Isaac takes a little milk." Gray prepared the coffee and passed Sam's cup to Tori. Gray carried Isaac's as they all walked back to the guestroom.

Sam was sitting up already. "Oh, thank god. I was worried you all left." They smiled, but their eyes betrayed a hint of real worry. They brightened as they noticed the mugs. "Is that coffee?"

Tori knelt beside them and passed the cup over. They took a sip and their gaze snapped back up to Gray, grinning. "You remembered how I like it!"

Gray smiled and set theirs on the floor to ruffle Sam's hair. "I've been watching you mutilate your coffee for a year now, Sam. Of course, I remember."

Finn and Ellis sat down on their mattress together. Ellis helped Finn take a sip of their coffee first. Gray made their way over to Isaac, and Vera and Tori sat together on her mattress.

Isaac was curled up on his side again, hunched into himself. His face was tight with pain. His eyes opened as Gray sat on the floor next to him. Gray pulled their hand through his hair and he trembled.

"Hey." Gray's voice was low. "Feeling good enough to sit up and have some coffee?"

Isaac bit his lip and nodded. Gray helped him sit up and leaned him against the wall. Gray clenched their jaw at Isaac's quick intake of breath. They took Isaac's cup and held it to his lips.

"We could probably get you out of that sling today, if you want," Tori said from across the room. "As long as it doesn't hurt too much, it should be okay. Just be careful not to reinjure your thumb. That brace needs to stay on for a few more weeks at least. What do you think?"

Isaac nodded. "That would be really nice. Thank you, Tori."

She made her way over to him, picking her way around the mattresses and everyone's tangled legs. She knelt by his side and undid the knot at the back of his neck. She guided the sling gently off his arm. Finn watched her work, longing written across their face. Tori's gaze lingered a moment on the bruises around Isaac's neck, fading to a purple-yellow. She swallowed and stood, returning to her spot next to Vera.

Isaac moved his arm, slowly rotating it in the socket. He gritted his teeth. "It hurts, but I think the pain is coming from the back. Where you had to give me stitches." He circled his arm a few more times. "Feels good to move it again." His gaze was full of gratitude. "Thank you."

Tori smiled. "Good. I'm glad there wasn't more damage." She looked over at Finn. Their eyes were downcast. "You made a good call, Finn. He'd be much worse off if you hadn't made the call to reduce it when you did."

Ellis nudged Finn's shoulder with theirs, a grin spread across their face. Finn shyly raised their gaze and ducked their head. "I just figured if it really was broken then it didn't really matter anyway, because that kind of break would need surgery and there's no way we could go to a hospital, so as long as there was a chance that I could make him better I would do that because dislocations can be dangerous if they're left unreduced too long and I didn't want to—" They cut themselves off as they saw Ellis's face, their lips pulled up into a smile, gazing at them radiantly. Ellis pressed a quick kiss to Finn's temple, and Finn blushed.

Sam's eyes were fixed on Isaac as Gray placed the mug in Isaac's left hand, their hands hovering in case Isaac's shoulder gave out. Isaac met Sam's gaze before looking away, pain straining his features. Sam's eyes filled with tears and they looked down.

"How's everyone doing today?" Tori's gaze moved around the room, starting with Sam.

"It still hurts, but less than before." They glanced down at their leg.

"Good. I think it's time we started getting you up and moving. You look just about recovered from the pneumonia, too. How are you feeling overall?"

"I'm fine," they said too quickly, glancing at Isaac. Tori lifted an eyebrow. They wilted. "Um. I still feel... um..." Their eyes flicked to Isaac again. Gray followed the look. "Things still... um... hurt." They looked down at their arms, a few bandages covering the still-healing cuts and burns. And I... um..." Their cheeks flushed with shame. "It still just hurts." Gray's hand settled on their shoulders and rubbed the back of their neck. Sam smiled shakily at them. Gray stroked their hand through their hair.

"Okay. I'll work on getting you some crutches so you can start getting around. Movement is going to do you a lot of good." She moved on. "Finn? How're the hands?"

Finn looked down at their hands. "Um. The swelling isn't as bad. The right one..." They carefully touched the tip of each finger on their right hand to the thumb. "It's still sore, but really it feels fine. Should be back to normal in a week, I'd say." They looked mournfully at their left hand, wrapped in a makeshift brace Tori had put together. "The left is... um... still broken, I guess." They shrugged, their shoulders bowing in.

"The left will heal, too." Tori smiled at them. "I promise."

224

They ducked their head. "I know."

Tori took a sip of her coffee and looked around the room again. "What else do you all need? You've been here for almost a week now. Do you need something from me you're not getting? Is there something I could do to help you recover better?" With that, her eyes rested on Isaac. He looked down.

Gray blew out a slow breath. "Honestly, we could use some information. You mentioned you heard about the explosion over the radios. How much do you actually keep track of the syndicates? If you could give us that info, we could start strategizing our next step."

Gray looked at Vera and Tori. Tori glanced up. Vera smiled at her. Encouraging. Gray smiled.

Tori swallowed. "Um." She raised her gaze and saw everyone looking at her. She blushed. "I... actually... know quite a bit about the syndicates' movements."

Gray's brow furrowed. "Why?"

"Because... um... I'm..." She bit her lip and Gray placed a hand gently on her arm. "...I'm... helping the resistance movements."

Gray's mouth fell open. "You... you are?"

Tori licked her lips. "Yeah." She lifted her eyes. Everyone was looking at her with... *awe*. Respect. She looked down again.

"Tori, why..." Gray shook their head in disbelief. "Why didn't you tell me?"

Tori looked around, wilting under everyone's gaze. "I didn't think we'd be having this conversation like this. Um..." She ran a hand through her hair. "Because I didn't know how to tell you. When I left you to find my own way, I thought I was doing the right thing for me. I thought the world would get better and I wouldn't have to sacrifice everything to make it that way." She shook her head. "But I was wrong. I... regret not going with you. I've wondered every day since I left if I could have made a difference if I'd stayed."

"Tori, I don't—"

"Gray, please..." She held out a hand, brows pulled together. "Don't do that." She took a deep breath to steady herself. "So, a few years ago I bought this house. I bought it with the express intention of running a safehouse out of it. Just for people on the run, or people who needed a place to crash, nothing special. Until I housed someone from the resistance. And I just... got sucked in. I couldn't *not* help him. So, I offered to keep him posted on anything I heard about syndicate movements. I bought a radio programmed with the syndicates' channels. Sometimes I'll let resistance members stay here between missions." She swallowed. "I know it's too little too late, but... I'm sorry. I didn't know how to tell you."

Gray abandoned their coffee and knelt in front of her. They took both her hands in theirs and squeezed hard. "Please don't apologize. Please. I don't blame you for leaving. I never have. I wanted a happy life for you then, and I feel the same way now."

Tori glanced around the room, cringing at all the eyes on her.

"I am so proud of you. This?" Gray swept their hand around the room. "This is enough. It's more than enough. Thank you, Tori. Thank you." They pulled her into an embrace. Her arms went around them and pulled them close. She buried her face in their shoulder. Vera's hand moved in small circles on her back.

Gray pulled away with eyes filled with tears. Tori blinked rapidly, hiding her own. "I just wish you'd told me sooner," Gray said quietly, and tucked her hair behind her ear.

Tori shrugged. "I didn't know how. But now you know." She squeezed their hand. "I'll tell you everything I can. All I can say for now is that Gavin hasn't left the hospital yet. I don't know if that means he's dead, or still recovering. They're being very vague."

Gray nodded. "Thank you. That's good to know." Their gaze jumped to Sam. Sam's face was tight with fear. "We can start planning our next moves to get as far away from him as possible."

Vera looked away. She took another sip of her coffee.

Chapter 40

Finn awkwardly shifted the book in their hand. They had it propped against their left forearm, their right hand holding the pages open. It was one of Tori's, from her small library of books people left behind when they moved on from her house. They could scarcely say what the book was about – some sort of historical fiction, but it wasn't engaging enough to really pull them in. The pages were dog-eared, and the cover was worn. It smelled like diesel fuel. Finn wondered if the people who had left it were truckers of some kind.

Their mind wandered. Who owned this book before it fell to Tori? Who were they running from? Were they still alive? Their eyes passed over the same line over and over, absorbing none of it.

"Hey."

Finn looked up, startled, to see Ellis standing over them. Finn hadn't even noticed them approach, they'd been so deep in their own thoughts. Ellis held a hand out to them. "Wanna take a walk?"

Finn swallowed. "Is it… is it safe?"

"Yeah." Ellis smiled. "I checked with Tori. These woods go for miles around and no one lives close. Just a quick walk."

Finn set the book down, wincing slightly as their fingers relaxed. They followed Ellis out the back door and into the sun.

It was midmorning, and still cool. Finn breathed in the smell of pine and dirt and chilly, sharp air. The sun filtered through the trees to the ground, dappling their face with shadow and light. Finn smiled at how it made Ellis's eyes change colors, a sparkling blue-green-grey.

The bruise that stained Finn's temple and cheek had almost faded away. Ellis gently took Finn's wrist and guided them further into the trees.

They walked in silence, stepping over fallen branches and winding around trunks. Finn was a little unsteady on their feet, still wobbly from their concussion. Ellis let their hand brush against the weathered bark, their fingers bumping against the surface. The tension seemed to fade from their face and they breathed deeper than they had in weeks.

"It's beautiful here," Ellis said softly.

Finn smiled. "Yeah." They lifted their eyes to the canopy, where the tops of the trees creaked together, opening to the sun and closing in an endless dance with the breeze. When they looked down, Ellis was gazing at them, warm and soft.

"Maybe when this is all over," Ellis murmured, taking a step closer to Finn, "we could build a house in a place like this. With the trees, and the sun, maybe find a lake or something." They took a step closer and touched Finn's shoulder, their fingers moving down to their wrist. "We could get a cat. Maybe a garden. Maybe we could..." They swallowed, tears suddenly pricking their eyes. "Maybe we could have kids. Adopt, or have some of our own. I don't know. I don't care." They carefully laced their fingers through Finn's. "I want a life. Not this constant running, the fear... We'd have a family together."

Finn looked at them with wide eyes. "You... you'd really want that? With me?"

Ellis's eyebrows pulled together. "Of course. Unless... unless that's not what you want."

Finn nodded. "No, I do." They looked down, their vision suddenly blurry with tears. "I do. A *lot*. I just... I didn't know if you'd ever want a family again."

Ellis's lips trembled. They pressed them together and closed their eyes. They opened them again when Finn took a step closer, their right hand pressing gently against Ellis's chest.

Ellis's hands rested gently on Finn's shoulders. "I'd want one if it was with you."

Finn's eyes fluttered shut as their lips pulled up into a smile. They leaned forward and rested their forehead against Ellis's. They breathed together, holding each other, listening to the wind and the birds and the rustling of the branches above them. Ellis stepped forward and gently pushed Finn back one step, then another. They pushed them back until Finn felt their back press against a tree. The rough bark scratched them through their T shirt. They shivered as Ellis's hands moved from their shoulders to their waist, as they leaned forward, their breath tickling against their neck. Ellis stood still for a moment, eyes closed, the length of their body pressed gently against Finn's.

Ellis raised a hand to Finn's cheek and kissed them softly.

Finn trembled. They pulled Ellis closer and hissed at the pain that lanced through their left hand. Ellis pulled back, taking Finn's wrists in their hands and pulling their arms in to rest against Ellis's chest. Ellis wet their lips and pressed Finn back against the tree. Finn melted. Ellis stroked their thumbs along the tops of Finn's hands. Their tongue moved gently against Finn's lower lip and Finn shuddered, opening their mouth. Ellis smiled and kissed them deeper.

"There's nothing but us," Ellis whispered against Finn's lips. Their mouth moved across Finn's cheek and up to their forehead, pressing a soft kiss there, then down to Finn's ear. Finn moaned in the back of their throat as Ellis brushed their lips behind their ear.

"There's nothing but us, and these woods, and the wind. It's just you and me. Nothing else in the world matters right now. Not... not the past, not the future. You..." They cupped Finn's cheek in one hand, pulling back to meet their eyes. Finn was almost desperate with longing. Their eyes flicked down to Ellis's lips. "...you're mine, and I'm yours, and there's nothing that can hurt us right now. It's just you and me, safe." They met Finn's lips with an open mouth.

"Safe," Finn whispered. Their eyes closed and they disappeared further into the kiss.

Chapter 41

Years ago

There was a knock at the door.

Tori shot up from her seat. She looked around at the family gathered around her at the table, the family that had placed their trust in her. Trusted her to keep them safe. She saw the terror in every single one of their faces.

"Who is it, mommy?" trilled one of the children. Alice. She was five.

Her mother clutched at her and pressed her hand over her daughter's mouth. "I don't know, sweetie," she breathed. She stared at Tori in horror.

Tori swallowed. "I'm going to go answer the door. Louis, you and Cara clean up the table as fast as you can. Put the dishes in the dryer in the laundry room. Laura, honey, I need you to take your sisters to your room and hide in the closet. You have to be very quiet. Do you understand?" Laura nodded earnestly. She was being so brave. She was twelve. Tori's hands shook. "I'm going to go answer the door. I'm going to see who's there and what they want. I'm going to keep them outside as long as I can to give you time to hide, alright?" They all nodded. Tori swallowed the lump in her throat and made her way to the living room. She folded up the fold-out couch where the parents had slept for the past three nights. She walked slowly to the door.

Someone knocked again, and louder this time. Like they were impatient. Or desperate. Her hand settled on the handle. She drew in a deep breath. Let it out. Opened the door.

There was a young couple on her doorstep. They were huddled together, soaked from the rain that had stopped only hours before, freezing and terrified. They both had a hunted look in their eyes that made Tori's stomach clench. *If they're running from someone, how close behind are their pursuers?*

"Please," the young woman whimpered. She was crying.

Tori steadied herself on the doorframe. "Who are you?"

"Edith. And Tobias." The woman placed her hand on the man's shoulder. "Please. They're right behind us. Please, can we just... can we just...?"

Tori's blood ran cold. "Did they see you come this way? Do they know where you are? Are they going to... to *follow* you here?" Her mind went to the children hiding in the closet. Alice, Melody, Alayna, Laura. Four girls with identical brown hair and freckles on their cheeks. Brown eyes, blue eyes, blue eyes, brown eyes. *Those children...*

"Please," whispered Edith. Tobias looked shellshocked. Too terrified to speak. He clung to his wife and stared at the floor in front of Tori's feet.

"I..." Tears pricked at Tori's eyes. "If you led them here I... I don't have any room to hide you. I'm sorry. You need to..." Her throat was beginning to close. Her voice wobbled. "You need to keep running."

"No," sobbed Edith. "Please, no... They'll kill us, please..." She tried to push past Tori. "Just for a few minutes, just—"

Tori thrust her arm across the doorway and squared up to the woman. *"No,"* she said, almost in a growl. "I have other people here who... I can't let you put any of my people at risk. I'm sorry. But you..." Her voice hardened. "You *have* to go."

Tobias made a noise in the back of his throat, halfway between a sob and a moan. He drooped against Edith as his eyes slid shut.

Tori moved to close the door. "I hope you make it. I do. But... I have people I need to keep safe, too. And if you brought them here..."

The woman sobbed desperately. *"NO—"*

Tori closed the door on her. Locked it.

Tori could hear the woman weeping behind the door. Tori slid down it and put her head in her hands. She felt the concussive *bang*s as the woman pounded on the door. Pleading. Making promises. Making threats. Tori squeezed her eyes shut.

She heard the crying move away from the door, and into the night. She got to her feet and pressed her hand against her mouth.

The others must be terrified. She made her way to the guest bedroom.

"It's me," she said softly. "They're gone."

The door of the closet swung open to reveal the family all clutching each other in panic. They relaxed when they saw Tori was alone.

"What—"

"It was just some people looking for somewhere to hide for a while. It's alright. They're going to keep running."

Cara, the girls' mother, stepped out of the closet and took Tori's hands in hers. "You're not going to—"

"No," Tori said quickly. "They were being followed. Couldn't... couldn't let them lead the... um... couldn't let them lead anyone here."

Cara's eyes filled with tears. "Oh. Those poor..." She gasped out a little sob. "Maybe we could—"

"No," Tori repeated, firm. "It would put your family at risk. But what we need to do is hide you better. In case anyone comes, um." She swallowed hard. "...*looking* for them. So, I need you to go to the crawlspace, behind the bookcase in my room. I'll fold up the beds and tidy up." She squeezed Cara's hands. "Don't worry. I'll take care of everything."

Cara wept. "Those poor people... Are they going to d—" She gasped and held her hand to her mouth.

"What's the matter, mommy?" Alice asked. Her huge brown eyes were fixed on her mother. Her lips were pulled into a pout.

Cara swiped her tears away and smiled at her daughter. "Nothing, honey. Everything's okay. We're going to play hide-and-seek now, okay sweetheart? Do you want to play hide-and-seek in a really fun place?"

The girl frowned. "I want to eat my food."

Cara nodded and took her hand, and Alayna's. "We will in a minute, honey. Let's go hide first."

Louis took the other two girls' hands. "Come on, girls. Let's go to Miss Tori's room for a little while." He was breathing so fast Tori wondered if he was about to pass out.

The girls put up a mild protest as their parents pulled them into Tori's room. She folded the pull-out couch up so it looked like any piece of furniture in an unused guest room. She hurried to the laundry room and pulled a few dishes out of the dryer. *If I wash a few at a time, I can pretend they're all just for me if someone comes in. And if the syndicates take long enough, I can have them all done by the time they get here.* The kitchen table was clear when she walked in. She placed the dishes in the sink and pushed in the chairs around the table.

She took a plate and began calmly washing it in the sink. Her eyes burned with tears and she bit down hard on her lip to keep from sobbing. *Maybe they'll escape. Maybe they'll make it. It's possible.*

Her gut curdled with guilt. *But I couldn't let them lead the syndicates right to those children. And from the look of them, they were very close behind.* A tear coursed down her cheek and onto the plate. *This whole family would be killed. I couldn't let that happen. I couldn't let—*

The sound of gunfire *popped* in her ears. It couldn't have been more than a mile away. The plate slid out of Tori's hand into the sink. She sank to her knees and wept.

Chapter 42

Isaac jerked awake and sat up with a scream. He squeezed his hands into fists, taking deep, shuddering breaths. His gaze moved around the room, slowly taking it all in. Concrete walls. No windows. Anchor points along the walls and floors.

"No..." he whispered. He looked down to see his hands cuffed in front of him, and twisted against the restraints. He squeezed his eyes shut, tears burning already. "No."

"Yup." Gavin sounded bored. Isaac's eyes flew open to settle on Gavin where he leaned against the wall, his arms crossed in front of his chest. His face was clear of scars, unbroken. Just like it was before... Isaac swallowed. "Sleep well?"

"What... happened?" Isaac's voice was a croak.

"You slept, dumbass. I went a little hard with you, I have to admit. Maybe shouldn't have hit you in the head so hard. Sorry about that. Or... not? I'm still not sure how I feel about it. I had fun, for what it's worth." Gavin chuckled. "So there's that."

Isaac felt tendrils of panic creep around his limbs. "What's... the last thing you did to me?" How much was a dream? Are they safe?

Gavin snorted. "Is that a serious question?"

Isaac swallowed hard. "Yes. I don't... I don't remember."

"Uh. Hm." Gavin's eyebrows shot up. "Yikes. I guess I really did hit you too hard. You don't remember them trying to exchange my cousin for you?"

Oh, god, oh god, no. That was real. They're here. He has them. *"No..."*

"Pfft. You don't remember their truly idiotic plan failing? You don't remember me torturing them?"

No. Please, no.

Gavin took a swaggering step toward Isaac, then another. "You don't remember me killing them?"

Icy dread crushed Isaac's limbs. His chest was encased in crushing steel. He couldn't breathe. "No…" He shook his head, dazed. "No, I don't—"

"Really? I shot each of them in the head in front of you and you don't remember that? That's weird. It seemed to make an impression at the time."

Desperate tears ran down Isaac's cheeks. "No… no…" This isn't real. It can't be real. This is a dream. I got out, I saved Sam… We got out…

"Are you seriously telling me you don't remember the last two months?"

Isaac blanched. "M-months?"

Gavin rolled his eyes. "Jesus Christ. One little concussion and you completely forgot all the shit I did to you? Are you serious*? That took so much fucking* work*, Isaac." Gavin aimed a kick at Isaac's chest, and Isaac was thrown backwards onto his back. He braced for the pain, the lance of agony through the lash marks, but it didn't come. He gasped.*

"You… when…?"

Gavin straddled Isaac's hips, shoving his hands up above his head with one hand and wrapping the other around Isaac's neck.

"Gavin… you… whipped me…"

Gavin rolled his eyes. "Yeah, fucking months *ago. I wanted to give you the chance to fully heal up. I love doing it on unbroken skin, you know, so much more…" His hand tightened around Isaac's neck. "Satisfying."*

Isaac choked and thrashed against Gavin's hand, loosening Gavin's hold for a moment. "They're… not dead," he heaved. "I… we got out, they got me out… we got out…"

Gavin's face darkened as his hand tightened. "I beg. To. Fucking. Differ." His hand locked around Isaac's throat and he squeezed. Isaac's eyes rolled back as he struggled against Gavin's hold, too weak to break it again.

"I'll show you when I'm done with this. At the moment, I just wanna see how many times I can do this before you pass out." Isaac convulsed against his hand, mindless with panic.

∴

Isaac was screaming. Gray was instantly alert. They rolled to their side and reached for him. He was twisting in the sheets, his teeth gritted, his eyes half-open and unseeing. Gray stumbled over to him in the dim light with their hands outstretched, their body hitching back for a moment as they tried to find a place to touch him without causing more pain. Their hands settled on his right shoulder, avoiding the lashes there the best they could. "Isaac!"

Isaac sobbed, writhing, turning away from Gray's hand.

"Isaac!" They shook him. He cringed away. *"Isaac!"*

Isaac jerked awake with a shuddering sob. His eyes were wide for a moment, looking around the dark room in a panic. He broke down, cowering away from Gray's touch, pressing his face against his hands as he sobbed.

"Isaac." Gray's fingers stroked gently through his hair. "Isaac, shhh. It's okay. You're safe."

"No…" he sobbed, cringing into himself. "No… you were dead…"

"No," Gray murmured. "It was just a dream. We got out, Isaac. Remember? You got Sam out. You're safe."

"Sam…" Isaac's hands dropped away from his face and reached out blindly, unable to find anything in the dim light.

"I'm here, Isaac." Sam's voice shook.

Gray stood and turned on the light. Vera was sitting straight up, head turned toward Isaac's voice. Her eyes were wide and her body trembled with tension. Finn and Ellis stirred, grumbling, disentangling their limbs as they tried to sit up. Finn's hair stuck straight up from their scalp as they blinked in the light.

"Wha's goin' on?" Finn mumbled

Isaac was pressed against the wall, his right hand extended out in front of him as if to shield him from something. His chest heaved with gasping sobs, his cheeks wet with tears. He whimpered quietly as Gray took a step towards him.

"Isaac, you had a nightmare." Gray's voice was low and gentle. They crouched down with their hands open and relaxed at their sides, eyes fixed steadily on Isaac. He still didn't seem to see them. "Isaac?"

His lips trembled. "Please…" He cringed further back from Gray.

Tori appeared in the doorway, steadying herself on the door. "What happened?" Her eyes darted around the room as she took it all in.

Gray turned momentarily towards her. "He had a bad dream," they murmured. They turned back to Isaac. "Hey. It's just a nightmare. It's not real."

"I just woke up from a nightmare," he sobbed. "And… after I woke up… you were dead… please…"

"Isaac. You're safe. It's okay." They reached a hand towards them.

"Please don't touch me!" he cried. He pressed himself back against the wall. "Please don't… I… I can't wake up from this and find out you're dead again… please…"

"Isaac." Sam's voice cracked, tears tightening their throat. "Please… it's okay…" Sam dragged themselves closer to him, pulling their broken leg behind them.

"No." Isaac squeezed his eyes shut. "No… not you. Please, Sam, not you. I can't…" He fell apart into sobs. "Please… I can't…"

Tears ran down Sam's cheeks. "Isaac, please… I'm not dead, okay? Remember, you got me out? You pulled me out of that building. Do you remember that?"

"No, no, no…" He slumped to his side. "I can't… please, Sam, I'm sorry… I can't wake up there again… with *him*… He showed me your body. He showed me where he…" Isaac choked. "I can't wake up there again. I can't do it again, not after this…"

"Isaac, *please*…"

"Please… just kill me, please just kill me, I can't look at you again… Gavin, *please*, just wake me up, please just kill me, I can't…"

"Isaac!" Sam's voice was terrified. "Isaac, *please*, please stop, this is real! You're never going back there, we got out!"

"I don't believe you!" he screamed. The room fell silent in shock.

"Isaac…" Tori's voice was low. "Isaac, it's Tori… Would you be willing to touch Sam? Would you be willing to touch them, see that they're real?"

"No," he moaned. "No, he made me touch them, he made me feel how cold their body was, made me…" He gagged with the force of his sobs. He pressed his forehead against the mattress, hiding his eyes.

Sam stared at him with their mouth open. Their face was pulled into a mask of horror.

"It was real…" Isaac whispered. "It felt real…"

"Isaac…" Tori's voice was thick with tears. "Isaac, please let Sam touch you. This is real, I… I swear."

Gray squeezed their hands into helpless fists. Isaac pressed his face into the mattress, shaking with sobs.

Tori walked carefully across the room to kneel by Sam. They jumped, their gaze tearing away from Isaac to stare desperately at her. "What do I do?" Their voice was strained with agony.

She ran her fingers through their hair and brushed the tears from their cheeks. She arranged her features into a calm expression. "Isaac, if Sam touches you are you going to hurt them?"

Isaac whimpered. "Never," he whispered.

"Okay." She nudged Sam forward. "Go ahead."

They crawled to his side, quivering with tension in every limb. They bit their lip and wiped their face on their sleeve. "Isaac…" Their voice was barely above a whisper. They reached out with one hand. "Please come back to me." Their fingers brushed against his shoulder.

He flinched and whimpered high in his throat. "I never left," he whispered. "I just failed you. I'm sorry, Sam… please forgive me…" His voice broke into a sob. "Please don't be dead…"

"I'm not dead." Sam's voice wavered. "I'm not dead, because you saved me, Isaac." They pressed their hand against his shoulder. He trembled at the touch. They folded one leg awkwardly under them and stuck the other out to the side, the brace still strapped on. They huddled against Isaac's side and draped their arms over him. Their head rested on his shoulder. "I'm right here, Isaac." Their voice didn't shake so much when they whispered.

Vera stood and made her way over to Isaac. She sat by him and ran her fingers gently through his hair, ignoring the tears running down her cheeks. She leaned her head back against the wall and breathed slowly. "We're here, Isaac. This is real."

Gray sat at the foot of Isaac's mattress and gave his ankle a squeeze. Finn and Ellis made their way across the room and squeezed onto Isaac's mattress, too. Ellis put a hand on his waist. Finn gently laid their right hand next to Ellis's.

Tori swallowed hard and sat behind Gray. She rested one hand on their shoulder, and the other on Finn's. She closed her eyes against the tears that kept falling.

Isaac lay still under their hands. "At least you're not killing me this time," he whispered.

Chapter 43

Isaac sat on the back porch, enjoying the afternoon breeze. The seasons had begun to turn; the air was cooler, the days shorter. The leaves on a few of the trees were taking on a yellow-green hue, and some were getting a red, burnished edge to them.

It wasn't so much that Isaac loved fall; it was that he loved the change. Spring and fall offered... hope. They offered the departure from what had consumed the world for months, be it cold or heat. He closed his eyes and breathed deep. He wondered, for a moment, if there were people out there enjoying the fall, free. He wondered if people were out there crunching through the leaves without fear. If they could be with their families and know they were safe. He thought he might be able to imagine how that felt. He reached out towards the feeling in his mind as a smile pulled at his lips.

"Hey."

Isaac jumped. He hadn't even heard Sam approach. Sam lowered themselves to the step beside Isaac and set their crutches aside. After three weeks, Sam's leg was healing well. In just a few more weeks, they could take the brace off.

Distracted, Isaac looked down at his right hand. It was still wrapped in the haphazard cast Tori had been able to pull together. He wiggled his fingers gently, wincing at the pain that still shot through. *At least my left hand doesn't hurt.* His shoulder was healed, and the stitches on his forearm had come out almost two weeks ago. He was healing, too. On the outside, at least.

He blinked as he realized he hadn't answered Sam. He cleared his throat. "Hey." He glanced at them. They were looking back, their eyes dark with worry. He swallowed. "What is it?"

Sam bit their lip. "I was just coming over to say hi. Um. I was wondering if maybe you'd want to go for a walk? I'm pretty good at using crutches now, and we could stay on the trails. We could... just talk." They searched Isaac's face.

He turned slightly away. "Um. That sounds like it would be nice. But… maybe later."

Sam's lips trembled. "Isaac…" Their voice was a whisper. "You can talk to me."

Isaac closed his eyes. He dragged his left hand down his face. "Sam…"

"You can. Please. I want you to talk to me. I want to know you're okay."

He shook his head. "Sam…"

"We're all worried about you. You're not acting like yourself. You won't talk to anyone." Tears welled in Sam's eyes and they swallowed hard.

Isaac pressed his lips together. *Except Tori, the one time.* His left hand pulled into a fist. "Nobody needs to worry about me. I'm f—"

"Fine?" Isaac cringed away from Sam's harsh tone. "You're anything but *fine,* Isaac! I know we don't know everything you went through, but…" They swiped their hand furiously at the tears that ran down their cheeks. "…but we saw enough! We watched Gavin torture you. We know that much. I know you're hurting. I know you're still having nightmares." Isaac flinched. Sam swallowed hard and kept going. "I know you didn't want anyone to see that but… we're all hurting because of Gavin, one way or another. And we're here for each other, Isaac." They put their hand gently on his shoulder. "I want to be here for you."

Isaac shook his head and shrugged off Sam's hand. "I'm sorry. I… I can't."

He stood, wobbling in place for a moment. It terrified him, how weak he still felt after weeks of recovery. *Finn says some of it is mental, too.* He steeled himself against the dizziness and walked away, leaving Sam grasping after him on the porch. He pressed his face into his sleeve and wiped away the tears that burned his eyes. Sam watched him go and crumpled into sobs.

Chapter 44

Vera laid on the couch, lost in her thoughts. Finn and Ellis were off on one of their walks, walks where they always came back with flushed cheeks and furtive smiles. Tori was somewhere in the back of the house, trying to give everyone some privacy and space. Vera hadn't seen her in hours. Sam was out with Gray in the back yard, doing some exercises to help Sam get their strength up again. Isaac was in the guest room, sleeping. He had slept a lot the past few weeks. *"A normal response to unimaginable stress,"* Finn kept saying. *"He's healing from a lot,"* they'd say, their arm around Sam's shoulders, holding them close when Sam was close to tears. Sam cried a lot lately. *"It's okay. He'll come around."*

I didn't sleep when I got out. She pressed her hands against her face. *I didn't sleep hardly at all for weeks after I was out.* Every time she had closed her eyes in those first few weeks, she was terrified she'd open them and find herself back in that cell. With *him.*

She shuddered against the wave of nausea that rolled over her. It happened every now and then, an unending barrage of fear and pain and sickness that overwhelmed her, filled her up, left her huddling on the floor, gasping for air. She could usually keep it at bay. She'd been holding it back for fourteen years. But every now and then – she didn't know what caused it, or why it happened, or how she could make it *stop*, but every now and then – she was dragged down into it. The only thing to do was to endure it.

There is was – that feeling that the floor had dropped out from under her, that she had to hold on to the nearest object to keep from being flung into oblivion, the knowledge that she couldn't *move* and couldn't *breathe* and couldn't do a *damned thing* because she was trapped, she was chained down in a cell filled with nothing but the cold and the pain and dear god *please* don't let him walk through that door with a knife in his hand and a smile on his face.

She convulsed. Sweat broke out on her brow and she trembled, squeezing her arms around herself, pressing into that hollow part of herself that threatened to consume her. She blinked, trying to clear her eyes of tears so she could *see*, but her vision was unfocused, her eyes darting around the room, looking for threats, looking for *him*. The room was empty.

She opened her mouth to call out to someone. She wanted Gray. She wanted someone bigger and stronger than she was to come hold her, protect her, hold the world at bay as she fell apart and oh *god* she was falling apart. She wanted Isaac. She wanted him back so badly, with his calm reserve and caring touch. She wanted her best friend. She wanted someone to lean on, someone to unravel with. She didn't want to be so goddamn strong all the time. She wanted to know someone would keep her safe while she lost herself. Her voice cracked, her dry throat breaking until the sound died on her lips. Isaac was lost in his own pain. Gray was too far away to hear.

They couldn't protect her from what was in her mind. She cringed away from the memory of Gavin, slapping her across the face, pulling her head back to inspect the scars around her neck, twisting her shoulders so he could look at her wrists. She felt herself slipping back in, the dull, heavy blanket of submission pulling her under. It blunted the agony.

No no no I can't I can't I can't go back there I can't... Another wave of misery broke over her. She closed her eyes and slipped under.

∴

Tori heard a sound that didn't belong, something like a sob. She put her book down and unwound herself from under her covers. She'd been hiding in her room for hours, reading, trying to give everyone else some privacy. She knew how stressful it could be to feel like a guest in someone else's house, never having privacy or time to themselves.

She padded across the floor, pulling a sweater on as she went. It was a cool morning and the house was still a little chilly from the night before. She rounded the corner and froze when she saw Vera.

Vera was sitting straight up on the couch, eyes unfocused, legs pulled in toward her chest. Tori couldn't help her quick intake of breath. "No..." she whispered. Slowly, she approached, hands at her sides. "Vera?" She didn't react. Tori swallowed. "Vera?" She stepped in front of her.

Vera's lips were trembling, her eyes wide and unseeing, her muscles pulled tight with strain. She didn't show any indication she had seen Tori approach. Tori bit her lip and slowly reached out a hand to touch her.

Vera flinched slightly away from the hand on her shoulder. Tori pulled her hand back. Vera stared straight ahead and a quiet whimper fell from her lips.

Tori took a shaking breath. "Vera, can you hear me?" Vera nodded. "What's going on? I don't know how to help you." Vera swallowed hard and pressed her lips together.

Tori stood up, her hands clenched into nervous fists, her eyebrows pulling together. She licked her lips. "I'm going to get Gray. Stay here." Vera nodded weakly.

∴

Gray sat in the damp grass with Sam, taking a break from their exercises. They both turned when they heard Tori open the door. Gray stiffened when they saw the look of desperate worry in her face. They quickly stood. Distracted, they reached down a hand for Sam and helped pull them to their feet.

They were almost too afraid to ask. They did anyway. "What is it?"

Tori shook her head. "It's Vera. There's something wrong. I think she's... I think she's *there* in her mind right now. I don't know what to do. She won't talk to me..." She pressed her hands together.

Gray swallowed hard. "Where is she?" They wrapped an arm around Sam's waist and moved with them towards the house.

"Living room. On the couch."

Gray supported Sam's weight as they walked through the back door, through the kitchen, into the living room. Gray took a shaky breath when they saw Vera on the couch, trembling. "Sam, I'm going to sit you in that chair, okay?" Gray indicated with their head. Sam nodded and limped to it, Gray still supporting them as they sat down. Their eyes were wide and fixed on Vera. Gray took a deep breath to steel themselves and walked slowly to Vera's side.

"Is this how she was with... with Gavin?" Tori's eyes shone with tears.

"I think so." Gray bit their lip, their stomach roiling at what they knew they had to say. "Vera, you can speak."

"Thank you, sir." Vera closed her eyes. Tori pressed her hand to her mouth.

Gray knelt beside her. "Vera, can I touch you?"

Her muscles were locked with tension. "You can do whatever you want." Her eyebrows pulled together in a shadow of confusion.

Gray recoiled slightly. They shook their head as if to shake off the words. "Do you want me to touch you?"

Vera trembled, opening and closing her mouth several times. No words came. She whimpered.

"Okay. I won't touch you. Not until you're out of... this. Do you... do you know where you are right now?"

She blinked. "I..." She stared straight ahead at the wall behind Gray. "No..."

"Okay. That's okay. We're at Tori's house. Do you remember? Do you remember coming here?"

She opened her mouth to try to speak and the words still wouldn't come. She whined high in her throat. "I'm... 'm sorry..." She cringed into herself as if expecting to be hit.

"It's alright, Vera. It's alright. You haven't done anything wrong. Are you scared you're going to be punished?"

A whimper escaped her as they said the word. She slid off the couch onto her knees, folding her hands in her lap and bowing her head. Tears rolled down her nose and into her lap. She shuddered and braced herself.

"No no no..." Gray whispered. They glanced up at Sam. Sam had their hands pressed over their mouth, silent sobs shaking their shoulders. Tori stared at Vera, horrified. "That's never going to happen to you again. I'm sorry. I won't say that word. You're safe. Vera, look at me."

She immediately obeyed. She looked at them, unseeing.

Gray clenched their jaw, revolted by their friend's conditioned obedience. "What do you think is happening right now, Vera?"

She gulped. "I am… going to be… punished."

"No." Gray's voice was hard. *"No,* that's not going to happen. I'm not going to do that." They searched her face. "Do you know who I am?"

She nodded once. "Gray."

Their heart sank. "Gray, your friend?"

Another nod. Her face broke into anguish as she began to cry in earnest. "Yes."

"And you think I'm going to p—" They caught themselves. "…hurt you now?"

She looked down. "If y-you want to."

Gray couldn't hold their own tears back. "What if I say I don't want to? That I'm never going to?"

She swallowed hard. "Then I can't be g-good."

Gray pressed their hands against their face. She flinched slightly as their hands went up. "Vera, are you going to do whatever I tell you to do?" She pressed her lips together and nodded. "Then I want you to come back to me. Right here. In Tori's living room, with me. I'm not going to hurt you. I just want you here with me. Can you come back to me? Be in your body right now?"

She whimpered. "No… please…"

"Why don't you want to?"

"There are… there are bad things… happening… in my body."

"Does it feel like you're being punished right now?" They tried to say the word as gently as they could.

She sobbed. "I am."

Tears ran down Gray's cheeks. "Can you tell me what you feel?"

246

She squeezed her eyes shut, a shiver moving its way through her body. "I... I am... c—" The word stuck in her throat like she was choking on it. Her mouth shut with a *snap*. "Take all punishments without complaint," she recited robotically.

"Vera, listen to me." Gray's voice was harder than before. "Tell me what you feel, even if it feels like complaining, okay? I want to know what's going on in your head so I can help you."

She swallowed. "I... am... c-cold." She shuddered. "He keeps it cold. It... hurts. I... f-feel..." She gasped. "I... feel... pain."

"Where?"

"M-my... head..." Each word seemed to cost her. "And... my stomach... my back... hurts..." She convulsed forward. "And it hurts... where... he... fucks me."

Gray squeezed their eyes shut. They had suspected what had happened, but it tore a hole right through their chest to hear her say it. They heard Tori whimper beside them.

"Vera," they said with a forced calm, "I need to bring you back. I can't leave you in that place, okay? I'm going to bring you back to me, in this house." They motioned to the blanket on the couch and turned over their shoulder to look at Tori. "Can you put that on her?" Tori nodded. "We're going to get you warm, okay? Not cold like where you are now." Tori knelt beside Vera and carefully wrapped her in the thick blanket. Vera remained motionless. "We're going to breathe together now, okay? Breathe in."

Vera obeyed. She dragged in a ragged inhale.

"Hold... and out." They exhaled together. "In." Mechanically, an inhale. "Hold." She trembled as she held the breath. "Out." It rushed out of her again. "Good, Vera. That's good. In." Her breath stuttered in as her lungs expanded. "Hold." She shook so hard she could barely keep her breath in. "Out." It came out in a whimper.

Tori knelt beside Gray and took their hand, her eyes fixed on Vera. Her cheeks were wet with tears.

"Keep breathing, Vera," Gray murmured. "As you do, I want you to feel it. Feel your lungs expand, feel it as you hold, feel the air coming out of your mouth as you exhale. Okay?" She nodded. She shuddered, nearly sobbing. Gray glanced behind them and saw Sam slumped to their side, curled up into themselves, crying hard.

"Okay. Keep breathing, nice and slow. You're safe. You're in Tori's living room. We're all here with you. Isaac's in the next room, Finn and Ellis are out in the woods nearby. You're never going back there. That's never going to happen to you again. And I... I am *never* going to hurt you. Do you understand?" They ducked into Vera's line of sight. "Do you believe me?"

Her eyes focused slowly, and Gray saw a dim spark of recognition. She pulled the blanket tight around her shoulders and shuddered, falling apart with a ragged sob.

Gray caught her as she slumped to the floor. They eased her up gently and guided her onto the couch. Her fingers latched into their shirt as she pulled them close and sobbed into their chest. Their arms went around her, and they held her carefully.

"Please don't let him hurt me again." Their shirt was already wet with her tears.

"I won't. He is never, never going to hurt you again." They squeezed her tighter.

"Please don't... please don't let him take me again. *Please.* I can't... I can't go back there..."

"Hey, shh. It's okay. You're never going back to him. He can't hurt you anymore."

"Please don't hurt me like he did. I know I asked you to but... please don't, *please*... I'll do anything..."

Gray swallowed hard against the lump in their throat. "I know you didn't want me to, Vera. I'm never going to. Even if you beg me to. Okay? You're safe from that. You're safe from... from me."

She sobbed miserably. "I'm sorry I'm so fucked up, I'm sorry I'm so... so *broken.* I never wanted you to find out. I never wanted you to see what he made me."

"Hey." Gray tilted her chin up so she could see their face. "You're not broken. You're *hurting*. And there's nothing he could have done to you to make me stop loving you, okay? We all love you, Vera. No matter what. You're just hurting. Not broken. And that hurt that makes you like this sometimes... is *his fault*. Not yours. Never yours."

She dissolved into sobs again, pulling her face out of their grasp and burying it in their chest instead. Gray held her tight as she rocked forward with each tortured breath.

"Can Sam and Tori touch you? Can we all be close to you?"

She gasped. "It's too much, it's too much, please no... just you." She gulped. "I'm sorry, I can't, I can't do a lot of people, I just need—"

"Okay. That's okay, Vera. It's fine. They aren't hurt, okay? Look." As she lifted her head and turned towards Sam and Tori, she cowered away from the anger she thought she was going to see in their eyes. She only saw warmth and worry. "They just want you to feel safe. Whatever it takes to make you feel safe, okay? Nobody is going to touch you if you don't want them to. Those are the rules, right? Nobody touches you unless you want them to."

She shook her head. "Not with... with *him*..."

"You're not with him anymore. You never will be again."

She sagged in their arms, each sob draining her. She curled in tighter against their chest.

"You're okay. We're gonna stay here for as long as you need. I'm not going anywhere. If you want to be alone, you just tell me. But until then we're all going to be right here." She nodded as tears poured down her face. Gray gently rocked her. Tori and Sam cried silently nearby.

Chapter 45

How many times am I going to wake up here before I realize the rescue was a dream? *Isaac rolled to his side, the now-familiar smell of the damp, dark room washing over him. He pulled uselessly against the rope tying his hands behind his back.* I'm never getting out of here. I'm going to die here. No one is coming for me. *He squeezed his eyes shut, tears running down his face.*

The first moments were always the worst. The crushing realization, the shiver of cold through his body as the cement floor sapped away his warmth, the burn of rope around his wrists. He was always *bound,* always. *He trembled, trying to hold on to the last few moments of peace. The last few moments free of pain. It always came eventually.*

"Hey, Isaac."

Isaac groaned and kept his eyes squeezed shut. "No…"

"Oh, come on. Rise and shine. I gave you a whole week to recover from last time." Isaac cringed away from the footsteps as Gavin approached him. "You know…" Gavin's hand tightened in Isaac's hair and wrenched his head back. "…it's taking you longer and longer to recover from things. Your body is getting used up, Isaac. It only took… what… four months? And you're already practically useless."

Isaac tried to pull away from Gavin's grasp. Gavin yanked his head back again, hard. "Open your eyes," Gavin ordered. Isaac whimpered. "Hey." Gavin slapped him across the face. "Open your fucking *eyes." Isaac swallowed hard and obeyed. Gavin's face was inches from his. Always uninjured, always unmarred by scars.* That's because I dreamed that I beat him. It was only a dream.

Gavin sighed. "I think it's time I start killing you, Isaac." Isaac's eyes went wide. "You've all but exhausted your usefulness to me."

The tears came in earnest now. "No… Gavin, please… I can…"

"You can what? Be better? Stronger? Withstand more? No, you can't. You're done, Isaac. Broken. Boring. This was fun while it lasted, truly. But I'm done with you. So, I'm going to kill you." He straddled Isaac's hips and wrapped his hands around his throat.

"No... pl—" Isaac was cut off as Gavin's hands tightened, cutting off his air. He writhed weakly against Gavin's grasp. Gavin was right. He was used up.

"I think I could probably make it last for days, if I'm lucky and if you can hold on long enough. I'd be content with that. Then when I'm done, I'm making good on my promise and going after Sam." Isaac bucked against Gavin's hand. "I know I won't get nearly as much time out of them. And, if your family isn't made up of complete morons, they're as far away from me as they can get. It'll make the search fun, I think. A good project to occupy my time." Isaac's eyes rolled back. Gavin smiled. "Maybe I'll take all of them. Or just Sam. I haven't decided yet. But I have decided one thing." He leaned in close, watching Isaac's face as he choked. "I'm absolutely going to show Sam your body before I start hurting them. They probably think you died months ago. I bet they can't even imagine that I've had you for all this time. That you've been suffering for all this time."

"Isaac."

"It's been a real thrill, I can tell you." Isaac's vision was getting fuzzy at the edges.

"Isaac."

"All I want you to do right now is relax, Isaac. Don't worry, you're not going to die today. That's all you need to know."

"Isaac!"

He gasped and shoved away the hands that held him. He sobbed brokenly, finally able to breathe again. *He's going to kill me. I'm going to die.* Gavin was still grasping at him, pulling at his clothes. Isaac screamed. He couldn't see. He threw an elbow and felt it connect. He twisted away from the hands as they let him go. He pressed himself against the wall, his face wet with tears, his fist pulled back. His right hand ached, making him gasp. The room came into focus.

Sam was kneeling in front of him. They were dimly lit by the sun beginning to stream through the window. The others were sitting up, trying to see what was going on. Gray got to their feet, looking over at them both.

Sam held a hand to their mouth. Tears streamed down their cheeks. They pulled their hand back to look at it. Blood ran from their lip.

Ice rushed through Isaac's veins.

"No... Sam... I'm so..."

Sam pulled their fist back and punched Isaac square in the face.

Isaac fell back against the wall, shocked to his core. He vaguely heard the others gasp. He put his own hand to his face and pulled it away. Blood dripped from his nose. He stared at Sam, dumbfounded. His mouth fell open of its own accord.

Sam still knelt on the floor, hands pulled into fists, chest heaving, face wet with furious tears. *"There,"* they sobbed. "Now we're even."

Isaac closed his mouth. "What—"

"I don't need one more thing for you to blame yourself for," they spat bitterly, trembling. "I don't need one more *stupid thing* for you to hate yourself for, to not talk to me about. So, we're even." Tears dripped down Sam's face and onto their shirt.

"I... don't..."

"Ever since we all escaped you won't talk to me. You won't let me in." Sam's voice was rising. Everyone remained frozen in place. "You won't tell me what happened. Because you have to be *strong*." The word was packed with anguish. "But he tortured me, too. I was there, too. Not as long as you, not as... it wasn't as bad as you..." They shook their head. "But I know. I know what it's like. And you... won't... *talk to me!*" They sobbed the words out.

"Sam..."

"We watched you get tortured, Isaac. And we risked everything to come get you. And I would do it again, in a heartbeat. I'd go back to Gavin right now if it meant I got you back. But you… you keep pushing me away, you keep avoiding me, you won't talk to *anyone*, except Tori…"

As if summoned, Tori appeared in the doorway, disheveled. She froze as she saw Isaac cowering into the wall, shock and bewilderment on his face, as Sam sobbed in front of him.

Isaac looked back to Sam and swallowed hard. "What do you mean…? Tori…"

"I heard you. I heard what you told her that first night. I was awake. I heard the whole thing."

Isaac blanched.

Sam gasped helplessly. "And I don't *care!* I don't *care* if you broke, Isaac. God knows I did. Gavin tortured you using things *I told him*." A shudder rolled over Sam's body. "And, be honest with me, did you ever *once* blame me for that?"

Isaac's lips trembled. "No…" he whispered.

"Then *why*…" Sam's voice rose to a wail. "…do you keep blaming yourself? *Why* do you keep pushing me away? Why won't you just… just *talk* to me?" Sam's hands went to their hair and they pulled, whining in anguish. "The worst thing Gavin ever did to me wasn't torturing me, Isaac." They pinned him down with their gaze. "The worst thing he ever did was torture *you*."

Sam collapsed into sobs and pressed their face into their hands. Tears started down Isaac's cheeks. He swallowed hard. His throat burned, his eyes fixed on Sam as they wailed miserably. He reached out hesitantly to Sam, afraid of being pushed away. His heart clenched at the thought. He steeled himself and brushed his fingers down Sam's shoulder.

They trembled and pressed their face harder into their hands. Isaac licked his lips, tears streaming, as his hand held firm on their shoulder. He was shaking.

Sam pulled their face up, was swollen and red from crying. They looked down at Isaac's hand, then slowly up to his face. They saw the anguish there. They gulped and hurled themselves into his arms.

Isaac wrapped his arms around them and squeezed as tight as he could. He swallowed hard and erupted into sobs as he pulled Sam against his chest, leaning back against the wall, cradling them. They wound their arms around his neck and wept bitterly into his shirt.

"I'm sorry. I'm so sorry," Isaac whispered. "I'm sorry I let him hurt you."

"I'm sorry I told him how to hurt you." Sam whimpered. "I'm so sorry."

"I'm sorry I pushed you away. It's not because I don't—"

"I know." Sam hiccoughed. "I just want you back, Isaac. Please just… just tell me what I have to say to get you back."

Tell me… Isaac convulsed around Sam, a sob drawing out almost into a choked scream. He whimpered against Sam's hair. "Tell me you forgive me," he whispered.

"Of course." Sam nuzzled into Isaac's neck. "Of course, I forgive you. I forgive you for everything."

Isaac swallowed hard. "For letting him take you… and taking so long to find you…"

"Yes. Everything."

"…and hurting you so I could go to him… begging for you to come for me… letting him hurt you again…"

"Yes, Isaac. I swear. Everything."

Isaac whimpered. "…for shutting you out for all this time… and for…" His thumb moved across Sam's lip, wiping the blood away.

"Yes. Everything."

Isaac's arms tightened around them and he buried his face in their hair. Sam sniffled and whispered, "Do you forgive me?"

Isaac shook his head. "There's nothing to forgive."

"No." Sam pulled away so they could see his eyes. "Do you forgive me for telling him how to torture you? For…" They swallowed hard and another cascade of tears ran down their cheeks. "…for not being strong enough?"

Isaac closed his eyes. He leaned forward and pressed his forehead against Sam's. "Yes."

"Say it. Please."

"I… f-forgive you."

Sam pulled Isaac into their arms again. They held each other as Isaac gently rocked them. Blood dripped from Isaac's nose and he lifted a hand to scrub it away. Sam didn't notice their lip bleeding, the drops running down their chin and into Isaac's shirt.

Isaac's eyes drifted up slowly and for the first time, he noticed everyone else in the room. Tori knelt on the mattress with Gray, hands clasped in theirs, tears running down both their faces. Finn and Ellis sat together. Ellis's eyes were averted, but they were smiling. Finn grinned from ear to ear, cheeks wet with tears. Vera's eyes shone with tears. She smiled, not seeming to notice them running down her cheeks.

Isaac swallowed. He tucked Sam's head under his chin and leaned back against the wall. The tears wouldn't stop. He didn't mind.

Chapter 46

She was there again. The cold seeped into her bones. Her hands moved to her neck and she shuddered. The collar wasn't there. I should be wearing it. It's how he marks me as his. It's how he chains me down. *She swallowed, the feeling almost alien.*

If I'm not collared, then what am I doing here? *She turned slowly, gaze moving over the walls. The instruments were all still there, hanging on their hooks, clean of her blood. The anchors on the walls and the ground. The cold cement floor. As she turned back, her stomach dropped.*

Her family stood in a line in front of the door. They stood tall and happy, looking at her with affection and pride. Maybe they won't leave me to die this time. Maybe they've really come for me.

Her heart jumped as the door opened and two more figures entered the room. Vera's eyes slowly adjusted to the dark. Her heart clenched as she realized one of the figures was Tori. Tori watched her as she walked in, a soft smile on her lips. Behind her was a man, half in shadows. The hair on the back of Vera's neck stood up. It was him.

"You have to run," she whispered. Her eyes went wide and desperate as she looked at her family. No one moved. "Please." The word was little more than a sob. "You have to go."

The man smiled. "I won't hurt them, sweetheart. You know I always loved hurting you. They're safe from me."

"Please…" She wasn't sure if she was pleading or thanking him. "Let them go. You have me back, let them go."

"They're free to leave. I think they're just… fascinated. Want to watch me work."

She bit her lip, the tears threatening to spill over. "Fine. Just don't hurt them. I'll take it. Just don't touch them."

"Oh, I should have mentioned my one exception to what I just said. I know you can take the pain so well. I remember." He winked. "It hasn't been so long that I've forgotten you, sweetheart. I could never forget you. I know you can take the knife, and the whip, all of it. By the end you were nearly... perfect. No, I know how to hurt you deep."

She shook her head, tears falling. "No. No. Please..."

The man took out a knife and pushed Tori to her knees, holding the knife against her throat. Tori's smile remained compassionate, her eyes locked on Vera.

Vera couldn't bear to see it. "Please!" She sobbed. "No. Don't touch her. She's good, she hasn't done anything wrong... please..."

"You ran away from me, Vera. You ran away and didn't come back for a long time. How incredibly... disobedient of you. What I'm going to do now is to teach you never to disobey me again. Do you remember your rules?"

"Yes," she gasped. "Yes, I remember."

"What are they?"

"N-never speak without permission."

"Good." The knife was pulled up against Tori's chin. Her hands were behind her back. Vera didn't know if she was bound, or if she was just holding them there. Still, Tori's expression was calm. Forgiving.

"Only eat or sleep when told to. Please..."

"Good. Keep going."

"N-never scream unless you let me." She was trembling so hard she thought she might fall.

"Good."

"T-take all p-punishments without complaint."

"We were doing so well with that one, too. Keep going."

"Never take off the collar."

"You're not wearing it now."

She shook her head, gaze still locked on Tori. "No."

"Put it on."

She looked down at her feet. The collar lay on the ground. She picked it up with shaking hands, the rough leather worn smooth from months of use. It felt so heavy. The small padlock dangled from the ring at the back. She felt sick in her bones as she raised it to her throat and buckled it on. She reached behind her head to snap the padlock closed, locking it around her throat forever. She sobbed miserably as she once again grew accustomed to the long-abandoned weight. She raised her eyes to the man. His knife was still poised at Tori's throat.

"Much better. It improves you, Vera. Elevates you."

Vera's throat felt like it would close completely with how hard she was sobbing. "Please... let her go... let them go..."

"I don't think so, Vera. Remember, this is a punishment."

"No..."

"Do you remember how I like you?"

A whine forced its way from between her teeth as she lowered herself to her knees, finally at eye level with Tori. "I'm sorry," she whispered.

"You've proven you can't be trusted when you're not chained down. Do it."

She looked down and saw the chain running down her shoulder from the lock on her collar. She took it in her shaking hand and clipped one end to an anchor between her knees.

"And?"

She folded her hands in her lap and bowed her head. She looked out from under her eyelashes to lock eyes with Tori. Tori was still looking at her with heart-wrenching compassion. Vera couldn't stand it.

"So much better. Take your punishment now, Vera."

"NO!" she screamed. "Tori no, I'm sorry... I'm so sorry, I never meant... no, please, please!"

The knife cut into Tori's throat. Vera threw herself against the chain, shrieking her despair. "NO! Please! No... I'm sorry, I'm so sorry, Tori, no... Tori..." She pulled harder on the chain. The collar held her back, closing around her throat more and more the harder she fought. She choked. A strangled sound tore from her throat.

Tori's kind smile never left her face as she bled out onto the floor. Vera reached out to try to hold her, to pull her away from the man. She couldn't reach her. Her hands left smears in the blood.

Chapter 47

Still shaking from the nightmare, Vera padded to the kitchen, her arms wrapped tightly around her. She didn't know what she was doing. She didn't know what she wanted. She hoped – god, she *hoped* – for something to relieve the pressure in her chest, the pull further into the house, to a different dark room. To Tori's room. She snapped on the light and stood at the counter, hands bracing herself up, head bent. Her hair fell around her face. She shook her head, gritting her teeth. *Go the fuck back to bed, you idiot. Just go back to bed. She won't—*

She turned to leave the kitchen and froze. Tori stood in the doorway, concern darkening her features. "Are you alright?"

Vera swallowed. *I'm fine. I'm fine except that I've been dreaming about you and all I want right now is for you to touch me again.* "Y-yeah. I'm good."

"You don't look... good." Tori took a tentative step forward. "More nightmares?" Vera nodded jerkily. "I'm so sorry. Do you want to talk about it?"

Vera crossed her arms over herself. "I... I dreamed about... um..."

Another step closer. "You don't have to tell me. It's okay. Do you want to go to the couch again? Just sit?"

No, I don't want to just sit. Vera's jaw clenched. "Um. I'm sorry. I didn't mean to wake you up."

"Occupational hazard, I guess. I don't mind." Tori's gaze was soft, her eyebrows still pulled together with worry.

"Tori, I..." Vera's throat clicked as she swallowed dryly. Tori's hands came up to rub against Vera's upper arms, and she trembled.

Tori's hands stilled on Vera's arms and she searched Vera's face carefully. "Is this okay?"

Vera nodded, hands shaking. Her stomach dropped as she reached out to Tori. She almost let her hands fall to her sides again. Tori's gaze was so warm, so concerned. Haltingly, Vera raised her hands and cupped them against Tori's face.

Tori's eyes went wide. Her hands tightened on Vera's arms.

Vera froze. *She doesn't want this.*

Tori smiled and pulled her close, arms snaking around her waist.

Vera closed her eyes and pressed a kiss to Tori's lips.

Tori drew in a quick, tremulous breath as Vera tilted her face up, pulling their mouths together. One hand went up to curl around Vera's wrist. Tori's fingers brushed the old scars there and she ran her hand back up Vera's forearm. Vera's fingers went back to tangle in Tori's hair as she opened her mouth, tongue brushing against Tori's lower lip. Tori moaned so quietly it was almost a breath.

Vera turned with her, pushing Tori back until her hips pressed up against the counter. Vera smiled as she lifted Tori and set her gently on the counter. Tori wrapped her legs around Vera's waist and pulled her even closer. Vera's hands moved down her back to her thighs, resting gently as Tori's hands moved to her face.

"I'm taller now," Tori whispered, grinning.

Tori cradled the back of Vera's head and lifted her chin with her other hand, running her thumb along Vera's bottom lip. She pulled Vera's face up to hers and met her with parted lips. Vera opened her mouth to her, her tongue pressing gently against Tori's. She sighed.

Tori's mouth moved across Vera's cheek, planting sweet kisses as she moved to her ear, down her neck. Vera took a shuddering gasp as Tori's lips pressed against the hollow of her throat. "Can I kiss you here?" Tori whispered.

Vera nodded vigorously, swallowing hard. "Please." Tori's hand tangled in her hair and she pulled Vera's head to the side, baring her throat to her lips. Vera gasped as Tori pressed open-mouthed kisses against her neck, moving back and forth from her jaw to her collarbone. Her fingers tightened on Tori's thighs. Vera shuddered.

"Is that still okay?" Tori pulled back, studying Vera's face. Vera nodded. "I just... I know if I set something off, you might not be able to tell me. I want to be careful."

Vera's eyes welled with tears as she gazed up at Tori. "Thank you," she whispered. "But I... I think it'll be different."

Tori tilted her head. "Why?"

Vera's lips trembled. "Because you're not... h-hurting me." She pressed her lips together.

Tori closed her eyes as her face crumpled in pain. She pressed her forehead against Vera's as her hands returned to cradle her face. "I... I'm so sorry."

Vera shook her head. "Don't," she whispered. "I just want to be with you right now." She opened her eyes to search Tori's face, imploring. "I just want to be with you. Please."

Tori nodded and leaned forward to press her lips against Vera's again. Vera opened her mouth hungrily. Her hands crept up to Tori's waist, slipping under the hem of her shirt and pressing against the soft skin of her back. Tori took a shaky breath as Vera's fingers moved over the sensitive skin. Vera was beginning to wonder if they should leave the kitchen in favor of somewhere more private. Tori's mouth traced a burning path back and forth along the side of Vera's neck.

"Oh heyyaaaaaahm I'm *so sorry*."

They both jumped to see Ellis standing in the doorway, staring at the floor and turning an alarming shade of red. "I'm so sorry. I didn't realize... um... I'll... I'm sorry." Ellis nearly collided with the doorway as they turned, leaving the kitchen with an almost desperate haste.

Vera's cheeks flushed red, too. Tori laughed. "What are they so embarrassed about? Catching you, or catching me?"

"Um..." Vera's cheeks still burned. "They're actually... uh... really awkward about this kind of thing in general. I don't think they've seen me with someone like this... maybe ever. They're really... um... private with Finn. And they're probably feeling pretty awkward about someone kissing our host." She swallowed, leaning away from Tori. "I'm sorry."

Tori used her legs, still wrapped around her, to pull Vera close again. She hooked a hand behind Vera's head and pulled her back in for a deep kiss. "Want to go somewhere a little more private? Maybe my room?"

If it were possible, Vera would have blushed harder. "I was just thinking that right before they walked in, actually. Um… yeah. That would be great."

"Great." Tori smiled warmly and hopped off the counter. She took her hand and laced her fingers through Vera's. She snapped off the light as she led Vera into the dark, into a part of the house Vera had never been before.

Chapter 48

Tori turned on the light again. Vera blinked as her eyes adjusted. The room was large, but cozy, with a thick, plush rug on the floor. The walls were decorated with paintings, pictures, collages – Vera guessed from Tori's guests over the years. Two bookshelves lined the walls, heavy and full of books. The bed was in the center of the room, the headboard against the far wall and the covers pulled back in a heap. Tori slowly led Vera to the bed, watching Vera's face with tender concentration.

Tori sat down and pulled Vera close, gazing up at her, lips pulled up into a smile. "Is this okay?" Tori's hands laced through Vera's.

Vera bit her lip, feeling Tori's fingers slide through hers, watching Tori turn her hand over and press a kiss into her palm. She nodded.

Tori pulled Vera's head down for a kiss and Vera leaned forward, straddling Tori's hips. Vera wrapped her arms around Tori's waist and held her, pressing a kiss against her hair and breathing the scent of her in.

Tori's lips caressed against her neck. "We only go as far as you want to, okay?"

Vera closed her eyes. It had been hard, finding something like this, in the years since she'd been captured. Hot mouths and clutching hands almost always seemed to send her into a panic, pushing against the body on top of her, cowering away from the touch, with both men and women alike.

Tori was different. Tori was so *warm*, and soft, and kind. Tori was gentle. Tori saw her, *truly* saw her, her wounds, her hurts, her past. And she was looking up at her like that anyway. Tori was gentling her and holding her anyway.

"I want to hear you say it, Vera." Tori's hand pulled Vera's head back so she could see her eyes. "I want to know you know that, that you believe me."

Vera's lips trembled. "I…"

Tori's eyes were so gentle. "It's okay. We don't have to go any further. We don't have to do anything tonight. We can just go to sleep, or you can go back to the guest room and sleep. Okay? I promise." She stroked her thumb along Vera's cheek, cupping her face.

Vera blew out a steadying breath. "O-okay. We only go as far as I want."

"Yeah," Tori whispered. "As *you want.*"

What do I want? Vera felt a warm flush go through her and her eyes flicked down to Tori's lips.

She leaned in to kiss Tori again, drawing Tori's bottom lip between her teeth and sucking gently. Tori's breath caught in her throat and she sighed.

Vera leaned forward and pushed Tori back against the bed, lacing her fingers through Tori's and pinning her arms gently above her head. Tori groaned as Vera's mouth moved to her throat. Vera moved Tori's wrists, so they were both pinned with one hand. She slid her other hand down Tori's arm, across her collarbone, and behind her neck. She drew her tongue down the edge of Tori's ear. Tori gasped at the hot breath on her neck, her mouth falling open. Vera pressed her forehead against Tori's temple.

"I'm sorry," Vera whispered. "I'm... um... rusty."

Tori laughed gently. "I'd say you're doing just fine." She arched her back, pressing herself up against her, lips searching hungrily for Vera's. "Please."

Vera smiled as she covered Tori's mouth with hers. Her tongue pressed deep as she breathed in Tori's intoxicating scent. A shudder passed through Vera, desire and fear and bittersweet longing all mixing together and moving through her. Tori opened her eyes and looked up at her, concern pulling her eyebrows together.

"Are you alright?" Tori's eyes were wide and incredibly vulnerable. She laid still under Vera's hands, wrists still pinned above her, gazing up at her in complete trust. Vera trembled.

"Um... I just..." Vera licked her lips. "It's been a long time since I felt... this... good." Tori smiled. "And I want to just..." Her hand tightened on Tori's wrists. "...*take* you, be with you, take you all in and just..." Tori trembled, her body reacting to Vera of its own volition. Vera pressed her lips together. "But I'm... um... scared."

Tori nodded. "I understand."

"No..." Vera's hand moved up to meet the other and she grasped Tori's wrists hard and pressed her down against the bed, burying her face in her hair. "I don't want to mess this up. And I don't want to... get scared and ruin it. It's hard for me to... um..."

Tori nodded. "That's okay. We don't have to go any further. And you won't... *ruin* this, Vera. You're..." She nosed against Vera's hair, pressing her cheek against Vera's. "You're perfect."

Vera trembled. "I want you."

Tori smiled. "You can have me."

Vera bit her lip and shook her head, pressing a kiss against Tori's neck. "I'm scared." She released Tori's wrists. Tori's arms came around her and held her tight.

"I'm not going anywhere," Tori whispered. "If this is all we do tonight, that's okay. If you... if you never want to do this again, that's okay too. I like this, Vera." Tori's hand went under her chin, guiding Vera's face around until she could see her eyes. "But only if it's what you want, too."

Vera's fingers pressed against Tori's back as Tori pulled her close. "Then can we just... will you just hold me? I want to..." She swallowed. "I want you. Just... maybe not yet. Please just... give me time."

Tori pressed a kiss against her forehead. "Take as much time as you need. Even if it never happens." Vera pushed herself up off of Tori and looked down at her. Tori smiled back at her. "I want you, too. I want you to take me. I want to have you, too. But only..." Her hand went up to caress Vera's face. "...if you want that, without a shadow of a doubt."

Vera stood up and let Tori push herself up and towards the head of the bed. Tori eased herself under the covers and held a hand out for Vera. Vera took it and crawled into bed next to her.

Tori opened her arms to let Vera get as close as she wanted. Vera cuddled up against her chest, her fingers hooking into the t-shirt Tori was wearing. Vera curled up in her arms as Tori pulled her close and tucked Vera's head under her chin. She pressed a soft kiss against Vera's hair. Vera listened peacefully to the sound of Tori's heart beating, soaking in the warmth and tender touches until she fell asleep.

Chapter 49

Isaac was busy cutting vegetables for dinner. He had his right hand, still bound in a brace, on top of the cutting board holding the vegetables in place. He handled the knife carefully in his left. Gray had offered to do it. *"The last thing you need now is to cut a finger off."* They said it with a laugh. Isaac insisted. *"I want to help. You don't need to keep me away from the pointy objects."* He'd been smiling, too.

Tori peeked past his shoulder. He moved back to show her his work. "Is this the right size?"

She smiled and nodded. "Perfect. Thank you."

Sam came into the kitchen, hobbling skillfully on their crutches. It was almost time to get the brace of their leg. Almost. "Can I help?"

Tori moved to shoo them out of the kitchen. "Nope. Thank you, though." She smiled.

Isaac turned, knife still in hand, a smile on his face too. "Come on, Sam. Be honest. You're here because you want a sample."

Sam froze, their eyes fixed on the knife.

They'd been around knives in the kitchen before. They'd helped Tori peel potatoes for shepherd's pie not even a week ago. But something was different this time. Something was wrong.

"If you think this hurts you're essentially fucked, Sam."

They stumbled back, losing their grip on the crutch as a hand went up in front of them. Pain lanced through their bad leg. They swallowed. *It's okay it's okay this is stupid it's just Isaac it's just a knife it's fine it's okay he's not here it's over this is stupid stupid stupid stupid.*

"Let me put it to you this way. I'm not going to stop unless you tell me the address of your hideout. It's entirely up to you how long this goes on."

They lost their balance and started to fall backwards. *Why why why no this is wrong why no this shouldn't happen I'm fine I'm fine I'm fine I'm fine.*

Gavin yanked Sam's head back, baring their throat as they sobbed. They pulled desperately at the rope binding their wrists behind them in the chair. Gavin waved the knife in front of their face.

"You sure you have nothing to say? Not a single clue *about the address of your little group's house?"*

Hot tears poured down Sam's face as they tried to turn their head away, against Gavin's grip on their hair. "N-no... no... please..."

Gavin sighed. "You'd think by this point you'd have figured out that I'm not fucking *around, Sam." He brought the knife to their left arm, just below the shoulder. Sam flinched away from the bite of cold steel on their skin. Their whimpers turned to screams as Gavin drew the blade across their arm. It left a line of blood as it went. They writhed away from the pain, but Gavin held them steady with an iron grip on their hair.*

"No! Please!*" they screamed. "No no no..." The knife left their skin and they slumped in the chair, sweating and shaking with relief. They swallowed hard against the rawness of their throat. It's only been a few hours... not even a day. They cried harder as they wondered how long they would survive.* It has to get worse. He's not going to stop.

"Anything coming to mind now?"

Sam gritted their teeth as tears streamed down their cheeks.

"Whatever." Gavin brought the knife to Sam's arm again and drew another line of blood.

Sam twisted as they cried out. They bit down hard on their lip. I can't tell him. He'll kill them. He'll hunt them down and kill them. *Their mouth opened wide in a scream of agony.*

Gavin finished with the cut. Sam moaned, gasping for breath. "Isaac will find me," they sobbed.

Gavin rolled his eyes. "That's the second time you've brought him up. Who the fuck is Isaac? Brother? Boyfriend? What?"

"He's my friend," they shrieked, blood rolling down their arm in a hot line. "He'll find me, he'll... he'll come, he won't let you do this..."

Gavin snorted. "Um... newsflash, buddy, but..." He waved his hand around the room in a lazy circle, knife still held tight. "...I'm kinda already doing it. How exactly do you imagine he's going to find you? If he's even looking. It was embarrassingly easy to take you, Sam. Are you sure this was an accident? How do you know he wasn't ready to just shed some dead weight?"

Sam shuddered. "No... he would never... he... he'll come for me, he will..."

"Don't you think he would've been here by now if he was coming for you? I've given him plenty of time. Plenty of hints, too. And he just..." Gavin knitted his eyebrows together, looking utterly perplexed. "...hasn't shown up. Weird."

Sam tried to deny it, tried to say it was all a lie and Isaac was coming for them. The words caught in their throat. What if he's telling the truth? They shoved the thought away. Isaac will save me. Isaac is coming.

"Welp, in the meantime you're stuck with me. And if your team is the group that's been hitting my satellite operations, I'd love the opportunity to return the favor. So. Your home base. Tell me or the next one is deeper."

"No! I can't, I can't I can't I can't no no no..." Isaac would be brave. Isaac wouldn't give him anything.

"Okay, hard way it is." The knife cut into Sam's arm. Blood flowed from the wound.

"NO! Please, no... please... it's 37 Rockrest Drive... in... in Teston... please..."

Gavin laughed. "There, was that so hard? Now I know the first place to go once I'm done with you. Honestly not sure how long that's gonna take, but..." He turned Sam's head, inspecting their face as they cried. "I'm not in any hurry."

Sam wailed in despair. He's going to find them. He's going to kill me and then go after them. "No..." they whimpered. "No... no, please... don't..."

Gavin tapped the blade against Sam's face. They flinched away, crying out weakly in terror.

Gavin grinned. "Thanks so much for that. I'll be sure to tell them who told me before I slaughter them."

∴

Isaac was frozen for a split second. His stomach dropped. He'd had a knife in his hand. Taken a step towards Sam. Maybe that was enough. Nobody else was able to predict their bad days, either. This day was different. This time, for Sam, something was wrong.

He watched Sam take a fumbling step back on their bad leg. Watched their knee buckle. Then another step. Sam was going to fall.

The knife fell from his hand and he was across the room in milliseconds. His good hand got a grip on Sam's shirt as his healing one fumbled against their arm. He didn't notice the pain as his fingers tried to close.

They collapsed to the ground together in a heap. It took a moment for Isaac to understand what Sam was saying between their hitched sobs.

"Pl— Pl— Pl-lease I-I'm so-sor-sorry nuh— no-o—"

Isaac tried to force down the ice in his gut. "Sam?" Their eyelids fluttered, their eyes darting around the room, unseeing. "Sam?" His hands shook as he reached out to hold them.

They gave reaction, no indication they even knew Isaac was there. They trembled so violently he could barely hold onto them. He pulled them up to sitting and wrapped his arms around them. They shrunk in his embrace, weakly raising their hands to protect their head.

Tori knelt beside Isaac. Gray was right behind her. Isaac swallowed hard, his eyes rising to hers, panicked. "W-what do I do?" He pressed his lips together to keep them from trembling.

Tori carefully brushed Sam's hair away from their face, her mouth twisted with concern. "You've never seen them like this before?"

He numbly shook his head. "I… I don't… I don't think they would keep this from me, I don't…" Tears brimmed in his eyes.

271

"I haven't seen them this way, either." Gray's voice was strained. "What do you think—"

"It was the knife." Isaac pressed his lips to Sam's hair, distracted. "That has to be it. I don't... I didn't mean to..."

Tori placed a hand gently on Isaac's shoulder. "Of course you didn't, Isaac. Now just... gently talk to them. Try to bring them back. Gently."

He nodded helplessly. "Sam..." he murmured. "Sam, you're okay... you're safe... you're right here with me..."

"Tell them where they are. Sometimes that helps."

Isaac's eyes were wide. "Do you want to... um... do it? Do you want to talk to them?"

Tori's hand rubbed Isaac's shoulder in soothing circles. "I think it should be you, Isaac. You're... well..." Tori licked her lips. "They trust you more than anyone. It's okay. You can do it."

Isaac swallowed hard and cleared his throat. "Um. Sam. You're in Tori's house... in the kitchen... uh..." He rocked them gently. "You're not with him. You're with me. You're safe. Sam?" He smoothed their hair away from their forehead as they whimpered. "Sam, you with me?"

The words that fell from Sam's lips were so strained with tears Isaac couldn't understand them. He moved his hand lightly through their hair. His arms shook as they tightened around Sam. *What if I can't get them back from this?*

"Sam? Sam, you're safe. Can you tell me what's wrong? Was it the knife? I'm sorry. I'm so sorry."

"N— n— no-o... no... pl-ease..."

"You're okay, Sam. It's okay. You're safe."

"H— he... G-Ga-avin..."

"He's gone. He's in the hospital. He'll never hurt you again."

Sam cowered into Isaac's chest. "P-please no..."

"I've got you, Sam. Is it okay that I'm holding you?"

They nodded weakly. "I... 'm s— sorry 'm s-sorry..."

"Shhh. You're alright. You have nothing to be sorry for." Tears rolled down Isaac's cheeks and into Sam's hair.

"I— If I had d-died if... i-if I'd ma— made him ki-ill me... he would n— never... you... never..."

"No." The word was a growl in Isaac's throat. "No. Don't say that. Don't say that to me. Ever. I'd take it all again, a hundred times, if it meant you stayed alive. Do you hear me?" He guided Sam's chin up. Their face was swollen and red and stained with tears. "Don't say that. Don't start that. Please."

Sam swallowed hard. "'m s-sorry I... I'm sorry..."

"Shh. Sam. You're okay, you're safe. Can you talk to me? Can you tell me what's wrong?"

"He... c-cut me... he... hurt me, Isaac... please..."

Isaac squeezed his eyes shut. "I know. I know he did."

"M-made me t-tell him... where to f-find y-you..."

"But we got away. Remember? He can't find us here. We're safe, at Tori's house."

"T-Tori..." They reached out blindly.

She took their hand in hers, squeezing gently. "I'm here, honey. I'm here, too."

"Th-thank you... T-Tori... thank you..."

Tori's voice was hushed. "Of course, honey."

"Isaac..." Sam huddled against his chest, hooking their fingers into his shirt and pressing their face there until the sound of their whimpers was muffled. "Isaac..."

He ran a hand through their hair and cradled their head against his chest. "I'm here, Sam."

They trembled. "P-please… just… will y-you hold me? I'm sorry, I d-didn't mean… I didn't…"

"Hey." Isaac pulled Sam into his lap as he pushed himself backwards, resting back against the wall. "I can hold you. No problem. Is this okay?"

They whimpered and pulled him close as tears burned on their cheeks. "Y-yes. It's… it's good. I'm s-sorry."

Isaac's cheek rested on the top of Sam's head. Tori moved closer and sat cross-legged on the floor next to them, rubbing soothing circles on Sam's back. Gray stood by, leaning against the wall. They crossed their arms, eyes filled with tears. They turned when they heard the others walking into the kitchen.

"What happened?!" Finn practically lunged forward, hands outstretched. Their eyes dropped to the brace still on their left hand and they stopped in their tracks.

Tori turned, holding out a hand. "It's okay. They're not hurt. They're just…" She swallowed. "Something happened. They got scared, thought they were back with Gavin. They're alright."

Vera crouched beside Tori. Their eyes met for a moment until Vera broke the contact, her cheeks flushing red. Tori's lips quirked up, before her smile fell for a moment. Among the lot of them, Isaac and Vera had the best idea of what was going on inside Sam's head. Tori gave Vera's shoulder a quick squeeze.

Finn and Ellis hovered just outside the circle surrounding Sam. Ellis put an arm around Finn's shoulder. Finn wound an arm around Ellis's waist.

"'m sorry." Sam's voice was small. Their eyes were still squeezed shut, their head tucked under Isaac's chin.

The room erupted into protest. Everyone scooted closer until they were within reach of Sam.

"Sam…" Isaac's voice was a whisper. "Is it okay if we all touch you?"

They sniffled and nodded. Hands went to their back, their hair, their shoulders. They shivered, unraveling a little and nestling closer into Isaac's chest.

Chapter 50

Vera hummed quietly as she dusted the furniture in Tori's living room. Tori had tried to insist that she relax, that they didn't need to earn their keep, that it was *alright,* but Vera was going stir crazy with nothing to do.

Almost two months. They'd been here for almost two months. Isaac's hand had healed, although the brace was still on to protect his thumb. Vera had raised her eyebrows when Tori said that. *"A dislocation takes longer to heal than a break?"* Finn had agreed. *"Thumb dislocations take forever to heal. It sounds weird, but it's true. Same with sprains. They heal slower than broken bones."* Sam was taking tentative steps on their bad leg. The brace was still on, but not all the time anymore. Finn's hand was healed, too. *It means it's almost time to leave.* Vera militantly pushed the implication away. Her throat felt tight every time the thought crossed her mind.

She moved from dusting a table to dusting a lamp. She started when she turned around and noticed Tori standing in the walkway watching her. She flushed red and straightened up.

"Sorry." Tori's smile was gentle. "I didn't mean to startle you. I was just… what were you humming? It sounded familiar."

"Just a song I miss. 'Work Song.' By, um, Hozier. It, um. It came out the year I went undercover." She chewed her lip. "I miss music. I had an iPod for a while but it broke. And we can't use phones while we're on the run. GPS tracking." She shrugged. "I just… like to remember my favorite songs. It's been a long time."

"I think I might have that song."

Vera's eyes went wide. "You… that song? How? Not on… not on a phone…?" She set the rag down.

"I have an iPod. Ancient thing. I'll go get it." Tori turned and disappeared down the hallway. Vera stood awkwardly in the middle of the room, waiting.

Tori reappeared, holding up the iPod. A battered pair of earbuds dangled from her hand. "Found it. Here." She reached out a hand to Vera and pulled her towards the kitchen. "I miss music, too. I miss dancing. Wanna dance?"

In spite of herself, Vera's lips drifted up into a smile. "I love dancing."

Tori guided her into the kitchen, to the middle of the floor. She handed the iPod to Vera. "See if it's on here." Tori fumbled with the earbuds as Vera began to scroll.

A well of longing opened up inside of her that Vera hadn't even realized was there as she swiped through the songs. She didn't know a lot of them, but there were so, so many more that she did. She couldn't remember the last time she heard music she liked. Some of the radio stations were still playing but it was usually nothing but news, curated carefully by the syndicates. *Even after they've won, they're still lying to us.*

She found it. It had been years since she'd heard the song – she wasn't even sure if she remembered all the words. Tori passed her an earbud as she tucked the other into her ear. Vera hit play and put the iPod in her pocket.

From the very first beat, Vera was catapulted back fifteen years. Her heart flooded with an ache so deep it took her breath away. Without thinking about it, her right arm wound behind Tori's back. She took Tori's right hand with her left and pulled her close. Tori let herself be guided forward until her head rested on Vera's shoulder. Vera started to shift her weight. Tori moved along with her effortlessly.

Vera hummed along. The deep notes rumbled through her chest; the high notes shimmered in her throat. She closed her eyes and felt Tori breathe close against her chest. Tori kept perfectly in step with her, swaying softly, their feet moving together. Vera wanted to ask her where she learned to dance. She held her tongue, letting the waves of music wash over her. Her face broke into a smile as she moved around the kitchen with Tori, perfectly in sync.

Vera's eyes filled with tears at the chorus. It touched something in her that hadn't been unearthed since she'd escaped Joseph: quiet, reverent joy, sweet and earnest and tenuous as a spider's web.

Tears fell steadily down her face. She rested her cheek against Tori's hair and breathed deeply. She drew her left hand in, holding Tori's hand to her chest and folding hers over it. She cradled Tori closer with her right arm and pulled her closer into her embrace.

Tori nuzzled into Vera's neck and pressed a small kiss there. Vera's lips trembled.

Tori's left hand crept up Vera's back until her fingertips brushed up Vera's neck. She cradled the back of Vera's head gently, fingers drawing lightly through her hair. Her hand went down to rest on the back of Vera's neck. For once, for the first time, Vera welcomed the weight. She shivered.

Vera pulled Tori in closer, her arms aching with the need to hold her. Tori's embrace tightened. Vera felt tears on her shoulder. Tori was crying, too.

They breathed together and for a moment, Vera felt like they were one person drawing breath. The music wound through them both as they moved.

As the music lulled with the last verse, Vera was rooted to the floor, swaying on the spot. Her hand left Tori's for a moment and she tucked Tori's hair back, away from her face. She pressed her lips against Tori's forehead. Vera tightened her embrace, trembling with longing and the sweet affection.

Vera moved in slow circles, her arms wound around Tori's waist as they danced in the middle of the kitchen. As the last lines faded Vera came to rest in the center of the room. She held Tori close. Her hand moved under Tori's chin and guided Tori's face up. Vera leaned down, blindly searching for Tori's lips. Tori clung to her as Vera pressed her mouth against hers. Tori brought her hands up to Vera's face, cradling her, wiping her tears away. The song came to an end. They stood still as the next one played, mouths moving slowly together.

Chapter 51

Someone sniffled. Finn rolled over, not quite connected to their body. They drifted, fading, almost falling back into sleep.

Another sniffle. They felt the dull spark of consciousness light up in their brain and their eyes drifted open begrudgingly. Their hand moved to Ellis's side of the mattress. They felt only cold blankets.

Panic rippled through their stomach for a split second before they woke up completely. *They're not gone. Not missing. Just not in bed.* They pushed themselves up, wobbling as they got to their feet. They took a step, paused, looked back. They pulled the blanket off the bed and wrapped it around themselves before padding out into the hall.

The lights in the house were all off. They stumbled through the dark, down the hall and into the living room. Their hand fumbled along the wall until they found the light switch and snapped it on.

Ellis was huddled on the couch, their arms wrapped tightly around their middle. They jumped as the light went on and scrubbed at their face, which was red and puffy, and slick with tears.

Finn frowned. "What's wrong? Nightmare?"

"No." Ellis's voice was husky. "I'm sorry if I woke you." They kept their head down, hiding their face.

Finn sat down on the couch next to them and their eyebrows pulled together, perplexed. "No, don't... Ellis, what is it?"

Ellis squeezed their eyes shut, swallowing the lump in their throat and drawing in a deep breath. "It's..." They slowly blew the breath out between their lips, trying and failing to keep their voice from wavering. "I... just..." Their face crumpled. They pressed their hands against their eyes and started to sob. "I j-just miss them."

Tears welled in Finn's eyes and they pulled Ellis into their arms. Ellis clutched at Finn, pressing their mouth against Finn's shoulder as they shook.

"And I... I d-didn't want t-to wake you, I didn't want... I'm... I'm sorry, Finn, I don't mean to make you f-feel like you're not enough—"

"No." Finn leaned back, taking Ellis's face between their hands almost roughly. "No. You're not. You're... Ellis... babe... you're allowed to miss your family. It doesn't make me feel... no." They pulled Ellis in close again, shaking their head. "It doesn't make me feel like I'm not enough."

Ellis keened softly into Finn's shoulder. Finn wrapped the blanket around them both.

"I always miss them," Ellis sobbed. "There are moments that I can... forget... just for a moment, but I miss them all the time." Their fingers dug harder into Finn's back. "And when Gavin... showed me the pictures..." Ellis shuddered. "It just brought it all back, so fresh... I thought I was getting over it, but it still hurts so much..."

"This isn't something you just get over, babe," Finn whispered. "You don't ever get over it."

"And I've been... I've been dreaming about them, about Christopher, about C-Chloe and Galen..." They wailed their names, pressing their hand hard against their mouth to muffle the sound. "Sometimes when I wake up next to you, I think I'm with him again, just for a split second before I remember, and I just... I hate myself so much for it because I love you, I love you so much, more than anything, and I almost lost you, but I just can't... I just can't stop thinking about them." They fell apart.

Finn pulled Ellis into their lap. Ellis clung to them and sobbed raggedly into their chest. Finn's tears ran into Ellis's hair as they rocked them gently. Gray appeared in the hallway over Ellis's shoulder, concern written over their face. Tori appeared behind Gray. Finn shook their head gently. They both nodded and walked backwards into the hallway, wearing the same expression of worry.

"I could never replace them," Finn murmured into Ellis's hair. "And I'd never want to. They were yours, Ellis. Your family. You never have to feel bad about missing them." They pressed their lips against Ellis's forehead. "I know you love me. And you love them too."

Ellis clutched at them. "I just... I want them back *so badly*, I would do... *anything* to get them back. I was happy. Our life was hard, dodging the syndicates, seeing our friends when we could, but it was *mine*. They were mine and they're *gone*..." They choked on their tears. "I don't even have *pictures* of them anymore... just the one I had in my wallet that day." Finn knew the one. Ellis protected that picture like nothing else: Christopher, Chloe, and Galen lounging on the couch in an adorable little pile. Smiling at the camera with real joy. Finn knew that when their family had been killed, Ellis was forced to run and leave behind everything they owned. Ellis had nothing else to remember their family by.

"And when Gavin showed me those pictures, it's the first time I saw them in *seven years*." Ellis shivered. "And I just... I want those pictures. I want to know how he got them." Finn's stomach clenched. "I wouldn't go back to him, but... if I could just see them one more time..." Finn swallowed hard. They rocked Ellis slowly.

"How old would they be now?" Finn already knew the answer.

"Chloe would be ten." Ellis didn't even have to think about it. "Galen would be thirteen." Ellis hiccoughed. "Jesus, he'd be a teenager now..."

Finn's lips trembled. "Would it feel good to think of them somewhere else? Those ages? Growing up?"

"Nothing fucking happens to us after we die." Ellis's voice was sharp with bitterness.

"Well... there's no way to know for sure... would you like to think of them growing up somewhere?"

Ellis's chest heaved. "It's all I wanted for them. To grow up... to be happy. A friend made a little baseball uniform for Galen. He never got to play it but... he might have liked it. Chloe followed me around the house every minute of the day trying to say lines from the movies she liked... Maybe she could have done plays, I don't know. If we could find a place far away where people did that stuff out in the open." Their chest heaved with dry sobs. "Christopher and I... we were thinking about having another one. We didn't know if it was going to work for us but... we just wanted another..." Finn's shirt was soaked through with tears. "I guess it wasn't fair to try and raise a family in a world like this.

But… I wanted it. I was selfish, and I wanted them… I wanted Christopher. I wanted the kids…"

"That wasn't selfish," Finn whispered. "They can't stop people from having lives, having kids, being happy…"

"They stopped me. They stopped my family. They *took them* from me." Ellis shuddered and sagged in Finn's arms. Finn pressed their lips against Ellis's temple. "I'm sorry…" Ellis's voice was small. "I love you. You're my family, too. And you make me happy."

"I know." Finn laid their cheek on the top of Ellis's head. "I know you love me. I know I'm your family. And… you're allowed to have me and still miss them. You're allowed. I can't ever replace them. I don't want to." Finn's fingers moved slowly through Ellis's hair. "The syndicates take things. It's what they do. Everyone's lost something. You lost…"

"Everything." The word was a whisper.

Finn swallowed. "You lost everything." *You almost lost me, too.* They shuddered to think what Ellis would do if they really *had* lost them. If Gavin had been able to follow through on his threat. *It's been almost two months. I might have been almost gone by now.* Even if they had all managed to escape eventually, there would have been no coming back from that. Finn knew that better than most.

"I just want to be with them again," Ellis whispered. Finn swallowed nervously. "Not… not *dead*, but… when I dream about them, or think about them, it hurts so much to know it's not real, that it's all in my head. I would give… I would give *anything* to see them again, just for a minute, kiss them, tell them I love them, I miss them… I would give *anything*."

The thought that had been tickling the back of Finn's mind ever since Gavin had tortured Ellis started to slip into focus. Their muscles locked as they tried to force the thought down, but it crept forward, growing bigger and more real no matter how hard they tried to crush it into nonexistence.

"It's just not the same with Finn, isn't it? It's tainted by the pain. You were happy and there's that part of you, deep inside, that would trade them to be with your family again."

Gavin's voice echoed in their mind. Finn wondered if Ellis remembered. If it had been true. *Gavin's a monster. He messes with people's heads. He was probably trying to torture me by saying that just as much as he was torturing Ellis.* They shuddered and pressed their lips against Ellis's hair. Ellis sobbed quietly into Finn's chest.

"I'm so sorry, babe," Finn murmured. "If I could bring them back for you, I would. I'd do anything, too."

Ellis's fingers dug into Finn's shirt. Finn pulled them close and wrapped them in a tight embrace. They rocked Ellis gently as their tears kept coming.

Chapter 52

Vera wrapped her arms around her knees and shivered slightly in the cool air. Dusk was settling in the sky, the sunset fading gently to tones of blue and grey.

It was peaceful here. The trees, the wind, the sky, they all made Vera feel calm. Like she was home, for the first time. She didn't feel that pull to go, to move, to flee before someone could find her. She didn't feel the need to escape.

It wasn't just the house that made her feel that way. It wasn't just the woods.

She stirred as she heard the door behind her open and close. As slow footsteps approached, she sat up and looked over her shoulder to greet whoever was coming.

Isaac smiled and motioned to the step where she was sitting. "Mind if I join?" She nodded and moved over to make room for him. He breathed deep, relishing the cool night air. "Nice night."

She nodded, closing her eyes. "I've been coming out here a lot. It's nice and quiet."

"I'm sorry, I didn't mean to—"

"It's fine." She opened her eyes and smiled at him, bumping his shoulder with hers. "I'm glad you're here."

He looked at his hands, folded together in front of him. The brace was off.

Vera's eyebrows went up. "All the way better, huh?"

Isaac smiled. "Sure. Physically."

Vera snorted. "About time. I hear the mental stuff takes years." Her smile slid off her face. "I'm... um... I'm sorry."

Isaac nudged her back. "Don't be."

"No, I... I shouldn't be such an asshole."

"You're not an asshole."

Vera met his eyes, a pleading apology passing over her face before clumsy sadness replaced it. He put an arm around her shoulder and squeezed. "You're not. Honestly, with what you've gone through, I'm surprised you're not a total headcase."

She laughed once, bitter. "How do you know I'm not?"

"Cuz I've known you for four years, dumbass." He gave her a playful shove.

She pushed herself upright, her lips quirking up again. "Careful, Isaac. You just got fixed up. It would be a shame to kick your ass all over again."

"You of all people could do it."

"Damn right I could."

They laughed quietly together and fell silent again. They watched the sky darken.

"How do you get over the mental stuff?" Isaac's voice was almost a whisper. Vera squeezed her eyes shut, taking a deep breath before she looked over at him. "I'm sorry. I just…" He hung his head. Vera watched him as he pressed his hands against his face. "It's been months. Almost three. Everyone's all healed up but I'm…" He ran his hands through his hair. "I still have nightmares almost every night. I still hurt sometimes. Even when… even when nothing is happening. Sometimes I feel like he's coming after me and I'm going to die. My heart won't stop beating fast and I feel like I'll pass out…" He squeezed his hand into a fist. "It shouldn't be this fucking hard. Not for me. Sam's never been through anything like that but I…" He shook his head. "I've been hurt before. I've killed before. It shouldn't…" He blew out a slow breath.

"There is no 'should', Isaac." Vera's voice was low and strained. "I was a fucking *cop*. I trained in interrogation; I worked the streets for three years. I saw all kinds of shit. I was punched, shot at, had people pull knives and guns on me all the time. And when that lunatic took me, I still fucking broke. I broke *hard*, Isaac, harder than you. I broke just like everyone else did, just like Sam, Ellis, Finn…" She squeezed his arm. "People break when other people break them. It doesn't say a damn thing about who you are."

284

Isaac stared at the ground and said nothing.

Vera swallowed hard. "Take it from somebody who knows, Isaac." He raised his head to meet her gaze. "You are fucking strong. You're the bravest man I know. And... what Gavin did to you would have broken anyone. It would have broken me." She held his gaze until he looked down. "Fuck, Gavin broke me after one slap. If that doesn't—"

"That doesn't count." Isaac's voice was hard. "You were—"

"Already broken?" Vera looked at him evenly.

"No. That's not what I meant."

"I know what you meant, Isaac." She leaned against him. "I don't know how to get better. I don't. If I did, I'd be better now. It's not something you just... *get over*. It's something you carry with you, and that's okay." He met her gaze, looking utterly helpless. "It's going to be part of you. You're going to have nightmares. You're going to have flashbacks. But they'll get less and less frequent. And when you have them..." She wet her lips. "We'll be there for you. We'll help you." He looked away. "I know it's hard. Believe me, I know. Okay? But you can talk to me."

He swallowed hard. "I know I can," he whispered. "I know I can trust you." When he looked up again he had tears in his eyes. "You know you can trust me too, right?"

Vera let out a shaky breath. "I... I know I can. It just... hurts. I didn't want anyone to know."

Isaac laughed, the sound coming out a little twisted. "Yeah. I understand that one. I didn't talk to Sam for weeks because I didn't want them to know about something they *watched happen*." He buried his face in his hands. "When they went through the same thing. Why can't I just...?"

Vera smiled. "Because you're a dumbass. Just like me. We're a family of fucking dumbasses."

He laughed, a little less bitter this time. "Yup. That's us." His shoulders relaxed a little. "I just... I know we're leaving soon. And I'm so scared I won't be able to protect them. Not when I'm like this."

285

Vera swallowed hard and looked away. Isaac watched her carefully. "You don't want to leave." It wasn't a question.

Her jaw flexed. "I'm…" She licked her lips.

He smiled. "You and Tori, huh?"

Her mouth fell open. "What… how…?"

He laughed. "Gray told me. Who heard from Finn. Who heard from Ellis."

She turned and looked back towards the house, like she was about to get up. "God dammit, Ellis, you *asshole*…"

"Hey." Isaac's voice was low and even. She turned her gaze back to him, embarrassed fury coiled in her chest. "You don't have to be embarrassed about it."

"I'm not fucking embarrassed. They just need to mind their own damned business."

"Vera." His hand was gentle as it rested on her shoulder. "You don't have to hide this from us, either. You don't have to hide at all."

She trembled with tension. Tears brimmed in her eyes as she looked at Isaac. He kept his hand on her shoulder, an anchor against her urge to leave. She drew in a breath, held it, let it out.

"You don't have to hide who you are, Vera. What you've been through… what hurts you… the people you love…" His eyes were soft. "We won't use them against you. No one will."

"You don't know that." She willed herself to be calm as the instinct to push him away rose.

He paused. "That's true. We can't stop bad things from happening. But we…" His hand tightened on her arm. "…*I* love you. I want to be there for you. No matter what it is, good or bad." He held her gaze. "I couldn't protect you from your past, or from Gavin. Let me be here for you for something good."

Her throat tightened, and her eyes burned. She dragged in a deep breath, closing her eyes and willing herself to be calm. "I'm sorry," she whispered. "I'm just… used to hiding it. All of it."

"I know." He pulled his hand away. "You're good at it. None of us had any idea what had been done to you. Tori, though…" His lips pulled up into a smile. "Apparently you weren't so good at hiding that." He winked at her.

She couldn't help the laugh that bubbled from her throat, unsteady and tight with tension. Isaac laughed with her. "Yeah, Ellis caught us mackin' it in the kitchen. Not the most private spot."

Isaac leaned against her. "I'm happy you found someone. I'm happy you found her."

Vera's face fell. "But we're leaving soon."

Isaac was silent for a moment. "Yeah."

Vera shut her eyes against the burn of tears. "I'm probably never going to see her again."

He shook his head. "No, I… I think you will."

She looked at him. "How?"

Isaac tilted his head. "Gray has been talking to her a lot about next steps recently. We knew we couldn't stay here forever. But now that we know Tori helps the resistance movements and runs a safehouse specifically for syndicate victims…" He shrugged. "They've been considering a lot of things, but I think the biggest thing is a joint endeavor. Depending on who else would be for it we'd continue to do raids and run interference, but with a bigger plan. We'd directly funnel people to Tori for recuperation, and then she'd send them out to other safehouses farther away from the syndicates, or out of the country entirely."

Vera shook her head. "Where else is safer? I haven't heard of anywhere else doing better than here."

Isaac shrugged. "There are a lot of rumors, but there are definitely places safer than this. The syndicates tend to clump in one place. There are regions to the north where there are huge swaths of land they hardly control at all. Tori thinks she could establish a solid relationship with some people out there. Get them to take people on the run and distribute them away from the syndicates. It would give us purpose and help a lot of people." He nudged her. "And have the added bonus of lots of time with your girlfriend between missions."

She blushed. "She's not my girlfriend."

Isaac smiled. "Sorry. 'Soulmate' seemed kinda intense."

She pushed him, a little harder than she meant to. Her cheeks blazed. "Oh my *god*, Isaac."

He laughed. "What? You guys seem… good together. Really good. She's good for you."

"She's *too* good for me." She looked down, cheeks still warm.

"Yeah, probably." She glanced at him. He was grinning at her.

She smacked his arm gently. "You're an asshole."

"Yeah, but I'm *your* asshole." He laughed. "Wait. That came out wrong."

She rolled her eyes. "Christ. I don't know how I deal with you."

"Frankly, neither do I. But you love me." He flashed her his biggest smile.

She sighed. "Yeah, I do. Idiot." She ducked her head. "Thanks for telling me the plan. I'm grateful for it. Tori is…" She shook her head. "I… I want to see her. I want to be around her after this. I'll have to thank Gray for the idea."

"Don't thank Gray." She looked up at him. "Thank Tori. It was her idea." Her eyes widened as his smile grew soft. "Sounds like she'd do anything to be around you, too."

Chapter 53

Vera's stomach roiled as she made her way down the dark hall to Tori's room. She moved her hand along the wall, her heart thumping with every step. Her fingers brushed the frame of Tori's door. Dim light shined from underneath. *She's still awake.* Vera felt like she had spilled a bucket of ice-cold water in her gut.

She curled her hand into a fist and pulled it back to knock. She froze. *What if she doesn't want to see me right now? What if she doesn't want me that way?* She swallowed hard and squeezed her eyes shut. *Isaac's right. I am a dumbass.* She bit her lip and knocked softly.

She didn't breathe as she waited. There was a rustle of fabric, then soft footsteps to the door. The door opened and Vera blinked at the silhouette that appeared, Tori's hair glowing in the light. It took a moment for Vera's eyes to adjust. Her chest felt tight as she realized Tori was smiling at her.

"Hey." Tori leaned against the doorframe.

"Hey." Vera's lips pulled into a smile as her cheeks flushed red. She looked down.

"You wanna come in?" Tori opened the door wider, moving to the side. Vera swallowed hard and walked in, ducking her head as her arms went up to wrap around her chest. Tori's eyes moved over Vera's body as she closed the door behind her. Vera was straining with tension.

Tori's eyebrows pulled together. "Everything okay?"

"Um… yeah." Vera's voice sounded calmer than she felt. "I was just… talking to Isaac."

"Yeah? About what?" Tori drifted to her bed and sat down, her eyes still fixed on Vera.

"Um…" Vera shrugged. "About the plan you've been talking about with Gray. To redirect people north, away from the syndicates. To work with us."

289

Tori's mouth pulled into a gentle smile. "Yeah. I think it'll work. We could do a lot of good."

Vera's eyes were riveted to the floor. "And... that would mean... I'd see you again. After we leave."

"Yeah. I guess it does." Vera slowly raised her gaze to Tori and saw her eyes shining in a soft smile. Tori watched her silently.

"Well..." Vera bit her lip. "I... would like that. Because I haven't come back to your room since... since we kissed... because I didn't know if could..." Her hands knotted together in front of her. "I didn't think I could... um... sleep with you... if I was never going to see you again once we leave. I didn't... I couldn't stand it. It would... um... break me." She glanced up at Tori. Tori's smile had only grown wider. "Because what I feel for you... these past few months... it's not just a fling for me. It couldn't be. I feel... too much for you." She pressed her lips together, the seconds ticking painfully by. She trembled. "Please say something."

Instead Tori reached out a hand to Vera. Vera approached her, hesitantly. Tori's fingers laced through hers. Vera's throat felt hot and tight.

"I want to make sure I understand," Tori whispered. "Do you want me? And you just... didn't want to take that step if you thought this would be a short-term thing?" She looked up at Vera, her eyes warm. "Is that what you meant?"

"Yes." Vera squeezed her eyes shut. "I... I couldn't walk away after that. My team is my family, but... I didn't want to give that part of myself to you because... if I did... I don't know if I could leave again." When she opened her eyes again, there were tears in them. "Because what I feel for you... is..." Her voice shook. "As long as I can come back to you, as long as I have... *this*..." She shivered as Tori pressed her lips against her palm. "I can give you that part of me."

"You know you still don't have to, right?" Tori watched her carefully from over her hand. "You know you don't have to do this, that my feelings for you won't change?"

A thrill ran through Vera's body. "W-what... *are*... your feelings for me?" Her chest felt too tight to breathe.

Tori took Vera's other hand. "I feel…" Tori swallowed and blew out a slow breath. "Ah. I feel…" Her eyes closed as she pulled Vera a step closer. "I want you, in every possible way. How your mind works, how you are so strong and capable and… *fierce.* I want all the thoughts that go through your head, good or bad. I want…" Tori's eyes opened and her lips curved into a smile. "All those quiet moments with you, like when we danced, I want to be there with you for sunsets, and mornings with hot tea. I want to lie with you under blankets and feel your body. I want…" Tori bit her lip. "I want your pain; I want to take it all away and be with you in all the things you are outside of it. I want everything you are, Vera, darkness and heat and light… I want to… *kiss* you, hold you… god, Vera, I want *you.*" Tori trembled. "I'm sorry. I don't know if you…" She gasped softly. "I'm sorry. That was a lot."

Vera gently pulled a hand out of Tori's grasp and guided Tori's chin up until she could see Tori's eyes. Tori looked up at her with a vulnerability Vera had never seen before, like Tori had opened up her own soul, her own throat to the knife, her own body to be taken… Like Tori had handed over something precious and fragile. Vera's hands began to shake. Tori's fingers wrapped around Vera's wrist and she squeezed gently, her thumb moving along the scars there.

"I love you, Vera." The words were barely a whisper.

The floor dropped out from under her. The world stopped spinning. The air froze in her lungs. She forced herself to take a breath. Then another.

"I love you, too."

Tori's face broke into a brilliant smile, her eyes shining. Vera felt rooted to the spot, pinned down under the comfortable, comforting weight of the words that had just fallen from her lips. Her hands went to cup Tori's face. She bent down and pressed a soft kiss against Tori's mouth.

Chapter 54

Tori's breath sighed out in a low moan as Vera pressed her lips against hers. She pushed herself back further onto the bed and reached out, fingers lacing through Vera's as she pulled her on top of her to the bed. Vera pressed hot kisses to the underside of her chin, and she gasped.

"If you… ah… if you change your mind… or if something happens… tell me and we can… we can stop…"

Vera dragged her tongue up to Tori's ear and let her teeth graze Tori's earlobe. "I know. Please." She let her body press down against Tori's. Tori's hands went unconsciously to the hem of Vera's shirt.

Tori's eyes rolled back as Vera's hand knotted in her hair and pulled her head to the side, baring her throat as she nibbled her way down from Tori's ear to her collarbone. "Vera… *please…*" she huffed. "Please promise me… you won't push yourself for me…" She whimpered. "Please…"

"I promise," Vera whispered. Her hands went to the waistband of Tori's pants and her fingers pressed against Tori's back. "I promise." She covered Tori's mouth with hers.

Tori trembled and came apart a little under Vera's touch. She tugged at the hem of Vera's shirt and pulled it up around her chest. "Is this okay?"

Vera pulled her shirt all the way off and threw it into a corner of the room. "Yes," she gasped, a little late. Her hand moved to Tori's thigh and she hitched her leg up around her hips. Tori's legs opened for Vera and Vera pressed herself against her, their bodies flush against each other.

Vera caught Tori's wrists and pinned them above her head like she had done the first time. She drew Tori's lower lip between her teeth. Tori gasped.

"I guess I should count myself lucky you don't have your handcuffs, huh?" Tori whispered as she pressed herself up against Vera.

Vera grinned at her wickedly. "I can manage just fine without them, don't you worry."

"Something tells me that's absolutely true." Tori's lips opened to Vera's tongue and she groaned. "Please."

Hearing Tori beg made something deep inside Vera burn with *want*. She had to clench her jaw against the urge that rippled through her to pin Tori down, taste her, press her mouth against every inch of her skin. Her lips moved to Tori's ear. *"Please what?"*

Tori blindly searched for Vera's mouth. Her voice trembled. "Please take me."

Vera moaned and pressed her face against Tori's hair. Her hands moved to the hem of Tori's shirt and she pulled it roughly over her head. Her mouth immediately found Tori's again and she pressed her down against the bed. Vera trembled as her nipples moved over the soft skin of Tori's breasts. Her mouth moved down Tori's neck, leaving a burning path as she kissed her way down to Tori's chest.

Tori's hand tangled in Vera's hair as her breath hitched in her throat. Her back arched as Vera's mouth moved to one nipple, then the other, licking and nibbling until Tori moaned. Vera slid her tongue down Tori's stomach to the crest of her hip bone. Tori panted as Vera bit into the skin there and soothed the sore spot with her tongue.

"Vera... Jesus Christ..."

Vera hummed in her throat, her lips pulling up into a grin. "You want me to go lower?"

"Yes... fuck..." Goosebumps rippled along Tori's body as Vera pulled her pants down lower around her hips, kissing every new inch of exposed skin. Vera guided Tori's pants off her hips and down her legs, leaving her panties in place. Tori whined as Vera bypassed her hips with her mouth and drew her lips down one leg. Vera's fingers stroked along the back of Tori's knee. Tori gasped. "Vera... you *fucking* tease..."

Vera laughed softly. "How am I a tease?"

Tori pressed her lips together and shook her head. "You're just... ah..." Her mouth fell open in a gasp as Vera nipped the inside of her thigh. Her hand tangled in Vera's hair.

Vera's met Tori's gaze, grinning. "You want me to go down on you?"

"Yes," Tori breathed.

Vera hummed. She hooked her finger on the waistband of Tori's panties and guided them down her legs.

Tori gasped at the feeling of complete exposure. Vera's gaze roamed hungrily over Tori's body as Tori's chest heaved with shaking breaths, her legs open to her, her eyes wild with desire. Tori's hand moved along the curve of Vera's jaw with trembling fingers. "Can I please... ask..."

"What is it?" Vera's voice was husky with need.

"Can you be naked too? I want... I want to see you, be with you like that... You don't have to if you don't want to but... I would like that."

Vera's hands shook as they moved to the waistband of her own pajama pants. She eased them slowly off her hips, her eyes fixed on Tori. Tori gazed up at Vera with perfect, exquisite longing. Gently, Vera pulled her pants and her panties down her legs until she could slip them off around her ankles. She let them both drop to the floor beside the bed.

Tori's hands went up to stroke against Vera's hips, her breasts, her face, her waist. "You're beautiful," Tori whispered. Her eyes shone.

Vera lowered herself over Tori, moving her thigh until she pressed between Tori's legs. Tori gasped and moaned under her, moving back and forth against Vera's thigh. She was already wet and aching. Vera licked her lips and kissed Tori deeply, her tongue pressing against the inside of her mouth. Vera gently kissed along Tori's cheek until she reached her ear. Her breath made Tori tremble as she lingered at the curve of her jaw.

"Beg me," Vera whispered.

Tori groaned. "Please," she breathed. "Please fuck me." A whimper started in her throat. "Please, Vera."

Vera shuddered. Her mouth moved down Tori's chest again, tongue pausing to lick one nipple, nibbling down her abdomen to her pelvis. Tori's breath caught in her chest and she trembled.

Vera kissed along the inside of Tori's thigh, drawing closer to her clit. Her lips hovered over Tori's clit. Vera's stomach bucked with anticipation. Tori's breaths came in fast, shallow pants.

Vera lowered her mouth and pressed her lips against Tori's clit.

Tori gasped, hands fisting in the sheets as Vera licked along her folds, tongue swiping over her clit with each pass back and forth. She sucked the sensitive spot into her mouth and swirled her tongue around it. Tori whimpered. "Ah... *fuck...*" Her back arched up off the bed as she opened her legs, pressing herself against Vera's lips.

Tori's wetness was slick on Vera's tongue. Vera trembled at the warm, musky taste of her, so good and safe even as it drove Vera wild with need. She stroked her hand along the front of Tori's hips, gently drawing the skin tight, revealing more of her clit. Tori whined high in her throat.

"Vera... can you... *please...* with your finger... *please...*"

Vera pressed her finger against Tori's vagina, testing gently. Tori gasped. "Yes... *please*, Vera..." Vera slowly slid a finger into her. She crooked her finger up, feeling for the sweet spot along the inside. When she found it, Tori cried out.

"Shh, girl, easy," Vera whispered. She rubbed her finger in a circle around the spot. Tori shuddered against her.

"I'm sorry, I'm sorry... I just... *Jesus*, Vera, you feel... so..." Her voice trailed off into a panting whine. "God, I feel like I could come from this right now..."

Vera grinned. "You can, if you want." She dragged her tongue against Tori's clit, savoring the sensation as it made her cry out again. Tori tried to muffle it with her own hand pressed against her mouth.

"But I... I want you to feel good too..."

"You can make me feel good. You can go down on me after, if you want." Vera's pulse raced at the thought.

"I mean... will you play with yourself? While you do this?" Tori's legs trembled as Vera sucked gently at her clit. "I... I really like knowing you feel good, too."

"Believe me." Vera pressed her finger against Tori's sweet spot. Tori gasped and bucked against Vera's hand. "I feel good right now. But... yeah. That sounds pretty great."

Vera lowered herself onto her belly, snaking a hand down to her own vagina as her other hand pressed against Tori's clit. Her stomach dropped with astonishment at how wet and sensitive she'd become as she'd been focusing on Tori. She slid her fingers over her own clit, the waves of pleasure that broke over her almost paralyzing. She moaned.

Tori trembled harder at the sound of Vera's pleasure. She gasped and pressed herself against Vera's mouth as Vera lowered her lips once more to Tori's clit. Vera eased another finger into her, moving them in small circles against Tori's G spot and rolling her tongue against her sensitive clit. Tori's eyes rolled back and her mouth fell open.

"Vera... god... I didn't... *fuck*, I feel like I'm gonna come..."

Vera flicked her tongue against Tori's clit, maintaining the deep circles inside her. "Do you want me to change something? Speed up? Slow down?"

"No!" The word was almost a scream. "I... I'm sorry... no, please don't stop... don't stop, *please*, Vera... ahh... *fuck*..."

Vera moaned as every hitched breath and groan made her own pleasure rise inside her. She shivered, forcing herself to maintain the steady circles with her fingers and tongue.

"Vera... ahh... oh... *fuck!*" Tori shuddered as her orgasm swept through her. Vera moaned as Tori's walls quivered and clenched around her fingers. Tori bucked her hips into Vera's fingers as she cried out, legs trembling, chest heaving with ragged gasps. She whined softly as the pleasure moved through her body in decreasing waves. Vera continued in steady circles. Tori whimpered.

"Vera..." Her voice was husky. "Vera... Jesus Christ..."

Driven by her own desire, Vera worked her fingers into Tori, pressing up against her sweet spot, sucking gently on her clit as she guided Tori's body up into another wave of pleasure, building and cresting inside Tori's body until she cried out.

"Vera… please… *yes*…" Tori screamed softly as she shook apart into another orgasm, nearly coming up off the bed. She clutched at the sheets as she rode out her climax with Vera still licking hungrily at her clit.

Vera could feel the deep tides of pleasure in her own body, building up into her own sweet climax. She trembled as her fingers circled her clit, her own wetness dripping down the insides of her thighs. She groaned.

"Vera…" Tori panted. "Are you…?"

"I'm getting close, yeah."

Tori's hand reached down and tangled in Vera's hair, easing her face up so she could see her eyes. "Can I get you there?"

Vera trembled, the warm, pulsing pleasure between her legs making her words clumsy. "I… if you want…" Her lips were wet.

"Please." As Vera withdrew her fingers from inside Tori, Tori gasped. She pulled Vera up towards her, catching her mouth with a kiss, her own taste thick on Vera's lips. "Please let me give that to you."

Vera lowered herself on her back, quivering as she began to tighten at the thought of Tori's mouth on her. Tori drew her tongue across Vera's hip bone, kissing lower and lower until her lips settled over Vera's clit.

Vera could never have expected the rush of pleasure and trust that poured through her. She whined as Tori began to lick gently along her folds, drawing her clit into her mouth and rolling her tongue against it. Vera's hands went up to grip her own hair. She pulled on it as she opened her legs wider to Tori.

She felt the tip of Tori's finger against her vagina and she gasped, her hand flying down to grasp Tori's hair. "Please, not… not inside…"

Tori paused and pressed small kisses to the inside of her thighs. "Thank you for telling me." Tori's voice was heavy with reverence. Her mouth went right back to work and Vera gasped.

"Tori... god, Tori... you're so... *fuck*, Tori, you... ah..."

Tori laughed. "Is it good?"

Vera moaned. "*Good*, fuck, you're... you're perfect..." She squeezed her eyes shut as the warm glow rose inside her, sweeping through her, burning away everything in its path until Vera was completely immersed and lost in it. She reached the peak of her climax, gasped, and came apart under Tori's mouth. She moaned, enraptured, completely at Tori's mercy. Her body rippled as the aftershocks rushed through her, one right after the other, coinciding with each swipe of Tori's tongue. As her pleasure cooled and eased inside her, she slumped to the bed, eyes rolled back, mouth open, sighing. As Tori drew herself up next to her and laid down beside her, she pulled Tori into her arms and pressed her face against her chest.

"Thank you," Vera whispered. "Tori... thank you... I love you... Tori..."

Tori closed her eyes, her lips pulling into a sweet smile. "I love you too." She kissed Vera softly, her lips still wet. "I love you." Tori cuddled closer to her, breathing in the smell of their sex. She reached down with one hand and pulled the blankets up over both of them.

Vera was already drifting, her brain seemingly untethered from her body, shaken loose by her climax. She pressed her lips unthinkingly against Tori's forehead. She slid slowly into sleep with her arms wrapped tight around Tori. Tori was asleep moments after.

Chapter 55

Months later

Sam babbled away happily in the passenger seat. "That was so cool, Isaac, thank you for letting me come with you this time, I can't even believe… I just… I can't believe we blew up that guy's boat, and then when the guards came, we just—" They slid one palm against the other with a smack. "I didn't know you could drive like that, Isaac! Oh my god—"

"Van," Vera said softly from the back, opposite Isaac. Sam fell silent.

"I see it," Isaac responded, reaching for his weapon under the driver's seat. "Sam, sit back and don't make eye contact."

The van slowly passed him on the left, the driver's gaze fixed on their car. Finn and Ellis warily watched it go by from the back seat. Isaac kept his eyes firmly on the road in front of him, his free hand clutching the wheel until his knuckles went white. The van pulled ahead of them and everyone let out a breath at once.

"Is that—"

"Syndicate, yup," Isaac answered Sam. "Probably transporting something."

"Are we gonna—"

"No. We don't attack without a plan. And right here is the worst possible spot to—"

Isaac slammed on the brakes as the van swooped into their lane, cutting them off. The van jerked into the next lane. Its brake lights lit up and the tires screeched. The van came even with the team's car.

"Vera." Isaac's voice was intense, but steady.

"On it." She was already rolling her window down, reaching for her gun.

"Everybody else get down!" Isaac's hand shot out and forced Sam's head down as the driver opened fire.

Isaac held the car steady as Vera took two shots and blew out the van's front tire. Another shot, and the rear tire burst. The van swerved. It careened into the middle lane, just in front of the team's car. Isaac slammed on the brakes again. The van crashed into the median.

Isaac swerved around the van and slammed the car to a stop behind it.

"Stay in the car!" Isaac bellowed. He jumped out with his gun. Vera was close on his heels. "Driver," he threw over his shoulder.

"Rear," she barked.

Isaac approached the van with his gun raised. He kept the engine block between himself and the driver in case he needed to duck behind it. The driver lifted his head and fumbled for something in the passenger seat. Isaac aimed and fired two shots through the windshield. The man jerked and slumped in his seatbelt, red blossoming on his chest.

Isaac carefully approached the van and looked into the open window. There was no one else up front. He held his fingers to the man's throat, feeling for a pulse. Nothing.

Isaac stalked around the van. Vera was aiming her gun into the open doors at the back. His hand tightened around his gun as he saw inside.

A man held a young woman – barely older than a girl – by the throat in front of him, shielding his body with hers. She was small, thin, and stared back at Isaac with empty eyes. The man had his gun against the woman's head.

"Back the fuck off!" he screamed. "Back off, or I fucking kill her!"

"Let her go." Vera's voice rang through the van. "Let her go, or you're dead. Right fucking now."

"Fuck you! Back off!"

Without a word, Vera raised her gun and fired a shot wide at them both. The man flinched out from behind the woman. Vera aimed and put a bullet in the man's shoulder. He let go of the woman's neck and fell back with a scream.

The gun flew from his hand. Vera launched herself into the van and put two more bullets in his head.

The woman slumped to the floor of the van like she was dead. Isaac leapt in beside Vera, reaching for the woman. He cradled her head as he swept her body once for blood and weapons. "She isn't hurt," he muttered. "I don't think."

"Finn can check her out in the car," Vera said, her chest heaving. "Right now we need to go."

"Come on," he said, his face close to the woman's. "We need to go. Can you hear me? Hello?"

"Isaac."

"Right." He scooped the woman up in his arms. She pushed against his chest for a moment, then went limp. "Well, we know she's responsive." He carried the woman around the van towards the car.

The rear doors of the car opened as he approached. "Ellis, you're up front," Isaac ordered. "Finn in back with her and Vera."

"Is she hurt?" Finn started to get out of the car after Ellis, their eyes fixed on the woman in Isaac's arms.

"No," Isaac barked. "We do everything while we're moving."

As Vera broke off from Isaac to go to the other side of the car, the woman's hand shot out and grabbed Vera's wrist. Her eyes bored into Vera's, focused for the first time.

"Okay. I sit next to her," Vera murmured. "Fine. Finn, move over. You'll be on the right." She slid into the middle seat. Isaac eased the woman into the seat beside Vera. The woman let go of Vera's wrist and her eyes went dead again.

Isaac slammed the door closed and jumped into the driver's seat. He put the car in drive and sped away.

"Who is she?" Sam whispered, turned all the way around in the seat to look at her with frightened eyes.

"No idea. Probably not syndicate, though. Probably a hostage. Or... or captive," Isaac ground through his teeth.

"Is she alright?" Sam asked, their voice tense.

Finn leaned across Vera, their hands moving over the girl, looking for injuries. "I don't see any reason she shouldn't be," Finn murmured. The girl sagged against the door of the car, unmoving, as Finn touched her.

"Let me get a seatbelt on her," Vera said softly. She reached across the girl and pulled the seatbelt across her body.

Isaac laughed softly, the adrenaline leaving his body all at once. "Holy... holy shit," he breathed.

Vera smiled at him. "We'll have a story for Gray and Tori when we get back."

Sam's shoulders relaxed. "Have you ever saved someone like that?"

Isaac chuckled. "No. Never like that."

Chapter 56

Years ago

Gavin's heart thumped against his chest as his father led him downstairs. He'd been downstairs before, plenty of times. He liked to watch his father hurt people.

Dad called it "having fun." And it *was* fun. Gavin loved it when someone screamed around the gag in their mouth, when their eyes were wide with panic and pain. He liked it when they said "please." *Please stop. Please, please, I'll do anything.* Gavin liked to think about that even when he wasn't downstairs. He liked to think about hurting people when he was at his lessons, when he was with his friends, when he was alone. He especially liked to think about it when he was alone.

Today, though, was a very special day. Today, his father was going to let him hurt someone for the first time.

He was ten now, and definitely ready. His hands tightened into fists as they rounded the corner together. Every step he took brought him closer to the door, closer to the room where there was going to be a person chained up or tied down and waiting to be hurt. He swallowed hard.

They paused outside the door. Dad put his hand on Gavin's shoulder and smiled down at him. "Are you ready?"

Gavin practically bounced as he nodded. He was ready. He was *so* ready.

His father smiled. "You get to have fun with someone today. I've got her tied up so she can't move. If you want, you can try some things that you've seen me do. Or you can try something new. You can use anything in the room. Okay?" Another nod. "Let's go in."

Gavin thought his heart would beat out of his chest as his father slid the bolt on the door out of the lock and swung the door open. The room was dimly lit. He knew his father liked to have fun like that. His eyes were wide as he focused on the form lying in the center of the room.

She was lying on her side with her hands tied behind her. Her ankles were tied together, too. She was dressed in a torn, dirty t-shirt and a pair of pants that were not any better off. She had a canvas bag over her head that concealed her face. The bag was tightened around her throat just above the collar around her neck. Gavin had seen that before. *Dad likes to put collars on people to show them they're his.* His throat burned. *Is she mine?*

His legs shook as they carried him into the room. His gaze moved along the walls to all the tools his father had. Whips, sticks, all kinds of chains and restraints. There was a cattle prod and tasers, too. And something that shot out a little stream of fire for burning people. There were other things, too, things he didn't recognize, but he didn't care. He knew exactly what he wanted.

He strode a little more confidently to the wall that held the knives. Gavin loved his father's knives. He loved how sharp they were, how they would cut his finger if he pressed it to the blade too hard. He loved to watch people's skin split apart as the blade went over it. He loved to watch the blood ooze down their skin.

He selected his favorite one. Jet black from the handle to the tip of the blade, all one shiny piece that was both scary and beautiful. He turned back to his father with the knife clutched tight in his hand. He felt a warm rush of happiness as his father nodded.

"Now," Dad said. "I have her gagged, and hooded, but I also have her ears muffled. She won't be able to hear very much. I did that because I want you to be able to have fun without her giving you trouble. She's been very good lately, and I told her she can scream as much as she wants while you do this. Unless you want her to be quiet. I can tell her that, too."

Gavin shook his head nervously. "I… um…"

His father smiled warmly. "What is it?" That hand went to his shoulder again, strong and comforting.

"I… I like it when they scream. I want her to scream."

His father's smile grew, and he nodded. "Of course. No need to be shy about that, Gavin. It's just fun. There's nothing wrong with how you feel."

Gavin nodded, vague relief washing through him. What he wanted was good. His father stood to the side, presenting the lady on the floor to Gavin with a sweeping hand. "What would you like to do first?"

Gavin bit his lip, the knife held tight in his little fist. He stood a step forward, then another. His legs felt like jelly. He felt like he might explode, he was so excited.

He got down on his knees beside her. He reached out one hand, the hand without the knife. His fingers brushed against the woman's skin.

She flinched back, whimpering into the gag. Shivers ran down Gavin's spine. He smiled and placed his hand on her arm, holding her steady. The woman whined as his hand settled. He brought the knife to her arm with the other hand and pressed the blade against her skin.

She gasped as the cold steel touched her. He drew the knife across her arm, barely breaking the skin. Blood welled in the cut, red and shining and so exciting. Gavin giggled in spite of himself. He felt his father approach behind him.

"Good. Was that fun?"

Gavin was nodding already. "Yes. That was… that was really good."

"Do you want to do it again?"

Gavin bit his lip. "Mm-hm." He brought the knife to her shoulder this time.

He made another cut, deeper, going through layers of skin and opening her up more. Blood oozed from the cut. Gavin licked his lips and looked her over, deciding where he wanted to put the knife next.

He pushed her gently onto her back and she rolled, following his silent command. Gavin shivered. *She's listening to me.* He held the tip of the knife against her stomach. She gasped, a scared little noise leaving her throat as the tip dipped against the skin. Gavin pressed down and she trembled. He felt a yawning cavern of want and excitement open up in him as the knife pressed into her stomach, poking through the shirt easily and piercing into her. He pushed harder and watched blood bloom around the knife, soaking into the shirt. The woman whimpered. Her muscles pulled tight as he pressed down. She was crying. Gavin swallowed hard and pushed some more.

He felt his father's hand on his shoulder. "Hey, buddy. Not too deep. She'll need surgery and I don't want that."

Gavin pulled the knife away and turned to his father, eyes big with worry and confusion. "But why? You've done this to people… and they bled and died. Do you want her to stay alive?"

His father nodded. "For the time being, yes. I want her to still be alive after this and I don't want her to need surgery." His eyes softened. "But you're doing great, bud. Are you having fun?"

Gavin felt a thrill of pride in his belly. "Yes. Thank you, Dad." He turned to look at the knife in his hand. He turned it back and forth, admiring the shine of blood on the tip. "Can I hit her?"

"You can do anything you want, champ."

Gavin handed the knife to his father and he set it to the side. Gavin's hands balled into fists as he looked at her, deciding where he wanted to hit her first. She was trembling and whimpering, curled around the wound on her stomach. It was leaking blood into her shirt. He took another contemplative moment and made his decision.

He raised his fist and punched her in the arm close to where he'd been cutting. She gasped. He looked at his hand. He was shocked at how much it had hurt his wrist. He wrapped his other hand around it.

"You okay, bud?"

He nodded. "My wrist hurts. Why…?"

"Here." His father kneeled next to him. "Like this. You make a fist…" He curled his fingers into his palm. "And fold your thumb over. Then, make sure your wrist is straight when you punch. Like this." He drove his fist against his other hand with a dull *smack*. "You try."

Gavin did as he was instructed. His father wrapped his fingers around his own and squeezed a little. "Tighter. Like that. See? Good." He motioned at the woman. "Go ahead, try again."

Gavin clenched his fist the way his father had shown him and threw a punch against the woman's back. She curled forward to get away from the punch, but it still didn't seem to hurt her the way Gavin wanted it to. His forehead wrinkled.

"What's wrong, buddy?"

"She won't scream." His arms crossed in front of his chest. "I wanted her to scream."

Dad took Gavin by the shoulders gently. "That's okay, Gavin. You're still young. You'll grow, get stronger, and soon you won't have to worry about that. If you want, you can try hitting her with something. That way it's a little easier. Does that sound alright?"

Gavin nodded, unsure. His father got to his feet and went to the wall, taking down a thin stick about three feet long. Gavin looked at it, skeptical.

"This," his father said, "is called a cane." He noticed his son's expression. "I know it doesn't look so bad, but believe me. It hurts." He threw a crooked grin in the woman's direction. "She would know." He placed it gently in Gavin's hands. "Use your wrist with this one, okay? I'll let you get the hang of it. Just don't hit her in the head." He winked.

Gavin turned back to the woman, the cane held in his fist now. He ran his hand down the length of it. He wasn't sure something this light could hurt anyone. He wound up his arm and brought it down as hard as he could against her shoulder.

The scream that ripped from her was so good it made Gavin gasp aloud. He could already see the skin turning red, the bruise blossoming where he had struck her. He turned to his father with wide eyes and a smile on his face. His father nodded, grinning fondly back. He turned his gaze back to the cane in amazement. His hand tightened around it and he raised his hand again.

He brought the cane down hard on her legs. She jerked, trying to push away from where she thought he was standing. He licked his lips and hit her again.

307

Gavin's mind was almost too full of happiness to bear. Every time he raised the cane and snapped it down onto her body, the muffled screams that tore out of her made him tremble. Again and again he brought it down, on her arms, on her legs, on her shoulders. He grinned.

"If you like," his father said, interrupting him for a moment, "I can hold her so she stays laying on her stomach so you can hit her on her back. I do that sometimes. Does that sound fun?" Gavin nodded. "Okay."

Dad drew a folding knife from his pocket and cut the rope wound around her wrists. She let out a shuddering moan as he pulled her hands forward in front of her. When he tied the rope around her wrists again, she started to sob. He rolled her onto her belly, pulling her hands over her head and pinning her to the floor. His other hand went to her collar, holding her down with his hand at her throat, too. Her whimpering cries made Gavin's mouth water.

"Go ahead, Gavin. Just don't hit me." He winked again.

Gavin nodded gravely, his forehead wrinkling with concentration. "I won't."

"Go ahead, son."

He brought the cane up and cracked it down against her back. The hollow, tortured sound she made sent a wave of goosebumps over Gavin's skin. He smiled, laughing a little.

He brought the cane down on her back again. And again. And again. She was sobbing openly now, each moaning scream drawing out into the next as Gavin beat her. He nearly vibrated with joy. He thought he saw stripes of blood soaking into her shirt.

He completely lost himself. He relished the sounds she made, the sounds of terror and agony and helplessness. *This is fun. I like this.* He laughed as the beating grew more vicious. She jerked with every strike of the cane, falling limp as the spike of pain faded momentarily before it wracked her again. Even the sounds the cane made against her body were beautiful. The dull *thwack* against her skin.

It sounded like she was begging, the words incoherent through the gag. He swallowed hard. He wanted to hear what she was saying. *Maybe next time. Dad gagged her for a reason, I guess.* Was she begging him to stop? Was she begging him to kill her, like he'd heard people beg his father? A deeper, darker wave of excitement rolled over him at that thought. *Would dad let me kill her?* He felt faint at the thought. He wanted to do it, deep in his bones. He hit her harder. His hand was going numb with the impact.

"Gavin." He didn't know how long his father had been trying to get his attention. By the tone of his voice, it had been a long time. His arm paused, the cane trembling in mid-air above the woman's back. She was whimpering now, the sound pathetic and dark and so, so good. Gavin's eyes met his father's. His father's face broke into a broad smile. "You having fun?"

"Yes." Gavin had to catch his breath. He looked down at the woman at his feet, shaking, bloody. Beaten. He'd done that. He'd done that to her. He shivered.

"You got a little into it there, bud. How you feeling?"

"Good." His voice was small, shaking. "Really good."

"Good." An even bigger smile. The woman lay on the floor, unmoving. Her breathing sounded painful. "I think we're going to have to stop for today."

Gavin looked up at his father, disappointment written all over his young face. "But... but I want..."

"Gavin, if you keep going like this, you're going to kill her."

Gavin pressed his lips together, trembling. "But..." His voice was a whisper. "But I want to kill her."

His father laughed, a happy, easy sound. "Okay, bud. I hear you. But not this one, okay? Not today. I want to keep her. She's in pretty rough shape, son. I'm not going to be able to do much with her for at least a few days." He winked. "You went hard on her. You did a good job."

Gavin ducked his head, his chest tight with pride. He was having so much fun. And his father said he'd done a good job. He grinned.

His father held a hand out for the cane. "Let me take that, bud. Head outside for me. Just wait outside the door. I want a minute alone with her." Gavin handed over the cane, eyes almost welling with tears, a mix of joy and disappointment. His father pulled him into a hug and pressed a kiss against the top of his head. "I'm glad you had fun. You did great, especially for your first time. I'm so happy you liked this." He ruffled his son's hair. "Go on. I'll be right out." He pushed him towards the door.

Gavin went, dragging his feet. He threw one more lingering, longing glance at the woman as she lay on the floor. Then he turned, leaving the room and pulling the door shut behind him.

∴

The man turned back to the woman on the floor. He loosened the bag around her neck and pulled it off her head. Her hair fell around her face, wild and soaked with sweat. He undid the tape holding the noise-canceling headphones in place and pulled them off her head. He eased the gag out of her mouth. Her face was wet with tears.

He drew his hand gently through her hair as she sobbed brokenly. Her body trembled with shock, each breath and movement agonizing. Blood rolled down her back from where she was split open in several places. She whimpered. He smoothed her hair away from her face, making soothing noises deep in his throat.

"Good job, sweetheart," he murmured. He cut the rope around her wrists again and momentarily left his spot by her head to free her ankles as well. Then he settled down next to her again, his hand still moving through her hair. She keened weakly with her cheek pressed against the ground. "Good girl. You're my good girl." He leaned down to kiss her temple, his hand tightening roughly in her hair for a moment as she flinched and shuddered away. He smiled gently. "Good job, Vera."

Chapter 57

Isaac glanced in the rear-view mirror again, checking for what felt like the thousandth time on the woman in the back seat.

Vera met his gaze in the mirror, and turned to look at their new rescue. *Rescue. Makes her sound like a damned kitten.* The woman stared out the window, wide-eyed, with a faraway look on her face, like she wasn't really there with them. Like she'd been kicked out of her own body, her mind sent to pasture until things calmed down. Vera swallowed hard.

The girl was stuck like glue to Vera's side, as close to her as was physically possible without actually sitting in her lap. Vera's hand carded through her tangled, bloodied hair every now and then, as soothing to her as she hoped it was to the girl.

Girl. She looked like she was seventeen or eighteen, around the same age as Sam and yet, horrifyingly, as broken as anyone she had ever met. They'd found her by accident, just like the resistance had found Vera. They had a long way to go until they got to Tori's house, and most of it was contested territory.

Vera had to hope they weren't being followed by the syndicate they had spent the last week sabotaging. Blowing up the roads they used to move equipment, drugs, and weapons, scrambling their radio and cell phone communications, stealing and destroying whatever tech they could get their hands on. It had been a busy week, and a productive one.

This girl, whatever her name was, was one of the things they'd stolen from the syndicates.

Now they were speeding down the highway towards Tori's place. Once they were there, she'd be taken care of until Tori could secure a place for her up north. The team would take the woman on the first leg of her journey, and then she'd continue on to the relative safety to the north.

Finn sat in the back seat next to Vera, with Sam and Ellis sitting up front with Isaac. Gray had probably arrived at Tori's place with their other car a few days before, having carried out their own mission on the other side of the county: a supply run. Much as they hated splitting up, it had become necessary in the past few weeks. Gray sometimes decided to skip the more dangerous missions. They couldn't keep up with the others as much as they had before, and between missions and rescues, there wasn't always enough of the family to go around.

The girl shivered again, trembling against Vera's side. She seemed to lean unconsciously into Vera, soaking up her warmth and the calm she was doing her best to exude. Vera wasn't sure if the girl was even aware that they'd taken her. She tried again to get her attention.

"Hey." Vera's voice was low and steady. The girl didn't bat an eye.

Vera leaned forward into the woman's periphery. She pulled the woman's hair back from her face, watching carefully for signs of fear or anger. She just saw more blankness.

"You with us, honey? You ready to talk to us?"

That got a response. At the word *honey,* her eyes snapped to Vera's, wide and unfocused. Vera leaned back. "Is that not a good word to use? Can I call you something else?"

The woman swallowed and turned her attention back to the window. She blew out a sigh.

"You got a reaction out of her, at least." Ellis turned and looked over the seat to focus on the woman. "What do you think's wrong with her?"

Finn bit their lip. "I didn't find any signs of head trauma. I wonder if it's just—"

"Psychological?" Vera didn't look up as she said it. Her jaw was tight. "Given who we're dealing with I'd put my money on that."

"What do we do about it?" Sam looked back with concern written on their face. They'd been uncharacteristically quiet since they'd rescued the girl. "Can we fix it?"

Vera shook her head. "Honestly, I have no idea. We have no idea what caused this. Until we figure it out we've just got to take care of her, keep her calm, and see if she improves once we're safe."

"I wonder if she knows what safety even looks like." Ellis's voice was bitter.

"We'll show her." Vera's hand went back to stroke the woman's hair again. Vera thought she could feel the woman leaning just a little into the touch. "But for now, we should stop talking about you like you're not here. I don't know if you can hear us, but we should act as though you can, right?" No response. Vera let out a slow breath. "You just talk to us when you're ready, okay?"

No one spoke again for a long time. Sam fell asleep, leaning on Ellis. Vera watched the woman carefully. She paid no attention to anyone in the car. The woman just watched the landscape go by. The trees became bigger and denser the closer they got to Tori's house.

Isaac pulled onto the long driveway. "You ready to see your girlfriend, Vera?" He grinned at her in the rear-view. If the woman hadn't been there, Vera would have punched him in the shoulder. She held off. Something told her it wouldn't be good for the woman to see casual violence, even if it was just a joke.

They rounded the bend and Tori's house came into view. The other car was parked outside.

"That's good, Gray's home." Isaac pulled in behind the car and shut it off. Finn got out of the car. Isaac climbed out of the driver's seat.

Finn was frozen, staring at the front door. It looked like it had been kicked down.

Chapter 58

Isaac lunged back into the car and grabbed his gun from under the driver's seat. "Everyone get back in the car," he murmured.

Vera followed his gaze to the front door. Her gun was still holstered at her hip. She pulled it out, hands shaking, and stepped carefully around the car to fall into step behind Isaac. He looked back at her for a moment to tell her to wait. His mouth snapped shut as he saw the look on her face.

The others were still frozen and staring at the front door of the house. The woman stood by the car, her eyes wide. Her hands were balled into fists.

Isaac stepped carefully over the threshold into the house. The lights were off; the only light came from the afternoon sun streaming in through the windows. Vera moved silently behind him. They swept the living room and found nothing.

They both jumped at a sound coming from the kitchen, a low thump against the floor. They shared a glance and moved together to the kitchen. Isaac's heart thundered in his chest as he stepped into the room. His stomach dropped and his gun nearly fell from his hand.

Gray was lying on the floor, gasping, in a puddle of blood.

"FINN!" Isaac screamed. *"Finn, get in here!"* He fell to his knees. His hands shook violently as he put them on Gray, trying to find where the bleeding was coming from. Vera stood behind him, sobbing, covering Isaac with her weapon as his hands became stained with Gray's blood.

Finn appeared in the doorway holding their own gun, their eyes wide and focused. A quiet *"shit"* left their lips as they saw Gray lying on the floor. "Is the house clear?" Finn's voice shook.

"No..." Isaac didn't look up, his hands slipping on the blood.

Finn knelt beside them, a hand moving to Isaac's shoulder. "Go. I got this. Go clear the house."

Isaac robotically got to his feet, finding his grip on his gun again. His hands dripped with blood. "Vera, you—"

"I'll cover Finn." Her voice broke. She raised her eyes to Isaac, wild and desperate. "T-Tori…" she whispered.

"I'll find her." Isaac's voice was hard. "Stay here." He stalked out of the kitchen and disappeared into the house.

∴

Finn's voice was steady as they turned to Vera. "Vera, turn on the light. If someone's still here they definitely heard Isaac, no point in me working in the dark."

She moved slowly to the switch on the wall and turned on the overhead light. A sob ripped out of her chest as Finn turned back to focus on Gray.

"Gray? Can you hear me? Gray?"

Gray stirred, moaning weakly. Their breaths sounded wet and painful. Finn's hands moved to their head, then their neck, then down to their chest where most of the blood was. Their fingers found the bullet wound, just below the left collarbone. They rolled Gray to the side and felt along their back for an exit wound. They didn't feel anything. *Probably for the best, all things considered.* Their hands moved quickly to Gray's abdomen, their pelvis, down their legs, and back up to their arms. There was nothing else.

They put their hand over the wound to their chest and felt a pulse at Gray's wrist. It was there, but faint. And fast.

Finn heard Isaac come back into the room and without glancing up said, "I need my bag. Can you get it?"

"Tori?" Vera sobbed.

Isaac looked first to Vera. "I… I didn't find her." Her hands shook harder. She swayed in place, reaching out and steadying herself on the counter.

Isaac wet his lips. "Finn, let me… let me get your bag." He turned and jogged to the car.

315

When he returned with the bag, he came back with Sam, Ellis, and the woman close behind. Finn barely heard the others react when they walked in. Their hands were vibrating with the need to move, to help, to fix this. They reached out for the bag and pulled it closer. "Isaac, I need you to put your hand where mine is right now." Isaac knelt and obeyed without a word. Finn grabbed their shears and cut Gray's shirt so it laid open over the wound.

The woman stood in the corner of the room with her eyes fixed on Gray. Sam had fallen to their knees and was sobbing, Ellis kneeling beside them, arms wrapped around them. Vera slid to her knees on the floor as sobs wracked her chest.

"Finn…" Isaac's voice was barely above a whisper. "Can you… fix this? Can you…?" He swallowed hard.

Finn's jaw clenched shut so tight they felt like their molars would crack. "I don't know." They pawed through their bag and found the airtight dressing they were looking for. They tore it open, their hands wet with blood. They stood quickly and grabbed a hand towel off the counter. "Move your hand." They swiped the towel across Gray's chest, clearing it of blood. They quickly placed the seal over the wound and smoothed it down with their hand. Their hand went back to their bag as they searched for their stethoscope.

"Finn." Isaac's voice was louder this time. "Can you fix this?"

Icy helplessness swept through Finn before they could stop it. They gasped. Their hands shook. "I…" They swallowed hard. "I can… decompress the chest… give them some fluids… I can help them…"

Isaac steadied his voice. "But can you *fix this?*"

No.

Fury at themselves bubbled up in Finn's chest, disgust at themselves that they had ever even *once* deluded themselves into thinking they were a help to their family. After everything, after all the years of dodging death and serious injury, they had really believed they could *help*. That their actions *mattered*. Their entire life disappeared into the crushing inevitability of this moment: when someone would be hurt and Finn would be useless to stop it. Their throat spasmed and a sound tore out of them that resembled a choked sob.

"No. No, I… I c-can't stop this…" They looked at their hands, stained red with Gray's blood.

"Hospital."

They all turned to look at the woman standing stock still in the corner of the room, her hands pressed over her mouth, like she couldn't believe she'd spoken.

Hot tears formed in Finn's eyes. "We can't go to the hospital, they'd kill them. We can't go…"

The woman gulped, her eyes moving nervously around the room. "There's… a hospital…" Her voice faded and she lost her nerve.

"A hospital where?" It was Sam who spoke, their eyes fixed on the woman.

"For… killers… thieves…" Her arms wrapped around her chest. "Saboteurs and fugitives…" She swallowed hard. "People like you."

"Where?" Finn's voice cracked like a whip.

"I… went there once. I can show you…"

Ellis's eyes narrowed. "How do we know you aren't leading us into a trap?"

She grimaced at Ellis, the first emotion she'd shown since the rescue that wasn't fear. "How do I know you all aren't a trap for me?"

Ellis fell silent and their mouth snapped shut.

"Let's go." Finn's voice was low and urgent. "How far away is it? Will they make it?"

"I don't know where I am." It came out almost as a whisper. The girl sounded terrified.

"We'll get you a map. You'll show us where it is?" Finn's heart pounded.

She nodded solemnly.

"Wait." Vera crawled to Gray's side, shaking too hard to stand. "I need… where's Tori, I need…" She took Gray's hand in hers. "Gray, Gray *please*… please talk to me…"

317

Finn pinched Gray's shoulder hard. They gasped, the sound rattling through the kitchen. Their eyes fluttered open. They moaned.

"Gray," Vera sobbed. "Gray, where's Tori?"

Gray whimpered. "They... he took her..."

Vera voice broke. "Who took her? Gray... please..."

They gasped, choking on blood as it bubbled in their throat. Their eyes rolled in their head, wide with terror and pain.

"Gray." The word was a sob. "Please."

Every breath looked like it cost them dearly. "He... Gavin... Gavin took her."

Chapter 59

Vera's throat closed around her strangled cry. Isaac shuddered next to her, his hands clenching into fists. His eyes blurred with tears.

Vera held out a hand. "Isaac. Phone and keys. Now."

He held his hand out to her, still red with Gray's blood. "Vera, no. No way. We've played this game with him before. It only ends in him having both of you. I can't let you do this."

Her hands were instantly on his shirt. She yanked him up to standing and shoved him backward.

"I wasn't *fucking* asking," she growled. *"Give me the fucking keys."*

"Vera…" He shook his head. "I can't let you sacrifice yourself."

"I'm not going to fucking *sacrifice myself*," she spat through her teeth. "I'm going to go find him and fucking *kill him.*"

"Vera…"

"What if it was Sam?" He couldn't help looking over at them, held tight in Ellis's arms. His stomach twisted as an image flashed through his mind, unbidden: Sam, trembling, marked with blood and wounds from Gavin's torture. Sam kneeling in front of him, Gavin's gun pressed to the back of their head. Sam. *His Sam.* His heart stuttered in his chest.

"I…"

"We don't leave our own behind." Vera's voice was a vicious snarl. "Tori is *mine*. You're not going to stop me from getting her back. You're not going to make me let her die. You need to take Gray's car. There's more room, and it's way less likely they've ID'ed it. I'm taking the other one. *Give. Me. The. Fucking. Keys.*"

"Isaac, we need to go." Finn looked up at him with desperate urgency.

Isaac's jaw clenched as he looked at Vera, half-wild with panic and rage, a trembling hand held out in front of her. "Let me find Gray's keys, make sure we have them."

"They're on the front seat." Ellis's voice broke under the tension. "I checked while we were outside."

Isaac swallowed and pulled his keys out of his pocket. He placed them in Vera's hand.

"Phone, too."

"How will you contact us?"

"Get another burner. Text this phone. I'll contact you once I have her."

"Okay." He handed the phone over to her. "Vera, I…"

She threw her arms around him. "Get Gray to that hospital. I'll meet you there." She was nearly tripping over herself in her need to get out. She dashed out of the kitchen and out the door. They all listened as she sped away.

Isaac shook himself, turning back in a haze to Gray and the others. "Finn, Ellis, Sam, you work on getting Gray to the car. You—" The woman's eyes widened as he turned his gaze to her. "I'm going to get a map and you're going to show me how to get to this hospital."

Chapter 60

Tori's wrists were tied tightly behind her, holding her down to the chair. She blinked as the bag was pulled from her head. The lights stabbed into her eyes for a moment as she cast her gaze around the room. Panic rose in her throat. An icy claw of terror pierced her chest as her eyes rested on the figure leaning casually against the wall, arms crossed in front of his chest. A smirk pulled at the corners of his mouth.

"You know who I am, right?" He raised an eyebrow.

She'd suspected ever since he and his men had kicked her door in. Ever since they'd grabbed her and shot Gray when they'd tried to stop them. Her heart dropped to the floor as she remembered the shot, the punching sound as the bullet tore through their chest, the blood as they'd collapsed to the floor. She had no way of knowing when the rest of the family would get to Gray. She had no way of knowing if they were still alive.

She swallowed the tears burning in her throat. "You're Gavin."

He smiled. "Yup. And you're the idiot who's been harboring Isaac & Co."

She gritted her teeth and glared at him. "Says who?"

"Says the spies I have who *finally* found you. I'm impressed. It took a while. Of course, I've been indisposed." He pointed to the scars that marked his face. "Courtesy, of course, of Isaac. I'll have to thank him for that."

She swallowed hard. "They probably know by now that you took me. They're far away from you, from where you can find them."

"Yeah, I was kinda surprised to find you alone there with Gray. Aren't you all a 'team'?" He punctuated the word with air quotes. "All for one and one for all? Together to the end?" She pressed her lips together. "I wonder how Gray is, now that I mention it. That wound didn't look good when we left. Sure hope they live long enough to tell them what happened to you. Otherwise I don't think you have a hope in hell of them coming for you. Which I'm sure they will, if they know where to find you." He bared his teeth in a grin.

She trembled. "They won't come for me. They won't risk it after… after what happened last time." An image of Isaac flashed across her mind, nearly dead, half-dragged from the car by Ellis and Gray. Broken. Bleeding. Bile rose in her throat. *He's going to do that to me. That's how I'm going to die.* An icy chill flooded her body. She could barely breathe. *He's going to torture me to death, like he was going to do to Isaac.* She gasped as tears welled in her eyes.

Gavin's smile grew. "That's disappointing. You don't think they'll even *try* to come after you?"

She was doing her best to hold back sobs. "Isaac won't let them. He'll make the right decision. He won't put everyone at risk."

"Do you want them to? Save you, I mean?"

She squeezed her eyes shut. "Yes," she whispered. *Vera would be brave. She'd be brave if it was her.* A sob caught in her chest. "Yes, please don't… please…" She knew it was useless. She couldn't help the panicked pleas falling from her lips. "Please…"

Gavin whipped a savage backhand across her face. She gasped and slumped to the side, stunned. The rope tying her to the chair cut into her wrists, keeping her upright. She tasted blood as the world spun around her.

"Fact is," Gavin drawled, "I don't want you. I was after Isaac. To be honest, you'd probably be dead right now if he'd been home. I want Vera, too. She's the one who blew up my warehouse, right?" He knelt in front of her. Tears poured down her face. "What do you think I'd have to do to you to draw them out?"

She was shaking so hard she could barely stay upright. "P-please…"

Gavin wandered behind Tori. He held a small purse when he returned to face her. "We found this at your place when we took you. Fascinating stuff. You know you can tell a lot about someone from the contents of their purse, right?"

Tori's eyes were fixed on Gavin's hand. She knew what he was going to find in there. She opened her mouth to beg again and the words froze on her tongue.

He rifled through the purse. "Let's see, you've got… some money… I thought you off-the-grid types traded in chickens or something. Weird. And… a knife, oh yeah, self-defense, very safe… a protein bar, can't forget that protein… a whistle… a pen… band-aids… and… now this is interesting…" He pulled a picture from the purse. The color drained from Tori's face. She felt like she might vomit. He turned the picture around to show Tori. "Now what's this all about?"

It was a picture of Vera. She was smiling at the camera, her face radiant. Tori had been flirting with her just as she'd taken it. *"I want something to look at while you're on the road. I want to have a picture of you."* Auto-printing cameras were hard to come by but finding places to develop film was harder. It was a risk she'd been willing to take if it meant she'd have a picture of Vera to keep. *"You're beautiful. I want a picture. Please…?"* They'd shared a kiss right after it was taken.

"It's the only picture in here. You'd think if it was like a 'team as family' thing you'd have a picture of the whole team, right? But you don't. You just have one." He knelt in front her, holding the picture close to her. She cringed away like it would burn her. "What's up with you and Vera, huh?"

She shook her head, terror gripping her chest. "She's the only one I have a picture of so far. I was going to get the rest."

Gavin shook his head. "Uh-uh. Nice try. What, you like her compliant? You ever do that trick with her that I discovered? Get her nice and subby? God, I can't even imagine what she'd let you do to her if you—"

Tori spat in his face. Her eyes blazed with rage. "Go *fuck yourself,* you *fucking piece of shit,* die in a *fucking car fire. I* will KILL YOU, YOU FUCKING SADIST PRICK, FUCK YOU!"

He wiped his face with his hand. "Well, your vocabulary went downhill in a hurry." He grinned. "Hit a nerve, though, didn't I? It's not my fault making her all submissive makes you feel yucky inside. It's fun, though, isn't it?"

Furious tears burned her eyes. "I never *touched her* when she was like that. I would never… I would *never fucking do that to her.*"

He raised an eyebrow. "But you did do something to her. What? Are you fuck-buddies or something? Need something hot and fast when you're on the run?

323

Or…" Her eyes widened. "…are you two a thing? A Thing with a capital 'T'?" He tilted his head. "Ooh. You are, aren't you? Damn. Well, there's someone for everyone, right?"

Her chest heaved with ragged sobs. *"Fuck you."*

He laughed. "Are you sure she wants you, though? You sure there isn't just some voice in her head telling her to do whatever you want? *Take* whatever you do to her?"

Rage shuddered through her body, forcing a growl through her teeth.

"Whatever. I don't much care what you're doing to her or not doing to her. I'm just… *so* curious…" He grinned wickedly. "About what would happen if she knew what I'm going to do to *you*. Would she come running? Or would she be relieved, that the person who holds her down and *fucks* her whether she wants you to or not is suffering, gone away from her?"

"You don't know a *fucking* thing," Tori spat at him.

Gavin shrugged. "Maybe so. Maybe not. I'm not in a hurry to get her here. Right now, I just want to hurt you. It's been… *so* long. I've been saving my energy for this since I got out of the hospital. You'll have to forgive me. I'm pretty rusty." His hand shot out, making a fist in her hair. He yanked her head back and she whimpered. "Now doesn't that sound like a good fucking time?"

She pressed her lips together and squeezed her eyes shut. Tears ran down her cheeks. *Be brave like Vera.*

Chapter 61

Vera's vision was blurred with furious tears as she tore out of the driveway. She held up the phone against the wheel and went to the previous calls. There were only six. She knew exactly which one had been from Gavin. She prayed he still had the same number.

Vera swerved, barely missing a tree. She choked down a sob and hit the accelerator again, spinning the tires around a bend and through the trees. Vera dialed it, put it on speaker, and dropped the phone into her lap. Both hands locked onto the steering wheel as the phone rang four times. Vera held her breath. The fifth ring cut off and her stomach dropped.

"Hello?"

She gritted her teeth. "You know who this is," she growled.

A laugh. *"Hey, Vera! How's it hangin'?"*

"*Fuck* you," she snarled. "Where is she?"

A snort. *"Like I'm gonna tell you."*

"Yeah, you fucking *are* gonna tell me, Gavin. You took her for a reason, and it wasn't to torture her. You want Isaac. You want me."

"So what if I do?"

"You can have me."

"...what?"

"You *fucking* heard me, you piece of shit. You don't want her. She hasn't done a damned thing to you. Take me instead."

He chuckled. *"Jesus Christ, did you people not learn from last time? How well did that go for you, exactly?"*

"It's not the others. It's just me. Trade her for me."

"Okay... I hate to be insulting but... don't you think maybe I'll just take you both? I'm sure you've thought of that already, but I just want to make sure..."

Vera tried to swallow the pressure in her throat. "Why the *fuck* did you take her if you didn't want one of us? Me or Isaac?"

"Did you ever think maybe you knowing I'm torturing a loved one is the best torture I can think of?"

She shuddered. "You're not that fucking subtle, Gavin. You're a sadist and you want Isaac and me to hurt the most. Take my deal, or I'll make sure you never find us again."

"And what about Tori? From what I hear you two are... well..."

Ice clutched her heart. "That's why I know you're going to take my deal. You can't fucking help yourself. You won't enjoy her as much as you'll enjoy me, and you know it."

"Damn, Vera, that was cold. If I didn't know better, I'd think you didn't care about her feelings. She's listening in, by the way. She's gagged. I didn't want her interrupting."

Vera's breath hitched like she'd been punched in the gut. "She can hear me?"

"Yeah, she's right here!" Vera heard steps and a rustling of fabric on the other side of the call. Over the phone, Vera could hear muffled screams getting closer and closer. Her mouth went dry. *"Hey Tori, I've got your girlfriend on the phone. Have anything to say?"*

"Vera, DON'T!"

Vera's stomach clenched. She almost lost control of the car as a wave of nausea crashed over her. "Tori—"

"Don't do it, Vera, please, don't be stupid!"

She set her jaw. "I know what I'm doing, Tori."

"No! Vera, you know what he's going to do... no..." Tori dissolved into a scream. Vera's hands spasmed around the steering wheel. The scream was muffled and Tori's cries faded until Vera couldn't hear them anymore.

"Well I guess we know her opinion on that."

"Give me an answer, Gavin, and a direction to drive in. Me for her. We both know you're going to do this."

"And what makes you think I believe you won't try something truly stupid? Like a rescue?"

A shadow of doubt passed over her face. "I'm not an idiot, Gavin. I know I'm not walking away from this."

"I'm genuinely curious." He sounded amused. *"This is exactly the situation you were in six months ago. What, exactly, do you think is going to stop me from taking you, and keeping her too, and torturing the locations of the others out of you? Or Tori. You might not break, but I bet Tori will. She's not used to this sort of thing. Are you?"* His voice faded like he was turned away from the phone.

"I'm not going to let you take me until she is safe. If you try to take us both, I will *absolutely* fucking kill you. I won't make the same mistake Isaac did." Her stomach burned.

"And that's it? We make the trade, she walks free, you're mine?"

No. I'm just going to fucking kill you. End of story. "Yes. That's it. Don't fuck with me here. You made a mistake by showing up to her house when we weren't there. This is the best outcome you could have hoped for."

"How is Gray, speaking of her house?" Gavin's voice was venomous. *"They weren't doing so hot last time I saw them."*

Vera's jaw clenched. In all likelihood, they were dead already. Wherever that hospital was, she doubted they'd stay alive long enough to get there. But if they did survive... *Gavin would never have to know. Gavin wouldn't be looking for them. Once they got better, they'd be a ghost.* Vera felt like she was going to fall apart. *They're probably dead. I can't think of them as alive. If they die...* Her throat closed in a bitter sob.

"They're dead." Her voice was flat.

A chuckle. *"Well I'll be damned. They'd still be alive, if they hadn't tried to stop us from taking Tori. You hear that?"* His voice faded as he seemed to turn

327

away again. *"Both Vera and Gray are dying for you."* His voice was loud on the line again. *"Sorry for your loss. Although with the number of my guys you've killed, I think we're still not even. Maybe once you're dead I might consider us square. Unless I decide to kill Isaac, too. Ugh, I don't know. I haven't decided."* He laughed.

"Are you done talking?" Vera's voice wobbled. "Where the fuck am I driving to?"

"We're not too far away. I didn't feel the need to be anywhere but close by. I assume you're leaving her house now?"

"I've been on the road for a few minutes."

"Great. You've still got a little ways to go. Take County Road 53 south until you reach 72. Take that east for about six miles. We'll be at 6535 East County Road 72. Big house, can't miss it. It's kind of a summer home, I guess."

"I got it."

"I think it's funny." He took a pause. *"You're not stupid. You have to know that whether you have a plan, whether you try to kill me or not, I'm going to try to take you and keep her. I can't help it. I don't exactly play well with others, you know what I mean? So... why are you doing this? You know exactly what I'm going to do to you."*

She swallowed hard and tried to keep her voice from shaking. "...I know."

"I'm going to put a collar back on you. I'm going to chain you to the floor and beat you until you can barely stand. I'm going to break you, just like whatever crazy son of a bitch broke you all those years ago. I'm going to make you obey me. I'm going to punish you if you ever, ever step out of line. I'm going to hurt and hurt and hurt you until your body just gives out and you die. I know you know this. There's no way you couldn't. So why, Oh Scary One, are you doing this?"

She shuddered at the wave of rage and fear that broke over her. "This is what you want, right? You want me. Better me than anyone else. I'm broken already. There's no need for anyone else to suffer." She swallowed the lie. She *hoped* it was a lie. *If Isaac taught me anything about you, it's that you can't help yourself with a self-sacrificial idiot.* She only hoped he'd be too wrapped up in his own fantasies to question what she was doing.

"That's… whatever, but what if I take you? What if you fail to save Tori, and I just keep both of you? What then?"

She swallowed hard. "Then…" Tears pricked her eyes and she pressed her lips together. "Then at least I get to see her again before I die."

"Aww. You two are adorable. Call me when you're ten out. I'll have her ready."

"If she's dead before I get there, I won't have to worry about accidentally killing her as I take you out." She hung up and hurled the phone at the passenger seat. It bounced under the dashboard. She pressed a shaking hand to her mouth and heaved out an agonized sob.

Chapter 62

The woman carefully pored over the map Isaac had spread on the hood of the car. She followed the line of a highway with her finger south from the city of Siding until she reached a junction, then followed it east. Her finger stopped on a small town called Beringer. It was in one of the few areas of the region that they avoided not because of the syndicates, but because of the hotbed of violence that had sprung up as people fought for what was left outside of the syndicates' control.

Isaac's eyes widened. "The hospital is in *Beringer?*" He looked at her, disbelieving.

She shrunk under his gaze, pressing her lips together. She looked down and seemed to brace for something. Isaac closed his eyes and blew out a slow breath.

"I'm sorry. I'm not angry at you. I just… it's a rough area. We stand the chance of someone else getting shot." Her eyes were fixed on the map. "Where in Beringer?"

She swallowed hard. "Um… F-fifth and Vassar."

Isaac's eyes went wider. "Jesus Christ. That's disputed territory, last I heard."

Her eyes were still cast down. Isaac noticed her watching his hands out of her periphery. "I… I don't know. I just know where it is." She drew in a shaky breath. "I… I told you where it is…" She held her breath.

Isaac folded up the map. "Thank you. Let's go."

"You… you're taking me with you?" Her eyes went wide.

"Yeah. The whole point of the last few hours was getting you away from the syndicates and moving you up north. Get in the car."

"But I... please..." She backed away from him, her hands held out in front of her in a silent plea.

He shot a glance at Finn, already in the car with Gray in the very back seat. They watched Isaac with desperation.

Isaac turned back to the girl, a placating hand held out to her. "We need to go. Okay? We need to leave right now."

"But I... I thought... can't you just leave me here, please...?" Her chest heaved with panicked gasps. "I'm sorry, I'm sorry... I'm sorry..." She fell to her knees, shielding her head with her hands as she began to sob.

Isaac watched her, open-mouthed, with his face pulled into an expression of pure horror. He turned to the car. His heart leapt in his chest as he watched Finn paw through their bag, looking through their supplies. He set his jaw and closed the distance between himself and the woman.

As he grabbed her, she immediately went limp in his hands. She forced down her sobs, whimpering softly as he carried her to the car. He roughly pushed her into the middle seat next to Ellis and jogged over to the driver's seat. He turned on the car, slammed it into gear, and sped away from Tori's house.

Sam turned around in the front seat to look back at the woman as she curled into herself. Ellis watched her with vague distrust.

"How long do we have?" Finn's voice shook as they prepped Gray's arm for an IV.

Isaac blew out a slow breath. "The hospital's in Beringer."

"What?" Ellis's voice was horrified.

Finn's head snapped around to stare at Isaac for a moment. "That's only an hour away!"

"I can make it forty-five minutes." Isaac's jaw ached from clenching it. "Do they have forty-five minutes?"

Finn's eyes darted across Gray's body as they considered the question. "I... I ha-have no idea. But we have to try. Isaac, please! We have to try!"

"I'm going, Finn. We're trying it, okay?" His knuckles were white on the steering wheel.

The woman wept softly next to Ellis, pressing herself against the car door, making herself as small as possible. Sam watched her for a moment before they noticed Ellis glaring at them. They raised their eyebrows as Ellis continued to stare them down. After a moment Sam pressed their lips together and turned their gaze back to the woman.

"Hey." Sam's voice was soft. "Hey... what do we call you?" She whimpered. "It's just a question. What's your name?"

She sniffled. "What would you like to call me?" She kept her head tucked behind her arms.

"Um... your name?"

She swallowed hard. "Edrissa."

"I'm Sam. And that's—"

"Sam." Isaac cut them off with a low voice.

They wilted for a moment. "Sorry." The girl still hid behind her hands. "Why are you so scared?"

She peeked out from behind her hands, looking Sam over with distrust. "I... I just want to go home." Tears rolled down her cheeks.

"Where's home?"

She crumpled into fresh sobs. Sam was perplexed. "H-home is... it's not... it's not *there* anymore... he sold me... he *sold me*..."

Isaac threw a horrified glance into the rearview mirror. "Someone *sold you?* Is that how we got you? You were being *sold?*"

She shivered. "You took me from my new o-owner. I thought you were going to claim me but I... please, just let me go home. If you don't want me then please just let me go home..." Her voice broke as she begged. Ellis stared at her with revulsion.

Sam's face was pulled into a mask of horror. "...*claim* you?"

With resignation, she pulled up her sleeve and held out her left arm. Just below the crook of her elbow was the remnant of a tattoo. It had been seared away, and recently. The flesh was still raw and open.

Sam gasped. "What... and did you expect us to... to do that to you again? To... make you our... *property?*"

She raised her eyes to them, confused. "Why else did you take me?"

"To rescue you?"

She shook her head. "There is no *rescue*. There is no *escape*. They told me..."

"Newsflash. They were wrong, because here we are." Ellis's voice was coiled with hostility.

Edrissa clenched her jaw. "What are you going to do with me?"

"I already told you. We're sending you north." Isaac glanced at her in the mirror.

"North...?"

He sighed. "The syndicates aren't everywhere. We have places that are safe. You can be free, if you want. Don't you want that?"

She trembled. "I haven't been... *free* in..." She fell silent as she tried to count. "What day is it?"

"December 30, 2029."

She gasped. "T-two years. Oh... my god..." She started to cry. "Oh my god..."

"Is there someone you would go back to? Someone you can find?"

"M-my br-brother, Micah... but he's... he's probably dead, he t-tried to stop them from taking me. They shot him... I don't know if he l-lived..."

"If he's alive there are people who can help you find him." Sam said, their voice tight.

"It doesn't m-matter anyway... They'll find me again. They h-have me chipped."

Isaac's head whipped around to look at her in horror. *"Chipped?* What does that mean?"

She pulled her sleeve higher to show part of her bicep. There was a faint grey mark on the skin there, covered by a small scar.

Isaac's stomach plummeted. "Does that track your GPS location?"

Her forehead furrowed. "Well... yes, if someone wanted to look in my file, they'd just pull it up. It pings my location every twelve hours—"

Ellis hurled themselves across the car to pin her against the door. She screamed and pushed weakly at their chest. "Isaac, give me your knife," Ellis growled.

Isaac's hold on the wheel slipped slightly. "Ellis, just... hang on... give me a second."

"Don't *bullshit* me, Isaac," Ellis snarled. "She's leading them right to us and I will be *damned* if these maniacs get their hands on us again for *her.*"

She whimpered and pushed harder against them. "No... *please...*" she begged.

"Isaac, give me your *FUCKING KNIFE!*"

Their roar of rage was cut off as Finn passed their own knife over the seat and bumped it against Ellis's shoulder. Finn barely looked up from their work over Gray. "Do it."

"No!" Edrissa shrieked. "No, please... please don't kill me..."

"I'm not killing you," Ellis growled. "I'm just making sure there's no way they find us again." They snapped the knife open and pressed it into her arm, just over the scar.

"No!" She sobbed raggedly. "No... please... if you take it out, they'll kill me... please..."

"That doesn't fucking matter if you're up north, does it?" Ellis pried the knife under the tiny chip and pulled it closer to the cut. They pressed their fingers

334

against the bloody wound and carefully removed the chip. It was barely the size of a pencil eraser. "Got it." They held it against the window and carefully pressed the tip of the knife into the center. It shattered with a tiny tapping sound as the knife went through it. Ellis rolled down the window and tossed the shards out of the car as it sped along the interstate.

Edrissa sobbed wretchedly. "No… you don't understand, I'm *marked*. If I'm ever found without that chip in my arm, they'll *kill me*…"

"They won't ever find you," Sam soothed. "We're taking you somewhere where it's safe."

"They'll always find me. You don't know what they're like, you don't *know*…"

"We do, actually." Isaac's voice darkened. "We know exactly how they are."

"Then you know they'll find me. They won't stop."

"At the moment they have a little more to focus on then one stray… what do they even call you? Slave?" Ellis's nose wrinkled.

"I'm not a *slave*." Edrissa sounded offended.

"What, then?"

"It… it depends on who's claimed you. For some it's *companions*, there are *pets*, there are a lot of different things."

"They're keeping people as *pets?*" Sam's voice rose.

She swallowed hard. "Yes. They've been doing it for a long time."

"What did they call you?"

Tears formed in her eyes and she bit her lip. She shook her head once. Twice. "I… I can't… Please don't make me say it…"

"You don't have to." Isaac was doing his best to keep himself calm. "You're alright."

"Fuck."

Everyone turned to look at Finn in the back seat where they were working over Gray.

"What?" Isaac's voice shook.

"I'm out of 10 gauges. And they need another."

"10 gauge... *what?*"

Finn licked their lips. "Needles."

Sam quailed. "You've been putting needles in their chest?"

"They need them." Finn forced the words out between their teeth. "And now they need more. I can't keep that *fucking* lung moving. What they need is a..."

Ellis's eyes widened. "A what?"

"A chest tube. But I've never done one before. Not by myself. And not in a moving car."

Ellis leaned over the seat, reaching for Finn helplessly. "What do you need, Finn?" Their voice was ragged.

"I... um... I mean, I have an ET tube, and a scalpel, I have all the stuff I need I just... never... *thought...*"

Ellis put a shaking hand on Finn's shoulder. "You can do it," they whispered. "What do you need?"

"I don't even have anything to... to *sanitize...*" Finn set their jaw and swallowed hard. "I need you to hold them when I'm ready. Let me get what I need first." Finn crawled over the back of the seat into the trunk to get their other kit. They grabbed a pair of needle-nose pliers from the tool kit and crawled back over the seat. "Gray?"

Gray was pale, bleeding slowly into the seat below them. Their eyes were half-open and faded from shock. They moaned softly.

"Well, that's a better reaction than it could be. Gray, I... I need to put a tube in your chest. It's going to hurt. But... we'll be at the hospital soon. They can help you."

Gray whimpered softly. Their hand searched for Finn's. Finn took it in theirs and squeezed. Gray's eyes fluttered closed and they wilted back onto the seat.

"Ellis... can you help me?"

Ellis stretched their body almost all the way across the seat. "Of course. What do you need?"

Finn stretched Gray's left arm over their head. "I need you to hold them like this. Okay? Don't let them move. I have a scalpel and I don't want them to bump me."

Ellis's hands wrapped shakily around Gray's wrist. "Okay. Tell me if you need more."

Finn squeezed themselves between the seats and huddled on the floor of the car. They took the scalpel in their blood-stained hand. They felt along Gray's ribs and marked the place with their finger. They drew in a deep breath and made the first cut.

Gray flinched and drew in a hissing breath through their teeth. As Finn made the next cut, Gray's mouth fell open into a scream. They pulled weakly against Ellis's hands, writhing mindlessly away from the pain.

"I know, I know... I'm sorry..." Finn bit their lip. Tears streamed down Ellis's face. Finn put the scalpel away and eased their finger into the cut they'd made.

Ellis swallowed hard. "Now what?"

Finn steeled themselves with a slow, deep breath. "Now I use the pliers to get through the muscle."

"...what?" The word dropped from Ellis's lips in a gasp.

Finn set their jaw. "Hold them." They pushed the closed pliers into the wound and began to twist.

Gray's howling scream tore through the car and made everyone shudder. Edrissa pressed her hands over her ears and trembled, cowering against the door. Sam began to sob quietly. Isaac's hands gripped the wheel so hard his fingers began to ache.

Finn scissored the pliers open, forcing the fibers of the muscle apart, boring a hole through Gray's chest. Over and over, they dug the pliers in, forced them open, and pulled them out. Gray convulsed away from the pain as Ellis strained to hold them still.

"P-please…" Gray murmured. "Please stop… please…"

Finn's eyes burned. They blinked quickly to clear the tears. "I have to, Gray, I have to. I'm sorry…"

"N-no please…" Gray mumbled. "No no nonono…"

With a terrible sucking sound, Finn breached Gray's chest wall. They worked the pliers into the tunnel between the lung and the outside and forced them open one more time, pulling the hole wide enough to fit the tube. They slowly guided it between the nose of the pliers. As it passed through, they pulled the pliers out. The flesh and muscle closed and sealed around the tube. Finn let out a shaky breath.

"Okay. Now I need to tape it in place and get a one-way valve going."

"Where are you gonna find a one-way valve?" Ellis's voice was high, panicked. Shaken. They looked pale.

"I don't know. I don't know, okay? But I'll figure it out." Finn's voice was quiet and intense.

Isaac's hands shook. "How much time did you just buy them? Enough to make it another thirty minutes?"

"They *have* to make it another thirty minutes," Finn almost sobbed. Blood ran from their hands and down their wrists, onto the slowly growing puddle on the floor of the car. A spatter of blood marred the right side of their face. Their breath caught in their throat. "They *have to* make it."

Chapter 63

I'm going to die.

Every nerve in Tori's body was screaming. She writhed under Gavin as he straddled her hips, her hands tied behind her and crushed beneath their weight. Gavin's hands were around her throat. Pressing down. Choking her.

Tears streamed down her face as she kicked out, legs jerking clumsily, trying to throw him off her. Her lungs screamed for air. Spots blossomed in her vision and her body began to tingle with numbness.

He let go. She coughed, dragging in lungful after lungful of burning air. She sobbed helplessly and tried to roll over, away from his twisted smile. He stood up and walked slowly around her.

"I've never had someone for this short a period of time before." He sighed. "Of course, I'm going to have you still after Vera gets here, but there's like a… definitive stopping point. I'm used to working with a lot of time on my hands. It's an interesting challenge, seeing how much damage I can do…" He kicked her viciously in the gut. She grunted. "…in such a short amount of time." He knelt down and turned her face back and forth in his hand. She whimpered. "Know what I mean? Vera really, really did not think this through. I don't even have to try to keep you when she arrives if you can't even walk. If you can't walk away, you're both mine on default." He grabbed her hair and tilted her head back, baring her throat. Purple bruises encircled it already. "Your girl is making a huge mistake, and she's making it for *you*."

She pulled away weakly, in too much pain to do much else. "Please…" Her voice was hoarse from being choked, over and over, and from screaming, when she had the air.

He snorted. "Please what?"

She trembled, closing her eyes. "Please… stop…" She swallowed a sob. "Please… you don't have to… I can't… I can't even stand up… please just… wait…"

"You misunderstood me. You think the goal here is to make sure you can't leave when she gets here?"

She met his gaze, eyes wide with terror and pain. "Please..."

He laughed. "Here's the thing. Over the phone you begged her not to come. *Begged* her. As if you hadn't told me earlier that you wanted her to come for you. I appreciate the attempt at bravery, really, I do. You've spent enough time with the others over the past few months, *something* had to rub off on you." He grinned. "What I want..." He placed a hand gently on her throat. She gasped and turned away, sobbing when his hand tightened slightly. "...is for you to already be so *broken* when she gets here that you'll beg her to stay, to take the torture for you."

"No..." She shuddered, turning her face away from Gavin's amused look.

"Because here's the thing: I truly do believe she thinks you're her new master, or owner, or whatever the fuck she had before. I think she thinks she belongs to you. And regardless of what you do to her behind closed doors, whether you hurt her or not, whether she begs you to or not... How does that work, by the way? Does she need you to hurt her? Does she beg you to do the same things to her the other one did?" He grinned. "Does she like to wear a collar when she's in bed with you? Does it make her feel like she's doing something right?"

"No..." Tori moaned. "We never... I... would never hurt her."

"Even if she begged you to?"

"She *has* begged me to." Tori choked back a sob.

Gavin stared at her for a moment. "...and you didn't capitalize on that? Damn. You are..." He chuckled. "You are missing out on some prime, grade-A torture there. Because she was..." He brought his fingers to his mouth, a chef's-kiss. "...just fantastic. Whatever. It doesn't matter. You'll see soon enough when she gets here." He shook his head. "I'm getting distracted. Fact is, I think she thinks she belongs to you, so if you begged her to leave, she actually might. But if you begged her to stay... to take the torture for her..." He laughed. "I bet she'd put the collar on herself."

Tori shook with sobs. "She doesn't... she doesn't *belong* to me. She would never think that."

He raised an eyebrow. "Really. You think there's *no way* – even though you just said she has *literally* begged you to hurt her, you think there's no way – that she thinks she belongs to you? Sweetheart, I tortured her friends in front of her and she *still* folded like she was born to do it when I had my hands on her. But with you? With you being so nice and gentle to her, she might even think she *likes* being owned by you." He grabbed her hair and yanked her closer as she tried to twist away. "Look. I've seen *a lot* of people like her, okay? Hell, I've even helped *make* a few people like her. And believe me, once we break them, there's no other way for them to be. They can't go back to who they were. They can't just... go out into the world and be a normal human being again. Granted, I don't know a lot of people like Vera who've been able to return to the world. Most of the time they die in captivity. Or are actively killed. That's what I prefer." She whimpered, trembling under his grasp. "I do have a kind of distant cousin who likes to play catch-and-release. Believe me, those people can never return to normal. They usually seek out people who are willing to own them again. It's a whole thing." He laughed. "Sorry, I'm getting distracted. I've been having issues with attention ever since Isaac fucked me up. Can you tell?"

He tossed her away from him and stood. She twisted, trying to get her legs under her to run. He kicked her onto her side and placed a foot on her ankle. He pressed down. She screamed and fell still as her body trembled with tension.

"Where was I... um... captivity, torture, Vera... oh yeah! We were talking about how you think she's with you willingly." He shrugged. "I mean, yeah, she's choosing to do it, but don't you think that's kinda... weird? Why would she do that? She shows up to your doorstep like a kicked puppy and you just... fall in love with her like that? Is that what happened?" She pressed her lips together as tears rolled down her cheeks. "Here's what I think: I think you like 'em broken, and she just wanted to be owned again. Isn't there something just... fucking *good* about knowing that if you wanted to, and I absolutely think you do, you can just..." He snapped his fingers. "...flip the switch, put her in that headspace where she's yours? She'd cut her own fucking throat for you if you told her to. And admit it." He knelt beside her and pulled her head back, forcing her to look at him. "It feels good."

She spat in his face.

He drew his arm across his face and laughed. "Your outrage is adorable. And sure, you can deny what I know about you. But... can you really deny what I know about *her?*" She squirmed under his hand. "Admit it to me. There have been times when you wondered, even for a second, if she wants to be with you at all. You've wondered if you weren't the steady hand she's needed all these years that no one in the group has been able to be for her. You've wondered if she doesn't just… *worship* you… because having someone to belong to again makes her feel like she's doing something *right*. And if you really want to tell yourself she's with you willingly, with no other weird bullshit about obedience and fear of you torturing her if she steps out of line, how would you ever be truly able to know for sure?"

The tears wouldn't stop. She tried to shut his words out, to deny it to herself. *It's just the torture. This is what he does. I saw what he did to the others. He tears people apart just by talking to them.*

But there it was. The tickle in the back of her mind. The doubt. The times when she would ask Vera if she was okay, if she needed space, if she felt like she was falling back into the black hole in her mind where she went when she was back *there*, in that cell… the times when Vera seemed a little *too* eager to please… the moments when Vera would zone out for a few seconds when they were together, making love, and Tori would stop and ask her if she wanted to keep going and she would say *yes, yes please, I want you, I want this*… Tori had been sure she was getting better at telling when Vera was far away. She was sure she could tell the difference between Vera getting lost in her thoughts like everyone did, and getting lost altogether. She was sure, *sure* that Vera knew the difference between her torture all those years ago and her life now.

But now, she wasn't so sure. Her body convulsed into a sob. *What have I done?*

Gavin laughed and stood again. "Here's the thing. I'm a fundamentally curious person. I've been dying to know who broke Vera first. So, I took the liberty of sending that picture you had of her to everyone I know. Someone's got to know something. Someone's got to recognize her. I've gotten a lot of no's so far. But whoever it was, I'm dying to talk to them. Get some advice. Because once she shows up… oh, honey." He nudged her onto her back. She went limp, quivering with shame. "I believe you love her, no matter how fucked up that relationship is. And I want to make you watch me break her all over again, with the advice of whoever did it first."

Chapter 64

They had a difficult time getting to the hospital door. The road had been destroyed; huge potholes torn into the pavement made the place look like bombs had been dropped there. Isaac swallowed hard as he wondered if that really was what happened. He turned back to look at Edrissa.

"It's here?"

She nodded, looking up at the fortified building as they approached. It didn't look like a hospital from what Isaac could see; it looked like a regular building, except with metal reinforcements at every window and armed guards at the entrance.

"What are they protecting?" Isaac eyed the weapons.

"The doctors."

He turned back to look at Edrissa in surprise. Her eyes were wide. "The doctors?"

"A good doctor or medic is hard to come by anymore. The gangs try to kidnap them every now and then. Sometimes the syndicates come looking for them too."

"And they can hold them off?"

She looked pale. "I don't think so."

"How do you know so much about this place?" He rolled to a stop a safe distance away from the armed guards and unfastened his seatbelt.

"I... I used to live here. In Beringer."

"How did you end up with the syndicates?"

Finn's voice rose from the back seat. "We need to go, Isaac." He glanced back and saw them fixing him with a look that bordered on panic.

He pulled his gun from under his seat and tucked it into the waistband of his jeans. He carefully got out of the car, his eyes locked on the guards. They were watching him just as closely.

"Stay in the car," he ordered.

Sam jumped out of the passenger seat and fell into step behind him.

"Sam... no. Stay in the car. It's not safe."

"It's not safe *anywhere*, Isaac. I want to come with you. Please." Their hand rested on his elbow for a split second as they looked up at him. "Please."

He glanced back at the car, at Finn's harried stare through the back window. They made a motion with their hand. *Let's speed this up.* He turned back to Sam, biting his lip. "Okay. Just... stay behind me."

He approached the guards slowly, hands raised. His eyes flicked to their trigger fingers as they moved over the trigger guards.

"That's close enough," one of them said. The guard shifted his weight nervously.

"We need medical attention. One of our family, they're hurt, they—"

"How're you paying?" the other one cut him off.

He blinked. "Paying?"

The first one to speak, the taller one, snorted. "This isn't a fucking community clinic. How are you paying? You have narcotics? Guns? What?"

Isaac swallowed. "We... we don't have anything. I'm sorry, we didn't know. Please. They've been shot."

"You think you're the first person to show up here with someone who's been shot? Big fucking deal. This place isn't for free. You want something you don't have to pay for, go see the syndicates. I hear they treat their captives *real* well." He chuckled.

"Come on." Isaac's throat was tight. "We're on the same side, here."

344

The other one laughed. "*Side?* There are no *sides*. There's us, and everyone else. People get shot. It fucking happens."

"They got shot fighting the syndicates."

"Who *doesn't* get shot fighting the syndicates. Be grateful they're even alive."

Isaac's expression darkened. "They *won't be* if we don't get them help. We can work something out. Please."

The shorter one smiled, his lips pulling into a sickening grin. "Oh, you want to *work something out*." His eyes fell on Sam for the first time. "You renting this one out? You could probably get more than just a surgery for them." He took a step forward with his eyes fixed on Sam. "How much do you go for, honey?"

Sam went still against Isaac's side. Isaac pushed them behind him, rage building in his chest. "They're not for *sale*, you sick—"

The other guard took a step closer. "Oh, come on. I thought we were bargaining. What's worth more? Your friend's life, or a few hours with this one?"

Sam stared at Isaac with wide eyes. "I can... I could—"

"*No.*" His hand drifted to his waistband almost unconsciously as they took another step towards him and Sam.

"I might not be asking at this point." The taller one leered at Sam.

Isaac's jaw was tight. "You'll have to go through me."

The shorter one smiled. "I don't think that'll be a problem." The barrel of his rifle inched up.

"*Isaac...*" Sam was breathless with panic. Their fingers were locked in a fist around Isaac's shirt.

The taller guard paused. "...Isaac?"

His stomach dropped. He pushed Sam further behind him, ready to bolt. *If I keep Sam in front of me and they shoot me in the back, they might still be able to get to the car... Oh god, I hope someone got in the driver's seat. They have to get away.*

345

The taller guard lowered his rifle. "Isaac Moore? *Gavin Stormbeck's* Isaac?"

Isaac's hand closed around the pistol in his waistband. "Sam, *run.*" He shoved them back as his other hand came up with the gun.

"Whoa, whoa, whoa. Wait." The guard dropped his rifle completely. It hung from the strap around his shoulder. He raised his hands and took a step back.

Isaac was already moving backwards, gun held up between them, left hand locked on Sam's shirt as he pushed them behind him.

"You can have the surgery." The guard stared after Isaac with eyes wide with disbelief.

Isaac froze. He let go of Sam's shirt and pushed them away. "Go to the car, Sam. *Now.*"

Sam scrambled back a few steps. "Isaac…" Their voice tightened in desperate terror.

Isaac kept the gun pointed directly at the taller guard's chest. "Why?" he demanded. "Why do you only offer help when you know who I am?"

The guard was staring at him, open-mouthed. Isaac thought he could see *tears* in the man's eyes. "You saved my family. You got them away from the syndicates and sent them north. They're safe now. Because of you."

Isaac's heart beat hard in his chest. "So what? We saved your family. Why would the doctor operate on our friend for that?"

"Because you saved her son, too." The other guard lowered his rifle. "Tell me my last name. I have to know for sure. Tell me my last name. My wife's name is Sandra. We have a boy and a girl. Roger and Sofie. What's my last name?"

Isaac swallowed hard. "I remember them. Sandra, Roger, and Sofie Barnes."

The guard let out a breath and stumbled forward a step. Isaac's hand tightened on his gun.

"That's right. Barnes. I'm Jeff. Jeff Barnes."

Isaac eyed the other guard. "What about you? Are we good? Will you let us through?"

The man stared between Isaac and the tall guard. "Barnes, you good with this?"

He nodded. "Yeah. Radio triage, tell them we've got a GSW coming in." He looked at Isaac. "Where've they been shot?"

Isaac's mouth was dry. His hand ached with his grip. "Chest. Our medic—" His mouth snapped shut.

Barnes's eyes went wide. "You have a medic?"

A good medic is hard to come by anymore. Isaac's stomach fluttered. He hoped he hadn't just put Finn in danger. *They would've figured it out soon enough. Chest tubes don't just happen.* "How do you know so much about us? I mean… how do you know my name?"

Barnes laughed darkly. "Oh, you've been causing the syndicates too much trouble to be anonymous. You've got a *lot* of people after you."

Chapter 65

Tori's blood stained the carpet. She lay curled on her side, hands bound behind her, trying desperately to shield herself from Gavin's blows. Over and over, he struck her with the cane, or kicked her, or just punched her. Her lip was split open and oozing blood down her cheek, mixing with the blood flowing slowly from her nose. Her skin was broken in several places along her arms, her back, her legs. She no longer had the strength to even try to push away from Gavin, to run. She lay still on the floor, under the relentless beating, her body jerking with each strike. She sobbed.

"What do you think, Tori? You had about enough? Will you be ready to tap out once Vera gets here?"

She gasped as he kicked her viciously in the back. "No…"

"Really? You want this to continue? You want her to leave you here to suffer like this?" The cane struck her across her shoulder.

She keened weakly. "Please… I… I can't…"

He knelt beside her and took her jaw in his hand almost gently. She cried out and shuddered away from his touch. "I don't believe you're that brave, Tori. Or that self-sacrificial. Why would you want this to continue when you can just transfer the pain to your plaything? She wants this, remember? She's begged you for it. Why don't you want her to take it for you when she comes?"

Tori's chest spasmed and she whimpered. *This is what she lived through, and I used that. I used this pain to make her be with me. I deserve this.* She turned her head away.

"That's one thing I never understood." Gavin's hand moved to her hair. He pulled her head back, admiring the blood and tearstains on her face. "Self-sacrifice. I mean, yeah, it fucking sucks when people you love get hurt, but why lay down your life or take torture for someone? Let's say Vera gets to you and can actually get you out, trade herself for you. Let's say you *somehow* get away from here on your own. What would be the point? She'd never get to see you happy and safe. She'd never be able to protect you again. She'd never be able to hold you, or let you fuck her, or obey you again. And you're going to die someday anyway. If you were able to escape, she'd be giving up the rest of her life to extend yours for a few years. And you could be taken, tortured, *killed* by someone else next week. I don't get it. It doesn't make any… *logical* sense." He turned her head back, forcing her to look at him. She let him do it, her body going pliant and limp. "Explain it to me."

Tori's lips were numb. "I… I don't know why she's doing it."

He snorted. "What do you mean, you don't *know?*"

Her lips quivered. "I know I've hurt her… I know I've used her. I didn't realize it… but I know it now. I don't know why… She could be free. She could be free of *me*…" She shuddered. "I don't want her to come, I don't want her to hurt more because of me…"

"Hm. Okay, now that I think about it, it does kinda make sense with you two. If she thinks she's yours, she might think she has a *duty* to do this. But… Isaac and Sam? That one *really* made no sense. Isaac gave himself over to me to keep me from torturing Sam, and he left his family vulnerable. The knight traded himself for a pawn. It's that kind of stuff that makes no sense to me." He laughed. "To think this whole thing could have been over, would never have happened at *all*, if Isaac had just… let me have Sam. They'd be dead by now, no question. But everyone else would be whole. Everyone else would be alive." He chuckled darkly. "My face wouldn't be all messed up like this." His hand went almost unconsciously to his scars. "This situation is more… the knight trading herself for the queen, I guess. I think I can wrap my mind around that."

What if he's right? What if she gives herself to him because she thinks that's her duty *to me?* She swallowed hard, tears cascading down her cheeks. *I have only one way to save her.*

"Kill me," she whispered.

His hand slipped out of her hair. He grinned. "…beg pardon?"

Tori pressed her face against the floor. She cringed away from him as her heart sank. "Kill me. Please."

He laughed. "Aw. That's so sweet. You're trying to sacrifice yourself for her, now. Around and around you all go."

"No, it's because… because… I can't take it. I can't take this until she gets here. I want it to stop now. I just want to die."

"Ha. Liar. Can you at least *try* to make it convincing?"

She closed her eyes, turning her face away from him. "Please."

"This is what I don't understand: your guilt right now. You like feeling powerful. You *like* it when Vera is broken at your feet, begging. Admit it. But you feel bad about that so you're trying to make up for it by punishing yourself. Why feel guilty? You like what you like, and you can't help that. There's not anything that can be gained from you doing this. So… why?"

"I… I never wanted to hurt her… I *swear*…" She choked on a sob. "I never thought… I never *knew* what I was doing to her. I…" She crumpled in on herself. "I thought she loved me like I loved her." Her chest tightened painfully with each sob. "Please… please kill me…"

Gavin chuckled. "I'm not going to. By all means, though, please keep begging me like that." He got to his feet and wandered over to a row of drawers against the wall. "I hope you don't mind. I took the liberty of getting Vera something. That was before my visit to your house went sideways and I got you instead of her, but… you can wear it until she gets here." He opened the top drawer and pulled something out, dangling it from his fingers.

A collar.

She pressed her face into the carpet, whimpering softly. "No…" she whispered.

He grinned at her as he approached slowly. "Yeah. I'm gonna put this on you. Then I'm going to keep hurting you, breaking you. When Vera gets here, you're going to beg her to take the torture for you. Then she's going to take this off you. And put it on herself." He kneeled beside her, a grin stretched across his face.

She turned her face away from him, pulling away weakly. "No no no… please…"

350

He pulled her head back and bared her throat to him. He buckled the collar around her neck. She sagged on the floor, the weight of it dragging her down into despair. She swallowed and it tightened uncomfortably around her neck. She felt cold fingers of panic clutch around her heart.

"...wow. Damn. You look... incredible in that. I'm going to have to get you another one after Vera takes that one from you." He turned her head back and forth, admiring how the leather pulled at her skin. She sobbed. "This opens up... so many other things I could do."

His hand tightened on the collar and he pulled her upright. She gasped and gagged against the pressure as he lifted her by the neck. Her legs scrambled to get under her as he pulled harder, closing the collar around her throat. Her body spasmed in panic. Tears streamed down her face. Her mouth opened and closed, but no sound or breath escaped as she choked.

Gavin's phone rang.

His hand paused as he dragged her upwards. His jaw clenched. He released the collar and Tori slumped to the floor, coughing and gasping.

"It's too early for her to be here by now," he grumbled. He sighed and pulled his phone out of this pocket, rolling his neck as he looked at the number. The frown disappeared.

"Hey, dad."

Tori lay shuddering on the floor as Gavin wandered away from her, listening to the man on the other end. After a few steps, he stopped. Frozen. "...what?" His mouth fell open slowly. "Oh my god... that is... oh my god. Yeah. Absolutely. Yeah, the summer house. Okay. Sounds good."

He hung up the phone and clumsily put it back in his pocket, half-stunned. He turned slowly back to face Tori. She stared up at him in terror. He started to laugh, softly at first, then uproariously, head thrown back, eyes streaming with tears.

"Oh my god. This is just... the best fucking day ever. Oh my god." He knelt beside Tori again. She shied away from his hand as it clamped down on the collar. He dragged her towards him, bringing his face close to hers. "Okay, Tori. New plan."

351

Chapter 66

Vera was shaking as she pulled up the long driveway. Her hands trembled on the steering wheel as she pulled the car up to the house. She angled the car so she could pull away without having to back up, put the car into park, and turned it off. She grabbed her gun. Her palms were slick with sweat as she climbed out of the car and made her way towards the house.

She didn't bother knocking. She turned the handle on the door, and it swung open. Her grip tightened on the gun as she made her way down the hall.

She had no idea where Gavin would be keeping Tori, but it didn't matter. Vera would clear the house and find them. She'd shoot Gavin dead and take down anyone else he had with him. Then she'd leave with Tori. *If she's not—*

She shoved the thought out of her mind. *She's alive.* She shook her head and willed herself to focus. She cleared the foyer and moved past the grand staircase, further into the house.

A coat closet. A guest bathroom. A living room. A kitchen, off to the right. She considered clearing every cabinet before she realized Gavin would choose to have this happen where there would be more space.

She suddenly realized that she hadn't seen anyone else yet. That worked out better; if Gavin heard gunshots, he would figure out pretty quickly that she was not here to make a trade. Still, it made her shiver.

She heard a rustling coming from the hall and snapped her gun up to the doorway. She slowly made her way out of the kitchen and stalked further down the hall to the room at the back of the house. A study. She swallowed hard and rounded the corner.

Her gaze found Tori immediately. Gavin's gaze snapped up to her face as she walked slowly into the room, gun ready in her hands, body as tense as a piano wire. Tori was on her knees with her hands tied behind her. Her hair was wild around her face and she was bleeding – oh god, she was *bleeding* – into the carpet. Her head was bowed, and she looked like she was on the verge of slumping to the ground.

Tori raised her head weakly. She was gagged. Vera's stomach roiled as she realized what was around her neck.

Gavin collared her.

She swallowed bile and a snarl of rage ripped out of her chest. Gavin's smile spread wide over his face as he crossed his arms in front of him, smugness showing in every inch of his stance.

Tori began to shake with sobs. She pleaded through the gag, shaking her head, and tried to stand. Gavin grabbed her hair and yanked her back to her knees. Her voice rose to a scream in her desperation.

"It's okay, Tori," Vera whispered through numb lips. "I've got you." She raised her gun and took aim at Gavin's chest.

"Hello, Vera."

No.

The world shattered with that voice. Her breath froze. Her hands shook. She nearly dropped her gun. For a moment, she completely lost where she was. She was in that cell again, she was so cold, she was on her knees and on her back and strung up from the ceiling and hurt, god, she *hurt*, she felt the whip on her back and the knife on her skin, she felt the cane breaking her open, she felt *him*, all over her, on top of her, inside her; it all came flooding back with that voice, those two words.

She blinked and two tears ran down her cheeks. She could see again. She was in that room with Gavin, she could see Tori, *her* Tori, on her knees in front of her, sobbing like her throat was tearing open. Behind her, she could hear that voice again.

"Lower your gun away from my son, Vera."

Her body convulsed. *Your... son?* Every muscle seemed to rebel against her. Her gun dipped an inch in her grasp, then another. Her arms moved slowly down until they fell to her sides, her hand wrapped loosely, uselessly around the weapon. Her lips quivered as her mind screamed at her. *There's something*

353

I need to say. I need to say I need to say I need to say, or he'll hurt me, he'll hurt me he'll hurt me...

"Yes sir."

Tori howled and sank forward, her forehead pressing against the ground. Gavin grinned from ear to ear.

"Oh, sweetheart." That voice was getting closer behind her. This must be a nightmare, this must be some hellish dream because Tori, *her* Tori was here, she was tortured, bleeding, and Vera was with this monster again after so many years. She'd been free, she knew that was real. She reached her mind back and tried to remember when she must have fallen asleep, when reality had stopped and this nightmare had started. There was a sinking, aching feeling in her gut like she'd been punched, and she knew, she *knew* it was real.

He appeared at the edge of her periphery and walked slowly around her, coming around to face her. Her mind erupted into agony and panic as her eyes focused on him. *No.* There he was, fourteen years older now, but still unquestioningly him. Seeing him brought everything back all over again. The beatings, the rapes, the bleeding. The times when he'd had friends over to play with her. The times when she'd begged him with everything she had, to just *kill her*, let her go, let her just be dead.

The force of it almost brought her to the floor: she could see it now. In the shape of the eyes, but bluer, the nose, the identical front teeth. *Gavin's father.* She wondered how she could have missed it all this time.

"It's been so long," he whispered, and brought a hand to her face. A cry of anguish punched its way out of her as his hand stroked her cheek gently. *Shoot him, shoot him, you still have the gun, shoot him, KILL HIM NOW.* She couldn't move. She was paralyzed with the weight of her pain and fear.

"I think you've met my dad." Gavin's voice was sickly sweet. "And apparently, we've met prior to our encounter six months ago. Would you believe," he sneered as he sauntered closer to her, "that I actually met you when I was a kid?" As he stopped at his father's shoulder, Vera shuddered in horror, seeing her torturers stand side by side.

Gavin's father looked at her fondly. "You were the first person my son ever hurt. And you were so good, Vera." He sighed out her name. "You were so good for me, almost the whole time you were with me. God, I missed you." His fingers moved gently through her hair. She cringed away from his touch before she caught herself. *He doesn't like it when I pull away.*

Over the sound of his voice, Tori's wails broke through and crashed over Vera like waves. Her mouth fell open in a silent scream as Gavin walked back beside Tori and yanked her up by the collar around her neck.

Vera's lips trembled. "P... please..." Her voice was barely above a whisper. "You have me now, l-let her go... please..." She closed her eyes and tears rolled down her cheeks. "Please, sir."

Gavin's father groaned softly. "How I missed hearing you beg. I missed... so many things about you." He drew back his hand and whipped it across her face. She gasped and stumbled, biting back a cry. "And the noises you make... when you're trying not to scream, when you're being so good for me..." His hand settled on the faint scars around her throat. "I'll have to get you a new collar. When you left me the people who took you cut it off you, didn't they?" He tilted his head at her. "I burned it. I thought I'd lost you forever. But now..." His face slid into a horrifying grin. "I have you back. I'll have a new one made, just for you."

"Please..." She whimpered. "Please let her go..."

"Not gonna happen," Gavin spoke up. "I didn't realize you used to belong to my dad. That, by the way, just seems like the craziest coincidence... I probably would have found out eventually if you hadn't managed to blow up my warehouse and escape, but finding out like this?" He laughed. "Just the best." He jerked Tori up by the collar. She gagged, her body writhing as she fought to breathe.

Vera took a step towards Tori. Her hand spasmed around the gun.

"Ah ah ah... no." Vera froze at the saccharine words at her ear. "Good girl. No, you're going to come back and stay with me."

"And I figured, why don't I stay with my dad for a while and bring Tori?" Gavin chuckled. "Let you two actually be together, considering how cute you are. And considering how much we can teach Tori about how to hurt you. She wants to so badly, you know."

Vera's eyes moved to Tori in a daze. Tori was slumped against Gavin, kicking weakly, trying to escape his grasp. *They're going to make her hurt me.* "Tori..." *I can take it. As long as they don't hurt her.* Gavin released Tori's collar and she dropped bonelessly to the floor.

"And," Gavin's father cooed as he brought his hands to her face, "You're going to be so good for us. Because if you don't..." He shook his head. "...I'm going to make you kill Tori. You were together for a few months, yes? You love her?" Vera nodded weakly. "Hm. Then you're going to behave for me, aren't you?" She nodded again. *Yes. Yes. Yes. Anything for her. I'll be good for Tori.*

Gavin laughed. "Wish I'd known this trick with you before, Vera. Coulda saved myself a lot of overhead. And a lot of hospital bills." He kicked Tori hard in the back.

Vera felt the blow like it had been dealt to her. Her mind was screaming. Her body was wracked with agony with every heartbeat. *I can take it. I can take it all for her. But I can't protect her from them. I can't protect Tori.*

She felt a knife in her heart as she realized what could save Tori this pain. She could take the pain herself and deliver Tori from it. She knew what she had to do. *I begged him to do it so many times.* If she took Tori's life, here and now, she could save her. She knew they would punish her for it. She knew she would suffer. But... *I can do it. I can...* She couldn't even think it. She couldn't put words to what she had to do. Her hand tightened around her gun, still miraculously in her hands. *They haven't taken it away because they know I'm theirs. They know I won't hurt them. They know I'm theirs to control.*

She couldn't feel that she was sobbing. She didn't feel it as her body was wracked again and again with agony, tears pouring hot down her face. She sobbed Tori's name. She couldn't hurt *them,* but she could save Tori. She had strength enough for that, at least. And once she was done, if they hadn't taken her gun away by then, she could turn it on herself. She could do it, for Tori.

She'd been put on her knees, she'd been raped, she'd been tortured, she'd been good, she'd been bad, she'd been *nothing,* but Tori was... good. *Truly* good, not the twisted kind of good Vera knew she was. Tori was kind, and strong, and tender. All Vera was good for was hurting. With that voice in her ear, she was reminded. She'd forgotten for so long, but she once again knew the truth that had been carved into her mind at the point of a knife. She deserved this, she deserved to be captured, to be collared, to be *hurt.*

But Tori didn't deserve this.

Something inside Vera snapped.

Neither do I.

Vera took a step towards Gavin's father. Her body came almost flush with his and she nuzzled into his neck. His hand rested on her hair and carded through it. "Hm. I might not even have to break you in again." She looked over his shoulder and her gaze fell to Tori. Tori squeezed her eyes closed, shutting out the sight. She wailed into the gag.

Vera raised her hand and took a single shot.

The bullet punched through Gavin's chest and threw him back against the carpet.

"NO!" Gavin's father struck the gun out of Vera's grasp, one hand locking around her wrist, the other closing around her neck. His eyes flashed with berserk rage. *"BAD GIRL."*

Her mind was gone. She lunged forward, his hand choking her as she shoved her face against his neck. She opened her mouth and felt the soft flesh of his throat against her lips, her tongue. She sunk her teeth in until she tasted blood.

The twisted howl that came from his torn throat was inhuman. Fire poured through her blood that razed everything else in her to the ground. She tasted his blood on her lips and she lunged forward again, sinking her teeth in again until she could feel the ridges of his trachea in her mouth. She bit down and tore at his flesh again.

A scream bubbled out of him, gurgling on his lips. Air rushed out of the gash torn in his throat. His blood ran in rivulets down Vera's chin, down her neck, staining her shirt. One more time she ripped her teeth through the gristle of his neck, her hands locked in fists around his shirt, supporting him as the life and blood gushed out of him and into the carpet.

Her legs gave out and she fell to the floor on top of him. Her eyes were wide and fixed on the growing puddle of blood under him. It was more blood than she had ever seen in her life. It was more blood than she thought was possible. His body was limp beneath her, and pale. It was grotesque, his throat torn open

357

and exposed, his eyes staring blankly at the ceiling, a vague look of surprise left etched on his face. She slumped off of him with jerky limbs that only half-obeyed her.

Vera turned and vomited onto the floor. She shuddered violently as the fire drained from her body, leaving only terror and pain. Her mind reeled with shock.

She jumped at the sound of Tori's sobs. She stumbled to Tori's side and fell on her knees beside her.

Tori flinched away from Vera's hands as they settled on her shoulder. Vera's mouth went dry. *She doesn't want me to touch her. She watched what I just did. She thinks I'm a monster.* She swallowed hard and her hands shook. She gagged at the taste of blood still in her mouth. She drew her sleeve across her face.

"Tori," she whispered. "I'm so sorry, I'm so… Please, just… let me untie you, let me help you and then I… I don't have to touch you again." Her hands went to the collar. Her fingers were clumsy against it as she fumbled with the buckle. Tori gave a tortured sob as it came away. Vera could barely see the marks on Tori's neck through her tears. "I'm sorry," she mumbled. "I'm sorry, Tori, I'm so sorry…" She bit her lip and moved to the gag. She pulled it from Tori's mouth and went to work on the rope around her wrists.

"No…" Tori moaned. "Vera… I never meant to… I never meant to hurt you. You must hate me… *Please…*"

Vera's hands froze. A well of icy dread opened in her stomach. *"…what?"*

Tori pressed her face into the carpet. "I swear to god, I didn't know… I didn't know I was hurting you. I'm so sorry…"

Vera swallowed the bile that rose in her throat and loosened the knot binding Tori. She pulled the rope away from Tori's wrists and tried not to look at the raw skin underneath. She placed a hand gently on Tori's hair. Tori shied away from it, cringing into herself.

"What did he say to you?" Vera's gaze moved over Tori's body, to the bruises she could see, to the blood soaking through her clothes. "What did he *do?*"

Tori sobbed. "Y-you d-don't have to f-forgive me but... p-please... no... Vera..."

"Hey." Vera shook Tori gently. She seemed to focus a little. "Tori. Stop. What did he say? You didn't... *hurt* me. What did he say to you?"

Tori gasped. "He... he said... I was using you... because you just wanted to be owned again. He said..." She groaned. "He said... I was using your past... to make you... let me do things to you."

"Stop." Vera's hands tightened on Tori's arms. *"Stop that.* You think I can't tell the difference between them and you? You think I can't tell the difference between what we have, between *love*, and..." She shuddered. "You weren't... *using me*, Tori." Her expression darkened. "So, don't... don't you *dare*... tell me you're sorry for being with me. Okay? Are you saying I'm incapable of really loving someone? Are you saying I'm so weak I need to be *'owned'*? Is that what you're saying?"

For the first time, Tori raised her eyes to look at Vera. Vera saw something written on her face, something like fear. Or maybe... *awe.* But there was no pity there.

"No," Tori whispered. "I don't... I don't think that."

"Then don't apologize to me. I'm so..." Vera squeezed her eyes shut. "I'm so sorry I let him get to you. I'm sorry I let him hurt you. But please..." She opened her eyes and grasped Tori's hands. "Please don't let him take you away from me now. He messed with your head, Tori. Just like he did to all of us. But it's a *lie*. Do you hear me? It's a *lie*. I *love you.* Me. I love you. I'm choosing it. I don't need to be... fucking *owned*." She spat out the word and pulled Tori upright. "Please don't ever say that to me again."

Tori threw her arms around Vera and erupted into sobs again. Vera wound her arms around Tori's waist and pulled her close, her own tears falling on Tori's shoulder.

"I thought he was going to kill me," Tori wailed. "And I... watching him do that to you..." Tori clutched at Vera. "Tell me you weren't going to sacrifice yourself, Vera, tell me you weren't going to do that... *please...*"

Vera buried her face in Tori's hair. "No. I was going to kill him. I was going to kill him and grab you. Get you out. I swear." Vera pulled back and stroked her hand through Tori's hair. She studied her face. Tori's lip was split, and her nose was bleeding. "Where are you hurt?"

Tori shook her head and swallowed down a sob. "I'm fine. He beat me, but I'm alright. I don't think anything's broken. Well..." She winced with her next breath. "Maybe a few ribs. But I'm okay." She turned her face into Vera's palm. "Really."

"Okay. Let's get you up. I'll wash my face in the kitchen and we can go."

Tori's face broke. "Gray! Oh my god... You said they were dead. Are they—"

"I don't know." Vera pressed her lips together. "We were bringing you a rescue and she knows about a hospital that takes in people who fight the syndicates. They all took Gray there."

"Where is it?"

"I don't know. I told Isaac to text the phone when he got a location and a new burner. Until we hear from him, we need to just lay low, stay off the main highways." She got to her feet and reached down for Tori, helping her to her feet. "You okay to walk?"

"Yeah." Tori swayed, her hand drifting to latch onto Vera. "I'm okay."

Vera wound an arm around her waist. "Okay. Come on. Let's get you out of here."

Chapter 67

Isaac spun the new burner phone in his hands, passing it back and forth, opening the screen, turning it off again. One of the nurses had found it for him, once she had found out who Isaac was, too. She'd pressed it into his hands, whispering, *"Thank you. You saved my best friend's parents. John and Christine Gillian. Please let us know if you need anything else."*

Isaac opened the messages and went to the only text that had been sent from the phone: *Beringer. 5th and Vassar. In surgery. Use my name to get in.*

That was it. That was all he could risk sending. If Vera was captured and the phone was taken... He couldn't risk telling Vera he knew they had people after them. He couldn't risk telling her they were there only by the generosity of the surgeon whose son they'd saved. He didn't want to put into words what the people here had been willing to do to Sam, were *going* to do to Sam, before learning who they were. *We're not safe no matter where we go.*

He looked around at his family, all crammed into the dirty waiting room. Finn paced, running their hands through their hair. Ellis was slumped on a couch in a corner of the room, rubbing their hands together, silent tears making their way slowly down their face.

Sam was curled up against Isaac's side. Isaac put the phone in his pocket and put an arm around them. They cuddled closer into his chest and latched onto his shirt.

Slowly, almost hesitantly, his gaze fell on Edrissa. She had pressed herself as far into a corner as she could get. Her eyes raked the room. Her arms were wrapped tightly around herself. She looked like she was ready to bolt at any moment. Or like she was going to be sick.

What am I going to do with her?

She'd stayed with them so far, but Isaac didn't know how much of that was even her choice. *Does she think we'll hurt her if she tries to leave? Is she afraid someone will kill her if she escapes and is found to be a—* He still didn't know what they'd called her. A slave? A plaything? Isaac's family had taken her as she was being bought and sold like a *thing*.

A dark, suspicious thought crossed Isaac's mind. *Would she betray us, go back to her masters and turn us in for favor with them?* He shuddered. He ached, remembering the pain and terror of being in syndicate hands for five days. His mind rebelled against the thought of even *imagining* two years of that torture. *If she betrayed us, I don't think I could even blame her.*

He shifted uncomfortably, feeling his gun press against his back. He swallowed hard. His hand moved to Sam's hair and stroked gently through it. *I'll have to kill her if she puts my family at risk.*

He ran his hand over his face. *How did this get so messed up? How did I get us here?* Gray, upstairs in surgery. Vera, god only knows where, going after Tori. In the hands of *Gavin.* He felt a wash of guilt roiling in his belly, burning him from the inside out. *If I had killed him, none of this would have happened. If I had just... finished it, ended his life, we'd be safe. Gray would still be...* He choked on the thought. *They're alive. They're still alive.* His hand tightened unconsciously in Sam's hair.

Sam raised their head to look at him. Their eyebrows raised as they saw the tortured look on Isaac's face. "...what's wrong?"

He huffed out a bitter laugh and pressed his lips into their hair. "What *isn't?*"

They swallowed. Their dark eyes widened as they looked up at him. "I... I'm sorry."

He chuckled darkly. "It isn't your fault, Sam. None of it is. If anything, it's mi—"

"Don't say it's yours. Please. Don't say it. We... we're here because of you, Isaac. If it weren't for you, we'd never have gotten here. Please... it kills me when you take the blame like this. When you hurt this way."

Isaac squeezed his eyes shut and swallowed against the burning sensation in his throat. He trembled at the voice that rose in his mind, the one that had once screamed silently but now spoke with Gavin's voice. *It is your fault. You decided to raid the outpost. You left Sam vulnerable. You failed to stop the group from coming for you. You begged. You broke. You didn't kill him, when he was there for you to kill, exposed, beaten, you didn't do it. You failed to protect them. You failed you failed you failed. Your fault.*

He blinked his eyes open at the touch of a hand on his cheek. He hadn't realized he was crying. He scrubbed his face with his sleeve.

"You have that look," Sam whispered. "I know what it means." Their eyes were brimming with tears. "I hear him still, too."

Isaac pulled Sam close and buried his face in their hair. His body locked up, resisting the sob that threatened to tear from his throat. "I'm sorry," he whispered. "I'm so sorry."

Sam shook their head and pressed their face into his chest. "No. Don't say that." They shuddered as they clung to him.

The phone vibrated in Isaac's pocket. He jumped. Sam flew upright, their small frame trembling with tension.

"Is it Vera?"

Isaac pulled the phone out of his pocket. Finn looked up. They put a hand on Ellis's shoulder and Ellis's head snapped up to look at Isaac.

Isaac's hands shook as he opened the message.

Got her. Both of us are ok. Headed to you.

He heaved out a sigh of relief that sounded more like a sob. "She got her," he whispered. "They're okay."

Sam dissolved into sobs and pressed their face into their hands. Finn sank to their knees beside Ellis and clutched at their hand. Edrissa's expression didn't change.

He hastily typed out his response.

Stick to back roads. Bounty on our heads.

After another moment, the phone buzzed.

If we didn't before we do now. ETA 3 hours.

Before he could text back a question, a nurse walked into the waiting room. Isaac was instantly on his feet.

"Is there any news? Are they okay? What's going on?"

The nurse looked tired. Harried. "It's a difficult surgery. They've lost a lot of blood. And... our supply just ran out." Isaac paled. "Our last universal donor was shot by the syndicates three days ago. Your friend is B-neg. Pretty rare blood type. If you want them to live..." The nurse made eye contact with each of them in turn. "...I need to test you all and see if you're compatible."

Isaac mechanically thrust his arm out. "Of course. Yes. Do it." He felt the press of bodies behind him as everyone shuffled forward, murmuring their agreement.

The nurse nodded. "I'll have you come with me." His gaze dropped to Edrissa, still huddled on the floor. "She's with you, right?"

Isaac cast a glance back towards Edrissa. "Yes. She's with us. It's up to her."

Edrissa's eyes went wide. She pressed herself back against wall, collapsing in on herself. Her eyes filled with tears and she pressed her lips together. She shook her head, trembling. "P-please..." She whispered.

Isaac nodded once. "She's not donating. She doesn't need to pay for her freedom like that."

Chapter 68

The guard guided Vera and Tori through the winding hallways of the hospital. If Vera had to guess, it had once been an office building. Now there were x-ray machines along the walls, big rolling cabinets full of medical supplies strewn about, beds pushed into every available space. Every room held at least one person. Vera shuddered and looked straight ahead. *This is a war we're fighting.*

Tori was tucked securely under Vera's arm. She looked like she was doing her best to walk upright, to conceal how badly she was hurt. To try to breathe without wheezing. To pretend the sweat that beaded on her brow wasn't there. She sagged against Vera's side. Vera suspected that Tori hoped she wouldn't notice.

She did. She pulled Tori closer and wound her arm under Tori's shoulders to pull her a little more upright. Tori tripped and stumbled into Vera's grasp. Vera paused and searched Tori's face, concern darkening her expression. "You alright?"

Tori nodded weakly. She was shaking and pale. "Just… need to sit down. Let's get to them. Then I'll sit down."

Vera nodded and started moving again.

After a few more hallways, the guard reached a door with *WAITING ROOM* stenciled on it in black spray paint. He pushed the door open and motioned them both inside.

Finn leapt to their feet as soon as they saw Vera come in. Everyone except Isaac was standing moments later. "Oh my… oh my *god*… Vera… you're…"

"It's not my blood," Vera mumbled, and passed Tori off to Ellis. Ellis eased Tori down onto the couch. Sam hovered behind Finn. Isaac sat up rigid on the couch, looking deathly pale.

Finn's hands jerked unconsciously towards Vera. "You… are you hurt? Where is this coming from?" Their hands settled in her hair, feeling along her scalp, not even noticing her trying to swat them away. "What happened?" Their hands moved to the back of her neck before she caught their wrists, guiding their hands off her.

"I'm fine." Her tone was hard. "I'm not hurt, Finn. Truly. I'm fine."

Finn backed off, their eyes still wide, raking her body for injuries.

Isaac stood slowly from the couch, Sam clambering to help him up. "What happened, Vera?" he breathed. "Whose blood is this?"

Vera's eyes flicked to Tori where she had collapsed on the couch. Ellis rubbed their hand against Tori's shoulder in awkward circles. "It's... um..." She bit her lip. "Gavin's father's."

Isaac blanched. "His... *father?* Why was his father there?"

Vera's eyes clouded with tears. She felt a rising tide of raw emotion threatening to drown her, to tear her apart. She trembled as Isaac brought his hand to her shoulder and squeezed gently. "Because... because Gavin must have found out..." She pressed her face into her hands. "Because he's the one who captured me fourteen years ago."

Vera dissolved into agonized sobs, each one feeling like it was taking a piece of her with it as it tore itself out. Isaac wrapped his arms around her and held her to his chest as she wept bitterly. She clutched at him, shaking hard, throat aching. He rested his cheek against her hair and cradled the back of her neck.

"I never knew," she sobbed. "I never thought I'd see him again, never thought he'd... he'd *torture* me again. He was going to make Tori hurt me. He was going to hurt us together... and... it's all... *my fault*." She gasped. "I was going to..." Her voice dropped to a whisper. "I was going to kill her, Isaac. I was going to take her life. I wanted to save her, I just wanted to save her..." Her fingers tightened in his shirt, her nails digging into his skin. He didn't move. Didn't say anything. "He had me... He said two *fucking words* and they had me. I still had the gun and I couldn't move; I couldn't kill them. I watched them hurt her and I couldn't stop them..."

"But you did," he whispered. "You did. You got out. How did you get out, Vera? What did you do?"

"I…" She swallowed hard. "I couldn't do it. I couldn't let them hurt her. I couldn't… let them… hurt… *me*." She crumpled in his arms, another sob aching through her chest. He guided her to another couch and wrapped his arms around her again. Sam sat on her other side and cuddled against her. Their thumb moved back and forth against her arm. Tori watched them, tears streaming down her face.

"I couldn't do it again," Vera sobbed. "I didn't… I *couldn't*. So, I… I shot Gavin…"

"You *what?*" Isaac held her at arm's length, his jaw falling open.

"I shot him… in the chest… and I… tore his father's throat out."

"…what?" Sam asked with a tremulous voice.

Vera gagged, the memory of the taste of blood on her tongue sweeping over her. "…with my teeth."

Isaac froze with his eyes wide and fixed on her. She closed her eyes, cringing away from the others' stares. *Now they all know. They all know I'm a monster.* She shuddered and stiffened in surprise as Isaac pulled her close again.

He pressed his lips against her forehead. "I'm so proud of you," he whispered.

That undid her. She wailed into his chest, shaking with sobs, clutching desperately at his shirt as he ran his fingers gently through her hair.

"You beat him," he whispered. "You found your strength and you beat him. You got away. Because of *your strength*, not anyone else's. I'm so proud of you, Vera. He couldn't destroy you. You saved yourself, and Tori." He squeezed her tight. "You did that. And you killed Gavin. You ended that fight."

She melted into his embrace. She felt Sam press gently against her back. Then she felt more hands on her. She looked up to see Finn and Ellis crouching beside her, their faces warm with concern. Tori sat beside Sam and draped her arm over their shoulders. She rested her hand on Vera's arm. A small sob broke from Tori's lips.

"We love you, Vera," Sam whispered. Their voice was small and scared and packed with conviction.

"What are you scared of, Vera?" Finn looked so earnest.

She bit her lip. "That you... that you think I'm a monster. You think I'm... dangerous."

Isaac snorted. "We're always known you were dangerous, Vera. But I've killed, too. For way worse reasons. And honestly?" He guided her chin up with his hand. "If there's any way he deserved to go, it's like that. And there's no one who deserved it more."

She looked up at him desperately, clinging to the love and acceptance she saw there. She pulled her face out of his grasp and pressed it into his chest. His shirt was wet with tears. He cradled her gently. For a moment, no one spoke.

"H-how is Gray?" Tori's voice was still raw from screaming.

Vera's head snapped up. "Oh my god... I'm so sorry, I was..." She wiped her face with her hands. "I'm sorry... How are they?"

Isaac blew out a slow breath. "Still in surgery. And... um... their blood bank has run out. They're B-neg, and we all got tested... except for Edrissa." Vera's gaze moved to the girl, to where she huddled almost forgotten in the corner. She watched them all with wide eyes.

Vera nodded, understanding. Isaac laughed bitterly. "Apparently B-neg is one of the rarer ones. And..." He pointed to Finn. "O-positive." To Ellis. "O-positive." To Sam. "A-positive." He pointed to his own chest. "I'm B-neg." He shrugged weakly. "What are the odds?"

"Low," Vera murmured. "Really low."

Isaac shrugged again. "Well, I've given some blood. They've come by just about every hour to get more. But... I don't know if they'll be able to take much more." He swallowed hard and Vera realized just how pale he was.

"I'm O-neg." Vera pulled up her sleeve. "Universal donor. They can take mine."

Isaac sagged in relief. "Thank god. I mean, I would give Gray all the blood I have, but..." He chuckled. "Almost feels like there isn't much left."

Vera nodded gravely. "They can have mine."

Tori spoke up. "I'm also A-positive. I'm sorry. If I could…"

Vera squeezed her hand. "I know, Tori. And so does Gray."

Isaac reached out and took both their hands. "I'm just curious… How do you two know your blood types?"

Tori pressed her lips together. "I wanted to know in case anyone ever came to my house needing an emergency transfusion."

Vera shrugged, her eyes distant. "We all got tested in academy. We had our blood type printed on the backs of our badges. It's relevant information." Her eyes focused again, and she drew in a deep breath. "So, is that where we're at? Just waiting for news?"

Isaac nodded. "Yeah. Just waiting now."

The door opened. The nurse's gaze found them all as he walked into the room, looking more tired than before. He was smiling.

Chapter 69

Isaac shot to his feet, a sort of strangled sob bubbling up in his throat. *They have to be alive, they—*

The room went black.

He came to on the couch, Finn's hand smoothing his damp hair away from his forehead. The nurse stood behind them, clearly concerned. His stomach roiled as he searched for his team, their faces spinning sickeningly above him. His hand clutched at the couch below him and he steadied himself.

His mouth was dry. "Are they...?"

"They're doing just fine." The nurse's features pulled into a tired smile. "All things considered. The bullet shattered two ribs and took a portion of the lung. The surgeon wasn't able to get it out. It's going to have to stay in your friend, unfortunately. But the damage has been repaired and they're out of surgery. They're recovering now."

"I want to see them." Vera's voice broke with strain.

The nurse pressed his lips together. "They're still intubated and sedated. It's going to be several hours until they wake up, at the very least."

"I don't care." Her hand clutched Tori's so hard her knuckles turned white. "I want to see them. It's my—"

"Not your fault." The words tumbled from Isaac's lips. He pushed himself up off the couch, the world going a little gray as he did it. "Not your fault. Not yours."

"Please." Tori's eyes were filled with tears. "Please, let us see them."

The nurse chewed his lip. "Okay. I can take you to them." His eyes flicked to Isaac. "You..."

"I'll be fine." He pushed himself up to sitting and froze as a wave of nausea crashed over him. His skin broke out in a cold sweat.

"I can get a wheelchair for you…"

"*No.* I want to see Gray. They're the one who's hurt, not me."

Sam's eyebrows pulled together in concern. "Isaac…"

"No." He clenched his jaw. "I'll be fine. Maybe I just need… a little help…"

Sam's hands were on him in an instant, supporting him. Isaac met their eyes for a moment, gratitude heavy in his gaze. They pulled his arm around their shoulders and wound an arm around his waist, taking as much of his weight as they could. They slowly stood together. Sam stumbled as Isaac's knees gave out. Finn lunged forward to catch him, wrapping their arm around his other side and pulling him upright again. Isaac squeezed his eyes shut, breaths coming faster. He swallowed hard and nodded.

"Okay. Come with me." The nurse's face was pinched with concern.

"What about her?" Vera's eyes went to Edrissa, huddled still where she had been for the past several hours.

"She's coming with us," Isaac panted.

Edrissa's eyes were wide as she looked up at Vera with a pleading expression. Then slowly, resigned, she got to her feet and followed the group as they left the waiting room.

The nurse wound his way through the halls, dodging equipment, beds, people rushing past. Every now and then he shot a glance behind him to see if the team was still following.

"What's your name?" Tori asked the nurse, her hand still clutched in Vera's.

"Thomas," he threw over his shoulder.

"Were you there for the surgery?"

"I assisted, yeah."

371

"Did it go…?"

He shook his head slowly as he sidestepped a machine that looked like it was for taking vital signs. "It was a hard surgery. Not as bad as it could have been, but… it went well. Doctor Trina is the best surgeon I've ever seen."

"How many surgeons have you seen?" Ellis was as close to Finn as the tight hallways would allow.

Thomas cast a serious look behind him. "Here? A lot. Most don't make it very long."

Sam looked at the nurse quizzically. Thomas pushed through a door into another corridor. Doors lined the hall. He stopped at the first room and put his hand on the handle.

"They look pretty rough," Thomas said in a low voice. "But they're okay. When you're ready to leave, do you think you could find your way back to the waiting room?"

Finn nodded. "Probably."

"Okay." Thomas pushed the door open and stepped aside. They all filed in one by one with Sam, Isaac, and Finn bringing up the rear. "If you need something, hit the call button and someone will come." Thomas left, pulling the door closed behind him.

Isaac's heart clenched when he saw Gray. They were tangled in a mess of wires and IV tubing, a series of monitors behind their head blinking with lights and making slow beeping sounds. A bag of blood ran into one of the IVs. Isaac felt dizzy. *That's mine.* An ET tube emerged unnaturally from between Gray's teeth, taped to the side of their mouth. The room seemed filled with the *whoosh*ing sound of the ventilator connected to the tube. Their chest rose and fell steadily with each artificial breath.

They all froze in shock. The person in the bed hardly looked like Gray at all. It was just their body, without their gentle smile, their strong and soothing hands, their soft gaze and kind words. Their heart pumped, their lungs moved, but the process looked almost mechanical. They looked… empty. Vanished.

Sam sobbed, a hand going to their mouth. Finn took Isaac's weight and lowered him to the floor against the wall, their hand locked on his shoulder as their eyes fixed on Gray. Sam fell to their knees beside the bed, their hands fluttering over Gray, settling at last on their hand.

Finn went to their side and wrapped their arms around Sam, whispering in their ear. "Shh… don't cry. It's okay. They're alive. You need to be strong for them now, okay? They need to feel good things right now. They need to hear us be happy and brave for them." They pressed firm kisses into Sam's curls. "I need you to be strong for them. If you need to cry, we can go out into the hall. But right now they might be able to hear you and we need to give them something good to hold on to so they can focus on getting better."

Sam nodded, wiping their nose with their sleeve. "Gray… Gray, we're all here." They sniffled. "All of us. We even brought someone new." Edrissa blushed. She stood huddled in the corner. "We're going to take her north when you get better. And you're going to get better, Gray. You had a good doctor. And Finn saved you." Finn looked at the floor and ran their fingers through Sam's hair. "We're all safe, Gray. Tori's here. Vera went to get her, and saved her. And Gavin is d—" They bit their lip. "We don't have to worry about Gavin anymore."

Vera drew closer to Gray, lightly trailing her fingers across their forehead. "I killed him, Gray," she whispered. "I killed the man who hurt me all those years ago. I… I broke free of his control. He couldn't hurt me anymore." She swallowed hard, tears welling in her eyes and spilling over. Tori tucked herself under Vera's arm and nestled her head on Vera's shoulder.

"You're gonna get better." Ellis pressed their hand to Gray's foot, standing at the foot of the bed. "You're gonna get better and we're gonna leave this place, go somewhere safer. We're gonna help you get better. We're all gonna take care of each other."

Isaac watched them all crowd around Gray, whispering their encouragement and love, pressing their hands against them, holding each other as they did. His eyes flicked to the corner, where Edrissa stood. Her arms were wrapped around her chest, her gaze fixed on the little group. Tears streamed down her cheeks.

Chapter 70

Something was wrong in Gray's chest. *I can't breathe, why can't I breathe right, why can't I...? Pain in, pain out. Pain in, pain out.* They pushed a sound out of their throat that was something like a whimper.

"They're awake. Finn, come here. Gray? Gray, can you hear me?"

The voice was coming from somewhere above them and they were underwater. *Why am I underwater? Might be why my chest hurts.* They opened their mouth, gasping for air that had to be nearby.

"Gray, it's alright... just breathe, there you go... just breathe..."

I am breathing. It just hurts too much. Pain in, pain out.

"I think they're in pain. Can you hit the button to call the nurse? Maybe they need—"

A strangled sound left Gray's throat. Their hand moved up to their chest and they pawed at where the pain was coming from. *If I can just dig the pain out...*

"Grab their arm. Gray, stop. Leave that alone. You'll tear your stitches. Sam... Sam... Help me. Grab their arm, there you go."

"Why aren't they waking up?"

"They're still a little sedated. Gray, you're okay. Squeeze if you can hear me."

I can try.

"Good! Good. Gray. Oh... come on, breathe. You're alright."

Where's Tori?

The thought crashed over them and froze their chest again. *Where's Tori? She's in trouble, someone... someone took her...* They whimpered as they tried to remember. They *had* to tell someone. Someone had to go save Tori. *Please, please help her, leave me alone and help her...*

"Gray, please! Just relax, Gray, let go..."

Please. Please, god, let her be alive. Leave me and go find her. Someone... why can't I...?

"That nurse should be here by now. Ellis, can you—"

"Of course."

"Isaac, come here, help me. Gray, relax, it's just us, you're safe..."

But where's Tori? Someone help Tori!

Gavin. Gavin has Tori. The thought punched them in the gut. They moaned, the pain spiking in their chest. *Gavin shot me and he has Tori.*

They thought they could feel tears on their cheeks, or it could have been the water. *Am I still underwater?* The voices around them sounded clearer. *Maybe...*

"Gray, stop... stop *pulling at that. Vera, can you find something to restrain them with? I can't..."*

SOMEONE FIND TORI! SOMEONE HELP HER!

They could hear someone screaming, far off in the distance. Screaming and sobbing. *God, someone else is hurt...? Help them too. Did Gavin hurt them too? Please... no no no please god someone help her... I couldn't save her... he shot me...*

They felt something winding around their wrists, tying them down. *Fine, torture me, hurt me, just please... don't hurt Tori, don't hurt my Tori...*

"Oh my god. What happened?"

"They woke up and started pulling at the bandages. They pulled one of their IVs, I'm sorry... we couldn't hold them down."

"Let me get them some more medication. Sometimes people have a bad reaction to the anesthesia..."

"Can we get some better restraints? These will work for now, but..."

"Let me see what I can find. Did they manage to tear the bandages?"

"No. Just the line."

"Okay. I'll be right back."

"Thank you."

God, my chest. What are they doing to me? My chest... hurts... They choked out a twisted sob.

"Gray, you're alright. You're in the hospital. They'll get you some more medication. You're safe, Gray."

Safe? Then why am I hurting? Why am I tied down? They pulled uselessly at the restraints. *Save Tori. Do whatever you want to me but save Tori.* They dragged in a gasp.

"Gray, please..." That voice. It was thick with tears, but... important. That voice was close. That voice was family. *"Gray, it's okay... you're safe. I'm okay. Vera got me. We're all here with you."*

They twisted closer to the voice, tears wetting the pillow under their head. Their lips trembled around the word. *"T- To-ori..."*

"Yeah, Gray. It's me. I'm so... I'm so sorry, I'm so sorry... you almost died, for... for me..."

"Tori, don't. You can talk about this when they're more awake."

"Sorry, I'm sorry..." A sniffle. A hand in theirs. It was warm, and they squeezed. *"There you go, Gray, hold on to me. We're safe."*

I'll never let you go. Never let you go again. Never let him hurt you again.

"He's d-dead, Gray, he's dead. We're safe."

A slow, rattling breath moved through their chest. *I believe you.*

"There you go. That's good, Gray. Breathe. There you go."

"Sorry that took so long. They're looking a lot better."

"I think they needed Tori. Needed to hear her voice."

"I'll still give some more fentanyl. It looks like they're still in pain."

Yes. God, it hurts.

"Will that put them under again?"

"Maybe, maybe not. It'll help with the pain for sure."

"Okay. Thank you."

"There. That should start working within the next few minutes. I'll look for some better restraints when I can. Come get me if they get agitated again."

"Will do. Thank you."

"No problem."

Still, always, that warm hand in theirs.

"Gray, that pain will start going away soon, okay? If you need to go back to sleep you can."

But I need to see her. Need to see Tori.

They felt pressure on their forehead. Hair brushing their face. And still, that hand in theirs. They held on like they were dangling over a cliff.

"They already look better."

"Yeah, fentanyl's good shit."

The pain in their chest was already ebbing away, settling and shrinking until it was a dull ache. Every breath still hurt. *Pain in, pain out.* But they could breathe. Their chest expanded and fell.

Their grip on her hand was loosening, fading. Panic spiked in them for a moment.

"It's okay, Gray. You can fall asleep. I'll be right here with you, the whole time."

Don't leave. Please don't leave.

The world faded away again.

Chapter 71

Pain in, pain out. Pain in, pain out. Gray moaned.

"They're awake again. Someone go get Isaac."

Gray's eyelids fluttered and their breath hitched in their chest. *Pain in, pain out.* They moved to reach for the pain and their arm stopped with a jerk. An icy stab of panic twisted their gut. *That's right. They tied me down. They were torturing me. Fine. Where's Tori?* They opened their mouth to beg for her.

"Gray, it's alright. You're safe."

There she is. Their heart swelled with fear and relief. *Is she here with me, being tortured? Did they hurt her?* They squeezed their eyes shut against the pounding in their skull.

They felt that warm hand in theirs again and squeezed.

"There you go. Can you open your eyes for me?"

I'm trying. Their eyes fluttered open and they saw a blurry shape beside them. Many blurry shapes. They swallowed and wet their lips.

"T- Tori…"

"I'm here, Gray. I'm safe."

Slowly, slowly, she came into focus, seated beside their… bed? They blinked and looked around the room, their mind swirling with confusion. They couldn't see the ceiling past the glare of the fluorescent lights above them. There were people packed into the room with them, blurs of people, shapes that seemed so familiar…

Their eyes returned to Tori and swept over her, taking her in. *She's alive. And…* Gray's jaw tightened as they saw the marks on her. On her face, her arms. On her… on her *neck.* They tried to reach up to touch her, and again their hand was stopped by the restraint on their wrist. They swallowed hard.

"T-torturing… us?"

Tori's eyebrows pulled together. "What?"

Gray glanced at their wrists, tied to the bed, and back up to her, at the marks on her neck. "Was he… torturing us?" Their chest throbbed with every word.

She pursed her lips. "No…" She squeezed their hand. "Are you worried about the restraints?" They nodded. They watched as her eyes filled with tears. They wanted to reach out and brush them away, hug her close. "We had to restrain you, Gray. You were fighting us when you woke up from the anesthesia. You pulled out your IV."

Their gaze drifted dizzily to their arm, where fluids were disappearing into a line in their vein. "Oh."

Her fingers brushed their forehead. "We can take them off, if you don't pull at things." She turned to someone… *Finn, that's Finn…* Gray was surrounded by people they *knew. Vera. Isaac. Ellis. Sam. Finn.* A smile pulled at their lips as they looked around.

Tori turned to Finn. "Right? We can take them off?"

"Yeah. Of course." Finn stepped closer to the bed and began untying the restraint from around Gray's wrist. They had dark circles under their eyes and their face was lined with exhaustion.

"You…" Gray wrinkled their forehead as fractured images flashed through their mind. *Lying on the floor of Tori's darkened kitchen, bleeding out. Being carried to the car, leaving a trail of blood behind them. Finn, cutting into them, forcing something between their ribs. Finn…* "You… saved…"

"No." Finn bit off the word and pressed their lips together, eyes brimming with tears. "Don't."

The strap around Gray's wrist came loose and they grasped Finn's hand, their gaze fixed on their face until Finn's eyes slowly came up to meet theirs. "I remember. You saved me."

A shudder ran over Finn's body and they shut their eyes, squeezing their free hand into a fist. "I… I just…"

"What is it?"

Finn pressed their lips together and shook their head, sending tears running down their cheeks. "I'm sorry, I'm... just..." Their voice twisted into a sob. Ellis wrapped their arm around Finn's waist and pressed a kiss against their shoulder. Finn buried their face in their hands, stifling another sob. "I'm sorry, god, I... I don't want to make this about me. I'm sorry. I'm just feeling... a little... overwhelmed..." Finn clutched at Ellis's arm as their chest began to heave with shaky, gusting breaths. They stumbled back, leaning towards the door, their fingers leaving marks on Ellis's arm.

"No." Gray's chest ached as they said it.

Finn paused, eyes wide and fixed on Gray. They licked their lips. "G-Gray... I..."

"*Please* don't go." Gray's fingers locked around the sheets beneath them, trembling with strain. "Please..."

Finn's eyes darted from Gray to the door as their legs shook under them. Tears rolled down their cheeks, dripping from their chin with each stuttering breath. They swallowed hard and took a slow step towards Gray. Then another. They sat down carefully on the bed beside Gray, lips quivering, eyes flicking down to the tube coming from Gray's chest, a *real* one, placed by the doctor during the surgery. They leaned forward, keeping their weight off Gray's chest, bracing themselves against the bed as their arm wound around Gray's neck. Gray raised their hand painfully to rest against Finn's back.

"Thank you for saving me."

Finn unraveled. They drew in a wheezing breath and wailed, pressing their face against Gray's hair. Their hand found Gray's again and held on like Gray was a life raft in a storm. Tears fell onto the pillow as Gray cried, too.

"I'm so happy you're alive."

"I'm alive because of you."

"I never, never want to hear you scream like that again." Gray's arm tightened on Finn's waist. "I thought you were going to die. I thought I was... going to..."

"I know."

Finn turned back towards Ellis, who had tears running down their face, too. Gray squeezed the back of Finn's neck and trembled in their embrace. After a minute Finn leaned back, scrubbing their face with their sleeve. They took small hiccoughing sobs. "I'm sorry. I'm sorry."

"It's okay, Finn. There's time to fall apart now."

"Yeah." They stood, taking a step back to make room for Sam. Isaac pressed close behind. Finn folded into Ellis's arms.

Sam bent down and pressed a kiss into Gray's forehead. Gray raised a hand to stroke through their curls.

Isaac looked like he was holding back tears, too. His hand wrapped around Gray's and held tight. Sam was glued to Isaac's side, an arm around his waist.

Gray held Isaac's gaze, the pain spiking for a moment, then easing. "You got us all here," they murmured. Their brow furrowed. "Where are we?"

Isaac bit his lip. "A hospital. In Beringer." Gray was punished for their sharp intake of breath with a stab of pain. They winced. "I knew where to go—" Isaac turned over his shoulder. "—because we had her."

Gray looked in the direction of Isaac's gaze, their eyebrows pulling together in confusion. As Isaac leaned back, Gray could see someone standing behind him in the corner, arms wrapped around herself, cringing away from their gaze. "Who's that?"

"This is Edrissa."

The young woman – small and willowy, and she couldn't have been older than Sam – shrunk at the mention of her name.

"A rescue," said Isaac. "We intercepted her as she was being…" Isaac paused, blowing out a slow breath. "…sold."

Gray's eyes bored into her. She stared down at the floor, trembling. "Edrissa?" Her head jerked up. "You saved me. Thank you." She jerked her chin back down at the floor. Gray shot Isaac a questioning look.

"She was in syndicate hands for two years. She's been… um…" Isaac bit his lip. "Shy."

Gray nodded, understanding. Their gaze traveled back to Tori, seated at their other side, her hand still firmly holding Gray's. Her lips pulled up into a smile. She squeezed their hand.

"I thought I lost you," Gray whispered.

Tori shook her head, sending a tear rolling down her cheek. "And I thought I lost you. But... Vera..." Tori reached behind her to take Vera's hand. "Vera came and got me."

Gray's gaze moved up to meet Vera's. Her eyes were dull with exhaustion and... fear? She wore a clean shirt, but Gray could see a dark red stain, almost black, marring the front of her pants. Her chin and neck were stained dark, flecks of dried red lingering above her collarbones and in the hollow of her throat. Her body was tense and guarded, in a way that made her look almost... *feral.*

I've seen that look before.

Gray wet their lips. "Vera?"

Vera pressed in close to Tori and put a hand on Gray's arm. "I... I got her out, Gray." Her shoulders loosened, just a little.

"How?" The word cracked on their lips.

"I..." She swallowed. "I killed him. Gavin's father."

"Gavin's—"

"He's the one who tortured me years ago. I killed him."

Gray's eyes went wide. "You *what?*"

Her lips pulled back in a fierce smile. "I killed him. He tried to take me again, and I killed him."

Gray's chest ached. "I promised you..." they whispered. "I promised you I'd never let him hurt you again."

"Now he won't." Her voice growled through her chest. "Because he's *dead.*"

Tori pressed a kiss into Vera's hair. "Because she tore his throat out." Tori's eyes shone with delirious pride.

"You... *what?*"

Vera's lip curled and her eyes darkened. "With my teeth."

Gray's mouth fell open. Vera shifted uncomfortably, the vicious satisfaction in her eyes congealing into a miserable sort of self-doubt. Her face fell a little.

Gray slowly closed their mouth. "I... am so proud of you."

Isaac grinned. "That's what *I* said." He laughed softly.

Vera's face slid into a smile, her shoulders shaking with half-laughter, half-sobs. She pressed a hand to her mouth.

Gray squeezed her hand. "So he's dead... where's Gavin?"

"I shot him." Again that fierce smile tugged at her lips.

"So he's dead?"

She hesitated for the smallest moment. "Yes."

Gray swallowed. "...are you sure?"

Slowly the smile slid from her face. "Pretty damn sure."

"Did you check? He's done this to us before. Are you...? I'm sorry, Vera, but are you *absolutely sure?*"

"I shot him in the chest, Gray. Yes, I'm sure."

"I was shot in the chest, and I survived, with way fewer resources. But definitely the best medic." Gray smiled at Finn. Finn blushed bright red and turned their face against Ellis's shoulder.

"Gray, I..." Her lips trembled. "I was focused on getting Tori out. I... I guess I wasn't thinking straight..."

"Hey." Gray pulled their hand out of Tori's grip to take Vera's. "Don't do that. I'm not blaming you, Vera. Having someone's throat torn out is one thing... you don't survive that."

"I watched the life leave his eyes." Her voice was a low rasp. Her lip curled into a sneer.

Gray's mouth pulled into a gentle smile. "Getting shot in the chest is different. But..." They sought her eyes until she met their gaze. "You got our girl out. That's the important thing."

Vera pressed her lips against Tori's shoulder. Tori smiled.

Gray turned their attention again to Tori. "But he... he tortured you first..."

Her face fell. "It's nothing. It's nothing compared to—"

"You were *tortured,* Tori." Gray's tone left no room for argument. "There is no comparing." They swallowed hard, their voice flattening. "What did he do?"

"He..." She bit her lip, tears threatening to fall. "He beat me. And he... um..." Her throat bobbed.

"He fucking *collared her.*" Vera's voice was a low snarl.

Gray's eyes fell shut. "Oh." Their stomach lurched at the thought.

"But now he's dead," Tori whispered.

Gray opened their eyes and nodded slowly. "What happens next?" Their gaze drifted to Isaac again.

Isaac huffed out a breath. "For now we stay here, at least until your chest tube comes out. After that you'll be alright to travel as long as we take it easy."

"When do we ever take it easy?" Gray asked sardonically.

Isaac nodded wearily. "I know. It'll be a rough road. But once we leave here we're going north. With her." He turned to look at Edrissa. She withered under his gaze. "Once we get her settled..." He pressed his lips together. "I'm going back on the road. Now that we know the syndicates are buying and selling people we have a pretty obvious mission: I'm going to intercept the shipments and make a pipeline north. I've been talking with some of the people here who have a pretty good idea of the major trafficking areas and how people get transported."

Gray nodded. "Makes sense."

"I'm going with him." Finn's hands were in fists at their sides.

"So am I." Ellis wound their fingers through Finn's.

"I am, too." Vera's jaw clenched. "I know what they do to people they've captured. I have to help."

"I'm going, too," Sam piped up.

"We'll talk about it later," Isaac grumbled. Sam looked at him, wounded.

Tori looked down at her lap. "I... I want to stay north." She wilted.

Vera put a hand on Tori's face and tilted it up. "If you want to stay north, that's what you're going to do."

"I want to start a safehouse for people when they arrive so they have somewhere to stay until they get resettled. I know it's not—"

"Please don't say whatever it is you were going to say." Vera pressed a kiss into Tori's hair. "If you hadn't had your safehouse and been willing to take us in, we'd all be dead. Dead months ago. You saved us. It's enough. It's more than enough." She pulled Tori into her arms.

Gray turned their attention to Edrissa. "And what do you want?"

Edrissa looked around the room, as if expecting someone to hit her for daring to *want*. She lowered her eyes and stared at the floor. "I... I want to find my brother. Micah."

"Where is he?"

"I don't know," she whispered. "He got shot when they... when they t-took me."

"I told her we'll help her find him," Isaac murmured. "If he's alive—" He flinched, throwing an apologetic look back at her. "We'll find him. We'll find someone who knows where he is and find him."

Her lips trembled and a tear ran down her nose and onto the floor. "Thank you," she whispered.

The story continues with:

Honor Bound: Book 2
Coming in 2020

and

Vera
Coming in 2021

Made in the USA
Monee, IL
28 July 2020